WOLVENGUARD

GEN-HEIRS: THE GUARDIANS OF SZIVERIA

SARAH WESTILL

To the extent that the image or images on the cover of this book depict a person or persons, such person or persons are merely models, and are not intended to portray any character or characters featured in the book.

All rights reserved. No part of this publication may be reproduced, distributed, or transmitted in any form or by any means, including photocopying, recording, or other electronic or mechanical methods, without the prior written permission of the author, except in the case of brief quotations embodied in critical reviews and certain other noncommercial uses permitted by copyright law.

This is a work of fiction. Names, characters, places, and incidents either are the products of the author's imagination or are used fictitiously. Any resemblance to actual persons, living or dead, businesses, companies, events, or locales is entirely coincidental.

WOLVENGUARD

Gen-Heirs: The Guardians of Sziveria – Book 7

Copyright 2023 by Sarah Westill

ISBN 978-1-955293-19-8

Cover Design by For the Muse Designs

OTHER TITLES BY SARAH WESTILL

The Guardians of Sziveria
(in reading order)

Levkaseon – A Prequel

Wintersfall

Raiventon

Kynhaven

Asherwick

Ericksen - A Wintervail Special

Survaine

Wolvenguard

Voklane (2024)

Bella and the Beast Master
(A Gen-Heirs World Novella Series)

Frozen Flowers Fallen

Perfect Melody Silenced

Dreams Never Seen

Fiery Nights Tempted (Feb. 14th 2024)

For world maps and to stay up-to-date on the latest
information, be sure to visit www.sarahwestill.com

To all the couples with age gaps who thrive in their love.

For my husband who saw past our age difference and trusted how I felt and the future we could build. Twenty-four years and I'm still thankful for us.

CONTENT WARNING:

THIS BOOK CONTAINS MATURE CONTENT,
INCLUDING BUT NOT LIMITED TO –

Consensual sex (non-graphic)
Action violence
Attempted rape
Loss of a parent and sibling

Reader discretion is advised.

WELCOME TO THE GEN-HEIRS
WORLD

In the distant future, a major cataclysmic event not only reshaped the world as humanity knew it, but left entire lands uninhabitable. As generations of survivors struggled to endure a fight for territory and resources, humanity regressed into what became known as The Primal Years. A dark and dangerous time that lasted for centuries.

Slowly, civilizations formed in the new nations. Limited means of transportation and communication began to develop in a resource-poor world. Powerful countries arose known as Sziveria, Ruthenia, Italyssa, Westica, and Cairo. New cultures, with their own standards of honor, became global powerhouses.

By 830 Post-Cataclysmic Event (PCE), strong talents are now inherited traits, passed down through genetics. The recipients of an unavoidable hereditary legacy are known as Gen-Heirs. Trains, ships, carriages and if one can afford them, small magnetically powered vehicles move people. Radios are the only means of quick communication besides handwritten messages. Heated water is a luxury. Extreme drops in temperature and harsh arctic winds have forced most food growth indoors, in greenhouses. A dangerously lethal virus known as Human Rabies Syndrome (HRS) plagues the globe. The inhabited world is growing at a slow rate, each unique country striving to exist in harsher, cold climates, and those who survive have become ruthless in their quest to thrive in this new, forsaken world...

THE RANKING SYSTEM:

Guardians of Sziveria

Queen/King Elect
    Prince/Princess Elect
    Arch Guardian
    Prince/Princess
    Shield Guardian
    Master Guardian
    Primary Guardian
    Key Guardian
    Guardian (anyone who serves the realm)

Other Key Terms –

First Intelligence Office (FIO)
    Sziverian National Investigative Division (SNID)
    Haven City Enforcement Services (HCES)
    Medical Science Officer (MSO)
    Medical Science Investigator (MSI)

Uninhabited Zones (UZ)
Human Rabies Syndrome (HRS)

1

Pungent smoke curling in the air mimicked the roll of anxiety in her stomach. Lucianna Castien squinted in the dim light. Scarred, grease-coated tables and mismatched chairs filled the narrow room. Patrons huddled over mugs and plates of food, keeping to themselves, glaring at anyone who dared venture too close to their claimed table. Cia picked a careful path through the slim spaces. Guilt gnawed at her gut, an emotion she couldn't afford to dwell on or allow to fester.

No one had noticed when she'd slipped from the meeting. Two years of training had given her an edge. Probably not enough, but she'd run out of time. She had one goal, one purpose. Nothing would stop her from achieving her objective. Not even the team who'd taken her in and made her one of their own.

Her contact, Hal, raised his cup in her direction. Cia took a bracing breath and continued his way. Sweet, burning tobacco tickled her throat and made her eyes water. She'd stink of it by the time she left.

"I didn't think you'd come," Hal said, wrapping both hands around his cup. "I sent a message two days ago."

"I've been busy." She pulled out an unsteady chair, taking a careful seat.

He leaned forward, excitement dancing in his green-brown eyes. "Busy getting my price, I hope."

Cia sighed and reached into the deep pocket of her jacket. Her fingers brushed aged leather. She laid the book on the table in front of her. When he tried to reach for it, she slapped his hand. "No. Not until we have a conversation, and I like what I hear."

Shaking his hand, he scowled at her. "You know I'm good for it."

Cia folded her arms over the book and leaned closer to him. "I know what I had to do to get this piece of garbage for you. Information. Now."

Hal sputtered. "Garbage? That's not garbage, it's art. Beautiful art of the—"

"It's naked men and women having sex, Hal. It's garbage." Granted, they *were* drawn in elegant sweeping lines of thick ink, but still. Cia had been too embarrassed to look beyond the first few pages to ensure she had the correct book.

He made shushing motions and looked around in concern. "Shh."

"No one cares."

"Do you know how much that book is worth?" he asked, his voice strained.

"I do." She pulled a folded slip of paper from the book. "The previous owner kept meticulous records."

And Cia had decided leaving the evidence of the book's purchase after she'd stolen it would be unwise. If the owner discovered the tome missing, he'd have no evidence to take to enforcement services. She spread the paper open with her fingers and tapped on the corners. "I figure this title is worth the information *and* an undocumented ticket. I'll cover the cost of the ticket. You'll need to ensure no one knows what ship I'm on."

Hal's brows crept up his forehead under oily locks of dark hair. "How do you know you'll need to travel?"

Cia leaned further across the table, a sinister smile tilting her lips. "I know enough, so don't bother trying to lie to me. You'll regret it if you do."

Hal flinched back. The chair creaked from the sudden motion of his large frame straining the already rickety legs. "All right, all right, no need to get agitated."

Huffing, he returned his hands to his cup, his eyes darting to the book and back down to the drink. "I couldn't get the name or location of the person you're looking for. I haven't even been able to learn if it's a man or woman. No one will say anything."

Hal leaned forward, looking around again. Cia mirrored the motion, hating that she had to get so close and smell his stink. Anticipation outweighed her disgust.

He licked his chapped lips. "But I did learn of a top man, way up, you understand?" Cia nodded. "He's been making sure we all get our money when we complete our assignments. I overheard them call him their secret weapon. That as long as they have him, they'll continue to have the resources to keep going."

Cia considered the information. A top man who ensured the money flowed would have access to every part of the organization. And the V Alliance was a large enterprise, of that she had no doubt. She wondered if the man Hal spoke of was the same one mentioned in the meeting she'd snuck away from. "Who is he?"

Hal's attention darted around the hazy room again. "Look, I'm not sure…"

Cia slowly eased the book to the edge of the table.

Hal held up a hand and took a labored breath. "Fine. It's your death, not mine."

"That's right. I told you when you agreed to snitch not to worry about me. I can handle myself." He looked her over. She knew what he saw. A young, skinny girl with no sense. "Now, who is he?"

"Joel Blackbain. Some financial genius."

Financial genius. That was a title she hadn't heard given to the man yet. Serial rapist. Drug addict. Dangerous. Former ranked guardian. Disgraced. Escaped convict. Those were things listed under his name. Not genius.

The First Intelligence Office was close to pinning down his location. They were likely giving the assignment of Joel's recapture to the highest authority possible to apprehend him this very minute. The only person capable of tracking down a mastermind criminal. Arch Guardian Wolvenguard, Deklan Ralston.

Cia kept a shudder of awareness to herself at even the thought of Deklan's name. Powerful, handsome, connected, and way beyond her reach, the beast master would do his job and do it well. Cia had to get there first.

"Where is he?" Cia asked, tapping her fingers on the book.

Hal licked his lips again. "New Columbia."

"Where in New Columbia?"

Hal patted his chest, reached into a breast pocket, and pulled out a folded scrap of paper. He held the slip out, the edges of the paper trembling. "I was in charge of sending this week's radio missive. The camp they're in needed more supplies. This is the location they gave. That's the best I can do. They'd kill me if they knew I shared this."

Cia plucked the note from his fingers. She held it up and tapped the book. "You get me here and back home, and when I return to Haven City, I'll acquire the next volume in this set for you."

Hal snatched the book from under her hand. He hugged the thin digest to his chest. "Deal."

Guilt tried to claw free from her chest again. She shoved the annoying emotion deep down and the fear of the unknown. She'd never left Sziveria. Her training hadn't reached the point where the First Intelligence Office felt she was ready for such a significant step. And once they learned what she'd done, they'd yank her guardian status away so fast she'd never be allowed into another position again, regardless of her Gen-Heir talent. Genetic gifts or not, there were some people you simply didn't betray.

Cia had to make the sacrifice count. She had to find the man who murdered her brother and mother. Who destroyed her father's life, and stole the last remnants of her childhood in a split second.

Chair legs screeched across the floor, yanking her from her musings—a dangerous thing to do in a place full of unsavory individuals. Hal held out his hand.

"Nice doing business with you, Shadow Lady."

The term made her cringe. He'd insisted on calling her something and had saddled her with the ridiculous moniker when she refused to give him a name. She waved her hand, unwilling to take his. "Yeah, with you too." She fluttered the piece of paper. "Thanks for this."

"Send the travel information to the usual place?"

Cia nodded. He gulped the last of his drink and then stood. Giving her another quick wave of thanks with the book, he left her sitting alone. Cia rose and went the way she arrived, easing through the sparse clientele and out the front door.

Outside, the moon was a thin slice in an inky, diamond-studded sky. The last remnants of the arctic winds chilled the night breeze. A couple more weeks and only the deepest hours of the night would become cold enough to leave frost behind, which would burn away with the first warm rays of morning. The ice drifts had finished their flow, and the world's oceans were again open for travel. Hunching into her jacket, the scrap of paper crinkling against her palm, Cia formulated the next stage of her strategy. To be on the next ship bound for New Columbia.

"CAN I HELP ALL OF YOU SOMEHOW?" DEKLAN RALSTON asked, arms crossed, surveying the small group collected in his foyer.

The most powerful of the intel guardians were gathered in his home. If someone had intentions of crippling the First Intelligence Office, attacking now would achieve the results. Deklan almost expected a small army to burst through his front door. Then again, if anyone could hold off an opposing force, the people before him would.

Ryan Voklane cleared his throat. The early morning sun streaming in from the windows above made his ice-blond hair nearly white. "Lucianna Castien appears to have boarded a ship bound for New Columbia late last night."

Deklan tried to pull the name from his memory since Voklane seemed to believe he should know the woman. Or at least know *of* her.

Katria Blackbain came to his rescue. Her vibrant blue eyes glowed against her porcelain face and midnight black hair fell in an unbound curtain down her back. "Almost two years ago, the assassin who killed my mother and sister murdered Cia's mother and brother." Katria's husband, Sean, stepped closer, his hand sliding along her back. "The crime was eerily similar to what happened to my family. Sitting on a blanket in the grass, only we were on our property, whereas the Castiens were in a public park."

"Daring," Deklan said.

"Very," Voklane agreed. "They kidnapped Lucianna, believing she had her father's Gen-Heir talent."

"She doesn't?" Deklan asked.

"No, she's an interceptor," Kevin Merrick revealed. "Like me. I've been training her since she came of age over a year ago."

Deklan gazed at their grim faces. "Is she on your team?"

"No, I haven't placed her yet. She isn't ready," Voklane said. "We had reached an understanding—"

"Yes, because that understanding worked so well last time," Katria snapped. "The only one who benefited was you, Ryan."

Sean slid Katria's hair behind her shoulder and murmured something soft into her ear. She waved a hand in Ryan's direction, her eyes wide. Sean raised his brows.

"Oh, fine," she bit out. "We all benefited." She pointed an angry finger at the guardian. "But you did not keep up your end of the bargain with either of us where the assassin was concerned. What did you expect Cia to do when she learned of that?"

"Trust us," Mason Dandridge said, arms crossed over his chest, his long black hair tied behind his back. His pale gray eyes flashed with anger. "She was supposed to trust us. We've done nothing but take her under our care, make sure she understood how the chain of command worked, and help her gain confidence in her talent. Since she's been training, we've made many new discoveries and come closer to finding answers. She wasn't supposed to go off behind our backs alone."

The situation coalesced for Deklan into an unpleasant picture. Sean Blackbain's guardian team had been betrayed by a teenager they'd taken in and begun to mold. They'd underestimated her need for vengeance. A demand he wouldn't have been able to deny if the circumstances had happened to his family. No one made an enemy of the Ralston's and lived without regretting their decision.

"And how does this concern me?" Deklan asked.

Voklane blew out a heavy breath and waved at Mason to answer the question. Deklan shifted to face the strategist.

"We think she went after Joel Blackbain."

Deklan blinked. "By herself?"

Mason nodded.

"Does she understand who he is? What he's capable of?" Again, Mason nodded. Deklan growled in frustration and turned his back to the group. He dug his fingers into his shoulder-length hair and considered the information. Nineteen and bent on revenge, the girl must have been confident enough with whatever she'd learned to go off alone. Deklan faced them again. "Does she know where he is specifically? Because I've only learned he's in New Columbia, but I have no idea where. We planned to leave at the end of the week to begin the hunt."

"We also know he's in New Columbia. We discussed the intelligence yesterday at our weekly meeting," Mason said. "She disappeared at some point during the discussion."

"I noticed she was gone, but not in time to follow her," Kevin said, his words laced with irritation. "Since she boarded a ship that left shortly after nine, she had to have learned an exact location before taking the MagnaRail to Port Scarbrough."

"She left from Scarbrough?" Deklan didn't wait for an answer. "If she left from Scarbrough, I can get to New Columbia possibly before she does if I leave in the next few hours."

"Or let her lead you to Blackbain," Ryan said, holding up a hand when angry shouts burst through the foyer. "She put herself in a bad situation. We should utilize it."

"Or how about just asking her for the information," Mason said between clenched teeth. "She's not bait."

"If she beats me there, it won't matter. I'll be following her regardless," Deklan said calmly. He looked at them all. "That's why you came here, right? To make sure when we apprehend Joel, we also get your girl?"

"How could you get there first?" Mason asked.

Deklan motioned for them to follow. He led them past the grand staircase, a monstrosity of space. On the second floor, a landing split into two arching stairways that led to the third level, where a balcony overlooked the foyer. Deklan figured sixty years ago when the first

Wolvenguard was told to build a house, the beast master had either been arrogant or wanted to make a statement of power. Perhaps both. The balcony rail was low enough for his wolves to peer over and survey their domain. Which they did daily. Especially his alpha, Neva. She wouldn't go down the stairs without gazing over the edge.

Deklan entered his study, nestled in the right corner at the back of the foyer. A world map covered the entire far wall, framed by lamps above and at each edge. He smoothed a hand along the Atlantic Ocean, in the vast space between his country and the small occupied coastal areas of what remained of South America. He tapped a finger along the Black Ocean side of Sziveria.

"She left from here." He drew his finger around the southern coast. "She has to cross either the Sovereign Channel here to the south or," he drew a new arc, "the Northern Pass. Unless they pick up additional passengers at Port Tabria or Ruthenia, I doubt they'll take the northern route. However, going through either adds at least an additional day of travel, perhaps two if the Sovereign Channel is temperamental."

He followed a line across Sziveria. "I will take the rails here, to Port Ice Hollows, and make a straight sail for New Columbia. Do you know what port she'll be docking at?"

Voklane reached into his pocket and pulled out a yellow slip. "She's chartered on the *Valdivia*. They're docking in Suri Ravi."

Katria stepped closer to the detailed map. "Why don't most passenger ships leave from Port Ice Hollows if traveling through the pass or channel takes so much extra time?"

"Port Ice Hollows is mostly a commercial port.

There's enough of an inlet for loading and unloading of merchandise directly to the rails, but not people. As the name suggests, it tends to collect ice, which doesn't always disappear when the drifts do. I'll have to radio the port to make sure ships leave from there and see who has one available for me to lease."

Kevin stepped forward. His fingers whispered along his short beard as he looked over the map. "New Columbia is a large nation. How are you planning on finding anyone there?"

Deklan smiled. "I find people. That's what I do." His gaze moved to Voklane. "I will recover your missing interceptor." He looked at Sean. "And your escaped brother."

Visible relief moved through the group. Deklan focused on New Columbia. "Do you know where she's going? Any information?"

"No," Mason answered. "And that's what's frustrating. A nineteen-year-old girl, with zero experience, obtained intelligence we couldn't."

Deklan leaned forward and studied the cities nearest to the Uninhabited Zones from the port. "Her cause is personal, her motivation different. She's likely convinced herself she has nothing to lose. She'd be willing to do things no one else would for information."

"Cia is honorable. She wouldn't—"

Deklan cut off Kevin's words, looking over his shoulder at the master guardian. "Is she or is she not on the hunt for an assassin that took someone precious from her?"

Kevin's jaw shifted. Annoyance flared in his storm-gray eyes. "She is."

"Then anything done to achieve that goal is honorable," Deklan stated. "Her time on your team, training and growing stronger, has also been an objective to learn what she can to accomplish what she needs. She agreed to your terms with her fingers crossed behind her back. Accept it, and either forgive or expel her from the fold when I bring her home. I don't care either way. I just need to know anything that will help me locate her and Blackbain."

Voklane scrubbed his hands down his face. Deklan figured the liaison to the arch guardian over intel teams didn't often find himself in an unfamiliar situation.

"All right. How long do I have?" Ryan asked.

Deklan glanced at the clock over the door. "I have to make a radio call and get my team together if there's a ship available. Four hours, at the most."

Voklane nodded and motioned to the group. They followed him out, and Deklan took a deep breath. He'd been given tough jobs in the past. Jobs he accepted, knowing once he captured his target, the world would be safer. Apprehending Joel Blackbain was no different.

Chasing down a wayward interceptor made things a bit trickier. His only hope lay in her jumping into her personal battle, unqualified and barely trained. Merrick was a legend in the community. His instruction would create a new weapon for Sziveria. But not yet. She'd learned enough to have confidence, not enough to keep herself out of trouble. Another year or two, and he'd have laughed in Voklane's face. Not even Sean's team could track and capture a properly trained interceptor. They were the secret weapon of any nation fortunate enough to realize one had been born in their country. Lethal ghosts.

Deklan moved to the radio behind his desk, checked the charge, and then made his calls. The port was open, and the ship he preferred was available. Next, he reached out to his team. Sabrie, his strategic coordinator. Tate, his medical scientist, and Galvin, his weapons expert. They would meet at his house in two hours.

Upstairs, his room took up the entire third floor. He packed a bag capable of being carried on his back. His wolves would hunt their meals once they left civilization. And Deklan had no doubt they'd be adventuring through the unknown. There were rumors of a rail line running to the location. If that were the case, they'd at least have a trail to follow. After packing a secondary bag with the things he wanted but could live without, Deklan left both bags by the back door.

He moved through the foyer, around the stairs, and to a double door leading into his training space. Exercise gear, a narrow rock wall rising to the ceiling, floor mats, weights, and other training equipment filled the three-story room. Two sets of double glass doors led out into a wild greenhouse. Dense foliage straining to reach the glass ceiling barely allowed light to penetrate the ground. Humid air rushed by, and the gentle trill of birds met his ears as he stepped out.

A bark of annoyance deep within the indoor forest made him smile. Nikita, the youngest of his pack, had been reminded of his place. Lifting his chin, Deklan called to his wolves, *"Sesay, archen'ya!"*

Excited yips tore through the air. Leaves rustled. Sticks snapped. Vegetation shivered high above, showing him their rapidly approaching path. Birds squawked in alarm and flew in various directions. The dogs burst through the undergrowth, eyes wide in excitement, tongues and ears flapping, tails raised in anticipation.

Deklan lifted a fisted hand. The Ruthenarc wolves skidded to a stop and sat in quiet obedience at his feet.

Nikita licked his muzzle, his midnight black front paws shifting in excitement. Neva, his golden female alpha, and Izia, her silver male beta, remained motionless, their eyes flickering to him and away, awaiting further instruction.

Deklan leaned forward, his gaze intent on his youngest pack member. "Nikita, *neriviztu.*"

Nikita stilled. His fur trembled from the effort. Practicing the command to remain perfectly still was necessary. At times, during assignments, his dogs could not make a sound. Much puppy remained in Nikita. Deklan had to work hard to guide the youthful exuberance out of him. At the ten-count mark, Deklan straightened and smoothed a pleased hand between Nikita's ears.

"*Dokhor vok,*" he praised. Each dog lifted their nose and demanded the same acknowledgment of being good dogs.

Deklan found Neva's bond, a beautiful golden thread. He called it forward. *How is Nikita's training going?*

He is not Vyshe, he is not.

The mention of his lost wolf made Deklan's jaw clench. He took a few steps back and opened the door to the house. *No one is Vyshe. He won't ever be replaced. Nikita will come into his own if you give him a chance.*

She chuffed air through her muzzle, her lips flapping. *Too much play in him, too eager, too young, too much.*

Deklan considered her assessment. *He did okay during our last overseas mission. This one will be longer and more involved. Will he be acceptable, or should he remain home?*

He will not jeopardize us, he will not.

Deklan teased her ears. *Thank you, that's what I wanted to know.*

Neva licked his wrist and waited with the others for him to enter the house first. Deklan led them through the downstairs and out the back door. A narrow brick path led to a railroad turntable, where his black engine waited, positioned to take the track out of the city. A snarling wolf, the fangs morphing into the V of Wolvenguard, took up the center of the engine house in brilliant yellow. Matching accents traced the aggressive lines of the exterior. Anyone seeing his train would know who it belonged to without question.

Deklan hoisted himself up the steep metal steps to the platform. He took two short steps to the door and popped the handle, the heavy steel door swung open. Angling his body, he motioned for them to jump up. They soared onto the platform and filed into the cab in leaping graceful bounds. When Nikita's black, fluffy tail disappeared inside, Deklan followed. In patient obedience, they waited at the kennels stacked in the furthest corner. Neva and Izia needed help into theirs. Nikita could walk into his bottom space.

Deklan patted the kennel floor. Neva lifted her paws, her nails scraping for purchase. Bracing his hands on her rump, he hefted her upward and let her scramble into the top kennel. He repeated the process with Izia, easier since the dog could pull his massive frame inside once Deklan provided a step for his back paws and then waited for Nikita to walk into his. He slid the locks into place, touching their noses afterward.

After double-checking that his wolves were safe and secure, he went down a narrow hall into the engine room. Like its much smaller counterpart, the Ariot, his locomotive engine ran on the power of magnetic energy. He checked the panel connecting all the components and started the process to begin the forces that would drive the propulsion. Once he had the important information from Voklane, he wanted to depart.

Back inside, he found the first two team members waiting for him. Sabrie, short and stalky, dressed in pants with an array of random-sized pockets, a t-shirt, and thick jacket, her cropped blonde hair gleamed in the muted interior light. A stuffed bag rested at her feet. Next to her, Galvin crouched, digging around in a chest.

"I'm just saying, we don't know where we're going," Galvin's voice floated in the cavernous foyer. "Or who we're after. I need options."

"There are options, and then," she waved a hand over the chest, "there's excess. This, my friend, is excess. We won't need even half of this."

Galvin huffed in annoyance, tossing tawny hair from his eyes, and yanked a rifle from the box in one hand and a gleaming long knife in the other. "Knife or rifle? Which one will we need, Rie-Rie?"

Her face twisted in disgust. "Don't call me *Rie-Rie*. Ever."

Galvin looked her over, from the top of her head to her leather-clad toes. "Fits you. I like it better than Map Mistress."

Sabrie kicked out, slamming the flat of her boot into Galvin's shoulder. Not expecting the sudden assault, his weapons specialist toppled over, gun and knife skittering across the floor in opposite directions. Galvin launched himself up from a prone position. In one fluid executed movement, he stood back on his feet, arms spread wide.

"What in the arctic was that for?" Galvin demanded.

"For being a scab," Sabrie shot back, her body angled for another kick.

"Know what your problem is?" Gavin asked, clearly unable to leave well enough alone.

"You."

Gavin clenched his jaw and narrowed his eyes, about to make a stupid mistake.

Deklan stepped out of the shadows of the stairs. "Enough."

The quiet, authoritative command stilled his operatives. Red flamed across Sabrie's cheeks. Gavin took a careful step away from her. Deklan stared at them in silence, his discontent clear. When neither made another move toward the other or offered additional immature barbs, he motioned at the back door.

"Load everything onto the engine and wait for me."

Sabrie snatched up her bag without looking at Gavin. Sighing, Gavin picked up the discarded weapons. After hoisting his belongings on his back, he lifted the chest. Wordless, he passed Deklan, giving a nod of acknowledgment.

Tate walked through the door a while later, a heavy backpack strapped to his shoulders and a canvas duffel in his left hand. Disheveled black hair framed his face. He wasn't much taller than Sabrie. Then again, to Deklan, most people were short.

"Where's everyone else?" Tate asked, using his foot to close the door.

Deklan tilted his head to the side. "Out at the tracks, waiting in the engine. Hopefully, they're behaving themselves."

Tate tsked and sighed. "Worse than siblings, those two."

Deklan grunted. "Do you have everything you'll need?"

Tate shrugged the weight on his back. "I always keep a med-bag ready, you know that."

"Just making sure."

"Don't worry, if it's in my power, everyone will return home."

Every job they took had an inherent danger, one they recognized. Tate had worked hard to save Vyshe, but in the end, the wolf's wounds had proven more than the medical scientist could treat. The loss had been the first for the team. The second Deklan had had to endure where his wolves were concerned. The echoes of fragile mortality now followed them on every mission. In time, Deklan hoped the tragedy would become far enough in the past to return to the more carefree nature the team had once shared.

Deklan squeezed Tate's shoulder in appreciation. "Can you please have Sabrie reach out to dispatch and ensure the rails are clear for us to Port Ice Hollows?"

"Sure."

A rapid knock sounded from the front door. Tate continued. Deklan reached the door before his porter. He waved the man off, who executed a shallow bow before turning and disappearing back into the depths of the house. If Deklan had a choice, he'd live alone in the massive house with his wolves. But as an Arch Guardian, he had a small staff. A porter for his front door. A guardsman for security when he wasn't home. A housekeeper to look after all the dust and dog hair. A chef to make sure he ate. He appreciated all their hard work yet wished the service he provided for his nation didn't come with all the embellishments. Between the staff, the parties he was expected to attend, and the reverence of those who weren't any different from him, Deklan often regretted accepting the high-ranking guardianship. He could secure escaped convicts and wanted criminals without all the flippancy.

Voklane waited on the doorstep. The FIO guardian held out a folder. "Here's everything I have, including maps with possible secret ports and rail lines. None of it's been confirmed."

Deklan accepted the folder. "Could she actually be entering one of these ports?"

"Unlikely since she took a known passenger vessel. However, one of them may get you closer to where she's going if you don't get ahead of her."

Voklane shook his hand, wished him luck, and left. Deklan searched out the household staff and let them know he'd be gone for an undetermined length of time. In his office, he went through his weapons. While he trusted his weapons expert to equip them, Deklan had a specific blade he wanted on his person. A gift from his father when he'd taken on the Wolvenguard position. He slid the knife into a sheath custom sewn into the back of his pants and then grabbed his bag on the way out the back.

The powerful rumble of the engine vibrated through the air and under his feet. Deklan sprang up the stairs to the narrow landing and opened the cab door. Sabrie crouched before the kennel, petting Nikita's nose through the narrow bars. She had a soft spot for the pup since they'd been introduced. Gavin tuned the guitar he kept in the cab from a short bench seat next to the kennels. The tight space housed the kennels, a bench, a driver, and a navigator seat. If all the seats were claimed, whoever was left out had to sit on the floor. Deklan went into the loud space housing the warming-up engine. After tossing his belongings onto the pile with everyone else's, he did his safety inspection.

"Everything good?" Sabria asked as he emerged from the back.

"Yes." Deklan stood at the control panel. He rarely sat. "Are we clear on the tracks?"

"Yes, we're authorized access, providing we leave within the next thirty minutes. After that, we'll have to wait five hours. There's a supply train heading to Glass Fields Correctional at seven."

The control panel gleamed in polished steel. Red paint marked the brake on his left. The throttle was black on his right, and the shifter remained silver. Gauges lined a small board. Various switches formed a neat line under the meters, including one that'd allow him to disrupt the magnetic force powering the steel beast. Deklan released the brake. A hiss sounded outside and the engine lurched. He pulled the gear shaft to first and eased the throttle forward, his left hand resting on the brake. The train glided along the tracks, slow and easy. Out the front window, he left his house behind, and Haven City passed, first slow, then faster as he shifted, demanding more power from the throttle. There were no crossings in Sziveria. A bridge or tunnel kept all traffic safe and flowing across the few areas where roads and rails co-existed.

A rhythmic *womp-womp* joined with the muted grind of steel-on-steel underneath. The first hard chord of Gavin's guitar marked the increase in speed outside the city borders. Sabrie slid a window open and leaned out, letting loose a loud whoop. Gavin played to her excitement, his fingers flying over the strings. Deklan grinned. How he loved his job.

2

ATLANTIC OCEAN
  Two days later

A COLD OCEAN BREEZE RUFFLED DEKLAN'S HAIR FROM HIS face. Salt tinged the air, leaving a thick sensation on his skin. He braced his forearms on the rail. Neva stood beside him, her claws sunk into the wood, her tongue lolling as she watched the waves move across the horizon. Wind rippled across her golden fur, her russet accents more red than brown in the late evening sun. Behind him, Izia barked at the seagulls, offended that the winged creatures dared even to consider landing on his vessel. Nikita couldn't decide between feeling the wind in his face or trying to catch a tasty bird from the sky and attempted to do both. Deklan sighed. At least the youngest of the pack would sleep well tonight.

A chunk of ice floated past. Beautiful in the setting sun, a sculpture of nature bobbing along in ever-changing hues of blue, pale oranges, and pinks. Deklan frowned and searched the vast expanse for larger obstacles. They were at the tail end of the ice flows, but ships had been sailing for weeks without any reported issues. Hopefully the few small stragglers were all that remained of the vast flowing sheets from the arctic. In the winter months, the Atlantic and Black Oceans became impossible to navigate, frozen solid in places and covered in treacherous chunks of ice in the rest, even beyond the temperate zones.

"We're all unpacked and ready if you are," Tate said behind him.

Tate stood hunched into his jacket, the chilly wind toying with his black hair. Red tinged his bronze cheeks, and he sniffled, dancing in place.

Deklan laughed. "Cold?"

"Not all of us have Ruthenian blood flowing through our veins."

Deklan clapped him on the shoulder. "Let me make sure we're still good for our heading, and I'll meet everyone in my cabin. You can get a fire burning in the woodstove if you want."

"Will do." Tate gave the signal for the small pack to follow him to the cabin to wait for Deklan.

At the helm, Deklan checked with one of the deckhands he'd hired for the voyage. He confirmed they remained on course and then headed to his cabin. The team lounged around the spacious room. A large bed, a nightstand, and a dresser were on the right wall. Windows across from the entry overlooked the endless sky and water. A desk and a small kitchen area were to the left. Underneath the windows, a couch and chair provided the illusion of a living space. Tate had started a fire in the woodstove and sat in the chair nearest to the growing heat. Lamps provided a warm, amber glow to the room.

Sabrie sprawled on the couch while Galvin sat on the floor rubbing Neva's belly. Izia had fit his body into the small space under the desk, becoming a shadow of silver fur. Nikita sat at the couch, his muzzle on the arm, a gaze of desperation on Sabrie for attention. The wolf had learned who the softy was in the group and took advantage of it whenever possible.

Deklan pulled on his bond, a sapphire thread connecting him to the young male. *Nikita, go lay by the bed.*

The wolf dropped to the floor with a dramatic whine, exposing his belly and folding his paws onto his stomach.

"He was fine," Sabrie whispered.

Nikita, Deklan chastised, pointing where he wanted the wolf to lay.

"He has to learn to obey," Deklan said to Sabrie.

Neva flipped onto her stomach and fixed her stare on Nikita. Deklan snapped his fingers. When her golden eyes switched to him, he nodded a fist up and down. She yawned, laid her head on her paws, and looked away. Continuing to grumble his displeasure, Nikita skulked to the bed.

Dog drama handled, Deklan went to the desk and opened the folder. "All right. Here's the maps of New Columbia." He handed them to Sabrie. "Supposedly, there are some ghost ports and rails. Take them into account just in case they're real, and we can utilize them."

"They aren't confirmed?" Sabrie accepted the documents, unfolding them on the seat next to her.

"No." He handed her a clean sheet of paper for her route planning.

Tucking a lock of blonde hair behind her ear, she leaned over the pages in concentration. "Then how do they even know about them?"

"I didn't get an explanation." Deklan sifted through the papers until he came to two drawings. Voklane had ensured the team was well-informed. Facing the team, Deklan held up the images. "Joel Blackbain and Lucianna Castien are our targets."

"Working together?" Galvin asked.

"Negative. It's believed Lucianna is after information from Joel, who was our primary goal until the girl involved herself. Nineteen and an interceptor-in-training."

Tate whistled, reaching out and taking the picture of Lucianna. "Sziveria wants her asset returned."

"Sziveria needs both of them returned," Deklan amended. "Blackbain is an escapee from Stonebreak."

Sabrie glanced up. "Why weren't we called in when the escape happened, like normal?"

Deklan half sat on the desk, bracing his hands on the cool surface. His fingers curled around the edge as he took a steadying breath. His team wasn't going to like what he had to reveal. "Because he didn't escape by normal means. He had help."

"Don't they always have some form of help?" Tate asked.

Deklan shook his head. "Not like this." Now, he had their complete attention. "Four years ago, a woman named Jessalyn Silverna came to my house with a unique request. She needed private access to her father, Arch Guardian Praekasdian. No one could know about the meeting because no one could know the secret information he was about to give her what I'm about to share with you. No one can know, understand? When we apprehend Blackbain, he will be quietly returned to one of the Northern Boundary prisons under a new identity."

He waited until they all acknowledged his order before continuing. "For over ten years now, Praekasdian has been at the mercy of a group calling themselves the V Alliance. Four years ago, when Jessi visited, Praekasdian came clean about the coercion. The group had ordered the assassination of his daughter, and when that didn't work, they threatened his wife, too."

"Summer sun," Tate said, swiping a hand down his face. "To have the arch guardian over the prison system in your pocket..."

"Yes," Deklan agreed, frowning. His fingers tightened over the wooden edge. "For those first six years, a lot of damage was done. The group funneled convicts out of the country via fake prison transfers. Where they sent them, we aren't sure yet, but one theory is they're using the prisoners for slave labor."

"For what purpose?" Galvin asked, draping an arm over his bent knee.

"Raiventon's wife believes they've been stealing resources from Uninhabited Zones outside New Columbia, Perazil, Westica, and possibly Ravenna."

Tate whistled again. "Wow, that'd be an untapped income source."

"Yes."

Sabrie tapped her fingers on the pages in front of her. "The slave labor would ensure no one knew about it, too. Keep everything secret and just distribute."

"Organization that large, though, someone is bound to start talking," Galvin said.

"Someone has," Deklan agreed. "They spoke to our girl there. Joel Blackbain is believed to be the brains behind the distribution. He ensures the products they obtain are being sent to the correct markets. Lucianna Castien is under the impression he'll have information she's desperate for."

Tate leaned forward, returning the picture of the young woman to Deklan. "What information?"

Deklan opted not to look too closely at the drawing. She seemed familiar somehow, and he didn't need the distraction. Without turning, he set the page behind him. "From my understanding, two years ago, the V Alliance had her family killed in front of her and then kidnapped her. She's searching for the assassin."

Galvin cursed, Sabrie covered her eyes, and Tate flexed his jaw.

Sabrie dropped her hand. "And, in their infinite wisdom, someone decided to train this girl as an interceptor?"

Galvin looked at her. "She can't help her Gen-Heir talent."

"No, but she's not stable, is she? And now she's out there running around, needing rescued because she's not ready to be a team player."

Deklan resisted the urge to rub his temples. "We aren't here to argue the decision to train her. She's important to many powerful people, and we're bringing her home. Obtaining Joel Blackbain is also necessary. He's the backbone of a very bad group and a terrible human. He was sent to Stonebreak for a reason. He'll be going back, probably to Northern Pointe, where he'll spend the rest of his life in miserable cold, alone in a cell."

"And what of this Alliance?" Tate asked. "What's being done about them?"

"They aren't our problem right now," Deklan answered. "You know how we function when I'm asked to carry out a mission with this team. We get our orders, we execute."

"In other words, they don't know much." Sabrie shook her head in disgust. "Great. Are they operating out of Sziveria?"

"I don't know enough to answer that," Deklan admitted. "I only know about where it concerns the prisoners."

Sabrie collected the maps and paper. "Can I work on this in my quarters? I want to look at my maps of New Columbia before I decide on a route."

"Of course," Deklan said.

She rose. "Thank you."

Galvin stood and followed Sabrie out. Tate waited until the door closed before standing.

"Is this Joel Blackbain, the former Wintersfall?" Tate asked.

"He is."

Tate sucked air through his teeth. "If he gets his hands on her, it won't be good."

"I know. I'm hoping she has enough training to get herself out of a bad situation, at least. And we have you."

"There are some things I can't fix, Deklan."

Deklan scrubbed his hands down his face. "Hopefully, it won't come to that."

Tate nodded and left. Silence settled around Deklan like a blanket. Outside, the gentle rush of waves against the wooden hull allowed him to gather his thoughts. Reaching behind, he picked up the detailed sketch of

Lucianna Castien. Name, age, weight, height, hair, and eye color were all stamped in neat letters across the bottom.

A tingle flowed across the ink covering his back. He flexed his shoulders, looking over the drawing of the beautiful young woman. Emphasis on *young*. And yet, the eyes staring out at him from the paper were anything but youthful. She was a study in the perfect subject for an artist to draw. Oval face. Long, straight, dark hair. Pale eyes, if the way the light caught them in the sketch were any indication. The text below the sketch stated her eyes were gray. Thin brows. Shapely nose. Even lips, neither the top nor bottom larger, and were slightly parted as though the artist had captured her mid-breath. He wondered if they were a natural pink or sallow like some women's lips tended to be without the aid of rouge. The faint shadow along her cheek hinted at sculpted cheeks and a soft jawline. The familiarity niggled at him again. How did he know her?

He'd have noticed if a beautiful woman like her had crossed his path. Unless she worked hard not to be seen. But he had crossed paths with her somewhere. An event with too many other people around for him to have been able to spend any real time looking at her. That had to be it.

Deklan knew of her father, the infamous assassin Henry Castien. He'd never met the man personally, though. Castien had retired before Deklan took over the Wolvenguard arch guardianship, and they didn't move in the same circles.

"What are you doing?" he asked the paper. The woman remained silent, her pensive gaze meeting his from the page, giving the sensation she was real, captured within the fibers. Sighing, Deklan returned the sketch to the desk. "I hope I find you in one piece."

TEN MILES OUTSIDE VALENDAVIA, NEW COLUMBIA
Five days later

CIA HAD UNDERESTIMATED JOEL BLACKBAIN. IF SHE WERE being completely honest, she would admit to having misjudged her entire plan. Yes, she made it across the Atlantic safely. Yes, she had somehow managed to get to this encampment by stowing away and sneaking through checkpoints meant to keep men in rather than out. The whole setup felt like a freaky outdoor prison camp, complete with the stench of misery and human filth.

Locating his office had been the easiest part. A three-story, rickety building, the top level had a wall of glass overlooking the pitiful domain. Cia had waited until night, huddling in the shadows of the building across, an unused space from what she could tell. Once the lamplight had gone out, she'd found a way in and up to the spacious room. Cold, hungry, and exhausted, her only goal had been to find the paperwork with the name of the assassin used by the V Alliance and get back to Valdendavia. To civilization, a hot meal, and if she were lucky, a cold shower and a real bed. Twenty minutes in, and she still hadn't found his filing system.

Anxiety clawed at her. What if she'd betrayed her team for nothing? Traveled all this way to leave empty-handed? No. She squeezed her eyes shut. *No.* She would find what she came for. She *would* learn the identity of the man responsible for the worst day of her life.

Cia went to the dark, sizable desk. She plopped down in the leather chair and surveyed the opulent room. Rugs covered the floor. Floor-to-ceiling shelves on either wall were lined with books, sensual figurines, and various other forms of sexual depravity depicted in forms of violence. A shudder raced up her spine. She shouldn't be here. She knew it deep inside, yet she couldn't bring herself to leave without the information she'd traveled so far and risked so much for. Perched on the corner of the desk, a particularly graphic bronzed portrayal of a man mounting some strange fantasy creature of indeterminate gender made her grimace. Her education in debauchery had grown in the past few months. If her father knew…

Cia quickly squashed that thought. If her father knew a lot of things, he'd be horrified. And disappointed. Ignoring the erotica, she took in the entire room. How would she store her files if she were a paranoid fugitive working for a malicious organization? The books drew her attention. Random in their placement, shades of gray in the faint moonlight, they appeared grouped by color. A sliver of excitement raced through her. Rising, she rubbed her hands together.

The first set of books she pulled down were regular leather-bound tombs, the printed words shadows on the paper. She checked the next group, moving closer to the window and the moonlight. Neat rows of numbers in three columns took up pages. His ledger. What her group wouldn't give to see the record. Cia stuffed the register into her shoulder bag and moved on. The rest of the books proved useless. She crossed the room and searched the other collection of shelves.

A polished stone figurine rested on a stack of thin notebooks on the middle shelf nearest the desk. Cia sighed, not wanting to touch the lewd piece. She pushed at the base until the statuette toppled off with a heavy *clunk*. The first book contained columns similar to the ledger she already had, except number groupings followed random symbols instead of all numbers. Turning the book, she shifted closer to the window and tried to make sense of the pages.

The number combinations were familiar. She gazed out the window in thought. Below, a few people milled about on a wooden walkway suspended over mud-saturated ground. Candles in jars stuck on posts provided enough illumination to walk by. Single- and two-story buildings crafted of wood stuck out in jagged silhouettes against the starry horizon. The sequences clicked in her mind. Radio frequency codes. Blinking, Cia flipped through the pages.

While she didn't understand the symbols that were likely the names associated with the radio identification, she *did* know which codes would belong to Szive-ria. None in the book made sense. How many radio calls did the man make? If all the slender books contained names and numbers, that would be thou-sands. Cia chose not to think about how vast a network would need to be to require so many contacts. She searched the next book, then the next one. Finally, she found one with familiar codes and stuck it into her messenger bag. She returned the stack to its original appearance, cringing as she replaced the questionable piece of art.

Patting her bag, she crept across the center of the room. A sense of accomplishment filled her with elation. Something useful had to be in the two books she had confiscated. Maybe the name of the assassin. Or maybe they would be enough to ease the damage she'd done by leaving without notice.

She opened the door. A tall, shadowed figure loomed in front of her. Shocked, Cia recoiled backward, a scream lodged in her throat. Sound didn't have a chance to escape. A hand shot out and grasped her neck under her jaw. Squeezing, her assailant leaned closer. His face came into focus, close enough for the meager light to reflect in his pale eyes.

"Hello, pretty," he whispered, his voice silky.

Cia gurgled and tried to twist free. He would have none of it. He spun her to face the desk and slammed her onto the hard surface. Breath rushed from her lungs in a painful burst. Adrenaline flooded her system. A familiar, unwelcome panic locked her muscles.

Everything sharpened.

Time stretched.

Her talent snapped through her body, useless in her moment of need. Kevin had been an exemplary teacher but only had her for a year of physical training. Not long enough to get her beyond the fear, the memory of that same adrenaline punch that had flooded her system when bullets tore her life apart. If given the chance, she'd have learned enough to move at super-human speed. An opportunity she wasn't granted.

The man licked her jaw, up to her cheek. *Eww.* Cia thrashed under his weight.

"Yes," he hissed into her ear. "Fight me. Please."

Her pulse thundered in her ears and pounded at her temples. She wrapped her hands around his wrist, still holding her throat, just loose enough to allow her enough air not to pass out. A grip requiring experience.

"No one fights me," he complained. "They bring me whores who whimper and sob but lay and take it."

His grip flexed, and the throb through her brain deepened.

"Don't just take it, pretty. Make me work for it." His mouth touched her ear, breathing the words into her. "Make me earn it."

Cia's mind scrambled to form a defense. Kevin had taught her, granted not a lot, nor had they worked enough for repetition to set in, but he'd still shown her plenty. Most of what he'd demonstrated had been standing attacks. The edges of the man's thumbnails bit into the soft flesh under her chin. His elbows dug into her ribs. Under her hands, the tendons of his wrist flexed. His hips surged forward, forcing his thigh between hers. Cia growled, and a flash of memory tore through her mind. Kevin's voice, calm and filled with authority, spoke in soft commands.

Put your hand on his shoulder. Press his weight away. Angle your body free. Use your knees. Your knees, Cia! She did all these things, trying a second time when he fought against her, breaking her hold. She curled her knee into her body, anchoring it into his hip, pushing off and rolling away using the force of his weight against him. A heavy *thud* echoed through the room as her foot collided with the bronze statue. She crouched on the other side of the desk, her eyes level with the flat surface.

The man matched her stance. Moonlight glittered in his gaze, meeting hers across the wooden expanse. "You won't get away again. Treasure the feeling of freedom. Your mine, pretty. All mine. All for me."

Cia eased to the left, closer to the door. He matched her movement.

"You come into *my* domain. Sneak around *my*

office." He tsked. "Did you expect I wouldn't know? Did you expect I wouldn't want to play?"

When she remained silent, he slammed a fist on the desk.

"Who sent you? What are you here for?" The harsh sound of his frustration filled the room. "Fine. Maybe you'll tell me after I've made you scream in pain and spent myself in your little body enough not to want you anymore. Or maybe you'll tell me to keep me from throwing you to the men when I'm finished. Hmm? What will it be?"

Joel Blackbain. The knowledge made a tendril of fear creep through her. Dark hair. Eyes pale enough to catch the light. An unnatural obsession with sexual violence. Her breath wanted to come too fast. She had to focus, get out of the office, and not lose what she'd managed to take. He hadn't realized what she carried, what she'd stolen, and she meant to keep it that way.

"Speak. I want to hear your voice," he said smoothly, all traces of anger gone. "Do you sound as beautiful as you look?"

Cia clenched her jaw and pressed her lips together tight. He laughed, a husky, unused sound deep in his throat.

"Oh, you will be such fun."

No, she wouldn't be. She bit the retort back. Even in the darkness, his amusement was evident on his face. He *knew* she wanted to deny his claim, to shove his evil dominance in his face. One would consider him handsome if his crazy weren't showing. Good bone structure. Well groomed. Strong.

Cia leaped from behind the desk and lunged for the door. He caught her mid-leap, fast. Too fast for her to anticipate or recoil. *Damn it*! All her stupid arrogance at thinking she was ready for the big, scary world flew away with her body sailing through the air and back onto the desk. Objects she hadn't managed to disturb when she'd crossed the desk earlier now scattered underneath her back. She kicked and twisted, but he outweighed her and took pride in subduing fighting women.

Flailing her arms, she searched for something, anything, to fight with. Her fingers brushed cold metal. Cia gripped the thin item. Joel landed on her, his torso crushing her to the desk, his hips slamming into hers and pinning her, making her unable to twist and get a knee between them like she'd managed before.

The bulge of his erection behind his pants ground into her, and she choked on a whimper. She would *not* let him know her distress. He fisted a hand into her hair and braced the other on the table beside her head. Cia blinked. The small black tattoo came into focus. SZ-SB-25225. His felon stamp. Unable to stop the scream of fury, Cia stabbed the metal straight through his hand and into the wood beneath.

He bellowed and rose enough for her to kick at him and scramble away. Pinned, he flopped to the side. The thin metal slid against his palm when he attempted to free it. Still, she wasn't fast enough. He grabbed her hair again and yanked. Fire spread across her scalp, and she cried out.

"There it is, there's my scream. More!" he roared, yanking her across the desk.

Cia flipped and bucked. His free arm wrapped around her chest, crushing her breast in his fingers. He pinned his abdomen to her butt, grinding her hips into the edge of the desk. With a hard yank, he tore his hand free from the desk. She made a feeble grab for the letter opener, still piercing his palm. Blood slid down his wrist and dripped onto the desk next to her. The click of teeth on metal sounded in her ear a second before the sharp point pressed under her jaw.

"Where should I return the favor? Where should I make you bleed first?" he asked, the eerie calm back in his voice. The door burst open. Joel slammed his forearm across her throat and pointed the bloody blade at the intruder. "Get out!"

"Master Blackbain, I apologize for the interruption, but we need to leave. The Wolvenguard was spotted two miles from here. He'll be within sight of the camp in twenty minutes. I have the train prepped and ready to leave."

"Is that what you were? A distraction for the wolf man to get to me?" Joel snarled. Grabbing the front of her shirt, he yanked her up and tossed her at the man. "Take her to a cell. I don't care which one. Lock her up, toss the key off the train on our way."

3

THE MUFFLED VIBRATION OF A TRAIN ENGINE COMING TO life in the distance compelled Deklan to pick up the pace. He cursed. "We've been made," he shouted to his team.

Behind him, their boots crunched on dead leaves and sticks. The dogs panted next to him. He had no scent for them to chase. If he did, they'd outrun the train when it finally started down the tracks, and if a way aboard were present, they'd find that, too. Wait. That wasn't correct. Deklan stopped long enough to sling his pack around to his side. He dug around in a front pouch and retrieved a small hair band. The personal article had often served them in their search for the missing interceptor. While the dogs knew her smell by now, they needed it again to know which scent among the many traces to isolate. They were close enough to the encampment to see foot traffic.

The train whistle screeched through the darkness, warning of impending movement. Night sounds went silent. An owl hooted and shot from the trees to their left.

"*Sesay, vae'ny,*" *Pack, owner*, Deklan ordered. The dogs gathered around him, sitting in expectation, eyes bright in the streaming moonlight. He held the band out to each of them. Their noses stretched close but never touched. "*Sesay, straes'ya.*" *Pack, seek.*

The small pack burst into motion, sprinting toward the camp. Deklan took a second to readjust his rucksack and then followed, pulling on the strength of the bond to saturate his muscles. They ran in long, silent strides. Leaves kicked up and fluttered around them, shimmering silver in the moon's glow. The human side of his team couldn't keep up, but they'd stay as close as they were able.

Low flames burned at a gate entrance. Two men stood watch, their backs to the woods. Deklan isolated the gold and silver threads between his wolves.

Neva, Izia, strivhat, he commanded, motioning to the guards.

Neva took down the left guard first, but Izia was swift enough to keep the other from sounding alarm. Deklan made quick work of incapacitating them. The stop allowed the team to catch up. He was finishing the bindings on the second guard's wrists when Galvin ran through the narrow opening, winded.

Bracing his hands on his knees, Galvin leaned over, sucking in air. "Damn, I wish I could run like you." Arching his back, he rose to height. "What's the plan now?"

"We need to know if the girl is on that train or not," Deklan said.

Sabrie and Tate arrived, gasping for breath. Both

leaned against the thin gate posts. Deklan waited until neither panted for air before moving deeper into the camp, ordering Neva to continue the search for Lucianna Castien. No one used the narrow plank walkways or came to investigate the stealth unit moving in their midst. Either they were locked up, or the train rumble in the middle of the night wasn't unusual.

Neva took several sharp turns, pausing every few seconds to sample the air. She stopped at a solid two-story, cement building with narrow windows up high. Two steel doors, side by side, were the only ways inside. Neva sat and lifted her paw.

Here, the scent ends here, she declared across their link.

Deklan brushed his fingers across her ears. *Good wolf.*

"Lucianna is in here, somewhere."

Deklan glanced down the vacant walk, his mind working. For whatever reason, the woman had been thrown into a building. If he could talk to her, maybe he could find out what happened to Blackbain, if anything. The train may be leaving for supplies or more incoming labor. Or, Deklan's initial belief was that Blackbain had learned of their arrival and fled.

The serial rapist couldn't be allowed to escape again.

Which left him with a choice to make. Split up the team, or waste precious time freeing the inceptor and stay together. And if he separated them, which wolf would remain at his side? Neva listened best, regardless of her leader. Nikita was still learning and needed one of the other wolves to stay on task. Izia was Deklan's alone. While he'd obey as a group, he largely ignored any individual commands a team member gave.

"The three of you take Neva and Nikita and get on that train. Find out if Blackbain is on it," Deklan ordered.

"If he is, do we apprehend?" Galvin asked.

"If you can without incident, yes. If not, no, just follow and collect information. I know it'll be harder with the wolves, so if you have to split up further, do it. We'll catch up."

Sabrie hesitated. Uncertainty crossed her face. She inhaled as if to speak and shook her head when Deklan raised a brow. Patting her leg, she urged Neva to follow with a whispered command.

"Be safe," Tate said, holding a fist to Deklan.

Deklan bumped his knuckles. "You as well."

The small team split off and disappeared into the night. Deklan heaved a breath and crouched in front of the door. Gnats swarmed around them. Izia sat next to him and shook his head, ears flapping. Scowling, Deklan waved a hand in front of his face. Where did these stupid little bugs come from? One tickled up his nose, and Deklan sneezed. Izia did the same.

The lock was a complicated series of bolts. There was no handle to open, which meant the door would likely swing open once the locks were released. Deklan dropped his bag onto the dirt-caked planks and dug around inside. He found his lockpicks and went to work.

A STRANGE SCRATCHING PULLED CIA FROM unconsciousness. Throbbing pain bloomed from her jaw, and her throat ached. A hard surface beneath her pressed into her bones. She blinked, the empty room an unfocused blur. Where was she? Grit met her palms when she tried to push herself up. Weak, everything hurting, her first attempt to rise failed. Grunting, Cia tried again, managing to get onto her hands and knees. Her hair fell in a tangled mess around her face. Her tongue a swollen, dry mass in her mouth. She smacked her tongue and tried to swallow, willing her memory to return.

Vague flashes of violence and fear made her draw in a ragged breath. Everything came back to her in a rush. She gasped and grabbed at her chest, feeling for the strap of her messenger bag. The thin leather belt crossed over her chest, and she followed it to the compact leather satchel. Patting at the contents, she breathed relief when she felt the books still inside. The man who'd punched her in the face when he'd dragged her down the stairs, literally, and thrown her into some kind of prison cell, hadn't bothered to search her. Why, she didn't know.

The odd, shallow scrapes caught her attention again, and she crawled across the cement floor toward the sound. Only a narrow window near the high ceiling allowed light into the room. Heavy shadows surrounded her, and she felt her way through the darkness. Her fingers bumped the edge of a wall a second before her forehead did the same. Scowling, she sat back and tried to force her eyes to see the room's edges. A *snick* echoed through the hollow space. Cia froze. Waited.

When nothing more than another round of scratching happened, she continued her journey around the perimeter of the room. A faint breeze against her fingers made her stop. She touched cool metal. The scoring was louder and vibrated across the surface. Another *snick*. Cia spread her hands across the smooth plane, searching for a handle, and found only steel. Then nothing. The door fell open, and she stared into the most stunning set of golden eyes against silver fur she'd ever seen. A massive wolf gazed back at her.

She didn't get the chance to figure out why a wolf was in front of her. The world trembled and bucked. A deafening roar filled the air. The dog launched into the room past her. A huge body followed, taking Cia along. She slid on her back across the floor, screaming as the room tilted and groaned. Heavy weight settled over her, shielding her as they continued to slide. The thunderous noise pulsed in her head, pulling another scream from her. They crashed into the wall in a heap of bone and muscle, and Cia again succumbed to the darkness.

Gasping awake, Cia attempted to rise, but something hefty and far too warm draped across her body. A wet tongue lapped at her cheek, and she swiped it away.

"Stop," she croaked.

The tongue disappeared, replaced by a cold nose. Cia turned and blinked. Amber eyes came into focus—the wolf from earlier. The dog whined and nudged at her again. Cia pulled her arms out from underneath... a man. Oh, summer sun, a man laid on her. Heavy and solid muscle. She rose enough to try to see him.

Bright light filtered in from above. The night had come and gone. The scent of smoke curled in the air. No noise, of nature or human, sounded. Cia pondered that for a moment before trying to scoot back enough to try and wiggle free. The wolf made another low cry of distress, nudging at the man's arm, laying limp at her side. She moved carefully to allow his head to remain cushioned by her body. Dark, wine-red hair, long without a hint of curl, covered his face. She figured the length fell at least past his shoulders. Cia brushed the strands from his face and jerked her hand free in shock.

Deklan Ralston.

"Stars above," she whispered, her heart jumping into her throat.

Trembling, she pressed her fingers to his neck. A steady pulse met her touch. Still shaky, she smoothed more hair from his handsome face. Wisps caught in the dark stubble covering his jaw. He'd found her. And she had no doubt with the beautiful wolf and him picking the lock for her prison cell, *she* had been his target. She clenched her jaw. Had Joel Blackbain escaped after all?

The acrid stench of smoke hit her again, and she glanced up. Haze floated in front of the barred opening. She kept one hand on Deklan and reached for the wolf. "What happened, I wonder?"

The dog had no answers to give. Cia sighed and continued to smooth her fingers through Deklan's hair. She took him in. His face relaxed in unconsciousness, she traced his strong jaw to his temple and brow. Everything about this man was perfection. She remembered the first time she'd seen him at Shield Guardian Terravine's annual Wintervail party. A force of his own, standing across the room, tall and imposing, she hadn't been able to stop staring.

Her uncle's wife, Melody, had noticed her ogling. Cia had blurted out how gorgeous he was. At which point, her aunt-by-marriage had burst her bubble by telling her exactly who she'd developed an instant crush. An arch guardian. *The* Wolvenguard. Who Melody also felt was too old for her. Well, Cia disagreed on the age bit. Her parents had shared a gap. Age didn't bother her. The ranked guardianship he held, however...

Cia was the daughter of a notorious assassin, raised in secret, only venturing into ranked society once a year before winter set in. Deklan's world was as foreign to her as her little secluded one would be to him. Working for the First Intelligence Office was a perfect fit for her. The organization was notorious for its secrecy. Cia would never have to reveal her guardian status unless she wanted to. And she didn't. She had zero desire to be thrust into the glitz and snobbery of ranked society. Once a year was enough for her, thank you very much.

A sigh of longing left her as she retraced the angles of his face. Disappointment filled her. She was bold enough to ask for what she wanted, and she definitely wanted to know this man. Before her mother's instant death, Cia hadn't been so audacious. But realizing in a single horrific moment how fragile life was had left an impact. Tomorrow wasn't promised. Leaning forward, she pressed a kiss to his warm temple.

"Too bad, wolf man," she whispered against his skin.

Tingles spread across her lips, and she resisted the urge to taste the skin beneath hers. She frowned at the odd impulse. His scent filled her nostrils, and she inhaled deeply, replacing the pungent odor of smoke with his unique aroma. The woodsy musk of juniper and sandalwood mixed with warm notes of cashmere wood. Masculine and comforting, Cia rested her forehead on his temple and allowed herself to be surrounded.

Deklan stirred, and she straightened. His wolf stiffened, staring intently. Groaning, he braced himself on his arms, and she shifted away from him. He fell back on his butt in an ungraceful heap, grabbing his head between both hands.

"What in the artic happened?" he asked, his voice gruff and raw.

"I'm not sure," she answered, looking up at the window. "Nothing good."

He released his head long enough to follow her gaze. "I remember the ground shook, and I saw something…" He pressed his fingers to his temples. "I don't know what I saw."

Cia eyed the barred frame. The bars weren't part of the metal but rather part of a grate that appeared to lift from the narrow rectangle. "How high do you think that window is?"

Using the wall to brace himself, Deklan slowly rose to his feet. He wobbled, found his balance, and eased across the space. His arm slid along the wall toward the window, coming short by at least two feet. "Maybe ten feet. I can jump it."

"But can you fit?"

He took a step back and tilted his head. "Nope."

"Didn't think so." Cia rose and dusted off her hands and butt. "Okay. I think I can fit."

"What about the…" he looked at the metal and cement wall and finished his sentence with a sigh, "door."

"Yeah," she drew out. "Not much of a door from in here."

With one hand braced on the wall, he dropped his head, shoulders tense.

Cia reached for him, hesitated, and pulled back. "Are you okay?"

The wolf nudged his leg, whining. Deklan reached down and spread his fingers between the dog's ears. "My head is killing me. I don't know if it's all this smoke, or... maybe I hit it or something."

"Let me see," she said softly, closing the distance between them.

He lifted his head and looked at her for the first time since he awoke. Cia forgot to breathe. Deklan had a unique shade of skin, not quite brown, not quite bronze, but some type of beautiful in-between shade only his family seemed to have. His mother was pale brown, his father a cinnamon bronze, and together, they'd made stunning children. The tone brought the expectation of dark eyes in shades of brown. Instead, he looked at her with vivid ocean-green irises, startling in their contrast to the rest of him. Even his hair was dark without the sun or another bright form of light, it looked maybe brown, maybe black. With enough light, the red highlights appeared.

Cia forced herself to focus and took in his face. He towered over her and had to lean over for her to reach his head. A thin line of blood trickled down his jaw by his ear. She touched his jaw and turned his cheek to look closer. A small cut marred his skin, and a bruise discolored his temple. She brushed her fingers under the contusion, and he flinched away.

"Let me see your eyes," she said.

He met her gaze. This time, Cia remembered to keep breathing. She moved them until he stood in a light beam and checked his pupil reaction.

"I don't think you have a concussion, but I'm not a medical scientist," she said, rechecking his pupils by covering and uncovering his eyes. Long lashes brushed against her palm.

His brows drew together as he closed his eyes. "All my wolves are still part of me, no broken bonds, so it's not that."

Cia brushed his hair away from his temple. "You're going to have a nasty bruise here."

Frowning, he touched his temple and winced. He straightened, and she took a step away. "Did you see my bag?"

She shook her head. "No. I only woke up a few minutes before you."

"Maybe it's still out there. I have something that'll help with the headache."

Cia looked up at the narrow window. "Did you get Blackbain?"

He tipped his head to the side, his stare unfocused. "No. They're stowed away on his train, which has been traveling all night. My logistics expert believes they're heading to a port."

"How do you know that?" she asked in disbelief.

"I told Neva to alert my team that I'm linked to her and can hear them if they speak to her."

Cia's eyes widened. "You can do that? Hear what they hear?"

"Yes, and see and smell. Thankfully, I can't taste, and I can't feel, either." He braced his hands on his hips and looked around the small, empty cell.

"That's incredible," she whispered.

"All beast masters share the same connection with their animal," he stated as if his skill were a boring, average fact.

"I know beast masters are more common in Ruthenia than Sziveria, so maybe to you, it's perfectly normal that you can talk to animals. I have never met anyone like you," she said.

A shallow smile curved his lips, revealing the beginning of a dimple on his right cheek. "Then we're even. I've never met anyone quite like you before, either."

Cia frowned and pondered what he could mean.

He didn't make her ask. "We're trapped in a cement cube. Something is burning out there. I hear no sounds of life." He touched under her chin, tilting her head back to expose her neck, and her heart attempted to leap out of her chest. "And it looks like someone tried to choke you to death. I have no idea if you're even okay. Yet here you are, calm, making sure my brain isn't about to leak out of my ears."

"Oh no. Should I be crying? Or freaking out? Or just generally making this situation more difficult?" she asked with big eyes.

He laughed, and yep, the smile launched him from gorgeous to devastating. "You're what? Twelve?"

"Nineteen," she corrected with a glare.

"Right." He waved a hand as if nineteen and twelve were the same age. "Most girls your age would do all the things."

"Most girls didn't watch their baby brother and mother die," she bit out and turned her back to him, looking at the window. "Most girls don't know how useless screaming is when the worst has already happened, and freaking out fixes nothing. Dead is still dead."

"Lucianna, I didn't mean—"

"Cia," she said to cut off an unnecessary apology. "My family calls me Cia."

He turned her around to face him, leaning close so their gazes were level. His mouth, full and so, so tempting, was *right there*. Cia clenched her jaw and dug her fingers into her hips to avoid touching him.

"I'm not your family, Guardian Castien."

Oh damn, he knew her position. She blinked at the stupidity of her surprise. Of course, he knew her position. He'd been sent to drag her sorry, betraying butt back home. "How much trouble am I in?"

"I have no idea."

Worrying about the unknown, yet inevitable return home, was useless. Time for a subject change. "I think I can fit through that window."

He moved to stand beside her, arms crossed. The sleeves of his shirt pulled taut over his biceps. Cia worked with fit men, sometimes daily, and yet she appreciated the flex of his strength on a different level than the men she trained around. Height-wise, he matched Kevin. Tall. If Cia were to rest her head on his chest, she'd be able to feel his heartbeat under her cheek. But where Kevin was lithe, Deklan had the same bulk as Mason. Big arms. Big shoulders. Big chest. She glanced down at his boots. Big feet. She doubted there was much *small* about the beast master.

"I won't," he said.

Cia shrugged. "That's okay. I can pick the lock on the door like you did last night."

He glanced down at her, brow raised. "You have the tools?"

Grabbing the leather strap across her chest, she lifted the bag from her side. "Everything I need is right in here."

His attention shifted back to the window. "All right. Do you want me to hoist you up there, or…?"

"I can climb up you and stand on your shoulders."

His head snapped around. "You can what?"

Cia pointed to the ground under the window. "Stand right here. I'll climb up and stand on your shoulders. Easiest and steadiest way. I will have to pull the grate free, so you'll have to anchor my feet."

He stared at her. "I don't think—"

Cia grinned. "So don't think."

4

A SPECIFIC MANTRA HAD TAKEN RESIDENCE IN DEKLAN'S brain. *She's too young. She's too young. She's too young.* Over and over, he repeated the phrase, the reminder, like the lifeline it had become. He could not, would not, feel anything but professional civility for the woman, *girl,* standing in front of him. Not exactly the picture of innocence with her challenging gaze full of attitude.

She was more stunning in living color than the artistic rendering he'd stared at for days. Eyes a peculiar shade of gray, bluer rather than steel. Her long hair had been braided at one point, but an obvious struggle and whatever had happened in the night had left the golden brown frayed and dust-coated. Underneath the grime, her rosy beige skin looked touchable. Soft. He tightened his crossed arms to keep from giving in to the impulse. Her full lips, a natural lush pink, were another temptation he had to look away from. Summer sun, but she was beautiful.

Deklan returned his attention to the high window. One way or another, they had to get out of here, and the small opening seemed the only option. He growled. Izia mimicked the sound, and Deklan uncoiled himself enough to soothe his wolf.

Cia took a small step away. "Is your dog all right?"

"He's fine," Deklan said calmly. "He sensed my agitation, is all."

"He's beautiful. What's his name?"

"Izia."

"And you're bonded to him, too?" she asked, her stare curious.

"I'm bonded to three wolves."

Her mouth fell open. "I… I didn't know that was possible."

"Generations ago, it was common for a wolf beast master to bond with a small pack. Now? It's unheard of." He shrugged. "My father chose to accept a bond with my mother. Her Sziverian genetics was a blank canvas for my father's stronger, more dominant Ruthenian traits."

"My parents were both Ruthenian," Cia said. "My father never spoke of why he left to serve Sziveria."

Everything in Deklan stilled. He wanted to flee to the opposite side of the room and not allow her to touch him again. Under any circumstances. Cia could forge an unbreakable connection between them with little more than attraction and thought. He wanted to know how much her parents had taught her about their genetics before he allowed her into his personal space. But they didn't have the time. They had to get out of this box and somehow find a way to follow his team.

He'd have to be careful on his end of the emotional spectrum. Not allow any errant desires to manifest. Deklan shoved all his feelings down deep and locked them away. He was being overly cautious, he knew. At no point had she given the impression she wanted anything from him in any capacity. And he refused to acknowledge the hint of disappointment.

"All right," he said. "Let's do it your way. The locks outside are tricky, but I can walk you through it to make it faster."

"Great." She grinned at him. Her teeth were white and straight, only adding to her overall beauty.

Deklan unwound one of many leather straps from his wrist to tie back his hair and moved closer to the window, looking up. "How do you want to—"

Her hands gripped his shoulders a second before her weight landed on his hips. Her bare toes dug into his side. She climbed him like a tree, rising onto his shoulders, using the wall in front of them to steady herself.

"Oh good, it's not locked. Whew." Her weight shifted, and Deklan wrapped a hand around her calf to ensure she remained stable.

The warmth of her skin seeped through the thin fabric of her pants. Her muscles shifted and flexed beneath his palms. Deklan stared straight ahead at the gray wall, his gaze tracing hairline cracks in the surface.

"All right, I'll need your hands to get higher," she said, slightly breathless.

Deklan inverted his hands and helped her balance on his palms. Looking up, he slowly lifted her. His biceps strained more from making sure she stayed steady than from her weight, which was less than one of his wolves. When her shoulders cleared the window, he pushed her, helping her launch the rest of the way through. An odd sound left her, but before he could inquire, her hips and legs disappeared through the opening. Deklan let out a breath and took a step back.

"Ready to get out of here, Izia?" Deklan asked, petting his wolf. The dog sat, tongue hanging out. "Yeah, me too."

Deklan picked up Cia's discarded shoes and moved to the door. "Are you out there yet?" he asked.

"Yeah," she answered, her voice muffled.

Deklan guided her through the process of navigating the heavy tumble bolts. The last one clicked, and the door fell open. Smoking ruins, as far as he could see, greeted him.

Cia stood, a singed bag in her hand. "I think the doorway protected it from the worst."

Deklan stepped into the harsh morning light. "What in the arctic."

"I know." A frown marred her pretty face. "The alarming part is there's no bodies that I can see. Do you think they evacuated them?"

"How many people were here when you arrived?"

"I don't know, it was nearly dark. I only saw a few."

Deklan looked around again, turning. Ash floated in the air and covered the ground in a thick, gray blanket. Only the smoldering squares of what once were foundations attested to anything ever having existed in the location. What had that amount of power? Bombs blew things to pieces. What could leave a fine coating of ash behind like snow? He turned and looked at their building. Scorch marks scored the exterior, but the structure remained strong.

"A volcano?" Cia asked, facing the forest, her eyes shielded from the sun.

Deklan followed her gaze. The trees stood, though the ones nearest were covered in the same fine powder as everything else. "We would have baked to death if it'd been a volcano, and none of those trees would be standing."

She wrinkled her nose and wrapped her arms around her waist. "I don't like this."

Deklan agreed. "There's a reason the UZ's exist."

"Last night, this was practically a swamp. They had boardwalks in place."

Cautious, Deklan pressed a boot toe where the walkway used to extend. His shoe met solid ground. He took a slow step forward. Izia whined. Deklan held his hand back, and Izia touched a wet nose to his fingertips.

What do you smell? Deklan asked across their bond.

Too much smoke, too much.

"We go slow," he said. Apprehension curled through him. Whatever had caused the odd destruction originated from the UZ, of which they stood within the boundary. He wanted to be far from here as soon as possible. "Single file, step where I step."

"All right."

A faint breeze tugged at his clothing, warm and balmy. Deklan glanced up at the cloudless, vivid blue sky. "I think it's going to be hot today."

"Hot? Does anywhere get truly hot?"

"There's still a desert in what's left of Africa, but I don't think it gets hot like it used to, pre-cataclysm. But for us, yes, it'll feel quite unpleasant." He tested the ground before each step, managing a steady pace. "I was uncomfortable yesterday walking during the day."

"I was warm, but not enough to remove my jacket."

"Today, you probably will."

Thirsty, Izia whined.

I know, but nothing here will be safe.

He didn't know at what point water would be safe. Not until they reached civilization or rain fell.

They eased along the barren landscape. Burnt plants and cracking mud crunched under their feet, mingling with their heavy breaths. The eerie lack of nature only added to his uneasiness. After an hour of walking, he shrugged out of his jacket and handed it to Cia to stuff into his pack. She'd tied hers around her waist at some point. Her damp hair clung to her cheeks and neck.

The flush of her skin and a glistening layer of perspiration had Deklan's throat constricting. He imagined she'd look similar after a strenuous round between the sheets. A bead of moisture snaked from her collarbone down between her pert breasts, where her once-white tank stretched tight. Deklan turned away from her, his heart hammering in his ears and another, more uncomfortable part of his anatomy.

"You weren't kidding," she huffed behind him. "I hope we clear this soon. I think the ash is making it hotter than normal."

"And the lack of shade."

"Oh wow, do you think we'll burn? I've heard of sunburns." She grunted. "I've heard they hurt. Do you think they hurt? Have you ever had one?"

Deklan shielded his eyes against the glare of sun coming off the ash. "Why so chatty all of a sudden?"

"I don't know. I'm boiling and sticky. We're heading in the opposite direction of the city all my things are in. I'm trying not to panic if you want the truth."

"You're an operative for the First Intelligence Office. Panic isn't an emotion they usually accept for their guardians in the field."

"Operative in training."

"And yet, here are you," he said, unable to keep the reproach from his voice.

"Were they upset?"

Deklan didn't pretend not to know what she asked about. "Yes. Did you expect them not to care?"

She blew a raspberry. "I don't know."

"Funny thing about teams," Deklan said, stepping over a large chunk of smoking wood, "they tend to care about what happens to each other."

"I'm aware of team dynamics."

"Really?" he asked skeptically.

"Yes, really."

Deklan clenched his jaw and looked over his shoulder at her. Some of his frustration must have shown in his eyes since she gasped and took a hasty step back. "And yet, here you are," he said softly.

Her already red cheeks deepened in hue. "I don't expect anyone to understand."

"They might have surprised you if you'd tried."

Her lips compressed in a tight line. Deklan went back to navigating the unknown path.

"You know," she began, "the tracks ran on the west side of the forest between the two mountain ranges. I bet they form a loop between the two cities. If we head in that direction, maybe we'llleeeaaahhh!"

Deklan whirled around on her shriek-morphing scream. Eyes wild and wide, she struggled in ash-coated mud up to her thighs. Deklan signaled for Izia to halt, seeing the wolf about to spring in his peripheral. Izia laid sphynx style and remained still.

"Freeze," he commanded on a harsh bark.

Cia stopped moving. Hands raised, she stared at him.

"It's sinking mud. The more you struggle, the deeper you'll sink," he explained.

"How far?" she asked, breathless.

"I have no idea. Some are only a few feet deep, others too deep to ever know."

Color drained from her face. "What do I do?"

"For now, just relax."

"Relax?" She sputtered and waved her arms. "How am I supposed to relax? I'm trapped in mud!"

"If you'd followed directions and stayed behind me, you wouldn't be, would you?" he said between gritted teeth.

She flapped a hand and looked away from him. "Fine. Be that way."

"What other way, exactly, am I supposed to be?" he asked, looking around for a long stick that wouldn't turn to ash when touched.

Dust floated around her, and she flicked at small, settled piles in front of her. "I don't know, charmed by my youthful innocence? Patient with my stupidity because, poor thing, I've lost so much."

Deklan stared in silence until her gaze rose back to his. Pretty eyes. So much bluer now when surrounded by the colorless world. "Is that how you've been treated?"

She shrugged. "I think my father finally agreed to allow my training, providing I was treated delicately."

Deklan spread his arms. "Nothing is delicate about real life or what this world *will* throw at you."

She held up soot-coated hands. "Hey, I get it. I know that more than anyone. I figured the team I was placed with knew that, too."

"Nuh-uh, nope," he said, popping his *p*. He returned to searching for a lever. "Stop trying to blame your team for your inability to follow a simple task. I'm not buying it. You may be young, but you've faced enough horror to have lost naivety. And you aren't stupid."

Using his foot, he brushed away ash and kicked at debris. When he glanced her direction again, he found her staring at him, her jaw clenched.

"Fine," she snapped and looked away on a glare and motioned to her right. "There are rails to the east of here. I thought if we went that direction, we'd find them and see if they were still usable. If we walk them long enough, we're bound to find civilization or a train we can hitch a ride on."

"I know about the tracks. I was heading to them on a safer route. However, even if I weren't, the proper way to have handled that would have been to call a halt and have a discussion, not be a brat and take off on your own."

She recoiled. "Brat?"

He snapped his fingers and tsked. "Forgot to add the spoiled to it, didn't I? Sorry, I won't make the mistake again in the future."

While she sputtered, he dug up a half-buried stick with his boot. He tested the strength to ensure it wouldn't break halfway through the rescue. He dropped his pack on the ground at his feet.

"I'm not a brat," she murmured, reaching for the stick.

"Fine, defiant rebel then. Either one will endanger you, therefore endangering your team." He braced himself. "Grab hold, and when you can reach my hands, take them. Don't let go, or we'll have to start over."

. . .

CIA WRAPPED HER GRUBBY HANDS AROUND THE STICK. SHE hated the odd, tight sensation in her chest. The knowledge she had disappointed him. She shouldn't care. He shouldn't mean anything to her. Yet, she did care. His opinion mattered, and right now, she didn't think it could get much lower.

As the rough wood bit into her palms and the mud acted like a jealous lover refusing to let go, Cia wondered what he would have done if she'd been honest. If she'd admitted his assessment about her lack of faith in her team had been too uncomfortable, she'd sought a means to deflect. All she managed to do anymore was disappoint those she wanted to please.

Mistakes and misjudgments were becoming a dangerous pastime of hers. His calling her a brat had also been a little too accurate if she were honest. She *had* allowed her vendetta to saturate her every waking action. But she wasn't ready to give up. Not yet. If she had to become a *defiant rebel*, as he stated, then so be it.

Inch by inch, he heaved her forward. At some point, he'd unbuttoned his shirt well past his collarbone, exposing a defined expanse of chest sprinkled with dark hairs. The sun gleamed off his burnished skin, highlighting the strain and flex of his muscles. A sheen of sweat coated him, racing trails down his temples and darkening sections of his clothing. Cia tested her reach, still at least a hand length away from being able to touch his fingers. The mud sucked and gripped at her. She had to fight the urge to help, to try to squirm and find some purchase in the muck.

Each small increment she moved, her shoes slipped further off her feet. She squeaked as her toes brushed the heel, leaving her shoeless. If Deklan noticed her increased distress, he didn't let it show. He grasped her wrist in a tight grip. Cia wrapped her hands around his forearms. Under her palms, the slide and flex of his muscles sent a little thrill zinging to her stomach. Ridiculous considering the situation.

Grunting, he pulled her up and forward. The mud released her in a sudden rush of goo. Cia careened into him, drawing in her legs to keep from getting stuck again. Deklan turned away from the bog, rolling into their fall. They landed in a heap of tangled limbs, sticky mud, and billowing ash. Cia coughed and struggled to rise. Her hand slid along his stomach. She had an unexpected impulse to skim her hand up his torso and lay along his body, find out how all his masculine lines would feel along her softer ones.

Where did these odd urges come from? Yes, she found him attractive. Immensely. He made her curious in a way the other men in her life never had. Which was saying a lot since the men she worked with were handsome, kind, and held the same physical standards as the one beside her. They, however, were all happy and married. Perhaps that was the difference. All the other men in her life were taken. Then again, Deklan might be, too. Cia knew nothing about his personal life.

Deklan remained on his back, his gaze on the sky, arms spread at his side. The blue sky reflected in his eyes, making their teal shade richer and more vibrant. The fine gray powder settled over them, sticking to his skin and leaving dark streaks behind. Using his hip for leverage, she sat up. Izia ambled over and nuzzled Deklan's temple. Deklan turned into the show of affection, rubbing under the dog's chin. Cia looked at her mud-coated toes.

"I lost my shoes," she sighed.

Deklan laid his arms across his stomach, continuing

to smooth his fingers along Izia's jaw as the wolf laid his head on Deklan's shoulder. "We'll figure it out."

Cia scrunched her face. "I'm sorry."

"Please just follow instructions. When we return to Sziveria, you can go back to however you function with your team. With me? Listen." He rose from a prone position in one smooth, flexible kick-up.

Cia blinked. She'd only ever seen Kevin pull off that move. She hadn't yet mastered the action. The rapid movement stirred more dust into the air, sparkling in the brilliant noon light. The oppressive heat weighed on her, and they hadn't even started moving again.

"Those pants are going to turn into brick," he said, picking up his bag.

Cia poked at the tacky mud covering her lower half. "So, what should I do? Walk around pantless *and* shoeless?"

He rummaged around in his pack and dropped one, then two boots at her side. Next, he pulled free a long pair of cotton pants and held them down to her. "All of this will be too big, but it's better than nothing."

Cia accepted the clothing, leaving behind muddy fingerprints. "Thanks."

With Izia at his side, he walked along the path they'd been forging, his back to her. Cia huffed and tried to peel herself out of the pants, but the fabric bunched at her ankles and stuck to her skin at every twist and yank. Her arms weren't long enough to pull, and kicking only tangled the mess.

She muttered a low curse and breathed against the frustration. "Hey, um, Wolvenguard?"

"Yeah?"

"I can't get my pants off."

5

DEKLAN FROZE AND FISTED HIS HANDS AT HIS SIDE. "COME again?"

Behind him, a huff of annoyance sounded. "My pants are stuck. Can you please help me?"

Slowly, Deklan turned. She sat, legs akimbo. The hem of her dirty shirt pooled between her thighs. The pants were twisted into a saturated mess around her ankles. Though streaked with muck, the pale, creamy length of both her legs was a sensual sight. Defined muscle flexed as she kicked at the offending garment, and he no longer had to guess what her bare legs looked like. Something he reminded himself he had no business thinking about. She wouldn't meet his gaze. Her cheeks were stained red, and her fingers toyed in the tangled fabric near her knees.

Deklan affixed his bag to his shoulders before leaning over and grasping the soggy fabric. Grit coated his palms, and he freed her from the pants with a quick yank. Squealing, she toppled over, legs spread, giving him a rousing view of her pink panties and bare

63

stomach where her shirt had bunched around her ribs from her falling backward. Deklan sucked in a sharp breath and spun on his heel, but it was too late. Arousal, hot and fierce, burst through him.

He... *wanted.*

Clenching his fists, he forced his breathing to remain neutral and took several steps away from her. While he liked to think he had control over his baser instincts, he was, at his heart, the beast he claimed to be a master over. His inner self wanted nothing more than to claim. Mud, ash, danger, exposure, none of those things mattered. She was beautiful, and she was currently half-naked. And she was also eleven solid years younger than him. Inexperienced in life, probably in love as well. Deklan *knew* better.

"Thanks," she said, closer than he expected.

Deklan chanced to look and found her dressed, *thank you stars above*, fiddling with the ties at the waist of the sleep pants he'd given her. Tangled hair, matted with sweat, dust, and mud, hung in thick strands around her shoulders. Sighing, Deklan unwound a leather strap from his wrist and shifted until he stood behind her. He gathered the tousled mess in his hands and tied it at her nape. The heavy weight settled over his palms, and it didn't take much to imagine how the long tresses, when clean, would feel brushing across his chest or stomach. Deklan let the mass fall from his hands to form a messy tail along her back.

"You're going to have a hard time getting the mud out," he said.

She touched the strip of leather he'd wound tight around her hair. "Thanks, and it won't be the first time I've had to wash junk from my hair."

"Ready?"

She nodded, adjusting the satchel she'd never been without across her chest.

"Good." Deklan pointed at the ground. "Every step, exactly where I do."

Using her index finger, she drew an X over her heart. "Promise."

Deklan narrowed his eyes on her. *Izia, ursla'viti ze'feminka.*

Izia fell back until he could follow Cia.

If she alters course at all, tell me.

He barked twice.

Cia jumped. "Did he see something? Hear something?"

"No, he let me know he understood my command."

"What command?"

Deklan tapped his temple. "The one I sent him."

Amazement filled her eyes, and she shook her head. "I may never get over how awesome that is, that you can *communicate* with your wolves."

A ball formed in his chest. He waited for the speculative interest to enter her gaze. The appraising curiosity. Then again, maybe she was too young for such games. She hadn't reacted oddly when he'd told her the first time. Though, she could still surprise, or rather disappoint him. At the last social event he'd attended, a girl her age had sashayed up to him and propositioned him right in front of her giggling group of friends. He almost said yes just to watch her faint since it'd been clear she'd taken a dare and had zero interest in starting anything with him. Instead, he'd gone another low route and insulted her. Loose women were dangerous, and he'd had no desire to contract human rabies syndrome. Only marriage would land a woman in his bed within the borders of Sziveria. She'd been appropriately outraged, had spat *animal* in his face, and stalked off, nose in the air. Apparently, her Mistress of Etiquette had forgotten the lesson on not making an enemy of an arch guardian. His younger sister had had a grand time reporting about the girl for the gossip column she wrote for.

But none of those things flickered across Cia's face. Only genuine wonder and something more innocent. A pure attraction he'd never encountered from a woman. Shocked, Deklan turned away from her and started searching out their path again.

The sun arced a brutal path across the sky. Every hour, Izia whined about thirst. A need they all felt. Deklan licked his parched lips and shaded his eyes as the level of ash lessened. In the distance, the fine layer disappeared, leaving green trees and grassy fields.

Deklan increased his speed. "I think we're out of it."

She sighed and coughed. "Great. Any sign of the rails?"

A glimmer beyond the field caught his eye. "Maybe."

Wind kicked up, and a deep, faraway rumble had him looking at the sky. Miles away, a line of black clouds had him frowning. Lightning snaked through the storm, rolling in their direction.

"We need to move," he said, increasing their pace. He sent Izia ahead, pulling on their bond to hear what his wolf heard.

"I can't go much faster," Cia huffed. "These boots keep trying to outwalk my feet."

Deklan paused, held up a fist, cocked his head, and listened through Izia. The low reverberation of steel-on-steel and the faint swoosh of a magnetic engine increased his heart rate.

Quickly, he shrugged out of his bag and shoved it at Cia. "Put this on and hop on my back."

She wrapped her arms around the bag and stared at him with big eyes. "What?"

"Do it!"

Startled, she shrugged the bag onto her shoulders. He turned his back to her and squatted, even though he knew she'd have no issues climbing up his frame. Her weight settled onto his hips and around his shoulders. Deklan gripped her thighs and took off. Her booted feet flopped and bumped into his upper legs. Clasping his hands, he moved them under her butt.

"Lock your ankles around my waist," he said, increasing his speed.

She obeyed and arranged her forearms around his collarbone, balancing her weight evenly between his shoulders and hips. "What's going on?"

"Train."

Her muscles tightened around him. Supple and firm, not so different from all the women he'd known in the past, yet very different from what Sziveria considered beautiful. The body wrapped so fully around him was a product of hours of training and strength-building. If he needed his hands, she could maintain her position on her own. He should allow her to, but he couldn't bring himself to release her. Having his hands full of her felt too good. Too right.

Her weight shifted to his left. "Where? How do you know that?"

"Izia can hear it."

"Your wolf told you?"

Deklan shook his head but didn't offer any further explanation. He'd already told her about the connection he could achieve with his animals. She'd either forgotten in the chaos or the discomfort at the extrasensory ability buried the knowledge for her. He was no stranger to a fear of his talent.

Hurry, alpha, hurry!

Deklan increased his speed. Cia squealed and tightened her hold, hugging until nothing but clothes remained between them. Every flex of her body seared across his back. Deklan's heart pounded from the intimate contact and increased physical demand. He struggled to maintain his focus. In his mind, visions of her wrapped around his front, clinging to him for an entirely different reason, left him struggling for breath.

The hum and rhythmic *chuh-chink-chuh-chink* of metal wheels sliding over steel rails grew closer. Louder. Deklan pushed harder. His feet pounded the grass. An opening between the trees ahead provided a clear path to the train zipping past. Cutting across, he called Izia to him. The wolf came charging through the narrow stretch of woods, eyes wild, ears pinned, tongue flapping.

Noise vibrated the air and the ground beneath his feet. Open cars clacked past, the chains and locks jangling with the motion. Deklan looked the containers over, noting only three in a row were empty. The rest were closed and sealed. If they missed those cars, they'd miss their ride.

Up into the car, Izia, Deklan commanded. When the wolf hesitated, he encouraged. *You can do it, dokhor vok.*

Izia put on a burst of speed, racing the moving compartment. Corded muscle bunched and released under his fur in a powerful spring of movement. He sailed into the air and through the gap, tumbling into the darkened interior. A second later, his gray nose and golden eyes appeared in the opening. He barked in a mixture of excitement and anxiety at being in the rail car alone.

A heavy gust of wind swept down the narrow corridor created by the woods on his left and the train on his right. Deklan fought against it, pulling on the strength of his heritage to push his muscles beyond their normal endurance and ability. Cia pressed her cheek to his. Her breath puffed across his jaw in jagged exhales.

"I'm going to have to throw you in," he tried to yell above the train and wind.

"What?"

"Just be ready!"

Her grip tightened, something he didn't think possible. "What? What are you saying!"

Deklan unwound her legs from his waist, and the moment he was parallel with the doorway, he grabbed her arms and slung her into the car. She screamed and flew through the air, landing on her back well inside the opening. To his relief, she recovered quickly. On her hands and knees, she scurried to the opening and reached her hand out to him.

"Come on!" she urged. The wind whipped strands of her filthy hair free from the binding.

Deklan made a hasty grab for the rusted handle low enough for a worker to reach from ground level. His first attempt failed. The tips of his fingers grazed the rough surface enough to make him stretch. Wrapping his hand around the cold metal, his arm jerked, and his thighs burned from the strain of maintaining his speed. Cia's small yet strong hands wrapped around his forearm and clutched at the front of his shirt. If Deklan failed, he'd pull them both free.

Sweat poured down his temples and ran along his

back. He clenched his teeth and dug deeper, launching himself into the train. He collided with Cia, sending them tumbling and rolling along the grimy, plank wood floor. They slid to a stop against the far wall. Sprawled on his back, Deklan gasped for air. Cia lay across him. Her hands fisted in the damp fabric of his shirt, and she pushed herself up, straddling his hips.

"Yeah!" she shouted, slapping his shoulder. Laughing, she leaned over him and pressed a smacking kiss to his lips before rolling away with another ecstatic whoop. "Did you see that, wolfie, did you?"

Her continued laughter echoed around the empty cargo car, joined by Izia's equally excited yips. Deklan laid a hand across his quivering stomach muscles. Above him, light strobed across the dark ceiling. A crack of thunder rumbled over the deep hum of the train. The steel walls trembled. Izia scrambled over to him and buried his nose under Deklan's shoulder. Deklan patted his head, smoothing his fingers along the wolf's fuzzy ear.

Cia's face appeared in his line of sight. She sat cross-legged near Izia's hunches, petting his side to his leg. "He's scared of thunder?"

"Yeah, most of them are. They don't like the sudden loud sound. Neva's my only wolf not to care. Nikita whines and cries. Izia wants to hide. He picked up that habit from Vyshe."

"Vyshe?"

An ache settled around his heart. "I lost him a couple of years ago."

Her hand brushed his, still lodged in Izia's fur. "I'm sorry. Connected as you are, their death must be difficult to endure."

"Yes." His voice caught on the word, and he

cleared his throat. "His was my second and probably the most difficult since he was from my original bond."

"I can't imagine it'd be any easier to lose this one here," she said, barely loud enough to be heard over the storm and train.

Deklan's fingers curled into the soft fur of Izia's neck. The wolf's hot breath puffed out his nose and over Deklan's shoulder. "No, losing him would not be any easier." He couldn't stop the scoff of pent-up hurt still left from the death of Vyshe. "I'll probably end up like my father and retiring to a life of support if I lose another one."

"A life of support?"

"Yeah, he offered to help with investigations, but he wouldn't do anything that jeopardized his wolf or his wife on purpose. He lost two and decided losing a third wasn't an option. Not if he wanted to remain sane. After losing two myself, I understand."

"How long will you have your wolves?" she asked, scratching between Izia's ears.

"For my entire life, if they don't get sick or seriously injured."

Her hand froze. "Decades? Really?"

"Yes. My father's wolf, Lunah, is over thirty, probably closer to forty."

"That's incredible."

"The Ruthenarc wolf is a remarkable breed."

"There is a lot that comes from Ruthenia that's pretty remarkable, including the human variety," she said, laughing.

Deklan tilted his head back, his gaze meeting hers. "Have you ever been?"

"To Ruthenia?"

He nodded as best he could from his awkward position.

"No. My father had no desire to return."

And she was too young to have considered venturing on her own before now. "Well, maybe now that you've made yourself a world traveler, you can visit."

"Ha, ha," she quipped.

The gentle *tink* of rain hitting metal made Deklan rise. Another roll of thunder reverberated around them. The mild patter turned into gushing torrents. Waves of rain blew past the open door, spraying a fine mist inside.

"Whoa," Cia exclaimed, crawling across the floor to the sheet of water. She held out her hand and sipped.

Izia shimmied on his stomach toward her. She laughed and held her cupped hand down. Deklan rose, his entire body protesting the movement, and watched her care for his wolf. He rubbed his chest against an odd flutter. Any member of his team would have done the same, he reminded himself. But something about her tenderly offering the wolf the one thing he was most desperate for had Deklan's heart expanding.

He forced himself to join them, his legs trembling from the built-up lactic acid of his earlier endeavor. Stretching helped, and he would, after he also quenched his thirst. Deklan didn't bother to use his hands. He stuck his head into the waterfall, pulling his hair free and letting the rain wash away the ash and sweat while taking his fill. Cold water soaked his shirt and ran down his chest and back, saturating the waist of his pants. He didn't care. He'd strip naked if not for the woman a few feet away.

She took off his bag and hers and tossed them into

the far corner, out of the mist swirling around. Deklan scrubbed his hands over his face and glanced at her again. She'd rolled the sleeves of her shirt up past her elbows and followed his lead, attempting to wash away the thicker muck covering her face and arms. Dark strands of hair clung to her cheeks and the sides of her neck. The soaked fabric of her top billowed and clung to her frame with each gust of wind, giving him enticing glimpses of the curves beneath.

"I don't know if this will make me look better or worse," she said, untying the leather strand and holding it out to him. "Do you think the rain is going to stick around long enough for me to try to get some of the mud out of my hair?"

He took the strap and wound both around his wrist. "I have no idea. I don't know the weather patterns here."

She shrugged. "Guess it's worth the risk."

Deklan sat, bracing his shoulder against the doorframe, letting the rain fall over his side. He leaned over every few seconds and took another gulp of water. Cia pulled her hair over her shoulder and let water sluice along the matted length. Deklan pulled his leg in and rested his elbow on his bent knee.

"There's a comb in my bag and maybe some soap," he said.

She sat back and squeezed gray water from her hair. "My luck, I'd get soapy, and the rain would stop. I don't know if I can comb this mess on my own."

His gaze transfixed on her elegant fingers, trying to tame the knotted mass. "Do you want me to help?"

6

Cia's hand stilled in the tangled length of her hair as she tried to figure out what his offer meant. Was he being nice? Or did he want to touch her? Because she really, *really* wanted him to touch her. Even if only her hair, she'd settled for that. Twice now, she'd been in his arms, and while she knew it was because she'd fallen there, the sensation was one she longed to experience again. She wanted to know how it'd feel when he wanted her in an embrace.

She licked rain from her lips and straightened. "Um, sure. Thanks."

Izia moved to the corner with the bags, circled, and laid with a groan. Aside from his pale eyes, he became one with the shadows. Deklan walked on his knees, pulling the backpack close when he was within reach. He dug around inside and removed a wide tooth, wooden comb. She sat cross-legged and pressed her lips together. A nervous excitement bubbled up within her. The emotion was new, and she tried to examine why this man attracted her so much.

His hands were surprisingly gentle as they navigated through her knotted hair. The rain continued to beat a soothing rhythm against the rocking car. Fine mist swirled around, sending droplets caressing down her face and neck. She closed her eyes and breathed in the moist air.

"You seem good at getting out tangles," she said.

A thick chunk of combed hair slid over her shoulder. "I am the fourth of eleven kids. At one point or another, we've all had very long hair. I have a lot of experience."

Cia drew her brows together. "All of you?"

"Yes."

She glanced over her shoulder. "Your hair was longer than now?"

"Almost to my hips at its longest." His fingers braced her scalp and made her face forward again.

She tried to imagine his wine-red tresses down to his butt instead of just his shoulders. "Why did you cut it?"

"It was hard to take care of, and my reason for having it long was no longer valid."

She waited for him to elaborate. When he didn't, she tried to turn back around. He huffed and made her face forward again. "What is a valid reason for long hair?"

"Culture."

"I know enough guardians to know it's not cultural among them, so what culture?"

"Ruthenian." More combed hair slid over her shoulder. "Didn't your parents teach you anything of your heritage?"

"No. Why would they tell me about fashion statements?"

"Because it's not…" He blew out a breath. "Never mind, it's too hard to explain."

The comb caught in a knot and yanked her head. She hissed and reached for her hair.

"Sorry," he muttered as he pulled the comb free. The cool brush of his fingers along the side of her throat caught her by surprise. "What happened?"

Cia moved her hand to under her chin, skimming the tender skin. "I got caught."

His touch feathered to the sensitive spot where her shoulder connected to her neck. "You never should have risked being alone with him."

"How do you know who caught me?" she asked, resisting the urge to turn.

"Were you caught by another violent, sadistic rapist?"

"It's possible, isn't it? If the intelligence is correct, that camp was full of criminals."

"And you walked right in." The disapproval in his voice made her stomach clench. "I'm still trying to understand your rationale for taking such a risk."

Her heart jumped at the reminder of how close she'd come to disaster. "He didn't get to be a rapist with me."

"I figured that since you weren't thrown into the cell naked. He wouldn't have bothered if you'd survived the attack."

And if Deklan hadn't come along, she wouldn't have survived, period. She'd have died of thirst within days, trapped in a natural catastrophe zone no one knew about. Then what good would she have been? Her heart kicked again. Lost to her father without explanation. Cia's mind shied from the uncomfortable truth she no longer wanted to think about.

The train rumbled on, and Deklan took the cue of her silence and returned to detangling her hair wordlessly, though his continued disappointment was tangible. The physical reminder of her recklessness had burst whatever camaraderie they'd managed. An apology formed in her throat but refused to be uttered. What would she be apologizing for? Attempting to find a mass murderer? No, she wasn't sorry for that.

Deklan gathered all her hair together, and gentle tugs told her he was braiding the length. Once finished, he tossed the plait over her shoulder. Cia caressed the damp strands, still coarse from the mud and ash. A problem she wouldn't be able to address until she could bathe.

Scooting up to her side, Deklan rested his elbows on his knees. "Did you find anything useful about Blackbain besides the strength of his hands?"

Anger bloomed inside her. Before she could catch her reaction, Cia twisted and shoved him. The unexpected push toppled him over. Laughing, he pushed off his side. Cia nudged him again, glaring. "Forget you, wolf man."

He grinned at her, the dimple peeking out at his cheek. His hair hung in damp strands around his face, a hint of curl at the very ends. Wet, it looked black. The wind rushing through the open door plastered his damp shirt to his muscular chest and arms. His beauty struck Cia like a knife to her gut, robbing her of coherent thought. Her irritation melted away, replaced by attraction and the chagrin of her outburst.

He tucked hair behind his ear and turned into the air, blowing the rest of the strands from his face. "So, is that a no, you didn't learn anything?"

She rolled her eyes and leaned across the space to grab her shoulder bag. "Sorry, I didn't mean to shove you."

"Yeah, you did, but that's okay." He shrugged. "My sisters do the same thing when I annoy them."

Cia frowned. She didn't want to be compared to his sisters. She dug around in the sack and showed him the two books she had stolen. "I took these from his office. Not sure if he managed to pack anything before he left, and the place became a memory, but I have this at least."

He leaned forward to glimpse into her bag. "Nice. I hope they're useful. Not sure if they'll be worth what you might have paid to retrieve them."

Frustrated, Cia snapped the pack closed. "You're really hung up on that."

He scratched at the whiskers under his chin. "I wonder why I have a problem with a young woman putting herself into the path of a wanted, psychotic fugitive? All alone, too, without the team she's been training with for over a year." The mask of indifference slipped from his face. "Do you know how lucky you are they cared? Or that they even knew where you went?"

Cia slid the bag back to the corner next to his. "Yes, I do know."

A shaft of light cut through the rain, turning the droplets into sparkling gold. Deklan pulled his legs up and rested his elbows on his knees, his attention shifting to the outside. The dancing light played across his bronze skin. Cia's fingers itched to touch him. In the quiet moment, the memory of her brazen kiss had her gaze dropping to his mouth. Then, his lips had been rough, dry, and dust-covered. Now, they were clean and looked soft. Inviting. Kissable.

Before her life had tumbled into dark despair, she'd once stolen kisses from a boy in a room they'd snuck off to during a Wintervail party. There'd been a lot of fumbling, heavy breathing and discovering how different their bodies were. Cia hadn't been ready for more at sixteen. At seventeen, her world had fallen apart, and now, at nineteen, she had bigger things to worry about than her sexual curiosity.

That's what she'd told herself, at least.

Her blood heated and rushed through her to curious places, simply looking at Deklan. What would happen if they touched? Kissed for real? Would he be better than the young man? Cia smirked to herself. Likely. And she'd probably catch on fire. What an exciting thought. Yes, she *definitely* wanted to experience a passionate kiss with him.

"Are you ever going to answer my question?" His deep voice broke through her musings.

Did she miss something he said during her little fantasy? She licked her lips and lifted her gaze to his. "What question?"

"Why you came to a foreign country and go after a violent criminal alone? You have to know your team was hours away from the assignment," he said.

Cia took a deep breath. "I knew."

Confusion tightened his brow and shone in his gaze. "Then why?"

She pulled her knees into her chest and hugged them. "Their priority would have been fugitive recovery."

"Yes, along with intelligence gathering on the operation."

Cia snorted. "And now we know if they'd come as a team and hung around spying, we'd all be dust. I suppose my little adventure actually saved the team."

"Maybe. Blackbain learned of us and fled. The plan was to let the team come in first, learn what they could make a positive ID on Blackbain, and call us in. Fugitive SZ-SB-25225 would have run, and the entire team would have chased him instead of just half of us."

"You memorized his felon stamp number?"

Deklan dropped his head back and laughed. "Out of everything, that's all you heard?"

Warmth bloomed across Cia's cheeks. She dropped her chin onto her knees. "Either way, the two books I managed to nab would have been destroyed had I not snuck into the office."

"Trust me, Raiventon would have done some sneaking of his own and not been caught."

Cia had to concede Deklan was right. "True as that may be, I had to see if he knew anything. I've tried everything I can to learn the identity of the man who murdered my mother and little brother. No one knows, not in Sziveria."

Deklan shook his head. "Someone knows. Someone hired and paid him in Sziveria. If you'd let your team—"

Cia slashed a hand through the air. "I did! Ryan Voklane told me that they'd continue looking for the assassin while I trained. All I had to do was learn what I could and be ready when they finally caught the culprit. So, I did. For an entire year. And when he didn't have anything new to tell me, I started asking my own questions. No one would talk to Guardian Castien, but a few would talk to little teenage Cia with a talent for being able to be an invisible shadow."

"For what price?" he asked, his words clipped.

For a moment, she debated not telling him. But he may fill in the blanks with something far worse than what she'd been willing to do in exchange for information. She shrugged. "A few books and trinkets have changed ownership."

Deklan shook his head again. "And why couldn't you trust Voklane?"

Anger set her jaw and made her teeth grind. "Did you know the same person who took out my family is also responsible for killing Katria's?"

"Yes, she explained when they arrived to tell me of your disappearance."

"For seven years," she held up her fingers, stressing the number, "*seven*, they've been looking for this assassin. Nothing. No name. They don't even know if the person is Sziverian or from somewhere else, like here, or maybe even on loan from Cairo."

"I know you want—"

"Need. Finding this scab isn't a want. It's a need. I *have* to find the person who took my family from me."

"Fine, but the assassin is only a part of a very large, complicated situation."

"I'm aware, and none of it concerns me."

His gaze searched hers. "Do you really believe that?"

Cia straightened from hugging her knees, lifting her chin. "Yes."

"Tell me what happened to you. To your family."

She scoffed and returned to watching the now gentle fall of rain mixed with a brightening sky. "Everyone knows what happened. We made all the papers."

"The articles are not your experience," he said softly.

No, they certainly weren't. The tale had been tragic, gobbled up for its titillating violence and sorrow by both *The Havener* and *The Haven City Chronicle*. She hadn't spoken to anyone about the ordeal. Not her uncle, who'd saved her, or her father, who'd laid with her in the nights following the disaster just so she could try to fall asleep. Even now, she couldn't put the horror into words beyond the basic facts.

"We were having a normal day, and out of nowhere, someone murdered them. In the chaos, I was kidnapped and held in an underground cell. They tried to convince me if I worked with them, I'd be able to avenge my family."

"Why did they want you to work with them?" he asked.

"They thought I was my father's genetic heir, that I had his sharpshooting talent."

"Voklane mentioned that."

Cia nodded. "Anyway, my uncle Vayden found me and brought me home."

"They never learned otherwise about your Gen-Heir ability?"

Dark memories threatened to intrude, and she pushed them down. "Not that I know of. They never handed me a gun to discover any differently."

He tapped his fingers on the back of his overlapped hand. "The person who killed your family was acting on an order. Someone else provided the information, made the request, and paid the money."

Cia's chest constricted. "The V Alliance."

"Yes. The same group that's responsible for the prisoner escapes. For Joel Blackbain being here, running whatever operation he was running. For the human trafficking that's been plaguing ours and other nations. They're all connected. Part of something bigger than one loose assassin. And if you think that doesn't concern you, you're mistaken. It concerns all of us. Every man, woman, and child on our chunk of the inhabited world." He met her stare, his aqua-marine eyes intense in the burgeoning sun. "For years, one very organized group has managed to secretly release prisoners, distribute drugs, kidnap people of varying ages, and coordinate on a global effort to steal resources. This is bigger than one killer and a personal vendetta."

"Maybe so," she agreed. She pressed a fist over her heart. "But it's not bigger for *me*."

THE SELFISHNESS OF HER WORDS MADE DEKLAN RECOIL. HE had to remind himself she was young and how narrow his worldview had been when he was nineteen, eleven long years ago. How all he'd cared about was his power and when the northern passage would open so he could go to Ruthenia and find a willing bed partner. He and his many lovers had bought into a lie about finding a suitable mate when they just wanted to experience a safe means of exploring physical desire without the commitment neither knew would follow. To them, he'd been a curiosity to appease. They'd been a pleasurable possibility for him to find a love his parents shared. He hadn't cared about the state of affairs in his home country or the future his father hoped for him.

"What happens after?" he asked.

"After I find the killer?"

Deklan nodded.

She shrugged. "I don't know. I guess if my guardianship isn't revoked, I'll serve on a guardian team."

"Why?"

Confusion pinched her forehead. "Why what?"

"Why would you serve on a guardian team?"

"Because it's what I've been training for."

"But you don't care about your country, why serve?

You could take your skillset and go into the private industry."

She stiffened and glared at him. "I care about my country."

Deklan stared at her.

"I do!"

He remained silent, and she huffed and looked away.

"Just because I want to see justice for my little brother and mother doesn't mean I don't care about Sziveria." Her jaw flexed. "Whoever the assassin is, they have ties to this Alliance group. Whatever I find will only help."

"Whatever you've found may have already helped if you'd worked with your team," he said, needing her to understand. "You didn't have to do anything alone. They came to my house, all of them, to ask me to find you. Does that sound like a group who'd stand by and do nothing if they knew, actually knew, how important finding the killer was to you?"

"It was important to Katria," she said. "And still nothing."

"Do you know why? Did you ask?"

Her cheeks flushed, and she looked away. "She doesn't like to talk about it."

"Ah, and neither do you, it seems. This giant weight must sit there in the room whenever the two of you are together." He inhaled the musty air swirling around the empty rail car. "Do you go to great pains to avoid each other and the discomfort of being in each other's presence?"

"Our training is different, so we aren't together often."

"And when you are?"

She didn't answer, her focus remaining on the landscape speeding past them.

"You should talk to her, Lucianna. Really talk to her," Deklan said gently. "Learn why and what's been done, if anything, to this point. Share what you've discovered."

She pulled her bottom lip between her teeth. "I don't know…"

"Think about it. You have the time."

"It's not…" She dropped her head onto her knees, her chest expanding with a deep inhale. He stayed quiet, allowing her the time to gather her thoughts. Sniffling, she turned her face toward him, laying her cheek on her bent legs. The agony in her eyes brought a tight fist to his chest. "I don't think I can stand her pain and mine together. I can't…" She took a shaky breath. "I just can't."

Before Deklan realized what he was doing, he'd pulled her into the shelter of his body. She wrapped her arms around his back and held tight, her face buried in the dampness of his shirt. Her legs tangled with his. Despite the day's ash, rain, and sweat, her feminine scent lingered. An enticing combination of midnight jasmine, warm vanilla, and something earthy. The warmth of her skin and supple flex of her muscles moved under his fingers, which had somehow slipped under her shirt to touch her hip. In gentle brushes, he caressed and marveled at the softness of her skin.

She gasped and trembled in his embrace, pulling back enough to look up at him, her arms still wrapped around his back. Her fingers pressed along his backbone. Tingles raced along his spine, from his hair to his tailbone. The beautiful cool gray of her eyes searched his gaze.

"I want you to kiss me," she said.

Deklan's focus shifted to her full pink mouth. His stomach and other parts of him jumped at the idea of tasting her. "Not a good idea."

A small smile toyed at her lips. "Seems those are the only kind of ideas I have."

She didn't give him the chance to argue further. Her hand shifted to his front and buried in the length of his hair, drawing him down to her parted lips. At the first tentative touch of her tongue to his bottom lip, Deklan was lost. He *knew* he shouldn't allow anything more. Should push her away. Their conversation had left her vulnerable. Not to mention, between his age and experience, his judgment should be better. But all his good sense faded at the first soft pull of her lips. Her fingers slid along his scalp, tightening in his hair, drawing him closer. Deeper.

The firm tip of her tongue teased again, and Deklan groaned internally, opening for her. She didn't take the invitation, instead retreating. If he wanted to do the right thing, now was the time. He could pull back and break the contact. But he was too curious, wanting to know how she'd taste. How she'd respond to his kiss. His tongue followed hers, sweeping into her mouth, exploring all the textures and responses she had to offer.

Her body pressed to his, her small breasts crushing into the wall of his chest. Deklan's grasp squeezed her hips to keep from pulling her onto his lap. Shifting their positions would be an easy thing to do. A quick lift, a swift adjustment of her legs, and she'd be astride him. Deklan wanted the simple intimacy so much he groaned at the mere thought. She mimicked the sound and rose on her knees between his legs.

A faint prickle danced along his scalp where she touched, arcing through his body and tingling into his fingers on her hip. Gasping, he broke their kiss and snatched his hands from her. "No," he breathed.

She stared at him in confusion, her swollen lips still parted and glistening from his kiss. "What?"

Deklan pushed her hand away and scooted back, putting distance between them. "Do you have any idea what you almost did?"

She blinked, and her face twisted in bewilderment. She patted her chest, stomach, and thighs. "Nope, our clothes didn't spontaneously combust. What's wrong?"

Deklan held up a hand and opened his mouth. Useless sounds emerged. How could she not know? Words wouldn't form, and he tried again when her eyes grew big, and she motioned for him to speak. "We can't…" Deklan shook his head and blew out a breath. "We can't touch again."

"I don't understand."

He raked a hand through his hair. "Yeah, I can see that, and it's not my place to explain it to you. Your parents should have."

Frowning, she crossed her legs and sat. "And why can't you explain whatever it is I should know?"

Rain shimmered behind her, surrounding her in a soft cloud of golden mist. Deklan's chest ached at her youthful beauty. At the innocence she had lost. And yet, some remained. That naivety stared at him now. Curiosity bright in her eyes. She was old enough to have taken a lover if she wished. Or to have already been in a yearlong marriage contract that had seen an end without renewal.

Deklan stared hard at her, searching her face for any sign that she understood the dangers of physical contact, let alone intimacy, with him. "You really don't know?"

She lifted her hands and shrugged. "What am I supposed to know?"

"Have you taken a lover before?" he asked.

An endearing flush spread across her cheeks and over her neck. She looked away from him. "Why are you asking?"

"You wanted to have this conversation, so please answer the question."

Her jaw worked, and slowly, she shook her head, continuing to look away.

A sense of possessiveness threatened to take hold of him. An emotion he had no right to feel where she was concerned. But she was unclaimed. Unknown to a lover's touch, and Deklan wanted to be the one to show her the remarkable beauty of passion. The questing tendrils of her bond still sizzled through his blood, arcing across his nerves, leaving him on edge. This was the last conversation he should have, yet it was the most necessary. "Are you sure you still want to discuss sex?"

She sucked in the inside of her cheek and wrinkled her nose. The blush of her cheeks deepened. Several seconds passed before she nodded. Resolute, her gaze met his, and her chin lifted. "Yes."

"You're Ruthenian. I'm half. A relationship between us has the potential to turn into something permanent."

Her brows drew together. "Doesn't every relationship?"

Deklan shook his head. "No, not like Ruthenians." He swept his hand down his face. "I can't believe your parents didn't tell you any of this."

"Is it specific to Ruthenians?"

"Yes."

She puttered out a breath. "Well, that's why. My parents never spoke of their homeland other than to say it's where they were from. But Jos—" Her voice broke, and she swallowed and tried again. "My brother and I were Sziverian."

"They should have told you about bonding. They should have explained."

She swept her hand toward him. "Explain away, wolf man."

Closing his eyes for inner strength and to isolate the beautiful silvery blue anchors of her bond floating around, Deklan forced them out, refusing what she'd unknowingly attempted to start. A rare ability his father had made all his male children learn to spare them from a pairing they didn't authorize. Only once before had Deklan needed to use the knowledge. And he hadn't been gentle with the woman that time like he would now. Though she'd experience a discomfort he had no way of avoiding. Cia gasped when he opened his eyes. He held his palm out to her. Her gaze shifted between his hand and his eyes. Slowly, she touched her fingertips to his palm. Regret made him frown as he slowly sent the tendrils back to her.

She cried out, snatching her hand away and pressing it to her chest. "What did you do to me?"

"I rejected you."

Discomfort echoed through Cia, a dull ache from her fingertips to her heart. Tears burned her eyes, and his words about rejection only made her hurt more. Worse, she didn't understand why.

"Rejecting a bond isn't something I can do if we were to become more intimate," he said, his voice deep and calm. "The more I allow you to touch me, the more I'll accept you until I won't be able to stop what you can build between us."

Cia tried to wrap her mind around what he explained. "What is this bond?"

"All Ruthenian couples share it, but between a beast master and his mate, it's more intense."

She considered his words. "And I control it?"

"Yes, the female initiates."

Thoughts whirling, Cia considered what he'd said. "And it's permanent?"

"Correct."

She nibbled her bottom lip. "And you don't want to have one?"

Pulling his legs up, he braced his wrists on his knees and tapped his fingers on his forearm. "Someday, yes, but I want the woman to know when she offers and to want the same."

And what if I do? Almost spilled from her lips. Which was ridiculous. Yes, she'd been curious about the man for months, but she didn't *know* him. Not really. "How do I learn to know? Can I control it?"

"Of course, but I don't know if you can learn now. Not without training..."

Which her parents should have done. The unspoken words made Cia frown. Why would they keep something so important from her? "Can you help me learn?"

He recoiled. "No. I can't... No."

She recalled his words from moments before. "Ah, if I keep attempting, you'll weaken." She couldn't stop the wicked grin. "Thanks for the information."

His chin dropped to his chest. The tendons in his jaw flexed. Cia's smile died. A bad feeling went through her at his reaction. She went to reach for him and stopped, curling her fingers into her palm.

"I'm sorry. I won't touch you again if I can help it," she said. When he remained silent, she asked, "Someone did, though, didn't they? Tried to force this bond thing on you?"

Izia padded over to Deklan. When the beast master crossed his legs, the wolf laid his torso across Deklan's thighs. Deklan sank his hands into the thick fur at Izia's neck. "It was a long time ago."

"Bad memory still."

A weak smile quirked his lips. He toyed with Izia's fuzzy ears. "Just something I won't allow to happen again."

Cia wanted to reach for him but squeezed her thighs instead. "What happened? Will you tell me?"

His gaze fixed beyond her to the scenery speeding past. Light and shadows played across his handsome face. "I suppose it would be unfair to cling to my weakness and say no when I know so much about you."

Cia pulled her knees up and hugged them. "Everyone knows so much about me. What happened isn't a secret."

"From your perspective, it is," he said, his words barely reaching her over the constant rhythmic *cha-chunk* of steel-on-steel.

Like him, Cia clenched her jaw and shifted her focus to a safer view. "I haven't told you much."

"You've told me enough."

She waited, patient and quiet, wanting with a desperation that shocked her to know more about this man. What had shaped him. Hurt him. She didn't want to be anything like the woman in his past who'd left such a deep scar he couldn't risk Cia's touch.

"Most women who agreed to test compatibility with me were only curious. The last one, however..." He took a deep inhale and braced his elbows on his risen knees. "She thought half-breed meant weak. Controllable. She didn't want a mate. She wanted a bonded servant. Her attempt to bond was similar to yours, a little bit at a time. Vyshe was the one who noticed. Who warned me." A small, sad smile graced his lips. "He didn't like her."

"I don't blame him," Cia muttered. "Did you do the same thing you did to me?"

He shook his head, his hair brushing his jaw. "No, I was careful with you." When she raised a brow, he chuckled. "I was, I promise. I let my emotions get the best of me."

"She tried to do a terrible thing. Anything you did to protect yourself isn't something to be ashamed of."

He shook his head again. "No, I *should* have been the better beast master. But I was so angry and... humiliated. When I returned her bond, I shoved all the energy into her chest. She was still sobbing in a ball on the floor when I left the cabin."

"Good," Cia proclaimed, chin lifted. "She didn't deserve anything less. Hopefully, she never attempted to force another man to her will."

"I don't know what happened to her. I haven't returned to Ruthenia."

The car rocked hard into a turn. Cia squeaked and toppled over, sliding across the gritty floor into Izia. Deklan wrapped them both in his arms and rolled away from the opening. Half sprawled across her and the wolf, he lifted his head once they stopped in the car's center. Cia blinked up at the dark ceiling. Izia licked her cheek and then bumped his nose along her jaw. With a gentle touch, she pushed his muzzle away.

"I'm alive," she croaked.

Deklan scrambled off her. "Sorry. I didn't want anyone bouncing out."

"Appreciate it."

Gripping her elbow, he helped her rise. He held her only where clothing was between them. A flicker of disappointment made her frown. The strength of his touch reminded her how exciting his fingers on her bare skin had been. She'd wanted more. Wanted his fingers to slide up or down and touch her places that had suddenly become desperate for him. The fierce desire his kiss had set off inside her was still a shock. She didn't want to halt everything between them. She wanted to explore. But her genetics wouldn't even allow the most basic contact with him. A growl of frustration left her.

"Can I touch a Sziverian man?" she asked before she could stop herself.

Deklan's hand fell away. "Have you before?"

"Well, yes, of course. I train with Kevin, Mason, and Sean. I touch them."

His brows lifted. "In training, not in…"

She scoffed. "They are very happily married."

"Intimate contact starts the process."

"I have… done some things," she admitted, looking away from him. "Nothing happened."

"What a shame," he said, his tone holding a note of laughter.

"That's not what I meant!" she said in disbelief.

A hint of a smile still quirked his lips. "No?"

Cia glared. "No. I meant nothing strange happened. At least, I don't think. Would I have felt something?"

A strangled sound left him, and he covered his face with both hands. Izia made an odd whining grumble and nudged at Deklan's wrist. "Woman, you're killing me."

Heat flared across her cheeks. She huffed and held up both hands. "Okay, look, whatever was supposed to happen… no, wait, that'll sound wrong too. Whatever experience I should have had… oh, stars above… You *know* what I'm trying to say!"

He threw his head back and laughed. His broad shoulders shook, and the dimple she'd caught a glimpse of earlier in the day reappeared. Once again, she found herself stunned by his masculine beauty. Her fingers twitched to touch him. To slide her hands up his corded forearms and explore his visible torso. Discover if the dusting of hair on his chest was coarse or soft. The humor dancing in his eyes only increased her urge to touch him. She crossed her arms and looked away.

"Let me see your hand," he said.

Bewildered, she snapped her attention back to him. "What? But you said—"

"We won't touch for long. Let me show you so you can understand."

The car rocked and rumbled around them. Thunder rolled in the distance. Only a faint mist of rain continued to swirl in the air outside. Cia worried her bottom lip between her teeth, taking in the brightening land. Sun twinkled and shimmered silver off wet leaves. The desire to touch him outweighed her curiosity over what he had to teach her. Slowly, she stretched her hand toward him.

His eyes stayed locked with hers. "Watch."

Cia dropped her gaze to her hand. Anticipation and desire rose deep within her, sending her heart into a chaotic rhythm. A part of her felt silly. He was only allowing her to touch his hand. Yet, the skin-to-skin contact seared through her nerve endings. She wanted so much more. Another kiss. The sensation of his fingers on her bare back. Her mouth went dry, and breath caught in her throat. Before her eyes, tiny white sparks danced between their touching hands. His breathing turned ragged, and his jaw clenched. The fiery glow she'd seen earlier in his eyes returned.

"Do you feel that?" he asked between breaths. "With this simple contact, you're trying to bond with me even now."

Cia snatched her hand away. She searched inside herself to determine how she was doing something she knew nothing about. "What am I doing? How do I stop it?"

Deklan set his wrists on his knees and opened his hands. "I don't know how it works for the female."

"So, I'll never be able to enter a short contract? To make sure the relationship works like the rest of the country?"

"You can, providing the partner in question isn't of Ruthenian descent."

Cia worked her jaw and stared at him in annoyance. "Then no genetic heirs since they're all Ruthenian to some degree?"

"I think four generations removed is the point where you won't have to worry about a bond any longer."

"Right. Ask for the family tree." She picked up an errant piece of grass from her boot and flicked it away in frustration. "Understood."

An awkward silence spread between them, cut only by the whoosh of wind from the open door and the repetitive pulse of metal wheels on steel rails.

"At least you'll have that," he said, braiding his fingers together. "If a woman has any Ruthenian in her, no matter how far removed, she can bond with me. Worse, she won't understand the significance."

"What will you do? Remain alone?"

Shaking his head, he looked away from her. "Forever is a concept most Sziverians shy from. And Ruthenian's..." He heaved a long breath and shook his head again. "They still have a stigma against a half-breed like me."

Cia recoiled. "Half-breeds? What? Do they issue pedigrees at birth?"

Deklan barked a laugh. "You... You're something else."

She held up a hand. "Wait. Your mother—"

"Had no idea when she bonded to my father. Thankfully, he'd fallen in love with her, and no harm was done."

"And your father knew when he married your mother that you'd be unaccepted in his homeland?"

He tilted his head toward her in affirmation. "He hoped, however, that he'd be proven wrong."

Cia looked at Izia, lounging next to his thigh. The massive wolf was content within his master's personal sphere. Cia could relate. She, too, would be happy to occupy a space near him. Her fingers flexed at the reminder of a sensation she couldn't quantify. A need she couldn't place.

"I am glad my parents let me believe myself wholly Sziverian. I'd rather not claim the heritage of a people so close-minded," she said. "How many times did they..." The words died in her throat. A horrible ache blossomed in her chest. "Did they make you think you weren't enough?"

"Ruthenia is a beautiful place with a beautiful culture. They are a proud people, and sometimes that pride overshadows all else."

Cia looked at him, brows raised. "Sometimes?"

He rolled his eyes and scoffed. "Fine. Most of the time."

"They're fools," she snapped, focusing on the damp landscape speeding past.

"Yes."

His agreement made her meet his stare. Not much emotion played in his greenish-blue gaze. Only a sort of quiet resignation she never thought to associate with a man of his power. She leaned forward, crossing her legs and resting her arms on her thighs. "Explain to me how an arch guardian, a position of power only beholden to the queen elect, who is a beast master of skill I've never heard of before, is rejected? Half-breed or not, do you have a weird habit or something?"

"A weird… habit?" he asked slowly.

Cia waved and rotated her hand in thought. "Yeah, you know, like you dig up insects for dinner or something. Or require all your wolves to sleep with you every night, even if you aren't alone. Or I don't know, shower with all your clothes on. Weird habits."

He covered his face with both hands and dragged them to circle the back of his neck. "You are so young. No, I don't have any weird habits. Innocent or otherwise."

Cia contemplated what an *innocent* habit would be and realized he'd again fixated on her age. "I am a grown woman."

"Grown is a relative term."

Incoherent sounds sputtered from her mouth. Forcing her irritation down, she rose on her knees. Grit and tiny pebbles dug into her knees through the thin cotton of her pants. She didn't care. No matter what he said, she *was* an adult. A grown woman, capable and old enough to be seen by him as something other than the girlish role he wanted to peg her into. "Relative to what? Experience? Years lived? Choices made?" She opened her arms. "What am I missing? Sex? Will that automatically make me a woman in your eyes?"

Wariness slid across his face. "Lucianna—"

"No, since you know so much about when I'm supposed to magically become mature, tell me, wolf man? Should I go find me a lover when we reach civilization?"

"That's very unwise, and you know it," he ground out.

"I do know, but I've heard there are parlors that cater to the uninhibited who vouch they've done a two-week self-quarantine between bed partners. You sign up and are matched. Am I right?"

"Yes, but they're still a dangerous risk, only the foolish trust."

She nodded. "I know that, too. Doesn't stop them from existing or people from partaking of what's offered." She leaned forward and poked his chest, daring to touch the exposed skin between his defined pectorals. "Just so you know, I didn't mention any depraved habits because you don't strike me as the sort of man to enjoy the horrors that the people who kidnapped me were set on dealing with their victims. Even if you only wanted a woman on her knees in bed, that wouldn't be enough for her to turn away the position of power or the chance of her children having the genetic capabilities you offer. I am truly confused."

An inner fire crackled through his irises like blue lightning, drawing Cia in until barely a breath separated their faces. She pulled her hand away to keep from sliding her palm up his chest.

"I am a beast to the women of Sziveria. I scare them. They think I'll be too dominant, and none of them are brave enough to discover what a night, let alone a year, in my bed would require of them. And I already told you, exceptional genetics aren't enough for Ruthenians. I am a passing curiosity they don't dare get stuck with. And you…" His fingers ghosted across her bottom lip, focused on her mouth. "Would risk far too much to learn."

"Don't you think it's mine to risk?"

"Not if we both pay the price for your curiosity."

"I'm right," she said, a heavy exhale blowing out her nose. "If I had more experience with a man, you'd take me seriously."

"I'm taking you very, *very* seriously."

The train lurched and increased speed before Cia could form a retort. They both shifted to the opening. Izia whined and returned to the shadowy corner with their bags. Cia grabbed the metal lip of the doorframe and leaned as far out as she dared. She searched the forest ahead and behind, then turned her attention to the sky. In the distance behind them, an arching ball of gray, trailed by plumes of dust, made her gasp and point. Lightning forked and danced around the object. Deklan stood, grasping the top of the frame. His arms bulged as he leaned out. The mass fell and disappeared from their view. Seconds later, a massive explosion of colorless particles bloomed into the air.

A cloud of dust sped toward the train. Cia squeaked in alarm and scrambled away from the opening. Deklan grabbed the door. Using the weight of his body, he shoved it closed with a roar. Debris pelleted and clanged against the steel. The car rocked and pitched. Terror seized her muscles, and breath sawed from her lungs. Deklan's body suddenly surrounded her, wrapping her in a warm, safe cocoon. Fur brushed her face, and she found herself padded in the front by a wolf, Deklan's arms around them both.

The screech of steel vibrated through the floor, rumbling deeper as their speed continued to increase. The constant ping of debris hitting the exterior lessened and faded. Slowly, the crazy sway of the car smoothed out until Cia figured they no longer had to worry about derailing. Deklan relaxed around her, easing away. Enough light bled in around the edges of the door for her to make out his crawl to the opening. Metal jangled and groaned as he slid the door open to peer outside. Cia joined him, learning around his large frame, her fingers curling into the back of his shirt for leverage.

Wind rushed by, blowing loose tendrils of hair around her eyes and mouth. She spit them free and untangled the strands from her lashes. The visible forest behind them was coated in a familiar fine gray ash. Sighing, she fell onto her butt, meeting his gaze when he glanced over his shoulder.

"I guess we know the dangers of getting too close to a UZ now," she said over the rush of air squeezing through the narrow opening.

Deklan gave the metal door a hard shove. It glided open, banging at the end of the slide rail. He joined her on the floor. Unwrapping a leather cord from around his wrist, he tied his hair into a small ponytail. She tsked under her breath, preferring his hair loose and framing his face.

"From my understanding, all Uninhabited Zones have different issues. The land north of Vativarsa and east of Siber and Latanus is a frozen wasteland. What's left of Africa south of the few established civilizations is sand, salt flats, and barren mountains. There's no fresh water. No one knows anything about what's beyond Westica's inhabited border."

Cia scrunched her face. "And the land west of New Columbia shoots out ash bombs. Awesome."

His focus remained on the forest speeding past. "I wonder if it's consistent. The camp was well established."

"Wood buildings can go up fast, and the cement one

we were in hadn't been damaged at all," she reminded him.

"And people were there when you arrived?"

"I saw a few. There were guards at the gate."

He nodded. "Yes, I dealt with the guards. So, they hadn't evacuated, which means the occurrences are likely random."

"Maybe random enough the site never worried about it before." Cia tapped her fingers on her knee. "I wonder if they'll rebuild."

Deklan shrugged. "With Blackbain in custody, I doubt they'll worry about the loss for a while. Not unless whatever resource they were stealing is worth more than the loss of him to their power structure."

"You don't have him yet," she said.

The smile he cast her direction was ruthless and a little bit unnerving. She resisted the urge to scoot away. Perhaps reminding him of the rescuing she'd needed, which had allowed his query to escape, hadn't been the wisest course.

"There's nowhere he can go that I won't find him," his deep voice promised.

Cia resisted rolling her eyes. "A rather arrogant statement."

Deklan shook his head, his smile still in place. "Not arrogant. Truth."

Doubt made Cia's eyes narrow. "You've never failed?"

"No such thing as failure, only setbacks."

"I hope the enemy doesn't have the same mindset," she said, frowning.

"I never said they wouldn't fail. I said *I* won't."

8

RICKETY WOODEN BUILDINGS ON SHORT STILTS BROKE THE space between the trees. Deklan rose, used the frame to hold on, and took in the change of scenery. "We're coming up on civilization."

Cia joined him at the doorway. The setting sun warmed her beige skin and made her chestnut hair glow. She was beautiful. More so since he'd tasted her passion. Since he knew she would accept him. All of him. The known and the unknown. An ache settled in his chest. He rubbed the discomfort and returned his attention to the burgeoning city.

Years ago, he'd acknowledged that love and a family weren't in his future. One little firecracker of a woman making him wonder, maybe even hope, for something different was borderline exasperating. He didn't want to hope only for her to change her mind or for him to have been nothing more than a passing curiosity. She was too young and couldn't possibly know what she wanted in a lifelong mate. But as he looked at her, she smiled. Genuine excitement twinkled in her sky-gray

103

eyes. There was no denying how honest everything about her seemed to be, including her desire. Yet he couldn't forget the whole reason he'd met her was due to her deception.

"How did you mislead your team?" he asked, his fingers tightening on the frame above him.

The light faded from her eyes, and she turned her face away. "How do you mean?"

"You know exactly what I mean. How did you go behind their backs without them knowing your plan?"

Her shoulders hunched, and she shoved her free hand into her pants pocket. "I never planned on… what I did. I was only trying to find information. But when I learned they'd found Blackbain, I had to get here first, like I told you. Guardian Voklane would never share what he r the team found, if anything, about the V Alliance. So, either beat them here or break into the First Intelligence Office later. I opted to commit the lesser of two treasons."

"The only betrayal is your lack of trust in them."

Her lips flattened into a line. "You've already given the lecture. I don't need it again."

Deklan couldn't stop the smirk at her teenage reaction. The youngest Ralston had just reached age sixteen. Dyna's attitude had become something of a legend in their household. As the baby, she'd been allowed to get away with more than any of the other siblings, making her life extra annoying when they teased her. Cia's answer echoed the same snide tone Dyna's would have been in the same situation.

"You remind me so much of my youngest sister," he said, chuckling.

Her scowl deepened. "You keep saying that."

"Because you keep acting like her." When she

narrowed her eyes, he rolled his. "Your petulance, not the..." he waved a hand, "other stuff."

"Thank goodness for that. I was about to wonder if Ruthenia had any other terrible habits I'm glad I don't know about." Her jaw worked. "And I'm not petulant."

"You haven't answered my question."

"I'm an interceptor. My ability to gather intelligence is the reason I'm being trained. Doing so on my own wasn't difficult, and why would they ever suspect I'd do it anyway? Once I was sure no one would help me find the killer, I started looking alone. I made a few contacts within the V Alliance."

Shocked, Deklan snapped his attention toward her. He tried not to be impressed. Or concerned. He failed on both accounts. "You've done what?"

Cia shrugged, pressing her arm harder against her side to close her body off more than she already had. "I told you earlier a teenager was no threat to anyone. You keep doing a great job reminding me of that. It wasn't a big deal. Lower-level people in any organization are susceptible to bribes. Their group was no different."

Through their conversations and her actions, he knew she hadn't ever crossed the line in trading information in exchange for her body. No, she'd mentioned handing over *things* instead of a few raimarks for the intelligence she sought. "What exactly have you stolen to meet their demands?"

Defiance hardened her eyes, and her chin lifted. "What I had to."

"Ah," Deklan breathed out. "Not something you're proud of."

"Sziveria does things all the time in exchange for intel. I didn't do anything I wasn't training for."

"I'm sure that'll come as a comfort to Master Guardian Raiventon."

"It's been two years." She held up her fingers. "*Two*. No movement. No new threads to follow. Nothing. Meanwhile, my father struggles to maintain some semblance of a positive attitude for me because he refuses to become like his fellow assassin Aleksandrov Nachemir and forget I even exist in his grief. Aleksandrov eventually snapped out of it, but his daughter was already gone." She fluttered her fingers in the air. "Given the same useless promise I was. Service in exchange for action. I already told you I'm not Katria. I *won't* let the past rest. If they won't get me the knowledge I need to find the scab, I'll do it on my own."

Deklan turned, keeping one hand hooked along the top edge. Her tenacity to avenge her family no matter the cost struck a chord in him. Deep within himself, he knew he'd be just as ferocious if the same tragedy had struck his home. But that didn't change the promise she'd made to her nation. "When you agreed to guardian training, you took an oath. You need to tell Voklane or Wintersfall what you've learned. I don't think anyone has managed to get inside the organization. You may have been surprised at their reaction if you'd told them when you made the contact."

"Yes, yes, I get it already, mighty and wise arch guardian. I should trust my team."

"No, I don't believe you do. Which is kind of shocking to me, considering you know firsthand how diabolical the V Alliance is. I've seen it too, Lucianna. And aside from a few lucky breaks, we're no closer to figuring out who is leading them or what they're hoping to accomplish, aside from wealth at the expense of others."

"Can't that be enough?"

Deklan shook his head. "History has shown us that's not usually the case. The procurement of wealth means something needs to be funded. But what?"

"Lavish lifestyles? Have you seen some of the parties these so-called Guardians of Sziveria throw? Why can't they want more Italyssan champagne, Thanzian cotton, or Ravennese silk? Someone figured out they could get away with selling people for a profit and importing drugs for the same, and they've done so. Seems pretty simple to me."

"Then why form a group so dedicated to its cause the members are tattooed with their emblem and are fanatical in their loyalty? No, whatever they want, whoever they are, it's bigger than prosperity. At least, that's what the members have been led to believe. Did you ever ask?"

"What they stood for?"

He nodded.

"No. I don't care. I don't want to know. I don't talk to them longer than necessary for the information I want."

"Or for your hate to show," he guessed.

She scoffed. "No, I didn't care about that. Though the low-end establishments I met them in probably helped mask any disgust I may have let slip."

Groaning, Deklan covered his face. Dropping his hand to his side, he looked at her in disbelief. "Have you no fear for your safety at all?"

"I was locked in an underground cage for weeks," she said, her face devoid of emotion. "A rundown bar near the Old City Ruins isn't scary."

No, he imagined not. And being locked away in the dark wasn't even the worst of the horror she'd endured.

Deklan resisted the urge to go to her, to pull her into his arms and offer comfort. His last attempt had ended in a hungry kiss he couldn't afford to let happen again.

"They never tried to recruit you?" he asked.

"They never knew who I was, and I never spent enough time in conversation for them to offer me a sales pitch. Once word spread, I was willing to... procure certain objects in exchange for information, I started getting offers. If what they had to say was good enough, I'd agree to another meeting with their desired item. Pretty straightforward. And their eagerness to work with me is why I think they're nothing more than a criminal enterprise hoping to earn wealth at the expense of other's health and freedom."

"And you haven't even told your father what you've learned?" he asked in disbelief, unable to reconcile her secrecy with the team dynamics he worked hard to maintain like any leader of a guardian team. Deklan *knew* Sean Blackbain was a fantastic leader. The primary guardian was legendary in part because of the tight-knit group of individuals he oversaw. Which now included Cia.

She shifted until her back pressed into the wall next to the opening. Wind made the end of her braid dance over her shoulder. "I didn't learn much, just a vague understanding of their structure, which the FIO had already figured out. I was getting them to trust me and know they could tell me things without worry. Learning about Joel Blackbain was my biggest score so far."

"And the FIO had learned it, too."

"Yes, but not the specific location, which I never would have been given even if they did know."

Understanding dawned on him. "You knew they'd ask me to apprehend him."

She nodded. "You and my team. And you know the rest."

Yes, he did. While she'd beat him here, she'd also managed to get herself captured. Something he knew she wouldn't appreciate being reminded of yet again.

She crossed her arms, her gaze tracking the outside speeding past. "Do you think this train is going all the way to the port?"

"I have no idea. I don't have the map, and I cannot communicate with the others to know where this set of tracks leads or meets up."

She pulled her bottom lip into her mouth and rubbed her biceps. "So, what are we going to do?"

"Once we stop, I'll find out where we are and where my team is and figure it out from there," he answered.

The buildings grew closer together. The vegetation thinned. Soon, dusty roads with equally dusty travelers appeared. Carts loaded with vegetables reems of colorful fabric, or clay jars drawn by single horses. Bicycles with wobbly wheels and laden front baskets. Skinny donkeys weighed down by riders and stacked crates on their backs. If the buildings hadn't conveyed the poverty they traveled through, the people made it clear.

"This is why we have to stop the V Alliance," Deklan said, sweeping his hand out. "They're stealing from these people in more ways than one."

CIA'S HEART TORE AT THE ABJECT DESTITUTION SPEEDING past. Not even The Rows in Haven City delivered such a sad state of circumstances. Meager patches of shriveled gardens hugged single-level houses built of salvaged material. The forest encroached on every inch of land. Vines slithered along the dirt road and clung to the sides of buildings.

"What do they do in the winter?" she wondered. "I don't see any chimneys or vents."

"Maybe these are still nomadic people, and they travel closer to the Perazil border."

The train decelerated, and the squabble of excited young voices rose. Soon, a line of children chased the slowing locomotive. Deklan moved from the door and retrieved their bags. He tossed hers over. Cia caught the satchel and looped it around her torso. Izia ambled over, gave a long stretch, and licked his nose.

"End of the line for us," Deklan said.

He didn't wait for the car to stop. Leaping off in an elegant burst of power, he rolled into the fall and rose in one fluid motion. Izia followed without hesitating. Cia stared in wonder and shifted her focus to the ground, not speeding past as quickly but still a blur of activity. Her heart pounded a frantic rhythm. He shouted and motioned for her to jump. Squeezing her eyes closed, she jumped. Terror ripped a scream from her throat as nothing but air and the thundering sound of a train roaring past met her. Deklan's shouted curse sounded a split second before his arms wrapped around her. They tumbled into the dry dirt. A cloud of grit exploded around them.

"Stars above, woman, why would you jump blind?" he shouted.

Cia's hands fisted into the front of his shirt, where she pressed her face. Breath sawed from her lungs. "I've never… jumped from a… train… before."

He went limp beneath her. His arms fell away, and when she rose, she found him spread out and staring at the sky, eyes closed. Brown dust added an extra layer to the gray ash still stuck to his skin, clothes, and hair. The sun glistened off sweat along his hairline.

Guilt tightened in her chest. Once again, he'd leaped to her rescue. She leaned close enough to whisper into his ear. "Sorry."

Izia nudged his temple and then licked her cheek. Deklan reached up and patted the side of his muzzle. "It's all right, boy, we'll live."

Cia stood, checked her bag, ensuring all the contents were still safe inside, and then held her hand out to him. A gaggle of excited kids rushed by, vivid fabric trailing after them from the wrapped style of their clothing. The tattered ends fluttered in the wind of the slowing train and their momentum. Passengers hurdling from the train must have been a common enough occurrence, for the children paid them no attention. Suddenly, Cia was thankful for the grime coating her, shielding her paler skin tone and, therefore, foreign presence from the gathering. Deklan fit right in, his complexion very similar in shade to the rich caramel of the locals. Only his teal eyes and the dark red tinge of his hair set him apart.

"Why do you think they aren't paying any attention to Izia?" Cia asked, helping him rise.

He dusted powdery dirt from his shirt and the front of his pants. "Ruthenians and their wolves aren't an uncommon sight in this nation. My father helped fight in two conflicts here over forty years ago."

"Does Ruthenia have a settlement here?"

"No, just interests." He hefted his pack onto his shoulders. Izia fell in step beside him. "There are two citadels operated by Ruthenia, however."

Cia raised a curious brow at the information. "Two? Does anyone else have a citadel here?"

"Not that I'm aware of."

The boldness of the V Alliance, their confidence in their entire operation, made her breath catch. They had no fear. No concern for repercussions or worry about exposure. They were so secure in their operation that they did so under governments and defending nations. Cia looked again at the raven-haired and chocolate-eyed youth chasing after a train. For fun or in the hopes something of value would fall free? She looked at the passing locomotive with new eyes, wondering if it contained products stolen from their land.

Guilt, sudden and fierce, ached in the center of her being. She shoved it away. Regardless of Deklan's words, anything she'd learned hadn't been new information. At no point could she have helped prevent the theft of natural resources that was surely happening before the camp had been destroyed. How many others were there? She had no idea, but perhaps the books she had now would hold such information. She tightened her grip on the strap. Maybe she could bargain when they returned to Sziveria. She would share what she had, providing she could be present when everything was translated. If she wasn't thrown into a correctional center for her unsanctioned actions first...

LIGHT DAPPLED THROUGH THE SPRAWLING CANOPY ABOVE. Colorful birds chirped and fluttered from thick branches. The path Deklan led them along could barely qualify as such, a narrow trail of trampled undergrowth and vines. Izia had confirmed through scent that people used the route, not game. A walk around the outskirts of town had shown no roads leading in or out of the settlement, only the footrails or the rails. Through his bond with Neva, he'd learned his team was northeast, so he found a path leading in their direction.

"Did you find out anything else from your team?" Cia asked, her words labored between puffs of air.

"They still have eyes on Blackbain."

"Are they still traveling?"

Deklan lifted a large leaf, waiting until Cia took it from him before continuing. "No, he had the train take them to the port city of Balendes."

The rustle of brush stopped behind him. Deklan glanced over his shoulder. Cia stood rooted in place, eyes wide.

"Are they still on the train? Is he staying somewhere? Is he on a ship?" she asked.

"No, they aren't on the train. I don't know anything else. I don't even know how far away we are. I don't speak this language, so I can't ask anyone. I'm hoping the next city has enough civilization for a printed name and a map."

"Maybe we'll get lucky, and the next city will be Balendes."

Weariness weighed on Deklan's shoulders. If only they could be so fortunate, he agreed. Chances were, they had another days-worth of travel before they reached the ocean. Not something he could worry about now. More pressing concerns, such as food, water, and shelter if they did get stuck in the elements after dark, had to take precedence.

An hour later, the sun barely cut through the trees, and Deklan knew they had precious little time left to travel. Darkness hit a dense forest much quicker than anywhere else. He strained to hear sounds of human activity.

Do you hear anything? he asked Izia.

Nothing yet, nothing.

Run ahead and scout for me.

Izia yipped twice in acknowledgment and shot off down the trail.

"Where is he going?" Cia asked quickly.

"To see if he can find people. If he can't, we'll need to find cover for the night."

"Stars above," she breathed.

Deklan subdued his laughter. "What? Never slept outside before?"

"No. I don't think anyone in Sziveria has slept outside."

"It doesn't get as cold here."

"Cold enough, I'm sure."

They continued down the footpath. Water steadily dripped from the leaves above, pattering on the brush and their heads. Deklan swiped an errant droplet from his eyes. "I wonder if it ever dries out."

"I've never seen so much plant life outside of a greenhouse before," she said. "Sziveria sees a lot of rain, but not with these results."

"Like I said, the temperature doesn't get as low here."

Darkness crept in like fog. The constant song of birds faded into a cacophony of shrill insect chirps and droning. Deklan tried to see through the inky depths of the forest for any manmade light.

People, there are people, Izia's excited words tumbled through his mind.

Excellent. Dokhor vok, Izia. The wolf's pride at being told he was good swelled across their bond.

"Izia found civilization," Deklan told her.

"Wonderful," she said with a long groan. "How much farther?"

"Hopefully, close enough. He can't tell me distance."

"Can we make it in the dark?"

"We're going to have to." Deklan reached behind his back. "Grab my shirt. I can see even in low light."

She grasped his shirt's tail, pulling it tight across his chest. Fifteen minutes later, the faint glow of humanity flickered between trees. Deklan increased his strides, forcing her to keep pace. Her grip gathered more fabric while her weight tugged on the stretched fabric.

"Not much farther, come on, you can make it," he encouraged.

Not a word of complaint left her, but the heavy huff of her breath and occasional hitch in her step let him know she was nearing the end of her reserves. The forest thinned. The trail split, one path remained narrow, little more than tamped down leaves and vines, the other wider, with hard-packed dirt threaded with exposed tree roots. Deklan opted to take the well-traveled route. Izia waited for them at the edge of town, snapping at a cloud of tiny gnats floating around his head.

Gentle musical notes from strummed guitar strings drifted on the night air. Only the occasional lamp on the stairs leading to low porches broke the darkness. The trail widened into a street rutted by wagon wheels filled with muddy water. Frogs hopped and splashed between the puddles. The annoying buzz and flit of gnats around his head made Deklan swipe his hand back and forth.

Cia coughed and gagged behind him. "I just ate one," she rasped.

"I'm glad we haven't dealt with these all day."

Light and laughter spilled from the windows of a larger building with a wide porch. A sign swaying over the stairs had a mug and sandwich etched into the wood. Deklan pulled Cia toward the canteen. The door was propped open, but fans on a pully system kept a steady breeze flowing enough to hinder the gnats. Inside, Deklan let loose a sigh of relief. The conversation dimmed but didn't stop. Curious stares followed them to the bar in the back.

"Do you speak any of the language?" he asked.

Cia joined him at the bar, bracing her forearms on the sticky surface. "No. Enough people spoke Atlantic for me to get by in Suri Ravi."

Deklan nodded. Atlantic was the common language spoken by at least five countries on different continents and as a secondary language in several others. "My father taught me a little Columbian."

A young woman wrapped in layers of colorful fabric accenting the dark brown of her skin nodded as she saw them. She dried a plate before setting it on a stack between the serving window and the dining area. Wiping her hands, she spoke in rapid-fire Columbian. Deklan shook his head. She asked slower, but none of the words meant anything to him. He tried speaking to her in Atlantic, and she mimicked his head shake and held up her hands.

"Great," Cia groaned, turning her back to the counter. "Think anyone in the crowd knows our language?"

"We just need to know where we are," he said.

"And if there's a room to rent in this town. I have some local currency. Hopefully, it's enough for a meal and one night, even if we have to share."

Deklan had to force his breathing not to hitch at the thought of a single room. He knew they had little choice, and he didn't want the escape artist out of his sight anyhow. But sharing a room with likely only one bed? He'd be in for a long night.

Cia straightened from the bar with a quick jerk. Deklan looked around the room for a threat. Nothing seemed out of place. Two old men played a mancala game, while at another table, a group of four played mahjong, and at a different table, a rowdy, colorful card game was happening. The diner appeared to double as the town's entertainment parlor. The two old men gestured between each other over their marble game. Cia moved in their direction.

"What are you doing?" Deklan asked, following her between the maze of tables.

"They're speaking sign. It's universal." She grinned over her shoulder. "What are the chances?"

At the table, the two men glanced up. Cia moved her fingers in beautiful, smooth motions. The man on the left answered in the same fluid gestures.

"He says we're in a town called Flower Valley. I don't know what that is in the native language, but that's what it translates to in sign. We're..." She signed again, looking at the man who'd taken charge of the conversation. "Ten miles from the nearest port city. I don't know what Balendes means in Columbian to ask if that's correct."

"What about lodging? Or a map?"

"He says the woman at the bar, Hannah, may be able to help. He'll go with us to translate."

They followed the man at a snail's pace back to the bar. Izia pushed ahead, going to Cia's side. Chairs jostled from his large frame, and patrons leaned out of his way, but no one seemed to mind the enormous wolf. True to his word, the old man helped them communicate their needs. Cia tried to pay him when everything had been arranged, but he shooed her money away and took her hands, clasping them with a smile. He released her and said something that made her laugh and hug him.

Hannah reached under the bar and produced a folded map, the creases and edges worn. She spread it out and tapped at a small dot. Cia signed again, and the man nodded and made the same gesture.

"This is where we are, and this..." She grinned and made a sound of excitement. "This is Balendes, which *is* the nearest port city."

"Ten miles, we'll make that easy tomorrow morning," Deklan said. A sense of relief triggered the exhaustion he'd been holding back.

"Rooms are in the back, and she said we can take our meals there, too. No indoor bathrooms, but there's a shower stall outside if we want to wash off." Cia waited while the man finished signing. "He says the water is heated by the sun, so it is not warm, but we won't freeze. It's not an endless supply, so we should..." She choked and shook her head and made exaggerated motions in return.

"We should what?" Deklan asked.

Red glowed across her face, and she shook her head hard enough to flail her braid. "Nothing. Just we should be quick. Very quick."

The old man laughed, teeth white against his chestnut skin, and clapped Deklan on the shoulder. He spoke in Columbian, his voice laced with humor.

"Should I be glad I have no idea what he's saying?" Deklan asked.

Cia pressed her lips together. "Probably."

Hannah led them down a narrow hall off the dining area. Weak candles burned beside each door. She unlocked the third door from a strand of keys hanging at her waist and opened it to reveal a modest but clean room. A small dresser sat across from a narrow cot, a round crocheted rug between them. The only other decoration was a window covered in a bright curtain made of crocheted flowers. The curtain matched the bedspread. There was nowhere to sit except the bed. Deklan resisted the urge to swipe his hand down his face. The three of them would barely fit in the closet-sized room.

Cia paid for the room and what he assumed would be their meal. Hannah lit a lamp beside the door and left after a quick bow of gratitude. Deklan swung his bag around and dropped it on the dresser.

"Did you need more money? I have some local currency, too," he said.

"No, what I had was enough."

"Okay. I'll pay for anything else we need from here on out."

She nodded and rubbed her hands on her thighs. Clumps of dried mud sifted to the floor. "You wouldn't happen to have another clean change of clothes in there, would you?"

Deklan shook his head. "Sorry, no."

"Right. No point in getting cleaned up then." She looked at the bed and pulled all the blankets off the bottom sheet. She dropped everything on the floor at the foot. "Don't want to ruin these."

A knock sounded on the open door. The fragrant scent of garlic, tomatoes, peppers, and fresh bread filled the room. Deklan accepted the tray of food from Hannah, smiling in appreciation. She closed the door behind herself. Generous helpings of bread, sauteed meat, and roasted vegetables covered the tray on various plates. Deklan pushed his bag to the side and set down the food.

"There should be enough for Izia," Cia said, picking up a slice of bread and loading it with meat and vegetables.

"Thank you," Deklan said, surprise and gratitude filling him.

He built a plate for the dog with a few bread slices and lots of meat. Izia lay on the floor, eyes bright and hopeful. His tail swished a rapid arc across the floor. Deklan held the plate while eating bread. When he finished the slice, he laid the plate at the dog's paws. Izia's gaze never left him. The wolf rose only once Deklan straightened and motioned for Izia to eat.

Cia finished her slice and went for a second. "You know some sign, too."

Deklan raised his brows in question.

Cia made the arcing gesture Deklan had delivered, permitting Izia to eat. "Sign."

"Ah, I suppose so, then. Is your method of signing the same as what the FIO uses for their operatives?" he asked, making up his food.

"I'm not sure. I haven't reached that point in my training yet. But I imagine it is. You didn't learn it?"

"Only commands for my wolves. My team has to be able to communicate verbal and non-verbal depending on the situation. All their Ruthenian commands can also be done in signals."

"Good to know," she said around a large bite.

Deklan smiled and dug into his food. Flavor exploded across his tongue. They ate in silence, Izia's loud snarfling and low groans of doggy approval keeping them company. When the food was gone, Deklan returned the tray to the much quieter dining area. Most of the patrons had left. The two old men continued to play their game, their gestures edgy, but their smiles betrayed their bluff of anger.

Cia had blown out the light by the time he returned. She curled into the wall, and Deklan took it as an unspoken request not to bother her. He closed the door and then spread out on the floor. Izia lay under the window, and Deklan used his soft side as a pillow. The wolf's fluffy tail curled around his chest while his muzzle rested on Deklan's shoulder.

"Goodnight," Cia whispered.

"Goodnight, Lucianna."

Eventually, her breathing evened out. Her hand flopped over the edge. Her fingers brushed over his forearm. Deklan *should* have moved, should have rolled onto his side away from her touch. Hopefully, she was too tired to acknowledge their attraction and cause any issues while she slept. Because as much as he should ease away, he couldn't. Slowly, he reached up and threaded his fingers between hers, drawing comfort in the simple touch. A dangerous and foolish risk. And when her fingers tightened around his, and she shifted to the edge of the bed enough to slide her hand onto his chest, he didn't deny that, either.

9

THE HOT FAN OF DOGGY BREATH PULLED CIA FROM SLEEP. Warmth surrounded her, a contrast to when she'd awoken in the middle of the night freezing. Had she managed to pull the blankets up in her sleep? She burrowed into heat, clutching handfuls of fabric... that moved. Gasping, Cia raised her head and stared at Deklan's face, still relaxed in sleep.

He inhaled deep through his nose and stretched underneath her. His muscles slid and bunched under her palms, stomach, and, whoa, her thighs. Like a living blanket, she was spread across him, head to toe. She'd even left a lovely damp drool spot on his shirt, which she slid her hand over to cover. His hands settled over her hips, sliding to knead palmfuls of her butt. A masculine sound growled from his throat a second before he nuzzled his face into the crook of her neck and flexed his hips upward. The hard length of his morning erection pressed into the sensitive flesh between her legs.

Pleasure arced through her at the intimate contact.

Even separated by clothing, the sensation thrilled her. She knew he wasn't awake enough to know what he was doing, but when he ground against her again, it felt too good for her to make him stop. Reaching up, she slid her hands into his hair. She pulled her legs up to straddle his hips. The action made the pressure building between them more intense. Cia moaned. Summer sun, she wanted to kiss him. Wanted to know the texture of his tongue against hers while his sensual motions continued to work her into oblivion.

His grip tightened, pressing her harder to his erection. The seam of her pants turned damp and she couldn't bring herself to care. Knowing she was so aroused only excited her more. The tip of his tongue traced the tendon of her neck, setting her blood on fire. Unable to resist, Cia returned the gesture. Salt and man burst across her taste buds. Her fingers shifted, digging into his scalp. Little sparks sizzled along her skin, crackling through her nerves.

Deklan cursed and scrambled to move out from under her. Cia squeaked in alarm, jumping from him and onto the bed. Breathing heavily, Deklan shoved himself against the wall between the small dresser and the corner. He dug his fingers into his disheveled hair, his elbows braced on his bent knees. He cursed again and folded his arms, dropping his head.

He flexed his fingers toward her. "I'm sorry. I'm…"

Cia tried to calm her breathing. "No, I knew better, I just…" She licked her lips, her body alive and thrumming with unspent passion. "I've never, you know, felt anything like that."

Deklan groaned and hunched deeper into himself. "Not helping."

"Would it be so bad?" she asked softly.

He lifted his head, his eyes startling in the early morning light. "Forever, Lucianna. There's no hey, this isn't working for me. The bond is for-ev-er."

She still didn't understand the issue. Looking at him, rumpled, the lines of his face more pronounced from sleep, a heavy stubble covering his jaw and framing his mouth, he was devastatingly handsome. Waking up to him every morning until those dark whiskers turned gray didn't seem such a hardship to her. Cia shrugged. "Okay, and? I thought we went over this yesterday on the train."

Slack-jawed, he stared at her. Then he tossed his hands up. "Never mind."

Izia stretched between them, shook a cloud of dog hair free, and then went to the door and whined. Deklan unfolded himself from the corner and picked up his bag. "I'll stop by the front and see if we can get some food and meet you outside. No rush. Izia takes forever on his morning hunt for the perfect spot to pee."

Cia tried not to lament yet another unfilled moment of desire in his arms. She knew he'd never allow anything to happen. Not while he was conscious, at least. The knowledge made her want to be all kinds of naughty and seduce him in his sleep. "All right."

Outside minutes later, Cia shielded her eyes against the rising sun. A low blanket of fog covered the damp ground, rising in faint tendrils. The sight was common on Sziverian mornings, and homesickness punched her gut. Deklan's and Izia's large frames were silhouetted in the distance. Cia adjusted her shoulder bag across her chest and kept a firm hold on their bag of banana muffins and grilled sausage wrapped in waxed paper. They were heading in her direction on a wooden walkway. Cia waved and joined them.

Deklan held up a folded pamphlet. "Found a map. Should only take us a few hours to reach the port."

"Too bad we can't find a carriage if there's passable roads."

"There is one road, no rails though."

Cia leaned closer to look at the folded map section he'd isolated. "Did the train keep going, do you think?"

"The tracks split where we jumped off, so it could have kept going or stopped at the port. No way of knowing now."

The wooden planks squeaked and groaned under their combined weight. Few people ambled about, dumping dirty water onto the road or snapping clothes onto lines hanging from their front porch posts. Two young girls chased squawking chickens, the fog swirling in golden wisps behind them. A cart laden with sheered wool and towed by a slow mule rocked past, creaking over each dip in the road.

The plank sidewalk lasted until the outskirts of town, where foot and cart traffic picked up. Men with loaded baskets strapped to their backs walked into the town, women and children trailing behind with what appeared to be the makings of temporary booths. Cia wished they had time to explore the town market, and the wares carted and carried into the small yet thriving township. A contrast to the settlement they'd seen when they jumped from the train.

Like yesterday, the day warmed up quickly. But the shadows of the forest helped keep the heat from becoming unbearable. They stopped at a small brook, ate their meager meal, filled up on water, and started out again. By the time they reached the outskirts of Balendes, Cia's clothes were damp from sweat and humidity, and she figured she smelled awful. Deklan stopped in the shadow of a tall stone building. Cia slouched against the wall. Izia sat, panting, his tongue curled and hanging between his bottom canines.

Deklan grasped a stone protruding from the wall, eyes closed. "They're across from the town square, near a fountain. I'm going to pull Neva to me, and she'll guide us back to the rest of my team."

"That's so incredible," Cia said, awed.

"Stay with me much longer, and you'll get used to the process," he said, a small smile tugging at his lips.

If Cia had her choice, she'd stay around him for a long, long time. "What?" she asked when his smile grew.

He shook his head and chuckled. "Nikita will be coming, too. Neva couldn't get him to stay behind. He misses me."

Cia smiled. "That's sweet."

"Nikita's still a puppy in so many ways despite being almost four. I keep waiting for the moment when he matures."

Sliding down the rough stone, Cia planted her rear on the ground. "When is the puppy stage usually over?"

Deklan dropped his pack and joined her on the ground. His fingers played in the thick fur between Izia's shoulders. "Two years."

"Did something happen to delay him?" She petted the wolf's soft coat on his hind quarter. Izia's tail swished against her thigh. His nose lifted, eyes closed in doggy bliss at being loved between two humans.

Deklan shrugged. "Who knows. He's the third in a pack and, therefore, doesn't have to shoulder as much responsibility. That may be what's caused him to remain juvenile. There hasn't been a documented instance of a beast master bonding to more than one wolf in centuries, so we can only guess how it worked before."

"Does that mean they're documenting *you*?"

Laughing, he dropped his head back onto the stone wall. "Probably. All of us Ralston hybrids with beast master genetics are a freak of nature to Ruthenians. They haven't seen what we're capable of in so long they'd forgotten what their genes once produced."

Curious, Cia tilted her head and regarded him. "What do you mean?"

"Ruthenians have ventured beyond their shores to explore the inhabited world and have fallen in love and not returned. They've had families in other nations, which spawned the first Gen-Heirs. However, they haven't allowed any of those offspring to return to their roots. Not until very recently, and with certification showing the chances of them having a genetically common child are almost nonexistent. My family was the cause of that decision."

Surprised, Cia stared at him wide-eyed. "Wow, why?"

He swept his hand over Izia. "Three wolves. My oldest brother, Darius, can bond with a bear and his twin with hawks. While there's one other beast master capable of pairing with a bear on record in Ruthenia, a bird of prey master hadn't been recorded in over a hundred years. My parents didn't just have wolf beast masters but a variety of predator pairings. It's... unheard of. The power of my genetics made the elders in the country reevaluate their rules, though they still put too many stipulations on them, in my opinion."

Cia dug through her memory for what she knew about his parents. "Because your mother wouldn't have qualified under their conditions."

"Correct. But her uncompetitive genetics allowed my fathers to thrive within us. Nothing held his genes in check. Each of his children were blank canvases for his powerful genetics to take hold."

Cia patted Izia's leg. "That's so amazing. Does that mean my children would be exceptional if I were to marry a gen-common man?"

"Maybe, if he could get you pregnant," he said, frowning.

"What do you mean, if?"

"Did your parents really not explain anything about a mate outside of Ruthenia?"

"I still don't understand the problem or why it matters where my future spouse may come from," she said.

"How much do you know about Ruthenian lore?" he asked, his fingers teasing Izia's flicking ears.

Cia bit her lip. "Nothing?"

Deklan sighed. "All right." He angled slightly toward her, resting his knee on Izia's flank. "If the legend from the start of the cataclysm is to be believed, Ruthenians are a genetically modified people. They were created in a lab with the sole purpose of creating more offspring with unheard-of genetic talents at the time. Now, we're used to people being able to communicate with plants or animals, catch a glimpse inside the human body, or even touch an object, and immediately know how to utilize the object to achieve maximum results. Such was not the case over eight hundred years ago."

He swept an arm out. "Most people were like the ones you encounter here. Normal, common genetics. Which, once again, if the lore is to be believed, were rejected by the genetically enhanced females. Only a genetically compatible male could produce offspring with her, and even then, she only accepted the genes that would give her offspring the strongest genetics. As a result, Ruthenian men know when their mates are in their ovulation phase, and they have a physiological response that allows them not to leave their bed until her phase has ended. Even then, they may not get pregnant for years. A non-Ruthenian has little chance of producing genes a Ruthenian woman will find viable."

Cia didn't want to believe her future was one without children. Not that she'd thought much about whether she wanted them. However, she didn't like the near-impossible odds he seemed to be casting for her. "But it does happen. Katria is like me, and Sean isn't Ruthenian. They had Anyka last year."

"Yes, but how long did it take them, and will they be able to have another? Ruthenians have seen a sharp drop in their birthrates. Their genetics have become too convoluted with competing genes. Will my brothers or I have the same success as my father, with or without a Ruthenian mate? We have no idea. So far, only our non-beast master siblings have married, except for my sister Damira, an equestrian talent."

Cia frowned. "Why?"

"It's a little different for beast masters. Only Drayke managed to get our mother's gift, and he's not ready to settle down yet." He chuckled, still playing with Izia, who'd gone from tolerating his ears being messed with to snapping at Deklan's teasing.

"What about you?" she dared to ask.

His fingers danced just out of Izia's reach. The wolf made low growls of annoyance, his head bobbing up and down. "What about me?"

Cia's heart thumped hard in her chest. She could fill in anything except the personal question she'd been asking. But she wanted to know. "Are you ready to settle down?"

"I'm thirty-one," he said as if the answer was enough.

She scrunched her nose. "Okay… and?"

"And yeah." He picked up a pebble and sent it skittering down the alley. "The idea of a family doesn't scare me."

Cia drew her knees into her chest, wrapped her arms around them, and dropped her chin. "I never really thought about a family."

"I don't want eleven kids like my parents had, but two or three?" He nodded, a wistful smile playing at the corners of his mouth. "I could handle that."

"I'm not sure if I want kids. Not after… you know." She blew out a long exhale. "Though after all you've said, it may not matter."

"Don't let the assassin take away your future family, too," he said softly. "Don't give them that power."

"I…" Words lodged in her throat, and she swallowed against the lump. "I'm afraid I'd be too paranoid to leave the house with my babies. I'm too aware of the dangers waiting for them outside."

"Most parents feel that way, I think. But every day, mundane things pose a risk to us. We almost derailed yesterday, but we'll still get on a train to get where we need to go."

He had a point. "I know."

"You're young. You have lots of time to decide."

She laid her cheek on her knees and regarded him. The tightness in her chest that always seemed present whenever she looked at him returned. Knowing he wanted something she may not for his future, which wouldn't include her, compounded the sensation. "So, you'd never bond with anyone who didn't want children?"

THE QUERY SHOULDN'T HAVE TAKEN DEKLAN BY SURPRISE. Lucianna Castien was bold. Let loose in ranked society, she'd likely offend every guardian she encountered just for the fun of seeing them squirm. There didn't seem to be such a thing as *too* personal for the young woman.

"No," he answered without hesitation.

A pouty frown pursed her full lips. Deklan looked away. He'd been too close to tasting her again this morning. Her warm, pliant body had been a blur of fantasy and pleasure in the in-between haze of sleep and awake. His palms still recalled the supple heat of her and the way she'd met his arousal, her hips rolling over his. Blood pooled south, and he shifted to alleviate the sudden strain against the seam of his pants. Damn, but he wanted her. He took a deep, calming breath.

"And I suppose a year-long contract is out of the question," she muttered.

"You'd be correct," he said. "While my Sziverian-born partner could walk away, *maybe* I'm not willing to risk being stuck in an unfulfilled bond for life."

"That's fair. But if you choose to be alone, then why would kids matter in the end?"

"Because I want them if I do find a mate." Deklan searched his mind for a new topic. Thoughts of babies led to thoughts of making babies. He didn't need that distraction to make things worse. "What would be a no-contract decision for you?"

"Wanting an outside lover, even one with a shadow contract," she answered quickly.

Lover rolled off her tongue, sending a shiver along his spine. "A man would be a fool to throw away anything he had with you."

She stared at him, glancing at his mouth before meeting his gaze again. "Yeah? I think all the women who threw you away were fools, too."

Deklan jumped up, shoving his hands in his pockets, and searched the intersecting streets for any trace of his wolves. He could call on their bond and see where they were, but he needed something to do. This scrap of a girl saw more than he wanted. And he struggled to see her as just a girl anymore. Not after feeling how very much a woman she'd been in his arms. How was it their conversations always ended up in intimate territory?

The air stirred behind him. "Did you ever come close?" she asked.

Deklan's jaw tightened. A forced attempt didn't count. Not for him. "No, not really."

Before she could inquire anymore into his private life, the scrape of claws on brick echoed from the right. Deklan took a long, slow breath, opening all the bonds connecting him to his wolves. The threads between them ignited across his vision. Gold for Neva, silver for Izia, and sapphire for Nikita. They shimmered in thin, delicate streaks from him, the gold and sapphire almost as strong as Izia's silver. The gold and silver arced around a corner into a narrow alley. Deklan picked up his bag. Izia stood, shook himself, and then took off with excited yips to find the rest of his pack. While his wolves could use the link to find him, the strands were only visible to him when the wolves were nearby.

"Come on, they're close," he said, motioning with a tilt of his head in the direction of Neva and Nikita.

The wolves raced down the narrow alley, not slowing one bit when they caught sight of him. Three voices exploded across his psyche. All excited, proclaiming their joint happiness at being reunited. Deklan laughed and dropped to his hunches. Neva launched herself at him, knocking him onto his butt. She licked his jaw and his throat with high-pitched whines of delight. On Deklan's left, Nikita rolled around on the ground. His paws curled, belly exposed, an upside-down grin splitting his face. Izia danced around all of them, barking his excitement.

"Oh my stars," Cia proclaimed. "They're beautiful, Deklan."

"Thank you," he said.

He gave Neva an entire body rub along her sides. Sitting as he was, he could bury his face in her neck while she rested her jaw on top of his head. Tension melted out of him. All his pups were within his reach again. Safe at his side. Resting his head against Neva's shoulder, he looked over at Cia. She'd sat in front of Nikita and rubbed her hands along his stomach. Izia hovered over her, his muzzle on her shoulder. Instead of acting a fool like he usually did, Nikita flipped onto his stomach and stared at Cia. She leaned forward until their noses almost touched, sinking her hands into the fur under his ears. The intensity of their gazes alarmed him. If he didn't know better, he'd swear she was communicating with the wolf. But he'd *feel* the bond necessary for such a feat, and Cia hadn't, thankfully, paired with any of his wolves without her knowledge.

She is different, she is, Neva whispered along their connection.

Yes, she is, Deklan conceded, unable to lie to his alpha female.

Nikita licked Cia's nose and nipped at her chin. *Mine,* he declared.

Deklan kept from slapping his forehead.

Not yours, Neva chastised, snapping at his hunches in a flash of movement.

Nikita yelped and cowered into the shelter of Cia's body. He bit at the air in front of Neva's face.

Enough, Deklan commanded. The wolves separated from each other. Rising, he adjusted the bag across his shoulders and then reached down to help Cia. "Come on, we need to get moving."

"What was that about?" she asked, brushing her pants in a useless effort since they were so coated in grime.

"Nothing," he mumbled, using a simple signal for Neva to take the lead and guide them.

Cia watched his hand and smiled. "Return."

"Yes, we're returning to my team, her last location."

Traffic, pedestrian, bike, and horse-drawn carts and carriages increased the deeper into the city they walked. Near the fountain, Deklan called a halt. Three huge wolves and his much taller frame compared to the locals would stand out to anyone looking over the square from a higher window.

Neva, straes'ya kechan archen'ya vae'ny, Deklan commanded her to seek the team and return to him. He didn't have to tell her to be stealthy in her approach. Despite her beautiful golden russet coloring, she managed to dash through and blend into her surroundings.

"What's going on?" Cia asked as they sank deeper into the small space between two buildings.

"My team should be here shortly."

10

"Miss Ralston! Oh, Miss Ralston!" a high-pitched, nasally voice called from deep within the throng of guests. A pale masculine hand waved over the tops of heads.

Delanee spun around and frantically searched for somewhere, anywhere, to hide. A curtain. A large potted plant. An open doorway leading into a space not occupied by the obnoxious man desperate to catch her attention. She hissed a curse and wished, not for the first time in her life, she weren't so tall. Since both her parents had been blessed in height, there'd been no hope for the Ralston offspring to be anything less than five-foot-ten.

Wine sloshed over the flute she carried, drenching her hand and splashed onto her pale lavender shoes. She didn't have time to worry about the mess. Pressing through the crowd, she tried to hunch down.

"Miss Ralston! It's me, Barnaby Ingerman!" he declared for anyone within range to hear. *And shoot*! He was gaining on her. "Oh, excuse me. Pardon me. Miss Ralston!"

The night had started with such hope, too. She'd been sent to the exclusive social dinner for a Thanzian diplomat to gather news for the society section of *The Haven City Chronicle*. As the leading writer for the gossip pages, Delanee received invitations to all the important social functions. Ranked guardians and wealthy members of society wanted their names in ink, and the best way for that to happen was to make sure she was present and given something worth writing about. While mingling among the upper fringes of Sziveria's elite, Delanee kept her ears open for more exciting bits of information. She wanted to be taken seriously as a journalist, and the only way to ensure respect was to write something genuinely groundbreaking.

Barnaby's annoying voice sounded closer. A woman let loose a cry of surprise. "So sorry, guardianess, I just need to get through here if you please."

There! Doubles doors opened into a greenhouse, letting in warm air tinged with the musky scent of soil and greenery. Tealights in colored glass illuminated a brick trail while lanterns suspended from trees twinkled deep within the foliage. Delanee shouldered her way outside, ducking behind the first tree she came to. Barnaby tumbled behind her a few seconds later, rising on his toes to peer along the path.

"Miss Ralston?" He trotted down the path, the tails of his long formal coat flapping behind him. "I know I saw you come out here. Please, I just want to talk. Miss Ralston!"

Delanee's grip on the slender stem of her flute threatened to fracture the glass. She peeked around the tree. Barnaby had stopped not three feet from her hiding place. Careful to keep from rustling ferns and vines tickling her ankles, she leaned against the trunk and willed him to move on. He stomped his foot and pumped his arms at his sides in frustration. He took a few steps deeper along the trail, stopped again, and did a slow turn. Delanee gasped and spun away, pressing her back into the tree.

"Oh, Miss Ralston," he drew out in a manner that made her skin crawl. "I know you're somewhere close. Don't be coy, we don't have to play games. I am already caught, already yours."

Delanee pressed her lips together to keep from gagging. She'd already told the infuriating little man she wasn't interested on multiple occasions. He'd taken one look at her in her grandmother's living room four months ago and proclaimed himself in love. That was the last time she allowed her matchmaking matriarch to get involved with her future, thank you very much.

Though, in all fairness, Madeleine hadn't declared Barnaby a suitable match; she'd simply invited him over to decide. Delanee's fault for continuing to insist on a beta male as an acceptable mate. Barnaby had taken the invitation as confirmation he was *the one*. Nothing Delanee seemed to do dissuaded him. She was reduced to pathetic hiding whenever their paths crossed. He may be a beta, but he was persistent. Delanee was his ticket to a better future, and he wasn't relinquishing the dream.

"Very well, we'll do it your way. I always loved a good game of hide and capture. Are you..." Leaves rustled. "...over here? Nope, not here. What about here?"

Her anxiety spiked. He'd find her in no time. She

should have disappeared deeper into the greenhouse, not so close to the door. Risking being seen, Delanee leaned around the trunk.

"Found you!" Barnaby leaped at a bush across from her, almost tumbling into the trimmed shrubbery. He snapped his fingers in disappointment. "Sly woman, where in the inhabited world are you?" he muttered.

Delanee grimaced and tiptoed toward the house entrance. The crowd swayed and parted near the door as a tall man maneuvered through, focusing on something across the room. His handsome face was a welcome surprise. The light gleamed off his short platinum-blond hair. In contrast to his pale coloring, dark lashes framed his silvery-blue eyes, making the shade even more startling.

Ryan Voklane.

Now, if *he* were to chase her around, she wouldn't run very far. The secret admission still grated. He was the last sort of man she should ever get involved with. Dominate. Powerful. Traits that would venture into a relationship, and she wanted to be under no man's control. Over a year had passed since she'd spoken to the FIO guardian. She'd spied him at other events they'd both attended but ignored him. At least, that's what she told herself since she hadn't found the courage to speak.

The last time she'd seen him, she'd gone to his work and learned some disturbing facts about crimes in her country. While she'd been forced to remain silent on the kidnappings he'd revealed to her, she *had* been able to draw attention to the forgotten orphanages where the children were being abducted. She'd managed to resist the urge to chase him down again when she'd learned Deklan had been sent off land to deal with yet another issue. When her brother learned of her attempt to interfere with his guardian duties, he had not been pleased.

Delanee clutched her wine in one hand, gathered her lavender dress heavy with beads in the other, and raced for the ballroom. Maybe she could use Ryan as a height shield and disappear into the crowd before Barnaby noticed. No such luck. His cry of surprise followed her inside, along with the pound of his boots. Delanee dropped her dress and grabbed Ryan's hand as she sped by, pulling him through the gathering. A sizzle of awareness tingled up her arm. His calloused hand was warm against her palm. More dark red liquid sloshed over her wrist, and she cursed, setting the useless drink down on a side table.

"Might I ask where we're going, Miss Ralston?" Ryan asked, his voice a deep rumble of silk along her nerves.

"Did you arrive in your own carriage?"

"No, I don't own a carriage."

"A two-seater Ariot, then?"

He sighed. "You know we can't get in an Ariot and leave together."

"Why not?" she asked. "I'm a grown woman."

"Unmarried."

She pulled him into the less crowded foyer. Cool air swirled around her damp skin, and she breathed in relief. "Who cares? I don't care. No one here cares. I'm a journalist, Voklane."

"You're the sister of an arch guardian. And I think your parents would care. I know your grandmother would," he argued, freeing his hand.

Delanee's hand immediately felt cold, and she brushed stray curls from her temples to distract herself from the loss of his touch. A loss she had no business lamenting. "Again, grown woman. My brothers don't have chastity rules, so neither do I."

Voklane's brows rose on his forehead. "Really."

Heat bloomed across her cheeks. "I mean, we don't care about baseless rumors. I can handle whatever people say—"

"Miss Ralston!" Barnaby huffed on a shout, trying to disengage himself from the crowd. "Wait! I must speak with you!"

Delanee squealed under her breath and grasped the edge of Ryan's sleeve. She tugged him to the door. "I need you to give me a ride home. Now."

"But I wasn't—"

"Please," she implored.

He stared at her for a moment, his gaze searching. "Straight home."

"Yes."

She opened the door into the chilly night as Barnaby burst into the foyer. They ran to Voklane's Ariot parked along the road. She waved him off when he went to get the door for her.

"Never mind that. We need to go!"

He laughed a deep reverberation that she wished she had time to savor. But Barnaby's heeled boots clicked a rapid pace on the bricks. Delanee yanked the Ariot open and fell inside, gathering as much of her skirt as she could manage, closing herself in when Barnaby's frame became illuminated under the nearest streetlamp.

"Ooohhh," she drew out in an anxious hum. "Hurry! Go, go, go, please!"

Again, he laughed, the sound so at odds with his usual solemn demeanor that she couldn't help but stare. "I didn't take you for the type to run away."

Delanee crossed her arms over her chest and resisted the urge to wave and stick her tongue out over a distraught-looking Barnaby Ingerman. He even flapped his hands in dismay as if attempting to wave them down to stop. Not going to happen. "For the first three months, I didn't run away. Now, the irritating man has left me no choice."

He guided the Ariot onto the road with a smooth turn of the steering column. "Not interested in a combover or pasty skin?"

Delanee scoffed and rolled her eyes. "Aren't you part of that particular subgroup?"

Ryan rubbed his hand through his short hair. "Last time I checked, I had all my hair."

"I meant the skin."

He angled his hand, inspecting himself. "Ah, yes, I suppose compared to you, I am rather alabaster."

Compared to her, most of Sziveria glowed in the dark. But, to call him pasty wasn't entirely fair or accurate, either. All of Ryan was pale, his hair, eyes, and skin. Yes, he was ivory-complected, but didn't look sickly or weak. On him, the contrast gave Delanee the most wicked urge to know how her skin would look pressed against his with nothing between them. Or her dark wine-red curls spread over his broad chest. Or her light brown hands laced with his while he... She quickly shut the thought down before she squirmed in her seat. When it came to Ryan Voklane, her fantasies were sadly never in short supply.

Amber light flowed through the tiny cab in ebb-and-flow waves, making her very aware of their proximity. If she shifted just a little, their arms would touch. She pressed her crossed arms into her breasts. What was it about this particular man that tempted her so?

"And no, I'm not interested," she said. "But the little man seems to think I'm playing some courtship game."

"Adding petite to his list of inferior traits. Poor man."

Delanee waved a hand up and down her sitting frame. "I am not short if you haven't noticed. The man barely comes to my shoulders, and that's when I'm barefoot."

He cast her a sideways look that had her wishing for more light to see his expression. His fingers drummed on the steering column. "Perhaps that's why he finds the appeal in you, Miss Ralston."

Delanee blinked and then blew her disbelief out in a huff. She had no disillusions about her body, including her lack of curves, another gift from her mother. "Oh please, he'd get the same view standing in front of *you*. I think it's more my family and the prestige he thinks he could have by contracting with me."

"Do you really believe that?" he asked.

"Since every man who's shown interest in me so far has seen me as nothing but a social ladder wrung to climb, yes. I have no reason to believe Mr. Ingerman is any different."

"Surely not *every* man."

Keeping her arms crossed, Delanee shifted in the seat to face him. "All but three people in my family is either a guardian, ranked or unranked, or will at some point become one by their own merit."

"Except for you."

By her choice, but she wasn't going to tell him that. "Right. I'm the most approachable means to my very connected family. A year with me would guarantee admittance into a very closed circle. I had hoped making all prospects go through my grandmother would weed the herd, but…"

"They aren't concerned about compatibility."

"No, they are not," she sighed, dropping her hands onto her lap. "They often never were. Some have even gone so far as to say we could live under the same roof but keep things completely non-intimate."

And why, oh, why had she said that? Mortification burned through her. She shifted to face the front of the vehicle, unable to look at him after her confession. How ugly was she by Sziverian standards if the men asking to contract with her didn't even want to explore a physical relationship?

"Delanee."

Her name from his lips slid across her skin like a physical caress. Gasping, she turned to look at him. The flare of light from a passing streetlamp caught in his irises, making them almost glow silver. Delanee blinked.

"That has nothing to do with how you look, you know that, right?" he asked.

She balled her hands into the embellished silk of her skirt. Tiny beads bit into her palms. "What do you mean?"

Slowly, he turned into the small parking lot of the apartment building she lived in with her grandmother. "All but you, two of your brothers and one of your sisters, are a beast master, correct?"

"Correct," she somehow managed to say without fidgeting. Technically, it wasn't the strictest truth. However, she'd already divulged far more of her personal life to this man than she should have. She would not reveal more.

He parked and then powered down the magnetic

engine. He exited, and she followed before he could reach her door. "You don't have to walk me up."

"I want to. We can finish our conversation," he said, his keys jingling in his pocket.

Delanee led him inside. A spacious greenhouse took up the entire front of the building, rising three stories. A bark-laden trail curved in multiple directions, leading in a circle to the ground floor doors or the staircases on either side. Night had fallen long ago, and the trails were vacant of any tenants. Only the occasional rustle of a nocturnal creature having found a way into the enclosure sounded in the quiet. The soft glow of tealights under glass to keep people on the trail created an intimate environment. Delanee increased her speed. The last thing she needed to dwell on was a romantic evening stroll through her residential garden with Voklane.

Ryan's arm reached around and grabbed the door handle before she could. She leaned back to make room for him to open the entrance to the stairwell. The scent of cement and metal floated in the air. Their footfalls echoed around them. He hadn't said another word, and her curiosity made her edgy. What remained if her physical attributes, or lack thereof, weren't the reason men weren't attracted to her?

Only a single candle under glass flickered on a kitchen counter in the apartment she shared with her grandmother. The open floorplan swallowed most of the weak light. Floor-to-ceiling windows comprised the entire exterior wall, showcasing a stunning view of the nightscape beyond. Potted plants, small trees, and indoor shrubs lined the floor or hung from the ceiling in front of the windows. Delanee loved this apartment, perhaps another reason she was picky about her future.

If she had to leave the warm comfort of her family home, she wanted to be in the presence of something far better. So far, no one had come close to being able to offer anything in comparison.

"Well, here we are," she whispered in relief. "Thank you."

Ryan wandered deeper into the apartment, and Delanee gently closed the door behind him to keep from waking her grandmother. A slight tremor of excitement danced in her stomach. For all intents and purposes, she was alone with the Intel guardian. She nibbled on her bottom lip. She knew he wouldn't welcome any advances from her, but just the thought of touching him again sent a thrill racing through her.

"What's all this?" he asked, his shadow looming near the windows at the dining room table.

Delanee let her hand fall from the door. "I'm researching all the orphanages in Haven City and the smaller outlining suburbs."

Paper rustled. "Why?"

Joining him at the table, she rested her arms on a high-backed chair. "Because I'm investigating a story concerning them."

The faint light behind him and the lack of moonlight left him draped in heavy shadows. Delanee considered retrieving the small tealight from the kitchen but then decided perhaps being unable to see him would be best. Ryan did funny things to her insides no other man to date had managed.

He shifted through the papers like he could see in the dark. Delanee tapped her fingers on the back of the chair. "What did you mean earlier? In the Ariot?"

"Here in Sziveria, beast masters are not born, they

are…" He rolled his hand as if hoping to pull the needed word from the air.

"Imported?" she offered, bracing an elbow on the chair and her chin on her palm.

He snapped his fingers. "Good term for it, yes. Our society knows so little about them, mostly by choice. Two of your sisters are married. One is a confirmed matchmaker, like Madeleine. The other is an equestrian talent, which worked well for her. One of your brothers is married, talent unknown. I'm suspecting something logic-based, maybe finance? Anyway, I digress. Only one beast talent has married, and it was a non-threatening talent. Horses."

Delanee straightened, not liking what he was insinuating. "She fell in love."

"Yes, with the son of the largest breeder of Icekutians in the nation. She married into a dynasty." He lifted a paper, angled it toward the light, and then let it flutter back to the table.

Pushing between two chairs, she pressed her hands on the table. "Because they fell in love."

If his gaze moved to her, she couldn't tell. "Mmm. I don't doubt you. And the rest of your siblings?"

A niggle of discomfort tightened in her chest. She resisted the urge to rub her breastbone. "They have not."

"Fallen in love?"

"Mmm."

His weight settled on the table, making the wooden slabs groan. He leaned across the space to her, and her breath lodged in her throat. The urge to close the distance drew her like a magnet. Paper crinkled under her curling fingers.

"Let me guess," he began, his soft words like a

silken caress over her skin, "Ruthenians don't want the risk of tainting a pure bloodline, and Sziverians are too scared of the nature of the beast."

Her heart thumped a hard fist against her ribs. She swallowed away the discomfort. "Yes."

The tips of his fingers feathered along the curls near her temple. Delanee's lips parted with a gasp. "You're beautiful, Delanee Ralston, but even I know there is more to you than the words you write on a page."

Alarmed, she pulled away from his ghosting touch. "What are you talking about?"

"Keep your secrets. I'm not asking for them." He straightened, lifting pages again.

Delanee wanted to flee. Fought the urge pounding through her veins with everything inside her. But she couldn't let him know how much his words alarmed her. Somehow, she kept her nerves from showing, smoothing a hand along the back of the chair to her left. "I have no secrets, Guardian Voklane. I really am just a journalist."

Laughter and easy conversation flowed around the room. Boxes of food went from one person to the next. Cia tried to ignore the sense of longing in the relaxed atmosphere. She missed *her* team. If only she'd trusted the process, she'd have her people to converse with, not the oddball amid strangers.

Rough floorboards pricked at her rear. She wouldn't make the mistake of trying to wiggle to get more comfortable. Her last attempt had left a splinter in her left butt cheek. Everyone else sat on something, a shirt, pair of folded pants, or a towel, and Cia now understood why. She'd hop up and do the same if she didn't fear being laughed at. She pressed binoculars tighter to her face, ignoring the sting of the splinter, and swept her improved vision across the windows directly across the square from them.

Sabrie, the group's lone female, had given Cia the task of watching the building while they conferred. Short and stocky, the blonde had left no room for Cia to argue, shoving the binoculars into her hand and pointing with authority at the window. Deklan hadn't countered the order, so Cia had sat. See? She could be a team player.

So far, watch duty had been a waste of time. There had been no movement from the windows, and Black-bain hadn't appeared in the courtyard. Supposedly, the only exits were the front of the building, and two fire escapes on the sides, both visible from the abandoned building Deklan's team had taken up residence inside. Cia panned the building to the roof, a flat space occupied by trees and benches for guests.

Izia flopped down next to her, laying his head on her thigh. The tips of his nails poked into her leg, and she resisted the urge to scoot away, which would result in another splinter. He curled his paws inward as if he realized her discomfort. Surprised, Cia smiled and patted between his perky ears. Nikita lay on her other side. Groaning, he rolled onto his back, paws folded over his chest, and a toothy upside-down grin split his muzzle. Weight settled against her back, and she blinked when a fluffy golden tail swooshed along her hip. Suddenly surrounded by wolves, she sat very still.

"Don't take their attention personally," Sabrie whispered from behind. "Everyone else is busy, and they need to be taken to the roof to pee."

Cia dropped the binoculars and twisted to see the woman. Her arms were crossed, pulling the sleeves of her maroon shirt tight across arms more defined than Cia's. While Cia had height on the woman, Sabrie likely outweighed her by at least thirty pounds. The only *soft* part of her was the color of her brown eyes, the straight hair tucked behind her ears, and the full swell of her breasts. Cia shifted her gaze to the rest of the room. To far left, Deklan leaned over a table, both hands braced, deep in discussion with the other two men on his team. Just the sight of him caused her stomach to flip. An awareness she couldn't seem to shake no matter how hard she tried. He didn't look her way, but his muscles bunched, telling her he wasn't immune to the invisible pull between them.

"Well, go on, be useful. Take them on their potty break," Sabrie commanded.

Cia slowly set the binoculars on the windowsill. She unfolded herself from the floor and rose to her full height. All the wolves stood with her. "Sure thing," she ground out through a forced smile.

At some point, Cia must have offended the strategist, for the woman had been rude and cold in her demeanor from the moment they met. Or perhaps it was simply Cia had taken Deklan from the team, and the behavior was a means of punishment. Whatever the reason, Cia had been placed under Sabrie's supervision, and the woman seemed to delight in her role, demeaning Cia every chance she could. Being petty and immature would be the easiest choice, but Cia opted to be her father's daughter. Calm outside, a storm inside, and no one would ever know if they didn't *know* her.

"*Sesay ursla'viti, Cia,*" Sabrie said, pointing at Cia.

The wolves fell in line behind her. Cia headed to the far-right door in the cavernous room. At one point, the space had once been an office of some sort, with short dividers separating workspaces. But the thin partitions had fallen over and were covered in a thick layer of debris. They clacked and warped underfoot, sending up plumes of dust with each step. Busted chairs and pieces of old desks littered the area.

A dimly lit hall led to a hollow staircase. The cement stairs were worn and cracked but still stable. Light filtered in from wide windows at each switchback landing. Her boots and the wolves' claws echoed off the concrete walls. At the top, a heavy wood door with rusted hinges creaked open with a hard shove. The dogs bounded out into the weakening light of day, panting in excitement as they let loose repressed energy. Cia wandered to the roof's edge and sat, ignoring the twinge of discomfort from the splinter still lodged in her flesh. She propped her elbow on her knee, her chin on her palm, and continued her vigil of the building across the square.

Women were wrapped in straps of vivid colors with no apparent reason for the choices. Just strips of rich tinted cloth, whatever shade struck their fancy, woven over their bodies and flowing in uneven lengths around their ankles and from their shoulders. The effect was beautiful and whimsical. All the children under ten were clothed the same way. Men and older boys dressed in simple pants and a tunic that fell halfway down their thighs. Again, color had no relevance. Bright blue tunic and purple pants, or yellow paired with red.

The square was a riot of color and vibrant life. Cia smiled. Not many from her home would ever experience such a wonder of culture. In the center of it all, a white marble fountain burbled crystalline blue water deep enough to splash in on a warm day. Metal twinkled and glittered within the shallow depths. Some things spanned all of humanity, such as offering meager sums of money to water—a custom shared by all civilizations.

Cia leaned forward and folded her arms on the broad ledge. A faint breeze tugged at the strands of loose hair freed from her braid. Behind her, the dogs romped and played, hopefully taking care of their business. By the loud slurping and lapping, someone had found collected rain from a recent shower.

Three men strolled from the hotel across the street. The man in front pushed a pair of tinted blue sunglasses farther onto the bridge of his nose and surveyed the busy square. Sunlight glinted off his black hair. Cia straightened but didn't dare rise. The sudden appearance of her frame silhouetted against the brilliant azure sky would give away their position. Dressed in shades of brown and cream, with tucked in shirts and vests, the men stood out in bland contrast to the bright locals. Anxiety stole her breath. What was she supposed to do? Joel Blackbain was just… walking away.

Cia squeaked and crawled across the roof to the door. The wolves perked up and trotted back to her. Nikita licked her chin, panting his warm, doggy breath all over her face. Her nose scrunched, and she gently pushed away his muzzle. She fumbled with the door, using her shoulders to wedge it open.

Before navigating the stairs, she waited for her eyes to adjust to the dim interior. The dogs panted and yawned, crowding the narrow landing. "All right," Cia whispered the moment she wouldn't break her neck navigating the gloomy stairs, "let's go."

Thankfully, whatever command Sabrie had given earlier held, all the wolves followed her back to their floor. She burst into the room, traversing the treacherous route of busted furniture and collapsed room dividers. Everyone stared at her.

Cia pointed at the windows when she noticed no one had taken her former position. "Joel Blackbain!"

Deklan cursed and dashed to the windows, grabbing a set of binoculars perched on the corner of the table they'd occupied with equipment and papers. "Where?"

"He just left the building with two other men," she answered.

The wolves flocked to their owner. Though, for her, that turn of phrase didn't quite work when applied to Deklan. The beast master didn't *own* the wolves, not really. Despite their time together being short, she'd observed enough to begin to understand the relationship he shared with his canines went so much deeper. The small pack sat behind him, alert and ready for whatever he would ask. And he'd be right there with them, in the same danger. Her heart turned a painful flip. She joined him at the window, picking up the binoculars she'd used earlier.

"Where?" he asked.

"There are three of them. They stick out like warts on a princess." She waved a hand at the window. "Ugly brown clothes in the middle of all that beauty."

"I see them," he said, his voice tight. Turning, he issued rapid orders that everyone, including the wolves, jumped to obey. Cia moved to join them, but Deklan's hand sliced through the air. "No. Stay here. We'll be back when we have Blackbain in custody."

"But—"

He shook his head. At some point, he'd pulled the sides of his hair into a knot at the top of his head, and the ends of his remaining unbound hair brushed his shoulders. "You don't know how we work as a team. The process or our roles. If you want to be helpful, pack everything up so we can move out when we return."

Sabrie, Tate, and Galvin waited at the door for Deklan. A pistol gleamed from Galvin's belt at his left hip, balanced by the handle of a wicked looking knife on his right. Tate adjusted the straps of his medical backpack on his shoulders. Cia liked the soft-spoken, dark-haired medical scientist. A good thing since she'd likely be dropping her pants for him soon if she wanted relief from the splinter in her butt.

The team filed out when Deklan gave the signal to move. All at once, the wolves whined and skipped around Deklan in an unhappy state. Cia blinked. Deklan's jaw clenched, and the pack settled. While he made not a sound, communication was happening nonetheless. Another pitiful cry left Nikita.

"What's wrong?" Cia asked, worried and confused.

Deklan shook his head. "Nothing. We'll be back." His gaze locked with hers. "Please don't leave this room."

"I won't," she promised.

His intense stare stayed locked on her for breathless seconds before he seemed satisfied and departed. The wolves' nails clicked on the floor behind him. Cia didn't realize she'd been holding her breath until he was gone from her sight, and air rushed from her lungs. Sweat dampened her palms, and she rubbed them on her pants. Would the man ever *not* affect her? When she was gone from the world. Perhaps only then.

Looking over the room, she spotted the discarded bags to load up the items. Sabrie's maps. A handful of Galvin's weapons. Anything Tate had, he kept on his person. Deklan's bag lay tucked under the table. The sight gave her some comfort, proof he'd be returning. Agitation at being relegated to the valet made her grumble. She shoved the items from the table into the proper bags, resisting the urge to go to the window and see if she could spot any of the team. The likelihood was low; they weren't an arch guardian team for nothing. Chances were Blackbain and his entourage wouldn't notice Wolvenguard until Deklan was securing the convict's hands behind his back.

Cia double-checked the space for discarded personal effects, knowing the group had been there much longer than she and Deklan had. Even dilapidated rooms could become *home* with enough time and familiarity. She set everyone's bags on the scarred table and returned to her post in front of the window. Leaning forward, she rested her forehead on the glass and watched the flurry of life in the square below.

Children chased pigeons, trailing ribbons behind them. Artists offered unique wares to the small tourist population and locals alike. A man perched on a stool next to a wagon full of bound tombs arranged by color on shallow shelves. The whole setup would fold in at the end of the sales day, protecting the precious books from damage. Food vendors sold paper-wrapped delicacies as fast as they could pull them from the heat. Cia wished she were down there, experiencing the scents and textures of everything the city offered.

A board creaked behind her. Cia twisted toward the sound. She crouched, jaw clenched, muscles bunched and ready. Adrenaline poured through her system, making everything come into sharp focus. The unwelcome spark of panic penetrated her nerves.

"Ah," the man said, his voice a dry whisper in the empty space. "You are much prettier in the light of day. Young." He licked his lips. "Perhaps I'll be so lucky and innocent, too."

And a man who looked like him shouldn't be evil incarnate. In the harsh noon light filtering through the windows, with only feet separating them, Cia finally had her first decent look at Joel Blackbain. She tried to find the family resemblance with the team leader she'd come to respect. Failed. Sean was *nothing* like his older brother.

Joel eased blue-tinted sunglasses onto his head, pushing the ends of his short, black hair away from his forehead. Predatory curiosity shone in his pale, honey-brown eyes. Clean-shaven, his face was a study of smooth masculine angles and pleasing bone structures. If not for the cruel promise reflected in his gaze and twisting his mouth into an ugly smile, he'd have been ridiculously handsome. But the ugliness of his insides bled into his features, stealing his humanity.

Cia regulated her breathing, knowing to give into the desire to panic at the onslaught of adrenaline would mean getting caught by the convict. This time, he wouldn't give her the chance to get free. Something crunched under his boots as he stepped fully into the room. She jumped up from her couch and put more space between them. While she couldn't be caught, she couldn't let him leave.

"So graceful," he purred, closing the door hanging on warped hinges.

He moved along the wall opposite her to the second door. Cia didn't know whether to be concerned he was trapping her in the room or thankful he also trapped himself. For a moment, he leaned against the door. Flakes of faded paint scattered onto the floor around his feet.

"My boys are leading your retrieval team on a merry chase around the city. We have lots of time. If you please me, pretty, I'll take you with me and leave you in Monaco Sands."

"Raped *and* kidnapped, how can I say no to that?" Cia asked, shifting further away from him.

He arched a sculpted black brow. "Would you prefer raped and murdered? I don't mind that option in the least."

"I'm sure you'll understand if neither option appeals." The surrealness of the conversation disoriented her mind.

His cold smile morphed into a heartless grin. "That's the beauty of it. You want neither and will fight me to prevent both."

Then he *moved*. The rush would have surprised an average person, but Cia wasn't normal. She dove to the right, out of his reach. His shoulder bumped into the wall, and he twisted, pressing his back into the crumbling brick.

"How did you know I was here?" she asked, moving backward in careful steps to keep from tripping.

"You were lovely surrounded by sun up on the roof."

Once again, her lack of experience played right into Joel's hands. "And evading the wolves?"

A laugh barked from him. "Want all my secrets, do you?"

He sprang from the wall and shot across the distance, separating them. Cia inhaled and braced, rolling into the collision. His weight settled over her, pinning her. Fragmented pieces of wood and framing dug into her back and hips. He hissed crude, cruel words, telling her exactly how she'd learn his secrets.

"Forget I asked," she growled.

With a twist, she shot her knee between their bodies, breaking the contact. His hands locked around her wrists. Squeezing, he pinned her arms to the gritty floor. Ruthless delight made his bronze eyes glow. Cia clenched her jaw to keep from making any sounds. Already, the heavy evidence of his desire pressed into her thigh. Her struggles were enough to excite him. She didn't need to add vocals and make things worse.

She arched away and planted her right heel. Pushing off, she twisted into the force and rammed her knee into his side. His ribs flexed, and he grunted. Before he could fully recover, she repeated the move two, three times until he howled and released her. She didn't rise. Instead, she spun on her back, braced her weight on her palms, and sent one foot into his chin and the other across his cheek. His head snapped back, and he rolled away. The sunglasses flew from his head and clattered across the floor. Cia flipped into a crouch and to her feet in a fluid motion. Bits of broken wood clattered as she scurried away from him.

Rising on his hands and knees, he glared. Blood trickled from a slice in his bottom lip and a split under his eye. Satisfaction flared through her. She'd managed two good hits. Kevin would be proud.

"Sit down and wait, and I won't hurt you anymore," she promised.

"Oh, pretty, the hurt hasn't even started yet," he snarled.

He launched from the floor and went for her legs. Adrenaline shot through her. Panic attempted to rise, but she shoved it away, knowing to give in now would cost her. Easily, she sidestepped his clumsy effort. He sprawled face first onto the uneven flooring. A cloud of dust plumed.

"Now stay," she ordered. "You aren't going to succeed. Not with me."

Breathing heavily, he pushed onto his hands and knees again. His arms trembled, whether from pain or anger, she didn't know. She hoped pain, since anger would motivate him to continue his attempts.

"I see I've underestimated you." He rose onto his knees and wiped his forearm across his mouth. "I didn't want to break you, not yet."

He shook his head as if clearing his thoughts. Uneasy, Cia put more space between them. When his gaze met hers, the desire and excitement were gone. Only fury and determination remained.

"Now you've left me no choice," he whispered and pounced.

12

Deklan took the steps two at a time, racing after Izia. Faint whines of distress joined the echo of his claws in the cement stairwell. His wolf couldn't get to the seventh floor fast enough. When Izia froze in pursuit, worry shooting through their bond and a proclamation that their quarry was not where they suspected, Deklan hadn't questioned. He ordered Neva and Nikita to continue with the team and set off with Izia to follow the wolf's instincts. Returning to the building they'd been occupying had been a shock and a concern.

The implications of Izia knowing Cia may be in trouble were too alarming to contemplate. He'd consider what that meant later when he knew she was safe and they had their target in custody. Or maybe there was nothing to wonder about. Perhaps Izia caught a scent neither of the others had and knew Blackbain had eluded them and doubled back.

On the seventh-floor landing, Izia waited for Deklan to open the door. The moment the wolf could fit

161

through the opening, he darted into the hall on silent feet. Deklan's heart leaped into his throat the moment he realized both doors were closed. He didn't bother with a knob, slamming his foot into the warped wood. The door burst apart in a shower of splinters. Izia vaulted through the space while Deklan kicked enough fractured wood free to get inside.

A snarl of warning was all his wolf offered before latching onto the back leg of the man, pinning Cia to the wall. A feat that should have been impossible if Cia's talent was what everyone, including her, claimed. Unless… his gaze narrowed, taking in the tremble of her limbs. The heavy rise and fall of her chest beneath her torn shirt. Blood smeared across her mouth and trickled from a split in her bottom lip. A small cut over her eyebrow tracked a red path down her temple. Desolation blazed in her eyes. She was scared. Anxious. Panicked. The emotions paralyzed her gift. Made the adrenaline-activated skill useless.

"Cia," Deklan barked.

Her wild gaze locked onto him. She blinked as if convincing herself he stood in the room. The man shouted in pain, falling to his knees. Izia growled and dug in deeper, his back legs braced.

"Snap out of it!" he ordered. They had no time for her to be wherever her mind had gone that'd robbed her of her birthright. Harsh of him, perhaps, but she'd brought herself to this situation, and he needed her functioning.

More rapid blinks and a deep inhale brought her gaze into focused reality.

He nodded in approval and turned his attention to the convict. "Is this our target?"

"Yes," she said, her voice shaky. She touched a trembling hand to her busted lip. "Joel Blackbain. His felon stamp is on his left hand."

Izia, strivhat, Deklan commanded.

Izia released his hold on Joel's thigh to jump onto his back, pitching them forward, and took the back of the convict's neck between his strong jaws. Joel raised his hands, his breath puffed in coarse gasps.

"I'm caught," Joel panted. "You can tell your mongrel to get the arctic off me."

"No." Deklan grabbed the man's arm and twisted until the inked identification on his hand caught in the light. "You made her bleed. For that, my wolf is content to return the favor."

Izia grumbled his agreement and, by Joel's sharp inhale and strangled cry, sank his teeth a little deeper into the man's vulnerable flesh.

"I didn't...make..." Rapid breaths punctuated each strangled word.

Deklan squeezed Joel's hand and leaned forward his focus intent.

Izia shook his head in warning. Joel licked his bloody lips and grimaced. The frown turned to a smirk. Challenge blazed in his caramel eyes. "Her... bleed... enough."

Anger raged through Deklan, hot and toxic. Izia snarled, catching the rebound of his volatile emotion, increasing the wolf's agitation. Cia's hand slid along his forearm and squeezed. Deklan pulled on his control. Forced himself into a sense of calm authority. He twisted Joel's arm enough to get the man's attention. Joel hissed and attempted to move to alleviate the discomfort. Izia refused to allow the convict even an inch.

"Are the men you're traveling with Sziverian?" Deklan asked.

"No."

"Were they being held by the Sziverian prison system?"

Joel clenched his teeth. Sweat trickled down his face. "No."

Is he telling the truth? Deklan asked his wolf.

He is.

Deklan reached into his back pocket and removed two thick leather straps connected by a strong magnet he could remove and, if necessary, use to restrain a convict to a steel wall or other equally sturdy piece of metal. Wrenching Joel's arms behind his back, Deklan secured his wrists. Ties wound through the thick leather ensured a snug fit for any size wrist. Only prisons and Wolvenguard teams could use the magnetic method of securing a prisoner since adjusting and ensuring a safe, comfortable fit took time. Izia kept Joel still through the process.

Once finished, Deklan rose and grabbed Joel's bicep. Izia leaped to Cia's side. She knelt on the floor and wrapped her arms around the wolf, her face disappearing into the thick fur at his neck. Deklan ignored the tightening in his chest and heaved the convict up to his knees.

"You can kneel or sit. I don't care. You will not stand," Deklan ordered, releasing his hold.

Joel plopped onto his butt, sighing. "What, no privilege statement?"

"You'll be returning to Stonebreak. You know your privileges. If you've forgotten them, they're etched in granite on your arrival at the prison, where you'll be placed to read them and can access them anytime you request." Deklan crossed the room to the bags arranged on the table and pulled his close. "I'm just your friendly retrieval specialist here to return you to your prison home."

Joel snorted but said nothing else. Deklan knew if he looked at the man, Joel would be fuming. Deklan focused on his link with Neva and Nikita.

Sesay, zars'tka zre archen'ya, he said across their bond.

A quick order to stop their search and return. Hopefully, the rest of the team followed the canine pair. A scuffle and the slap of a warped board being stepped on made him turn. Cia stopped behind him with Izia. His wolf inched closer until his fur brushed her thigh. Deklan wished he could have such natural contact with her, too. But any touch he offered wouldn't be simple. Blood still smeared across her chin and caked in the hair near her temple.

"Tate will be here soon." When she drew her brows down in confusion, he elaborated, "My medical scientist."

"Ah, right." She brushed a hand near her eye and winced. "I must look awful. Could you... help?"

"My training is rudimentary."

"I'm not dying. Plus..." She glanced away, her cheeks flaming, and went to gnaw on her lip only to wince at the first touch of her teeth.

Deklan shifted his attention to Joel, still seated and silent. Cuts and bruises marred the man's face and neck. He held himself at an uncomfortable angle as though something else hurt, and he didn't want it to show. Cia hadn't been frozen the entire time they'd been alone, a small relief. If Joel had managed what Deklan suspected, Izia would have snapped his neck at Deklan's command. One he wouldn't have hesitated to make. Her superficial injuries were bad enough. At least, he'd *thought* they were only shallow. He leaned forward and met her stare until the various shades of gray were visible in the depths of her irises.

"What else did he do?" he growled low to keep the words private between them.

She blinked. "N-nothing. It's..." She exhaled. The heavy puff of air teased across his lips. Leaning closer, she whispered, "I have a splinter. It really hurts, and I know I won't be able to walk a long distance unless it's taken out."

A splinter? He leaned back and looked her over. "Where?"

She twisted and popped her left hip in his direction, angling her butt toward him. Oh, good grief. Sudden dryness coated his mouth, and he swallowed.

"Do you want Tate to handle it?" she asked, the blush creeping to her hairline.

Izia's snarl mirrored the haze of red over Deklan's vision at the thought of her dropping her pants for anyone but him. He clenched his hands into fists. Not good. The wise course of action would be to, yes, let his medical scientist handle the *medical* needs of Cia. But the beast part of him so eloquently embodied by his wolf answered for him.

"No, I'll do it," he answered between gritted teeth. He calmed the spike in his pulse and soothed the bond linking him to Izia. The wolf's hackles smoothed, and he licked his muzzle. Deklan held out his hand. Izia pressed his wet nose to Deklan's palm. "We'll have to wait until the team returns, though. We can't leave Blackbain alone."

Cia nodded. "Understood. And thank you."

Deklan sent a mental command to Izia to guard Joel.

Though Deklan noted the wolf's discontent at leaving Cia, he didn't hesitate to take a sentry position in front of the prisoner.

You're keeping her safe by guarding, Deklan reminded his sulking wolf.

He will not touch her again, he will not, Izia growled through their bond.

No, he won't.

Commotion in the hall minutes later announced the arrival of the remaining team. Neva and Nikita bound through the broken door and went to stand guard with Izia. Tate slung his pack onto the table. Galvin grumbled about not being able to use any of his weapons while Sabrie crossed her arms, leaned against the wall across from Joel, and glared. The convict leered but wisely kept his foul mouth shut.

"What's the plan?" Tate asked, his attention snagging on Cia before he rifled inside his bag.

"Patch up Cia and then return to Suri Ravi and our ship," Deklan answered.

Tate held out a bottle of saline, cotton pads, and a small glass jar. "Does she need anything covered?"

"I don't think so." Deklan accepted the items, not questioning how Tate figured no one else would be touching the young interceptor. "But I need tweezers, too."

Tate searched through his pack again. Silver flashed as he handed the utensil over. "If you need any help—"

"I won't," Deklan interrupted too quickly if Tate's grin were any indication.

"All the same, I'll be here."

Deklan's gaze caught Cia's, and she followed him from the room and up the stairs to the abandoned eighth floor. They didn't go beyond the entrance. Whatever offices had existed on the floor were vandalized, the walls crumbling, doors lying in the corridor. Enough light seeped through the broken windows for him to work by.

"Guess whoever occupied this floor didn't leave happy," Cia noted, lifting her shirt over her hips.

Deklan's breath caught, and he grabbed her forearm. "We'll do that after I treat your face."

She kept her eyes averted, still looking over the ruined office floor. "Is it so bad?"

Deklan held her chin in his hand and took in her injuries. "I've seen worse."

He went into the dilapidated office to his left and found a small table still with all its legs. After setting the table next to her, he arranged all the first aid supplies he'd need once he cleaned her face of blood. Wetting a cotton pad, he set to work wiping away dried blood.

"How did he catch you?" Deklan asked, trying to focus on anything other than Joel's hands causing her damage.

She kept her gaze downcast. "I'm still learning."

Deklan squeezed her chin until her eyes lifted. "No. The truth."

Shame and a hint of anger darkened her stare. He didn't let her hide behind either. Simply waited, patient.

"I... I have some sort of latent traumatic response from when, um, when—"

Deklan didn't make her finish the awful sentence. "A post-trauma stress reaction."

She nodded.

"And it interferes with your interceptor talent?"

Cia touched a trembling hand to her chest, over her heart. "When my pulse races and my muscles engage, and everything slows, I think I'm powerless, right back on that hill. Kevin has tried to help me get past it, but..." She shrugged.

"Real world scenarios are different than in practice."

"Something like that," she agreed.

Deklan figured there was more, too, but he wouldn't know until he witnessed her attempt to engage her gift. He clenched his jaw from giving her yet another lecture about coming to this country alone. She knew her mistake a hundred times over now. Gently, he wiped away the mess, leaving behind her pretty peach skin. The cut over her eyebrow still trickled, so he applied the paste Tate had sent to stop bleeding and help with the bruising. He smoothed a little underneath her lip, swelling from a bite or hit. He couldn't tell and didn't want to ask.

"Spicy," she said, wrinkling her nose.

"That'd be the black pepper. Helps stop bleeding."

He crouched down on her left side. Their eyes met as she gathered up her shirt and held it out of the way for him to loosen the tie of her pants and slowly, inch by inch, reveal her bare hip. His pulse raced when he realized she wore no undergarments. Perhaps she had at the start of her journey, but now all she wore were the loose cotton sleep pants he'd given her from his pack. A small snagged hole along her rear told him where he could expect to find the splinter lodged in her flesh.

"Can you hold up the right side of your pants so I don't have to make you completely drop them?" he asked, sweat beading along his hairline.

"I don't mind," she whispered, her gaze trusting and, damn it, heated.

This woman was determined to drive him insane. "I do," he ground out.

Her eyes searched his, and she gave a slight nod of concession. She grabbed the waistband in her fist at her right hip and held them in place.

Deklan tried not to notice how the shadows dipped and flowed over her exposed hip or the flexing muscle of her shapely butt. Resisted the urge to trace the bared curves with his tongue. Lust settled thick and heavy in his groin. He ignored that, too.

The skin around the wood fragment was puffy and red with irritation. He looked at the tweezers and wondered if they were big enough or if he should see if Galvin had needle-nosed pliers he could use. "This is going to hurt. It's pretty large."

"How large?"

"I'm surprised you've been walking at all."

"Great," she muttered.

Deklan had no good place to brace his hand, so he steeled himself against touching her and filled his palm with her silky skin. His fingers contracted into her hip and the yielding flesh of her stomach. Yet, beneath the female softness, the shift of muscles enticed and teased him to discover more. To learn her strength and see how her sleek form would look wholly exposed to him. Oh, summer sun, it'd be so easy to slide his hand over her ribs and discover how supple her breasts would be in his hand. How responsive she'd be to his touch. His skin was a dark contrast to hers. A warm honey-brown to her delicate beige. The increased rush of her breathing didn't improve matters. The intimate contact equally fascinated her.

Deklan dug his fingers in deeper and focused on the task. Carefully, he grasped the splinter and eased it from her flesh. She gasped and tensed but remained still. Blood surged to fill the void, darkening the damaged skin before dripping free. Deklan set the tweezers with the sliver onto the table and picked up a clean bunch of pads and the saline. He thoroughly cleaned the wound before applying a thick layer of salve.

"Oh wow," she breathed. "That was big."

Deklan spared the sharp fragment a glance and nodded. "Yes. You're a tough woman. Anyone else would have been cursing and flinching when I removed it."

"Including you?" she asked, laughing.

"Probably," he conceded and stood, taking a necessary step from her. He busied himself with gathering everything while she adjusted her clothing.

"Thank you," she said. "I would have been mortified to have anyone else see my bare butt."

A very nice bare butt. Pale and plump, yet firm with muscle. Oh, the things he'd do— he cut the trail of thought before he could get any harder than he already was. Talk about mortification. "No problem. Ready? We have a long trip to Suri Ravi."

"Can I go to my hotel room and get my things?"

"You left a lot behind?"

"My clothes." She plucked at the loose cotton covering her legs. "Not that I don't appreciate the loan."

Deklan considered the logistics of separating once they reached Suri Ravi. He'd have to keep a team member, or a wolf, with her to ensure she returned to the ship on time. "I'll see what we can manage."

Her smile was brief but bright. "Thanks."

Like everything else about her, Deklan tried to disregard the spark she ignited in his blood. And like every other attempt, he failed.

13

GOLDEN LIGHT SPARKLED OVER WAVES SO CLOSE IN COLOR to Deklan's eyes that Cia found herself transfixed. The undulating glide of the green ocean was broken only by the glitter of the setting sun and the occasional white peak. Sitting cross-legged at the rail, she brushed her fingers through Izia's fur. The wolf lay with his head on her left thigh. Nikita lounged to her right, occupying her other leg, while Neva curled at her back. The wolves had been a constant companion to her for the voyage. A contrast to their master, who had avoided her at every turn. By the third day, Cia had given up any attempt to find him, let alone engage in conversation.

Already, he put distance between them. A depressing thought to know once they reached Sziveria, she'd be relegated to seeing him only at the few functions they both attended—a scenario she didn't want but couldn't see any other alternative.

Joel had been sequestered away below. Twice a day, one of the men walked with him around the deck with the wolves trailing close behind. Deklan had insisted he wore a floatation device with a rope attached in case he had any ideas of jumping, they could pull him back onto the ship before he drowned since he'd be unable to swim restrained. Cia made it a point to be anywhere else. He'd tried baiting her the first day of the voyage, or rather, she figured he was baiting Deklan. She had no idea what he hoped to accomplish by angering the Wolvenguard. Nothing good.

Now, they were within hours of arriving at Port Ice Hollows. She was excited to see the cliffside docks but nervous about returning home. She'd have to face Sean and Kevin, figuring even laidback Mason would have a few choice words for her. The trepidation of their disappointment grated on her nerves. As did the unknown of whether they'd be at the port or awaiting her arrival in Haven City.

The wolves, sensing her anxiety, crowded closer. She had noticed that about them. They flocked to her whenever her emotions reached an extreme level. Cia didn't understand how they knew but was thankful for their companionship. Another loss she would keenly feel upon arriving home. One of the wolves was never far from her reach. Even at night, one of them accompanied her, curling at the end of her bed or alongside her like a big, warm, fluffy pillow. None of her usual nightmares plagued her with them present. They seemed to wake her before the worst memories could yank her into the horror.

"Wish I could take you with me," she whispered into the fur between Izia's fuzzy ears. Nikita whined and shoved his nose under her elbow. She laughed and scratched under his chin. "You too, pretty baby."

"You better be packed," a snide female voice said

from behind. "No one is going to wait for you when we dock."

Cia twisted and met Sabrie's glare. For three weeks, Cia had dealt with the woman's rude, almost near hatred. Neva's head lifted, and a soft growl only Cia could hear emanated from her.

"Shh," Cia urged, spreading a calm touch through the shivering fur at Neva's shoulders. "It's okay." Louder, to be heard above the waves, wind, and hopeful seagulls, she addressed Sabrie, "Tate stacked my bag with all the others after breakfast."

Sabrie lifted her nose into the air and turned on her heel. Cia sighed and returned to the view. In the distance, the faint outline of the cliffs rising from the ocean lined the horizon. The sails snapped and billowed above her. The captain shouted orders from the wheel, and the deck became a flurry of activity. When a deckhand rushed for the ropes tied near where they sat, Cia and the wolves moved to a new position.

Tate joined her, leaning against the rail on his elbows. The breeze ruffled through his short, black hair. "She's jealous."

"Who, Sabrie?" Cia asked.

"Yes."

"What in the inhabited world does she have to be jealous of?" Certainly not Deklan's non-existent attention toward her.

Tate motioned with his chin. "The wolves."

Cia's fingers curled into the fur of Izia's head. "What about them?"

"The only other person they behave this way with is Deklan."

She wasn't sure how the revelation was supposed to make her feel. Confused, awed, and a little excited, all the emotions clamored for a place. "I didn't do anything."

"Not that you're aware of," he conceded. When she frowned, he angled to face her, bracing his weight on her left arm. "You're Ruthenian. They can bond with you, one of them, completely, just as they can with Deklan. Maybe all three, since no one knows exactly how this bonding thing works between couples or beast masters and their animals. You offer something no one outside of Ruthenian can offer them."

Cia ruffled the fur between Neva's ears. "So, they're what? Courting me?"

"Perhaps they are."

Somehow, she kept from snorting. The wolves didn't need to convince her to be their mistress. If their master wanted her, she would fall into his arms without hesitation. "Too bad it's not up to them."

The ship turned to begin docking. A few seagulls turned into dozens, all fighting and squawking in the sky over the ship, hoping to steal something edible. A woman screamed from a vessel making port next to them as the aggressive birds dove, picking at feathers and baubles on her hat. Tate snickered. Crews awaiting cargo shouted and guided ships into their harbors. Cranes groaned, and rope hoists jangled, adding to the constant thunder of waves crashing into the cliffs. So many noises and sights competed for her attention.

Cia turned to watch all the action involving their approach. Workers lined up at huge metal dock ties. Knit caps were pulled down to their brows, and heavy wool or leather jackets covered their torsos. They all wore bright yellow canvas pants tucked into black boots. Brawny men and women used to constant, grueling labor. Windburn reddened their cheeks and noses. The captain eased the ship into the birth while the deckhands threw ropes to the workers below. Shouting and grunting followed the ship, forced into a stop by ropes on either side. Once secured, a plank was lowered to the docks on either side.

The crew, already packed and ready, wandered off the ship, joking and laughing. Cia looked up— way up — the cliff face looming over the collection of ships below. Pulleys attached to lifts and switchbacking stairs crisscrossed the sheer slate, broken in places by an intrepid tree or tufts of grass. Birds nested in crevices. A wide wooden walkway was constructed from the wall connecting the piers. The space rose and fell with each ocean swell rising beneath them. Cia wondered how anyone walked so easily along the floating mass. She'd have to manage. She wasn't wearing bright yellow to avoid getting lost in the swirling waves.

Joel emerged from below between Galvin and Sabrie. Deklan, conversing with the captain, made a motion the team seemed to recognize, for Sabrie nodded and continued off the ship with their charge. Tate tilted his head. "Come on, we're off, too."

"With the wolves?" she asked, picking up her packs from the remaining few on deck.

"Yes. Deklan has to settle with the captain. We'll meet him clifftop. He won't be far behind."

Cia looked up at the hundreds of stairs to the top and groaned. "I hope there are places to step off to the side to let others go past."

Tate laughed. "You'll do fine. It's not so bad."

The wolves divided to flank her front and back. Neva and Nikita were at her front, while Izia was at her back. Every few steps, his nose would bump her lower back, reminding her of his size while encouraging her to keep moving. At least she'd have a soft landing pad if she tumbled backward.

Dripping with sweat, shaking from muscle fatigue, and gasping for breath, she finally reached the top. The rest of the group waited in a loose circle with Joel between them. Sabrie looked out over the ocean while Galvin surveyed the bustling crowd. Crates were being loaded and off-loaded from manually pulled rope lifts. Vendors were selling quick, prepacked meals to eat on the go. A stiff ocean breeze whipped through Cia's hair and carried the scents of brine, unwashed bodies, and rich tobacco smoke. She wrinkled her nose and fought a sneeze. Neva had no such compulsion, blowing mucus from her nose all along Cia's hand.

"Ugh, gross," Cia complained, wiping the snot off her thigh.

Tate laughed. "The price of their affection."

Neva and Nikita moved from the path and sat beside Sabrie while Izia stayed at Cia's side and watched the stairs with a hard focus. Cia patted his head. "He won't be much longer."

Cia kept her hand on Izia's head and looked back at Tate. "Should I worry if—"

A gunshot cracked.

The crowd reacted in a collective dive and shout of fear. Cia's earlier fatigue disappeared. She spun around, searched the pedestrians, immediately dismissed anyone among them, and turned her attention higher to the cramped buildings erected nearly on top of each other in the available flat spaces between massive boulders. Some intrepid builders had managed to use a few flatter ones for foundations, putting the structures higher than the rest. One such stone monstrosity, roofless and crumbling, grabbed her attention.

Without a second thought, she took off. Someone attempted to assassinate Joel Blackbain upon his arrival, and Cia wouldn't miss this chance. The possible identity of the assassin, the author of all her nightmares, was within her grasp. No way would she allow the person to walk away without a fight.

CHAOS MET DEKLAN AS HE STEPPED OFF THE LAST STAIR and onto the main street of Port Ice Hollows. The worn stone felt odd beneath his feet after the constant motion of waves and the stairs' creaky, often questionable stability to the top. Neva and Nikita barked while Izia bounced in a frantic *pay attention to me!* pattern. By the disorganized excitement of his wolves, he knew something bad had happened. He searched out his team and found Tate kneeling on the ground, throwing bloody bandages away while motioning for Sabrie to hand him something from his pack. Galvin knelt across from him, speaking to someone, a man, if the large boots were any indication. People scrambled around him, rushing to the stairs or nearby buildings, jostling him in their frantic bid to escape something or someone.

Deklan shoved his way to his team, gritting his teeth. Joel lay staring at the sky, blinking, a grimace of pain twisting his pale face. His shirt had been torn from the left shoulder, where Tate wrapped a long cotton bandage. Galvin held Joel's side up off the ground enough for Tate to slide the roll under Joel's shoulder and back over.

Tate glanced up long enough to make eye contact. "I need to get him somewhere indoors to clean and suture, but he'll live. Nothing vital was hit."

"Think it was a bad shot or a warning?" Deklan asked.

Tate shrugged. "No idea, though I'm leaning toward bad shot. What's the point of a warning? Nothing he says will reduce his prison sentence. He has limited incentive to talk."

Unless they used torture. Deklan met Joel's cold stare and knew the same thought had already crossed the man's mind. Since Deklan wouldn't be involved in that mess, he tuned out the bleak speculation.

The wolves continued to desperately get his attention. He'd silenced their link while concluding his business with the captain. Now, as he searched for the one person he wanted to find, he opened their bond and almost fell to his knees. Their distressed cries slammed into his mind in a wall of sound.

Bad man, bad!

Gone, gone, gone!

She ran, must follow, tell me to follow, she ran!

They all repeated their own worries, their own focus, and goals. Deklan made a fist and silenced them with one sharp command. Only once the pack sat, eyes on him, muscles quivering with the need to move, did he sift through the individual words and land on the one he needed more information about.

Izia, where did Lucianna run?

This way, she ran this way. Izia turned, his nose pointing toward the infernal woman who had obviously gone hunting an assassin on her own.

Izia, ursla'viti, he ordered and then commanded Neva and Nikita to stay.

His gray wolf bolted into the dissipating crowd, weaving through a few stragglers or those who didn't care about a single fired shot. Deklan released his link to his other wolves and pulled deeper on Izia's, merging their senses. The sweet scent of jasmine and warmth of vanilla mingling with the earthy undercurrent of patchouli filled his nose. Unique to Cia, easy for Izia to trail, like a delicate iridescent pearl thread for the wolf to follow. His ears picked up the distant sound of someone shouting to hold a rope steady while a woman heckled with a sailor about mending a vest and pair of pants. Wheels on push carts squeaked. A cat chittered at a bird. Deklan kept his gaze on Izia, sifting through the information provided through their bond, hoping wherever Cia had run wasn't far.

Broken and sagging wood stairs led to a crumbling stone building perched on a boulder. Izia wove and jumped his way to the top. Deklan moved slower, having to avoid rotted or missing sections. Fragments littered the usable rungs where someone, either Cia or the assassin, had made an error and stepped where they shouldn't have. Izia's bark echoed to him.

Inside, inside! Izia's words punctuated each yip.

Deklan used the side of the boulder for balance and leaped up the last few steps. The final one cracked beneath his weight but held. Inside, something crashed and broke. A feminine shriek. A masculine grunt. Deklan paused in the opening, allowing his eyes to adjust to the dimmer interior and get his bearings. The wood ceiling shuddered, sending dust sprinkling down.

Do you see the stairs? Deklan asked Izia.

This way, they are this way.

Deklan followed the winding thread of the wolf's bond through cluttered rooms littered with broken chairs, clay pots, and various other indiscernible objects to the back of the building, where a narrow set of stairs led to the upper floor. Izia was already on the second floor. Growls and warning barks joined the clatter of objects falling and breaking.

Vye, Izia, do not approach, Deklan warned, not wanting his wolf to get close to the action and potentially be hurt before Deklan could observe.

His warning came too late. The harsh retort of a gun expelling a bullet sent a red haze of pain across his bond with Izia. The wolf yelped. Deklan sprinted over-thrown and fallen debris through a broken wall into a room. Izia still stood. Blood saturated his pale gray pelt and right front paw, dripping in macabre splatters to the filthy wood plank floor beneath. Cia spun through a kick, knocking the smoking pistol free from the hand of a sweaty, tall, wiry man. The would-be assassin took advantage of her back to him and Deklan's split atten-tion to sail through an opening to the outside.

"No!" Cia screamed and ran to the sagging framed window, her hands clutching the exposed stone. "Come back here, you coward!"

Deklan dropped to his knees and pushed bloody fur from the wound to see the extent of the damage. Fear burned in his stomach. He couldn't lose a wolf again. Couldn't go through the death of another bond. Couldn't lose another piece of himself.

Cia spun, eyes wild, hands fisted. "Send Izia after him!"

Deklan shook his head, not trusting himself to speak at her command.

"Send him!"

"He's been shot, Lucianna!" Deklan bellowed.

Okay, I am okay, Izia assured, licking Deklan's chin. When so deeply connected, the bond went both ways. Izia experienced Deklan's all-encompassing panic.

A deep gash split the skin of Izia's shoulders, cutting through the deltoid. No bullet had penetrated his body. Deklan fell to his butt and dropped his arms on his knees and his chin to his chest. Izia licked at his fingers and whined.

"Is he okay?" Cia asked softly, her touch ghosting across his forearm.

Deklan took a grounding breath before looking up to meet her stare. Guilt, concern, and regret all flickered through her gray eyes. All the emotions were wasted on him. He had room for nothing else except the anger that had seared away his fear.

She was a mess.

Bruises were developing on her cheek and neck, where the ones from New Columbia had finally healed on the voyage. Rips in her clothing dotted with blood told him one of the crashes he heard was likely her being thrown through one of the busted tables downstairs. The visible trauma to her beautiful body did nothing to alleviate the fury pounding in his temples.

"Why did you come here?" Deklan asked.

Drawn back to the window, she braced her arms on either side of the opening. "He was… right here. If not him, then he'd know. I *know* he'd know who I searched for."

Deklan pressed his hand to Izia's chest. The steady beat of his heart pulsed against Deklan's palm. "And if we hadn't arrived? Would you have won?"

14

Cia's shoulders tensed. Loose mortar crumbled beneath her fingers. Mortification and shame kept her from turning, even as his booted steps shuddered along the decaying floor beneath her feet.

"Would you have?" Deklan demanded.

No. He knew the response. And her desire to have information had once again nearly cost her life, along with Izia's.

"You can't keep doing this," he whispered behind her. "What good will answers do if you aren't here to learn them?"

Remnants of the fight raced through her mind. Cia had been so sure of herself when she'd walked into the building and spied the thin, sweating assassin reloading the rifle with shaky hands. Certain she'd kick his butt all the way back to the team. Then he'd turned, and the crazy in his eyes should have been her first warning. But she'd been busy trying to see any sign of recognition. Any indication of guilt. Her second warning of imminent failure should have been when he launched

183

an empty shelving unit at her. Just, *wham*, sent it hurtling across the space faster than she could react. Nor had he given her time to adjust to a piece of furniture knocking her senseless. He'd been right on her, clawing, punching, squeezing... She shuddered and forced the violence from her thoughts.

Deklan sighed. A long exhale of frustration. Cia turned and rested her back against the rough stone.

"I'm sorry," she said. Pain tugged at her lip, and she winced, touching a swollen split still sticky with blood.

He stared at her for a long moment. His gaze tracked over her, a muscle jumping in his clenched jaw. "Gather what you can of the belongings he left downstairs. I need to get Izia to Tate and check Blackbain's condition."

"No lecture?" she asked, a bit mystified.

"Didn't do any good in New Columbia. Why should I waste your time or mine?" he threw over his shoulder on his way to the stairs.

"Ouch," she whispered, rubbing her chest.

Izia limped after him, leaving blood behind with each step. The crimson splashes were unnaturally bright on the filthy floor. Had the wolf not burst up the stairs, fangs bared, hackles up, dangerous intent quivering in every muscle of his body, Cia would have taken a bullet to the head. Instead, the gun had been turned in terror on Izia. The distraction had been enough for Cia *and* the assassin to get free. The beautiful beast had almost taken a bullet to save her. Which never should have happened.

Cia collapsed against the wall and dropped her head into her hands. Tears stung behind her eyes and nose. Sobbing like a weakling would get her nowhere. She breathed through the urge. Her lack of proficiency had once again resulted in catastrophic failure. No longer could she ignore that she wasn't ready for the fight she was so desperate to accomplish. When would she be capable? How long would she have to wait? Fear of the answer had her biting her lip to stop another, stronger impulse to cry. Deklan had given her a task, which she'd complete and worry about the rest later.

Shoring up her wayward emotions, she skirted Izia's trail and went downstairs to the nest the assassin had made for himself while awaiting their ship's arrival. Only the occasional groan and pop of the wind buffeting the structure broke through the silence. A bird hopped on the nearest sill, chirped, and fluttered away. The tiny creature probably had a home built somewhere in the rafters. Cia toed a pair of boxers away from a sleeping pad before kneeling and lifting the thin cushion. Her heart fluttered in excitement at a small collection of papers until she realized they were nothing more than pornography. Sighing, she refolded them and kept them. Evidence was evidence. The rest of her search found a small food stash, a daily log of dock activity, and a glass vial with fine pink powder. She shoved everything into an empty backpack lying at the head of the mat.

Rising on protesting muscles, she took one last look around. Satisfied she'd found everything worth finding, Cia returned to the last place the team had been. Neva waited for her. The golden canine stood, trotted a few steps, and glanced over her shoulder. Cia caught up and kept pace with the wolf's guidance. They weaved through the congested street that had recovered from the earlier scare. A quaint, covered train station sat at the edge of a yard seven tracks deep. The single teller in a shack meant to keep out the wet elements glanced up, noted the wolf, and returned to the novel on the counter. Neva continued beyond the station, hopping over tracks.

Cia hesitated. All good Sziverian parents warned their children of the dangers of rail tracks. Roads and pedestrian walkways never crossed them. Either bridges or tunnels provided safe routes, which only stressed the hazard of venturing onto tracks. The fear was ingrained, a lifelong habit to never, under any circumstances, set foot on a track. The wolf didn't seem to care, trotting over the risen steel as if she did it daily.

A behemoth of a black engine snagged Cia's attention. Painted in vibrant yellow, a vicious wolf snarled from the side. The fangs morphed into the V of Wolvenguard, leaving no doubt about who the engine belonged to. Cia looked left and right, listening for any approaching engines. When nothing but the crash of waves and croon of seagulls filled her ears, she took a chance and touched a toe to the first line. The ground didn't tremble. A steel monster didn't burst into existence and attempt to run her over.

Neva bounded up the narrow steps to the open door, disappearing inside. Deklan leaned his upper body out, shielding his eyes from the sun kissing the low horizon. The red glow of sunset glinted off his hair, turning it blazing red instead of the normal near black. Neva and Nikita's heads popped out on either side of him, flanking their master as he surveyed the yard. Cia's stomach flipped at the powerful sight.

The Wolvenguard.

Deklan stepped onto the platform, bracing his hands on the railing running the length of the engine. Cia gripped the shoulder strap of the pack and rubbed her sweaty palm on her thigh in nervousness.

"Is Izia okay?" she asked at the bottom of the steps.

He took two steps down and held out his hand. "Yes, he'll be fine. Tate is stitching up the gash now."

"Blackbain?"

"Also, fine. I've already radioed Haven City. Enforcement and First Intelligence will be waiting for him when we arrive."

Cia worked her bottom lip between her teeth. "Sean?"

"I don't know if Wintersfall will be there or not. It might not be... advised for the brothers to see each other before Joel is in complete custody."

Her attention flickered to his open palm. "Not scared to touch me anymore?"

"I doubt you'll try to bond with me being helped up steps," he said, his mouth quirking with a hint of smile.

Wouldn't she show him if she did? But she didn't want him that way. Stuck with her against his will. Especially since she seemed determined to frustrate him at every decision. No, if by some incredible twist of fate, she did manage to capture the beast master, she wanted him as excited about their future as she would be. Forcing away any hint of emotion and clearing her mind, Cia pressed her hand into his. The warm roughness of his palm whispered along her fingers. She wanted to squeeze, to feel more. Instead, the moment she had balance, she let go and nodded that she could handle the rest on her own. He turned and went inside. Neva followed, her fluffy golden tail swishing. Nikita danced in place, waiting for her.

"Hey, pretty baby," Cia crooned, petting his head. He nuzzled her palm, his damp nose pressing to her palm before his tongue licked her wrist.

Greeting given, he waited for her to enter before

following behind. The small space inside the engine was cramped with people and belongings. Tate was ushering Izia into a bottom kennel. Neva peered out from a thin metal grate on the front of her wooden enclosure. Nikita waited his turn, lifting his front paws when Tate motioned for him to hop inside. With a little push on his butt, he managed to get up on his own. Cia glanced around and noted there'd be nowhere for her to sit. Joel slouched on the seat closest to the kennel. Sabrie glared beside the convict. Galvin sat with his arms braced on a risen knee at Sabrie's feet. Tate took the small folding seat on the other side of the kennel.

"You can use this seat if you want," Deklan offered, motioning to the driver's chair next to where he stood at the controls.

Cia shrugged the pack off next to her duffel bag, laying on the edge of all the other personal belongings. "You don't need to sit?"

"He prefers to stand while operating," Sabrie answered.

The woman's reminder that she knew more about Deklan than Cia made a frustrating niggle of jealousy arise. And out of spite, which Cia knew was immature of her, she planted her butt in the seat beside Deklan. Fine, she'd enjoy the dual views of the tracks in front and Deklan's back. The way the muscles in his shoulders, forearms, and thighs flexed each time he adjusted the controls or his stance as the engine accelerated and swayed along the rails.

Instead of the lurching motion, she was used to with traditional engines, Deklan eased the heavy car forward to glide at a faster speed. His left hand braced on the accelerator while his right worked controls and the brake when necessary. Soon, they were flying down the rails at a speed she thought only a MagnaRail engine could manage. She hadn't felt the faint rise from the tracks, so knew they weren't riding in one. Cia wondered if the machine was custom for the Wolvenguard team.

The noise from the engine humming behind them kept conversation away. Cia settled and took in the details about Deklan. He'd pulled his sides back again into a knot at the crown of his head, leaving his straight hair to brush his shoulders. Leather straps wound around both his wrists, and the sleeves of his navy sweater were pushed up to his elbows, drawing attention to the flexing caramel skin between. Cia sat on her hands to keep from touching. He hadn't shaved since rescuing her, and the scruff became him. She wondered which she'd prefer, the smooth angles of his face or the rougher texture of his beard under her fingers.

As if he felt her attention riveted to him, he glanced over his shoulder and met her stare for the briefest of seconds. Hiding her curious desire was impossible. His jaw tensed, and his lips flattened before he looked away. Perhaps, if she hadn't managed to injure one of his babies, she could have made a more compelling argument for him to see past their age difference. But she had, and now she had to deal with the disappointment of her actions.

Hours later, after a beautiful trip across the country, where the tracks crossed over multiple rivers, spanned expansive fields that turned to ice in the winter and colorful bursts of flowers in the early summer, they didn't stop at the Haven City MagnaRail station like Cia had thought they would. The engine kept cruising through, maintaining a steady momentum along the farthest rail, and veered off a single track into a wooded area. Deklan eased into a slower, coasting speed. A vast gray structure came into sight. Behind the mansion, a glass conservatory rose an additional two stories, stretching beyond view.

Deklan brought the locomotive to a drifting stop. The brakes hissed as he parked and locked the engine into place. They'd arrived. Acid burned in Cia's stomach. She didn't want to move from her seat. Didn't want to see if her team was waiting with the authorities present to collect the escaped convict. She waited until everyone gathered their belongings. Deklan freed the wolves, motioning for them to follow everyone off before lifting Joel by his elbow. Only her things, scattered with Deklan's, remained. The engine still idled, filling the now empty space.

Cia bit her lip and regarded the backpack and her duffel. She shouldered her belongings and crept down the stairs. Everyone gathered around Joel, who scowled. The wolves were in strategic positions, even the injured Izia. Cia licked her lips, not noticing any familiar faces among the guardians. Seeing a chance and unwilling not to take it, cowardly as she was being, Cia snuck away.

"Why?"

Cia rinsed a plate and shook the excess water free before placing it on the drying rack. The soap stung the minor abrasions on her knuckles. Her father never did the dishes, and all the ones in the sink when she'd left had still been there when she'd walked back in the front door. No new ones. Stress made her father forget to eat, and her disappearing on him again brought back some bad memories. Cia tamped down another rise of guilt.

"Why didn't you eat?" she asked instead of answering his signed question.

His gaze narrowed on her face, focusing on the bruise along her jaw, and morphed from concentration into a parental glare. "My only child was missing. Again. No one had any answers. No one would tell me anything. Again. All Vayden could learn was you were no longer in the country, but not if you'd gone on your own or if someone had taken you." His fingers moved in angry, exaggerated motions.

When she said nothing, drying her hands, he asked again, "Why? Why would you do this to me, Lucianna?"

Cia dropped her head, the rag clenched in her fist. "I thought I could find the assassin."

Henry came around the counter, took her face between his hands, and searched her eyes in question. He had no idea what she'd spoken because she hadn't been looking at him.

Cia took a deep breath and sniffled back the tears threatening. "I thought I could find the assassin. Stop him. I-I didn't have time to tell you."

The tips of his fingers pressed into her jaw. His mouth flattened, and he shook his head. "You had time. You chose not to say anything or even leave me a note."

His words were gruff from a voice not often used. Cia couldn't deny the accusation.

"You would have told me not to go," she admitted, whispering, even though only she could hear the cowardice in her voice.

"Perhaps. You will never know what I would have said." He brought her forehead to his. "I want you to have a full life, Cia. I don't want you consumed by vengeance or trying to chase the impossible."

She pulled back until he could see her speak. "My life is mine to live, and I choose to find the person who took everything from you."

He tsked and brushed a thumb down her cheek. "Ah, my beautiful daughter, how I have failed you. Whoever took your mother and brother from me did not take everything. I still have you. Give this up. If you must be a guardian, fine. Protect this country. But forget about the shadows that will always slip through your fingers."

"And if I can't?"

Henry kissed her forehead. "You will become a shadow yourself."

A tear slid down her cheek, and she swiped it away, extricating herself from her father's embrace. "Let me see what I can find to feed you," she signed.

He moved around the counter and sat on one of the stools. "I should be cooking a meal for you."

Cia made a face. "We tried that, remember?"

His fingers drummed an uneven beat on the countertop. "I've been reading recipes. I think I could do better."

Searching through ingredients in the cabinets, she paused long enough to look at him. "Have you tried any of these recipes to test your theory?"

His lips pursed, and Cia laughed.

"I'm good with cooking, Dad."

Pans clanked and skidded along the cast iron stovetop. Henry nudged her aside, and he prepped the stove while she prepared the ingredients. They worked in silence, signing when communication was necessary. The everyday routine helped calm her frayed nerves and return her to normalcy.

Thankfully, Henry wasn't a grudge holder. When

she'd first walked into the house and found him sitting at his desk sorting through papers, he'd taken one look at her filthy body, and the stark relief in his eyes had almost made her cry. A nod of acknowledgment was all he offered before returning to his task. Cia had known he'd needed a chance to process her safe return, and she'd needed a bath, so she'd left him. Once clean, she'd avoided him for another reason.

The confrontation.

Another round of personal condemnation for her mistakes.

Cia knew she needed to reevaluate her plans. Make new ones. Figure out where to go and what to do next. One of the V Alliance assassins was in Sziveria, maybe *the* assassin. She may have been fighting the man responsible for killing her mother and brother. Might have had him in her literal grasp, and she'd been too untrained to do anything more than defend herself. A harsh lesson.

Fishing out a peeled potato from a pint jar, she set the wet white lump on a cutting board and chopped it into cubes. With a fresh onion, rosemary from her mother's greenhouse herb garden, and some shredded jarred chicken, she sautéed it all together. Fresh carrots, sliced cheese, and a pear to share from their root storage would round out their meal.

Henry set plates on the counter for them to eat. Neither had sat at the six-person table since the murders. The empty chairs hurt too much. Cia wished he'd get them a small table for the two of them, but her father refused. Fiona had chosen the table when they'd arrived in Sziveria from Ruthenia. Their first piece of furniture together held too much sentimental value for

Henry. For Cia, the table was just another reminder of everything they'd both lost.

Cia pushed the food around on her plate, her mind wandering to what Deklan and his wolves may be doing. She wondered at what point he'd realized she'd disappeared. She knew he was smart enough to figure out where she'd gone. Thoughts of him led to the barrier between them, and she turned, looking at her father.

"Why didn't you tell me about the Ruthenian mate bond?" she asked.

Henry blinked. "We're in Sziveria. The bond… you won't ever have to worry about it."

Cia pressed her lips together. How much to reveal? If she mentioned Deklan and his claims about her accidental attempts to force her bond on him, her father would know they'd shared a level of intimacy. Not exactly a conversation she wanted. Yet, she had no one else with whom to discuss the problem.

"How did you even learn about the bond?" Henry asked, his head tilted in confusion.

Cia poked at the potatoes, and her father nudged her foot until her gaze met his again. "Deklan Ralston told me about it."

"The Wolvenguard?" her father asked, eyes wide in shock. "How… why… why would he talk to you about that?"

Heat flared across her cheeks. "I might have accidentally tried to forge a bond with him because I didn't know. I still don't know how I would have attempted to do anything."

"When in the inhabited world did you spend enough time with Deklan Ralston to," he waved a hand and continued, "for that to be a concern?"

"He's who found me in New Columbia. He brought me back to Sziveria."

"Ah." Henry braced his arms on either side of his plate and faced the kitchen. "I owe him much then. Did you—"

"No." She touched his shoulder and answered verbally and by signing before he could finish the thought. Cia blew out a long breath. "The thing is, I care about this man, Dad. A lot."

"He's much older than you, Cia."

"You and Mom had an age gap, and you made it work just fine," she pointed out. "And his wolves... What does the bond mean?"

"It's permanent, that's what it means." He twisted on his stool and grasped her hand between both of his. "Lucianna, you can have a normal Sziverian relationship. Test out a pairing for a year before worrying about making a mistake. Forget the beast master."

"But you and Mom—"

"And when she died..." He squeezed her hand and then resumed by signing. "The loss of her bond almost took me with her. There's a reason Nachemir became a shell and didn't even notice when his surviving daughter disappeared on him. The only reason I pulled myself from the void was because of when they took you from me, alive and fighting."

He paused, squeezing her hand again before continuing. "Your mother and I chose Sziveria because your talent would be recognized, but you'd have to worry about none of the things Ruthenian's pride or demand."

"Deklan is Sziverian. He won't demand anything." She pressed a hand to her chest. "I was the one making the demands, apparently. How do I stop it from happening again?"

Henry brushed a finger along her jaw, sadness in his gaze. "The stopping is only temporary. If you allow things to progress, you won't be able to prevent the bond from happening. He won't be able to resist accepting and then forging the connection himself. It's a personal, very intimate thing, daughter. And it's forever."

Cia's heart clenched. Forever with Deklan Ralston? She had already considered the future and liked the outcome. Her father confirming what Deklan had explained only solidified her determination. If the beast master would change his mind and have her, she'd happily live life at his side. But her mistakes were many. She hadn't exactly shown him the best parts of herself.

"It may not matter," she signed. "I made him pretty mad."

Henry's jaw tightened. "What did you do?"

Besides leaving without saying goodbye? Where was Cia supposed to start with that question? Digging deep, she scrounged up her courage and recalled everything that had happened in New Columbia, leaving out the times Deklan's tongue had been in her mouth or his hands on her bare skin. By the end of her recollection, Henry had dropped his head onto the counter, and she waited until he looked at her again to finish.

"I am a failure as a father," he croaked out.

Cia gasped and shook her head. She touched his shoulder. "No, you're not. What a ridiculous thing to say."

Henry scrubbed his hands down his face and turned toward the kitchen again. "Wolvenguard's parents told him all he needed to know about his Ruthenian half, and I couldn't even tell my daughter when she was whole. To attempt a bond when neither has agreed is…" He blew out a long breath and held his hands open. "It's forbidden, Lucianna. His parents would have informed him so he knew proper etiquette when searching for a spouse."

I rejected you.

The memory of Deklan sending her bond back to her caused pain to echo through her chest. She touched her collarbone in an attempt to ease the discomfort. The flicker of movement brought back Henry's attention.

"He knew how to, um." She licked her dry lips. "How to refuse me."

Sadness welled in his eyes, and turned down his mouth. "Tell me he didn't do that to you."

Cia brushed his arm and hoped she could make him understand. "I left him no choice. I didn't understand what I was doing or what I would have done. Deklan wanted me to *feel* that what I was forcing on him was tangible to me as well. I still don't know how to recognize it when I touch him, but I certainly felt it returned to me. He said his mother didn't know when she forged a bond with his father. While it worked in their favor, his father didn't want his children to have the same fate."

Henry shook his head. "I never thought you'd have to worry about a bond. I figured the worst it would be is the adoration Wintersfall shows for his Ruthenian wife. And how horrible is that, really?"

Cia smiled. Sean Blackbain's love for his wife, Katria, was a thing to behold, she agreed. "Not horrible at all."

Henry returned her smile, though it didn't quite reach his eyes. "I would have had that for you."

"Isn't it my decision?" Cia took his hands. "And did

you not share the same adoration for Mom? Was your love not as deep?"

"Deeper."

"And you'd deny me that?"

He waved a hand and rubbed the other along the back of his neck. "The bond, it's very complicated."

Cia straightened on the stool, clasping her hands between her knees, an image of rapt attention. When he looked at her, she said, "Explain it to me."

Blush darkened his face. Rising, he collected their plates. "This is not a conversation a father wishes to have with his daughter."

Heartache swelled within her. She tapped her finger on the counter in his line of sight. "Had you and Mom made any plans at all to talk to me about what my Ruthenian heritage may mean in a relationship?" she asked by signing.

"We'd thought about it after you turned sixteen. There are things you need to know."

Cia recalled the limited conversation Deklan had been willing to have with her. "Deklan told me how it might be difficult for me to start a family here."

Henry swiped a hand down his face. "Yes, that is one of the things. But," he shook his head and squeezed his eyes shut, "I just don't think I can tell them to you."

"Then who?"

He shrugged helplessly. Cia heaved out a long exhale and waved him off. "Go, I'll take care of the dishes."

Henry kissed her temple and squeezed her shoulders. "Thank you for coming home."

Cia watched him head into the library off the dining room, his shoulders stooped as if carrying a heavy weight. Had she added to his already burdened thoughts? Probably. If he was a failure as a father, then she was equally a failure as a daughter. She scraped food off the plates more forcefully than necessary.

After cleaning the kitchen, she checked in on her father. A fire crackled in the large hearth, the only light source in the spacious room. The amber glow reflected over the dark windows of the greenhouse. The windows would reveal a lovingly tended space in the light of day. Fiona Castien had cultivated the garden to become her sanctuary. Henry hadn't allowed her hard work to disappear into a tangle of weeds and rodents. Now, only a black void stretched, cut by the occasional hint of something large within the shadows. Cia shivered.

Henry rapped a snifter of amber liquid on the side table. The constant *tap-tap-tap* only felt as a reverberation on the glass between his fingers. She alone suffered through the noise of his frustration. He stared intently at the dancing flames. Cia contemplated leaving him to his thoughts. But he'd be hurt when he realized she'd gone to bed without a word. She'd been the source of enough heartache where he was concerned.

Conscious to be in his peripheral, Cia brushed her fingers along his bicep. He glanced up, took a slow sip from his glass, and returned to gazing at the fire.

Cia moved fully into his line of sight and signed, "I wanted to tell you goodnight."

Henry fiddled with the rim of his cup before meeting her gaze. His hands moved quickly, asking, "Will you be here in the morning?"

A fair question, one she regretted he felt the need to ask. "You know I will be."

"I never wanted you or…" His hands clenched into fists. When Cia reached for him to comfort, he began again. "You know I never wanted you to have my talent. But now that I know nothing of how to help you make sure if you're going to continue this ridiculous path of revenge, you at least have the full advantage of proper training. I can't help you."

"I have all the help I need," she assured. "I went off on my own before I was ready."

Henry tilted his head and regarded her for silent moments until she felt the urge to squirm under his assessment. "And when, Lucianna, will you be ready?"

15

Sweat rolled down Deklan's forehead to his nose, splashing on the floor beneath him. He ignored the sting of salt in his eyes and the protesting muscles of his arms, forcing himself into yet another push-up. The burn in his shoulders, stomach, and lower back temporarily drove away the frustration he couldn't stop focusing on without a distraction. So, he distracted. Pushing his body to the limit.

Izia lay resting in the corner on a fur rug. In the greenhouse, the doors open to the humid indoor garden, Neva and Nikita howled. Deklan had silenced the bond between the two playing wolves but left the connection open to Izia in case he needed anything. The injured wolf had been the one to realize Cia had snuck away upon their arrival. No word of goodbye. No thank you. No apology. No waiting to disclose the information she'd potentially uncovered.

Gone.

If uninjured, Deklan didn't think he'd have been able to stop his gray wolf from chasing after the young interceptor. The knowledge was yet another thing for him to worry about. For him to physically exhaust himself to keep from dwelling in apprehension.

Booted feet appeared in his line of vision. Deklan continued the controlled lower and rise of his torso. A small puddle formed on the hardwood beneath his face. The soaked fabric of the shirt he hadn't bothered to remove clung to his back. Joints popped as his visitor sat cross-legged in front of him. Clasped large hands with silver rings and wrists wrapped in familiar leather bracers replaced the boots.

"Hello, *Ahtyshka*," Deklan greeted mid-push.

"You have found her," his father said. Despite decades spent in Sziveria, a Ruthenian accent still flavored his words.

"I have found no one," Deklan huffed, increasing speed, demanding more from himself.

Markus remained silent. Waiting. Aggravation slid through Deklan, and he shoved off the floor back onto his haunches. Ignoring his father would only prove the truth of his words. Markus handed him a towel. Deklan pressed his face into the soft, clean-scented fabric and resisted the urge to growl. When had he lost control of his future? Oh, yes, he remembered. When he rescued a wayward guardian from herself. Now, he was the one needing rescued from himself.

"Who told?" Deklan asked, sighing in resignation.

"Why does it matter?"

Deklan dropped the towel and stared at his father. Gray streaked through the dark red hair Deklan and most of his siblings had inherited. Markus's golden stare held a level of patience only three decades of parenting could master. A suspicion rose in Deklan, and he narrowed his eyes.

"It was Tate, wasn't it," Deklan guessed.

Instead of confirming or denying, Markus asked, "Why are you fighting this?"

Deklan shoved off the floor, draping the towel around his neck. He hopped onto a curved, manual treadmill. Excess nervous energy still thrummed through his veins, made worse by his father's questions. Using the rails at the side, he pressed his weight into the treads, forcing them into motion. Once the belt glided effortlessly beneath his feet, he let go and ran, his speed increasing with each footfall. Izia lifted his head, surveyed the distance between him and Deklan, and attempted to rise. Deklan motioned for him to stay.

"Your wolf wishes to comfort you," Markus said. He went to the front of the treadmill and leaned his weight against the front bar with crossed arms. "Most beast masters are pleased to know they've finally found their mate. Why aren't you?"

"She's a child," Deklan ground out, running faster.

Markus's brows shot up. "A child? I've never heard of this happening before."

Deklan clenched his jaw and tightened his fisted hands. "Not literally. She's... Donovan's age."

"Your brother is an adult, coming into adult responsibilities." A frown moved across his face. "You've already made him meet one challenge."

Yes, Deklan had. Donovan's talent wasn't just as a beast master but an incredibly rare judge. Not only could Donovan declare a beast master unacceptable, but he could physically *remove* a master's ability to bond. While Deklan could pull a wolf bond from an unfit master, he couldn't eradicate the actual ability to connect with a wolf like his younger brother could. Beast masters feared the talent Donovan had inherited.

Once, every generation had the fabled judgment capability. Donovan was the first documented in over a century. To say a wide birth was made when he set foot in Ruthenia for the first time was an understatement. A year and a half ago, Deklan had returned from a mission with an abused wolf. He'd brought Zhenya to Donovan to help his brother understand the importance of his gift. Their bond had been immediate, and Donovan could no longer ignore his responsibility.

"What is her name?" Markus asked.

Deklan's already pounding heart kicked harder. "Lucianna Castien."

Surprise flitted across Markus's face. "Henry and Fiona Castien's daughter?"

"You know them?"

Markus shook his head. "Not personally, no. I know they're Ruthenian."

"Fiona was murdered over two years ago."

"Yes, I recall hearing something about that. And the girl was kidnapped. Darius was involved in the subsequent investigation." Markus studied Deklan. "You have been given the opportunity to have a full bond, not the weak echoes I share with your mother and none of the prejudices of Ruthenia. Why are you not rejoicing in this fortune?"

Deklan grabbed the bars and hopped off the treadmill. He flipped his head to send his drenched hair away from his face. "She's nineteen."

"And she can't know what she wants at nineteen?"

"No."

"Yet she's old enough to serve as a guardian. To die for this country." Markus grabbed Deklan's arm when he moved to walk past. "If she's mature enough to make such a choice, why isn't her judgment where you're concerned acceptable?"

"Because she doesn't *know*," Deklan stressed. "Henry told her nothing, *Ahtyshka*."

Markus's gaze narrowed. "Define nothing."

Deklan swiped a hand down his sweaty face. "Exactly what I said. She knows no Ruthenian. Nothing about the mate-bond. She doesn't even know that if she bonds with one such as me, one of my wolves, probably that one," he flicked a hand at Izia, "will bond with her, too. The existence she knows would be turned upside down. How can she make that decision without all the facts?"

Izia lifted his head and whined.

Deklan cast him a glare of annoyance. *Yeah, I'm talking about you.*

The gray wolf let loose a long groan and laid his head on his paws, gaze averted, brows twitching.

Markus ran his fingers along his silver-streaked beard. Over the decades, his father's facial hair had changed from a full, bushy beard to a cropped goatee and everything in between, but always present, delighting his children. Now, his young grandbabies were teased and tickled by the bristles. One of Deklan's first memories was of his father brushing his prickly chin on Deklan's belly while Lunah nudged him from the other side with her cold nose.

"Your *makyshka* had none of the facts when she decided to accept me," Markus said.

"I thought it was the other way around?" Deklan crossed his arms. The towel pulled tight across the back of his neck.

"I still had to ask her. She didn't completely understand what she'd done, only that her bond with Lunah was irreversible for both of us. While yes, we had to accept each other, I still asked her for forever before she even fully knew if forever with me was something she could live with. The bond takes care of the rest, son." Markus grabbed Deklan's shoulder and squeezed. "And you'll get the full spectrum. Everything."

"Do you regret not having that with *Makyshka*?"

"No, just a curiosity for what our unique bond would have been like at full strength. Your *Makyshka's* bond is the only one I've ever wanted and the only one I accepted. Together, we've accomplished amazing things through our connection, which always made me wonder what we could have done if it'd been stronger." Markus's grip tightened, his gaze intent. "How do you feel about your *strazhruna*?"

His guardian. The thought sent a shiver of awareness up his spine. She wasn't his. Not yet. But she *could* be, without a second thought on her part. Deklan knew this, and the possessive power of the knowledge made him want her near enough to protect. To claim. He shook away the compelling sensations.

Deklan scowled and shrugged free of his father's grasp. "I should be feeling nothing where she's concerned."

"And yet, you do. For the first time? Or perhaps the first time it's mutual," Markus guessed. Sighing, he ran his hand over the top of his braided hair. "None of my boys listened to my advice when I said don't go to Ruthenia for a mate. Yet, all of you did, and you are all paying the price. She is not those women, my son."

"I know she is not them. She is also not old enough. Maybe in a few years, when she has time to learn. To experience life—"

Markus's widened his eyes. "To fall in love with someone else?"

Deklan ignored the sharp stab of pain those words elicited. "Then she wouldn't be mine, would she?"

"No, I suppose not, since your stubbornness would have lost her."

Deklan tilted his head back and sought patience. "*Ahty—*"

Markus waved a hand. "I know, I know, your life, let you live it. Just be glad I was the one who arrived and not your *makyshka* or, for the love of the stars, your *bakishka*."

Deklan stared at his father in alarm. "*Baki* Madeleine knows?"

Sympathy filled his father's gaze. "Everyone knows. Your teammates came to the house during our weekly dinner, and your *makyshka* did not fail to notice you were missing."

And the entire family could have descended on his house. Deklan envisioned the chaos of all ten siblings, plus his matchmaking grandmother, demanding the details on Lucianna Castien. Dread made him groan. No such thing as personal in a large family. Especially not when he had a snitch on his team who announced Deklan had found a potential mate and wasn't happy.

Markus clapped him on the shoulder again and squeezed. "You have a week to figure yourself out. Either show up with her for next week's family dinner or give a good excuse for your mother why she's not getting grandchildren from you anytime soon."

SLEEP ELUDED CIA. NO WARM, FURRY BABIES TO COMFORT her. No masculine strength to make her feel safe. For almost two weeks, she hadn't slept alone. Curling into a ball, she wrapped her body around a pillow. Since losing her little brother and mother, she'd battled with loneliness in her silent home. Now, the awareness of solitude suffocated. She wanted Deklan, even if he only slept on the floor as he'd done in New Columbia. Or without him, she wanted Izia to hug instead of the poor substitute she currently clung to for solace.

Tomorrow promised to bring the confrontations she'd managed to avoid today. Her team hadn't shown up at her door, probably because they had debriefed with Deklan and helped transfer Joel to wherever Sziveria decided evil incarnate belonged. Something she should have been involved in but had been too cowardly. Her hold tightened on the pillow. What was she thinking being a guardian? She'd failed on so many levels.

Sniffling, she took a deep breath. No. Self-deprecating thoughts would get her nowhere. Would accomplish nothing worthwhile. *When* her team arrived, she'd take responsibility and do better if they allowed her to remain with them. Her quest for retribution would continue, but she knew she needed to approach the pursuit differently.

The muted hiss of a window opening in the room beside hers sent Cia upright in bed. Joshua's room. Neither she nor her father had been in her little brother's space since his death. Neither of them could move past the doorframe. Not even to ensure the window was secured. A foolish mistake for a former assassin and guardian-in-training to make. Had it been left unlocked, and now some thief was sneaking in? Cia tossed the covers aside and slid out of bed on silent feet. Her father would never hear the danger. She didn't take the time to put pants on, sneaking from her room in nothing but underwear and a silk camisole.

Hushed voices whispered behind the closed door. Cia pressed her back to the wall and closed her eyes, visualizing Joshua's room. Dresser to the left, next to the door. Bed between two windows, far wall. Toy chest in the right corner. A wooden train set wound around a block city, cutting a path across the entire floor. The project had taken her brother weeks to accomplish.

Cia waited. Clattering and a hissed curse made her jaw clench. They'd knocked over one of Joshua's buildings.

Slowly, she turned the knob and let the door fall open by its weight. Cold air wafted into the hall. Goosebumps rose across her skin and sent a shiver along her spine. She ignored the chill. The hinges creaked. The room fell silent. Whoever was inside stilled, betraying nothing to Cia. She continued to wait, tense seconds ticking by.

"Maybe the window caused the door to open," a man whispered.

"Open windows make doors close, you moron," the second intruder murmured. "Now shut up."

Cia raised a brow. Moronic housebreakers? She crouched weight on the balls of her feet. Angling toward the door, she braced her left fingers on the wall for balance.

"There's no one there," the one labeled a moron whispered.

"Shut. Up."

"We came here for a job. Let's get it done. I'm tired of waiting." When the leader didn't answer, he tried again. "Come on, man. It's one little girl, you saw her earlier. Everyone is still sleeping. Let's finish this."

"Fine," the leader snapped in a hushed tone. "Just watch where you're walking this time."

A plank creaked beneath the men's weight. Cia leaned forward enough to glimpse the room but not be seen by the intruders. Glowing silver moonlight blanketed the area in long shadows. She searched for anything to use as a weapon. A wooden sword lay half under the bed, next to an open box of marbles. Uneasiness bunched her muscles. The pain in her hip and ribs from her earlier confrontation reminded her of the failure and stole her confidence. She released a slow, moderated breath and forced calm through her jumbled nerves.

Henry wouldn't hear the fight unless she ran to his room and awoke him. And she knew she didn't have time. Their safety was up to her, as was ensuring her father didn't awaken to find his remaining child dead at the hands of assassins. Cia couldn't focus on answers with these two, only on eliminating the threat they posed. Maybe she'd get lucky, and they'd have something useful on their person.

Maintaining a sense of calm to keep from triggering the adrenaline rush associated with her talent, she prepared for her first move. The next time she saw Kevin, she'd apologize and ask him to help her finally get past the anxiety of her interceptor talent engaging. If she couldn't overcome the panic attacks, she'd be useless as a guardian. Nor could she find the answers she desperately sought. Thankfully, Kevin believed in defensive training regardless. If she kept centered, the hours and hours of drills would hopefully give her a different outcome. Yes, she'd failed with Joel twice and the convict's would-be killer. But not this time.

Without a second thought, she dove for the sword.

One of the intruders yelped. More blocks tumbled and scattered, ricocheting off her legs. The mattress squeaked and bounced, mixing with a masculine curse. Cia rolled away. Bringing the sword up, she caught her would-be attacker across his face as he knelt on the bed and attempted to reach her. The blunt edge cracked along his cheek. She didn't waste a second, flowing through the swing, twisting, and bringing the total weight of her upper body into the strike. Catching him under the jaw, his head jerked back. She flipped the weapon and used the handle to punch him in the chest. Air rushed from his mouth as he tumbled backward to the floor from the impact.

Cia hopped onto the bed. The soft mattress sank beneath her weight, providing enough bounce to jump at the second intruder. Her heart thudded in her ears, and the rush of adrenaline she'd hoped to avoid flooded her system. The room warped around her, threatening to transition into a sun-drenched hill. Air lodged in her chest, burning and swelling. She faltered, stumbling, and collapsed to one knee on the wobbly bed. Aware of her weakness, the second man dove for her, settling his heavy weight across her body.

In her mind, a wolf howled.

16

Desperate, furious barking ripped Deklan from sleep. He flew up in his large bed. The sheets tangled around his waist and legs. Tossing the covers aside, he slid from the mattress and padded to the wolves' corner. A large safety-gated area kept them contained. Stuffed pillows lined two of the walls, forming an L. Leather and rope toys littered the center. Water shimmered in a shallow basin sunk into the floor against the left wall.

Deklan resided on the third floor in a spacious loft-style flat. The only doors were to his closet and bathroom. Windows on the back side of the room overlooked the greenhouse, which left the space muted in the day and near complete darkness at night. A crackling fire provided the only source of light. Behind the gate, Izia whined, barked, and paced in agitation. Deklan stopped at the barrier, resting his hands on the cool wood, and opened his bond to the frantic dog.

What's wrong, Izia?

The gray wolf whined and barked. *Trouble, she is in trouble!*

Only one *she* could broadcast her distress to his wolf. Lucianna. No longer could Deklan deny Izia— for whatever reason his doggy brain had decided— had accepted a bond from Cia. And if Deklan hadn't rejected her many wayward attempts, he'd have known she was in danger before the wolf. He wasn't sure how to feel about that, so he ignored the tightening in his chest and waved the wolves back from the gate. All the dogs backed up, sat, and waited as they'd been trained to.

Deklan engaged the bond between Neva and Nikita. *Izia, you'll stay here—*

No! Izia barked in fraught, high-pitched yelps.

You're injured and won't be any good to anyone if you rip out your stitches, Deklan tried to explain in a soothing mental tone.

How will you find her how? Izia yipped, lowering his upper body to the floor.

Deklan almost slapped his forehead. Without Izia's connection to Cia, Deklan would never find her unless he radioed someone who knew where she lived. But, hoping he'd wake whoever he called, wait for them to find her address, and hopefully give him directions would take much longer than allowing Izia to be their guide.

Fine. He pointed a stern finger at the wounded dog. *But you will stay back, no fighting, and let Neva handle whatever problem we encounter.*

Yes, I will, yes! Izia hopped on his front paws and stood, tail wagging, waiting for the signal to leave their corner.

Deklan left the gate open, but the wolves remained while he searched for something quick to wear. He threw on a pair of bamboo sleep pants and a sweater and slid on boots without socks. He'd be cold and look exactly like his clothes implied: he'd been pulled out of bed in the middle of the night. Worrying about his appearance wasn't a priority. Every second they took was a second. Cia may not have to wait.

What are you getting from her now, Izia? Deklan asked, slapping a knit cap on his messy hair and motioning for them to follow.

They bolted from the enclosure and followed him down the dark stairs. The clicking of the dog's nails on the wooden steps echoed through the empty house. All Deklan's staff lived in their own homes, except for the staff supervisor, who resided in spacious quarters off the laundry room. Phin Ellington wouldn't hear the dogs or Deklan leaving the house.

Must reach her, must! Izia shouted through the bond.

What are you feeling from her? What's happening? Deklan asked, trying to keep his distress at bay.

Fear. Scared, she is scared.

They ran through his office and out a side door into the garage and stables. Horses nickered softly at their movement. The musky scent of hay and livestock assailed his nose. Two of the wolves sneezed. In the center, the hulking shadow of the carriage loomed. His rarely used Ariot was parked near the door under a cloth tarp. Deklan threw the cover off, tossing the dusty fabric to a far corner. He opened the passenger side door. The dogs piled in, knowing their respective places inside the small interior. Nikita in the back space, Neva on the passenger floorboard, and Izia in the passenger seat so he could see out the windshield. While they settled, Deklan opened the garage door. Faint moonlight and chilled air swept inside. After closing the passenger door, he climbed into the driver's side and eased out onto the road. He returned to close the garage to keep the horses from getting too cold.

On the road, ice glimmered silver in patches on the brick sidewalks and buildings. The city slept. Devoid of the usual congested traffic, he navigated the streets faster than normal. Izia guided him, following a thread only the wolf could see. Haven City thinned until he left the town limits, heading to Caris. Had he known she lived in Caris, he would have taken his rail engine. He pushed the Ariot's magnetic engine to its max.

Izia's agitation grew closer to her home. He directed Deklan down a quiet residential street, his front paws working in the seat's leather. Two bicycles lying against the hedges surrounding a single-story house grabbed his attention.

Is this her house? Deklan asked.

Yes! She's here, she's here!

Deklan parked and leaned across the short distance, opening the passenger door. Izia shot out, followed by Neva. Nikita scrambled between the seats. In his haste, his front paws twisted on the soft front seat, and he fell on his face before righting himself and hurrying after them.

Neva, vunmir zre straes'ya, Deklan instructed on his way from the Ariot.

Neva touched her nose to the bike seats and then took off like a shot, racing across the yard and around the corner of the house. Nikita followed. Izia whined, waiting for Deklan. He ran after the wolves, sliding on the slick, frost-laden grass as he rounded the corner. The tip of Nikita's black tail disappeared through an open window. Warning growls and deep curses of alarm filtered through the small opening. Deklan hoisted himself through the frame, twisting his shoulders to fit. Izia barked and cried below.

Wait, I'll let you in once it's safe, Deklan said to the pouting wolf.

Deklan had barely set foot on the ground before someone launched at him. Cia's scent wrapped around him briefly before her entire body clung to his. Her legs around his waist, her arms around his neck. He held her tight to his chest and supported her butt with his forearm.

"Are you okay?" he asked into her hair.

She pressed her face into his throat. Her warm breath fanned along his collarbone. "I-I'm fine. How did you know?"

Relief flowed through him. Deklan squeezed his eyes closed and hugged her closer. "Izia."

Opening his eyes, he took in the room. Toys lay scattered. Nikita sat on his charge while Neva held hers by the throat, growling in warning anytime the man attempted to move. Sweat poured from both the intruders, who trembled. One appeared to have urinated if the wet crotch of his pants and puddle beneath him were any indication. Deklan toed between them and out of the room. He didn't want to let Cia down, but his fingers brushing the bare skin of her thigh distracted him. Desire was an entirely inappropriate emotion to be feeling.

"Where is your father?" he asked, grasping one of her ankles behind his back.

"Still sleeping."

Deklan frowned. "He—"

"Is deaf," she whispered, "say nothing to no one. He doesn't like anyone but those he trusts to know. I don't want you to confront him for something he has no control over."

He hadn't asked how or why she knew sign in New Columbia. Now, her fluency and comfort in the signal form of communication made sense. Deklan sat her down, careful to look only at her face. She had no modesty standing before him in a pair of panties and a tight camisole. The heavy shadows curled around her small breasts and settled in the smooth curves of her hips. He wanted to trace each subtle angle, assure himself in a different way that she stood before him safe. Unharmed. Her confidence didn't help, almost daring him to touch.

"Go get dressed," he rasped. "And wake up your father."

She opened her mouth and started to point down the dark hallway.

Deklan grasped her wrist and lowered her hand. "Lucianna, Henry may be deaf, but he's still a renowned assassin. I'm *not* going to wake him."

Sighing, she nodded. "All right. I'll meet you back in... Joshua's room."

His head snapped back to the open doorway. The toys and small bed finally registered. The bastards had broken into her little brother's room, attacking her not only in her home but amongst painful memories. He growled.

Cia's hand gripped his forearm. "Don't. They're contained. Doing anything else would make us no better than them."

"Should I move them before your father sees them?"

"Please. If you follow this hall, it'll lead to the dining room. Take them in there." She released his arm. "Thank you."

"What about a radio?"

"At the end of the block is an enforcement radio box."

Deklan rounded up the wolves and the intruders, marching everyone to the dining room, where he instructed Neva and Nikita to stand guard. Izia waited for him at the front door and, after being let in, joined the other two in keeping the men contained. Deklan returned to Joshua's room and closed the window, then the door. He stood between the hall and the dining room, keeping both in view while he waited.

Henry emerged first with a handgun gripped in his right hand. His dark hair stuck up at odd angles, and his shirt was inside out, but otherwise, he looked every inch a furious assassin. Cia trailed behind him, cotton sleep pants hid her legs and an unbuttoned shirt covered her arms. She wore the same thin tank, her pert breasts outlined through the sheer fabric. She wrapped the shirt around herself and folded her arms before appearing to the men. Deklan let out a breath he hadn't known he'd been holding.

A match flared as Henry lit a wall lamp. The men winced. One sported a nasty bruise along his jaw. The other had a split bottom lip and a cut above his left eyebrow. Yes, Cia had needed help, but she'd managed to hold her own for a time and deliver some critical blows. Deklan gave her a quick smile of pride.

"I'm going to go radio for someone to pick up these two."

Cia nodded. "My dad wants to question them."

"I'm taking Nikita with me. Izia will listen to you if anything happens, and Neva will follow his lead."

Izia wandered to Cia. She reached out, her fingers burying in the fur of his neck. "All right," she whispered with relief, as if touching his wolf brought her... peace.

Deklan swiped a hand down his face. He knew that particular sensation. His world righting itself when he made a physical connection with his beasts. Cia would only experience the same if she'd forged a true bond. Would only *need* the contact if she'd been deprived for too long. All the nights Izia had spent at her side on the journey. In her bed. Deklan hadn't known they could bond on such a deep level without one happening between him and Cia first. Would it grow if something developed between them? Too many questions and concerns for him to worry about now. He'd deal with their errant link later.

Outside, he waited for Nikita to move to the passenger side before hopping into the Ariot and driving the distance to the radio box to save time. He debated who to radio first and, in the end, settled on Voklane. He put in the guardian's private transmission number and waited.

"Voklane," a half-awake voice crackled along the line.

"It's Wolvenguard," Deklan said, scanning the dark, quiet street. Ice flecks danced in the air. He shivered. "Two men attacked Lucianna Castien in her home tonight."

A beat of silence, then, "Is she okay?"

"She's fine."

"Were you with her when they broke in?"

"No."

"Ah. Then I take it congratulations are in order?"

Deklan ground his teeth and ignored Ryan's implication. "What do you want me to do about them?"

"If Castien doesn't decide to use them as fertilizer for his greenhouse, I'll be there in... twenty minutes."

Deklan disconnected and closed the radio box. Nikita sniffed around the curb, and Deklan waited for him to do his business before letting him into the Ariot. Not in such a rush this time, Deklan spotted a narrow driveway for the Castien house. The brick strip led to a bicycle shed but was large enough for him to park the Ariot off the street. Nikita jumped out from the driver's side.

Inside the house, an alarming silence made him pause. Deklan sought Izia's bond. *Everything okay?*

Fine, all is fine.

Despite Izia's assurance, Deklan crept to the dining room. Henry straddled a chair, arms crossed over the back. Cia stood behind the kitchen bar at the sink, picking lint from a discarded drying cloth. The two intruders watched the wolves with shifting eyes, never meeting the staring canine's gaze.

"They won't speak," the Ruthenian assassin said without looking at Deklan.

Deklan raised his brows. Henry might be deaf, but he was attuned to his surroundings enough to know when a new presence entered his space. Of course, he would be. Deklan had been wise not to underestimate him.

Deklan ensured he was within Henry's line of sight when he spoke. "No matter, Guardian Voklane is on his way. I've heard a rumor he has an impressive record of being able to get information from those he wants."

Both men tightened their lips. Deklan grabbed a bar stool and carried it to the kitchen. He sat beside Cia and pulled her around to stand between his legs. He couldn't explain the need to touch her or bring himself to deny the urge. Draping his arm around her chest, he hugged her to his body. Henry frowned at them but said nothing. They both knew he had no recourse. Cia welcomed Deklan's embrace. She was safe because his wolves had stopped would-be killers from taking Henry's remaining child.

"Are you sure you're okay?" he whispered into her ear.

"Yes. Neva jumped through the window before…" She licked her lips, and a shudder raced through her shoulders. "Anything could happen. I'd taken one of them out already. Nikita sat on him to keep him down."

Deklan's hold tightened. "Your talent?"

She shook her head. Her silky hair caught in the stubble along his jaw and tickled his nose. "Just regular defensive training."

Deklan rested his chin on her shoulder and wrapped his arms around her waist. "We're going to have to work on that."

She stiffened. "We?"

"Yes. You've gotten someone's attention. They aren't going to go away, and you need to know how to defend yourself properly. Your talent makes you almost invincible. It's not something you can afford to suppress."

Relaxing her weight against him, she turned until she could meet his stare. "Kevin can handle my training."

Deklan's gaze settled on her mouth, so close all he had to do was move an inch, and he could taste her again. "Like he already has? I don't think he can train you properly. He doesn't know how your talent works."

Her expression fell flat. "He has the same gift."

"He has a gift by the same name, but you're full-blooded Ruthenian. Different than him on many levels."

A knock echoed through the foyer. Cia broke free of his hold. "I'll get it."

Izia trailed after her, and Deklan leaned back to keep her in view. Henry noticed their movement and stood. Deklan noted him fist his hands to keep from speaking in the manner he was used to in his home. Cold air wafted through the foyer and into the kitchen. Cia held the door for Ryan. The pale-haired guardian removed his ivy cap, fixing his mussed hair while waiting for Cia to lead the way.

Voklane accepted Henry's extended hand. "Castien. Wish we could meet under better circumstances."

"Me as well." Henry motioned to the now fidgeting men. "Here they are."

Ryan grasped the hat in both his hands, turning the cap in a slow circle. "Can I have the room, please?"

"Wolves, too?" Deklan asked.

"Yes."

Deklan snapped his fingers. Neva and Nikita looked at him. He signed for them to follow. Izia would trail Cia without instruction. Henry led them into the living room, closing the door behind Nikita. Cia lit a table lamp. The wolves explored the unused space.

"What will he do?" Henry asked.

Deklan shrugged. "I have no idea. Nothing bloody."

CIA GLANCED AROUND, MEMORIES GHOSTING PAST IN THE room her family had once lived in and enjoyed. The corner of the couch where her mother had curled up and read, her hand dangling over the arm. The recliner her father had gently rocked, his fingers toying with his wife's. The floor where her little brother had built elaborate train tracks they'd step over for days. After their death, her mom's book still lay spine up where she'd left off on the couch arm. Joshua's wooden Ariots were still lined up near the wall for a race they'd never perform. Cia had picked up the discarded Wintervail decorations Henry had torn down two years ago, but nothing else had been touched. Their home had become a mausoleum to the deceased Castiens. Even her parent's bedroom remained unoccupied, Henry having moved into the spare room.

Fatigue weighed down her shoulders, and she collapsed onto the couch. Henry shuffled closer to her, concern pinching the corners of his mouth.

"Are you sure you weren't hurt?" he asked.

"Not by the men," Cia signed. Henry stiffened, and she kept from rolling her eyes. "Deklan knows, Dad. I had to tell him so he knew why you didn't hear the break-in."

The beast master lounged against the wall, arms crossed, curiously looking over the meticulous room. All the emotions from the eventful night converged on her at once. Sorrow. Anger. Fear. Panic. Relief. Safety. She took long, slow breaths to force back the burn of tears. Izia laid his head on her thighs, groaning. Cia folded herself over him, burying her hands in his warm fur. A hand brushed her shoulder, and she lifted her head, meeting her father's worried stare.

"Lucianna?" Henry signed.

"I'm just..." She searched for the right word. "Tired."

Of so much. Situations she'd put herself in and ones she had no control over.

"You both need to stay with me at Wolvenguard," Deklan's deep voice rumbled in the silence.

Cia glanced between him and her father.

Henry spun around. "What? What is being said?"

Using her toes, she poked Henry's leg to get his attention. "Deklan has offered his home to us."

"We're fine here."

"I don't think so," Deklan argued. "Don't be foolish. This won't be the only attempt on her life."

"Then we'll stay at Terravine."

"Does Terravine have my wolves?" Deklan shook his head and pointed at Cia. "*She* will be safest in the Arch District. In my home. Whether you come or not makes no difference to me."

"There would be speculation. You'd hurt her reputation," Henry said, his hands fisting at his thighs.

"Not if you're there," Deklan said.

Cia chewed on the inside of her bottom lip. If she had her way, her father would go to Terravine and reside with his best friend while she stayed under Deklan's roof. Alone. Working her limited feminine wiles to convince the man to give them a chance. He wasn't immune to her. She figured after how he looked at her in the shadowed hall, something fun and interesting might happen if she walked around half-naked in the light of day. Desperately, she wanted to test her theory. Knowing she'd be around the wolves again was also a giant check mark in the pro column.

And she wanted out of this house. Hadn't realized how soul-crushing each room had become until tonight, when she'd been forced to acknowledge how little *living* had been happening. How much neither she nor her father had been able to let go of Joshie or her mother.

Again, she bumped Henry's leg and signed, "We

need to leave with him. Leave…" She waved a hand around the room. "All this behind. The bad memories are piling up here. We have an excuse for change. Let's take it."

Henry's bleak, heartbroken gaze wandered the room. "I don't know."

Cia stood and took his hands. "For me. Please. You asked me to live my life earlier. I'm asking you to do the same. For both of us."

Slowly, Henry nodded. Cia threw her arms around him and hugged him tight, knowing how much the concession cost. Would continue to cost until he fully decided to either wither away in this large home or finally move forward.

She leaned back. "You'll stay at Wolvenguard with me?"

His gaze flickered to Deklan and then back to her. "For a time, yes."

A quick rap of knuckles sounded on the door. Deklan leaned over and let in Voklane. The ivy cap was back on the guardian's head. While dark circles weighed down his eyes and exhaustion drew harsh lines from his mouth, he was as dangerous looking as always. Cia had never bought into the liaison role the man claimed as his only use. She wished she were trusted enough to know the truth.

"A man hired them to watch for Guardian Castien to return home. If she arrived alone, they were to eliminate her in her sleep. If she arrived with others, they were to report back descriptions of who and await further instructions," Voklane said, leaning against the doorframe.

"Any idea who this man is?" Deklan asked.

Voklane shook his head. "No. They work for the

local carriage company and were involved in Lucianna's abduction two years ago. Whoever hired them knew they were open to illicit work."

Voklane moved from the entry when Deklan pushed past him. Moments later, he returned, frowning. "They *told* you all that? Made a full confession?"

"Yes. As much as they knew, anyway. The man who approached them and made the offer gave no further information besides the job and a bag full of raimarks." Voklane looked at Cia, then Henry. "I'd not stay here after tonight. When your death isn't reported, whoever wanted you eliminated will likely try again."

"We figured that," Cia said. "Deklan offered to let us stay with him."

Voklane nodded. "That's a good idea. No one will get past the wolves."

"They may still try," Henry said.

A dark smile curled Deklan's lips. "Let them."

17

Shrill screaming echoed from the second floor. Deklan dropped his mug of coffee in the foyer, having been passing through on his way to the training room, and raced for the stairs. Ceramic shattered and skidded across the marble. Hot liquid splattered on his bare calves. He ignored the sting. The wolves were in the greenhouse, doing their morning run. Whatever the problem, he'd have to handle it on his own.

He took the stairs, curving to the left. Last night, he'd shown Cia and her father the right and left wings, letting them decide from there which room they wanted. He'd expected Henry to sleep near his daughter and had been surprised when he'd chosen a room in the right wing when Cia had chosen the largest room on the left half of the floor.

Deklan barreled down the wide corridor. Lamps flickered above small tables holding potted plants or fresh flowers. He could care less how the vacant second story looked, but his housekeeper took pride in her position. Cia's door was open, a dark maw at the end of the hall. Light suddenly flared in the room.

"Who in the arctic are you?" a woman shouted.

Deklan grasped the door frame and let out a breath. Then he glimpsed Cia, and all thoughts of relief collapsed in a rush of hot desire. Legs braced on the bed, the blankets tangled around her feet. She balanced with her hands on her hips. The skimpy navy camisole she'd had on last night barely reached the top of her white panties. In the harsh light of morning, he saw everything that had been hidden in the shadows. Toned, muscular legs attested to the hours of training required to build such definition. A flat stomach. Small defined arms. Cia may be lean in size, but her strength could not be ignored. She'd be unstoppable once she embraced the full level of her talent.

And damn if he didn't want to tackle her to the bed and feel that sleek physique moving beneath him.

"Why are *you* in *my* room?" Cia asked, anger coloring her words.

Deklan shook away the haze of lust fogging his brain and entered the room. "Miss Nikas, this is Guardian Castien. She'll be staying at Wolvenguard for the foreseeable future. Ellington was supposed to inform you this morning at the staff meeting."

Analeisa's ivory skin flushed, and she swept imaginary dust from her maroon apron. "I was… late this morning. I missed the meeting."

"Her father, Henry Castien, is also in residence on the other side of the house. Please do not disturb him," Deklan ordered.

The housekeeper's dark bun bobbed on top of her head as she nodded her understanding. She shifted to her basket of cleaning items on the floor near the bed and picked it up. "My apologies, Guardian Castien."

Huffing, Cia dropped onto the mattress, legs crossed. Her hair fanned above her before settling in tangled waves across her back. "It's fine. Sorry, you were scared."

"Surprised," Analeisa amended, clutching the basket until her knuckles turned white. She turned her attention to Deklan, her golden green eyes softened. "I'll save this floor for later in the afternoon. Are your quarters ready to be cleaned?"

"Yes, the wolves are in the greenhouse. Thank you."

"Excellent." Chin lifted, Analeisa left the room.

Cia sucked air through her teeth. "Well, someone is jealous."

Deklan looked at her. "What are you talking about?"

In languid motions, she stretched her bare legs out, locking her ankles, and settled her weight back onto her elbows. The position caused her tank top to shift upward, stretching tight across her small breasts and revealing a perfect little belly button. The pose was relaxed yet provocative. Her stomach flexed, drawing attention to the smooth angles of her exposed hips. More of her creamy skin was visible than covered, and Deklan's heart pounded in response. Blood rushed to collect in his groin. What was the minx up to?

"She doesn't like me being in the house," Cia said, flicking her top foot back and forth. The action drew attention to her slender ankle and small toes.

Transfixed by the motion, his mind wandered, imagining a slow, sensual journey from those perfect toes up her calf to her thigh. He stifled a groan and barely stopped himself from palming his aching erection. "What are you doing?" he growled.

She arched a brow. "Nothing."

Her gaze wandered from his face to his chest and lower. He wore nothing more than shorts, which were now embarrassingly tented. She smiled, not at all uncomfortable or shy. The coy smirk only heightened her already sensual appeal.

"What were you about to do before you ran here to save me from your housekeeper?" she asked.

"My morning routine."

"Oh good, I'll do that, too." She sprang from the bed and crossed the room to the bag she'd thrown in an overstuffed chair near the window. After digging around, she removed loose cotton pants and tied her hair into a high ponytail. Next, she pulled out a sage green cotton bralette and reached to lift her shirt.

Deklan spun around. "What are you doing?" he felt compelled to ask again.

She gasped, and Deklan squeezed his eyes closed. Most everyone who knew him personally had seen what he kept hidden.

"Wow," she whispered, and the air disturbed behind him.

Was she dressed, or was she staring at his back topless? His fingers curled into his palm.

Her touch ghosted along his back muscles, barely touching, tracing the details of his intricate wolf tattoo. "This is stunning."

"Every beast master has one."

"This exact one?" she asked, still tracing the design with gentle fluttering caresses too light to cause harm.

"No, they are unique for the master." And more personal than anyone but a beast master or their mate could comprehend. Before he could stop himself, he asked, "Do you like it?"

"I… love it," she whispered.

A shiver raced through him. "Are you dressed?"

Cool air brushed his back moments before fabric rustled, and she sighed. "There, you're safe."

He turned back around. Safe was a matter of opinion. She'd traded the camisole for the finely knit bralette. A wide band wrapped around her ribs for support while the scooped neck covered her breasts. The tight fabric hugged the perfect globes, leaving nothing to the imagination. Muscles shifted beneath her flat abdomen as she tossed the camisole into the clothes hamper beside a chest dresser.

"Can I eat first, do you think?" She ran her tongue along her upper teeth and made a face. "Well, after I brush my teeth."

Deklan turned on his heel. He should have left so much sooner. "I'll meet you in the training room."

The slap of her feet on hardwood followed behind him. "Where is that, exactly? Your place is huge."

"Down the stairs and to the right, last door, you can't miss it."

"And food?" she asked, still chasing after him.

Deklan paused. He hadn't considered his guests and their needs this morning. He wondered if Ellington had. "I'm not sure. Do you want to eat in the breakfast room or the training room?"

"Training room."

Deklan nodded. "I'll have something brought there."

After locating Ellington and requesting food for Cia, he went to the training room to work off excess energy. He started with a warm-up on the treadmill. Minutes later, Cia strolled in with a plate full of cold meat cuts, fruit, a muffin in her hand, and a large glass of water in the other. She sat cross-legged against the wall nearest to him.

"Wow, is that a climbing wall?" she asked after swallowing.

Deklan's gaze flickered to the two-and-a-half-story wooden wall in the center of the spacious room. Handholds of various lengths and sizes stuck out at uneven intervals, some indented, others protruding. "Yes."

"Impressive." She took another bite, taking in the room. She pointed to the three open doors set into a glass wall rising three stories. "And through there?"

He increased his speed. "The greenhouse."

"This house is something else."

"The first Wolvenguard apparently had a lot to prove. He took the funds as an Arch Guardian to build his house and made…" He waved a hand around. "This monstrosity of a residence."

Cia shrugged, popping an orange slice into her mouth. "I like it. Fits the whole beast master mystery."

Deklan couldn't help but grin and waggle his eyebrows. "Did you see my bronze wolves?"

"No, it was too dark when we came in last night." She hopped up, half a muffin in her hand. "Out front?"

"Yes, at the entrance." He jumped off the treadmill and grabbed a towel to wipe the sweat off his face.

After she disappeared, he went to the weight lifting bench, careful to keep the amount within his ability without help. She returned, running in.

"Those are amazing!" she proclaimed.

He laughed, having to pause halfway through a lift. "Not the word I used the first time I saw them."

She sat again and put the plate on her lap. "That's because you don't like attention, and those scream, 'You will fear me'."

Deklan hung the bar back in the press and sat up, wiping his face and chest. "What do you mean I don't like attention?"

"Do you?"

"No."

She smiled, sticking another orange slice into her mouth, a glimmer of triumph in her eyes.

Deklan braced his elbows on his knees, the towel loose in his right hand. Only his siblings understood his need to be obscure. The house he lived in grabbed attention. His wolves demanded the same. Even his physical features drew stares. Everywhere Deklan went, people watched. Sometimes in curiosity, more often in fear. Not even Ruthenia had offered a sense of normal since the extreme level of his talent was an oddity among any population. Five of the other Ralston offspring understood, for they, too, were freaks among the gifted.

Yet Cia had never seen him as the powerful beast master some wanted to claim and use and others longed to eliminate. *She* had looked at him as nothing more than a man. One she desired. Deklan swallowed. Even now, she watched him, a challenging lilt to her chin.

He rose and stalked to her. "You think you know me, Lucianna Castien?"

Unfolding herself from the floor, her gaze never left his. Her fingers grazed the waistband of his shorts, damp from sweat, stopping just shy of the skin contact he'd forbidden. Her knuckles brushed like butterfly wings across his abdomen. "I'd like to know you more."

She didn't give him a chance to answer, though he doubted he could have, his throat too dry for conversation. Flouncing past, she made a running leap onto the climbing wall, catching a handhold three feet above. Her laughter echoed around the cavernous room. Deklan swung the towel around his neck, holding onto the ends. He moved to the wall, looking up, watching each graceful move she made on her upward journey.

"Does my butt look good from down there?" she asked, amused.

All of you looks good from down here, almost tumbled from his lips. He cleared his throat. "Just making sure you don't fall. You didn't rope up."

She paused and glanced around. "There are ropes?"

He pointed to the thick black ropes dangling to the left of the wall, anchored from support beams along the glass ceiling. Deklan figured at construction, this was supposed to have been part of the greenhouse, but the Wolvenguard changed his mind and erected another glass wall. The room would have made a dazzling starlit ballroom if any of the beast masters had been inclined to hold social events. None were.

"Should have looked or asked. I don't allow my team to climb without being secured," he said.

"No safety ropes in life," she grunted, stretching for a handhold.

Deklan shifted. "And a preventable training accident is a stupid risk."

Sweat glistened on the exposed spans of her back and trembling arms. She was almost to the end of the climb. After figuring out her trajectory should she fall, he adjusted his position again. At the top, she let loose a whoop, her delight filling the room. Deklan couldn't stop the grin at the sound of her musical laughter. She kept going until she straddled the thick wall and swung her legs, continuing to giggle.

"Wow, I bet on a clear night this would be something else," her voice echoed down to him.

"I have a balcony off my room inside the greenhouse with the same view."

She leaned forward, propping her elbows and resting her chin on her palms. "Really? You can see the stars?"

"Unless it snowed or iced heavily, yes."

"And are you inviting me to your room to see for myself?" She pivoted on the ledge until she laid flat on her back, the movements swift and graceful. One foot braced on the ledge, her knee bent, while the other dangled. "Or maybe I'll just come back here."

Deklan glanced over his shoulder to the open doors and shook his head. Their conversation wasn't private. "Any part of the house is open to you except the third floor, which is my personal space."

Her leg swung harder. "Ah, so not an invitation."

"*Not* an appropriate conversation, Guardian Castien."

Her heavy sigh whispered throughout the room. "Very well."

She braced her hands on the ledge and swung both legs around. Deklan's heart leaped into his throat. Her toes found purchase, and he forced himself to relax. Her journey down was as easy as the one she'd taken up, elegant and confident. When only three feet remained, she dropped and landed with a flourish and a grin of accomplishment.

"Sean needs to install one of these in his training room," she said, sliding his towel free.

Sweat slicked the defined planes of her stomach and chest. An appealing flush reddened her cheeks. Wisps of damp hair clung to her forehead and neck. Deklan had never wanted to kiss a woman so desperately in all his adult life. Taste the exertion on her skin. He spun away and headed to the greenhouse.

"I'm going to find my wolves," he said. "Use anything you'd like in the room."

"I thought you were going to help me train," she called after him.

"Another time." Right now, he needed to get away from her, fast, before he did something neither of them could take back.

A SHATTERING CRACK OF THUNDER TORE CIA FROM SLEEP, screaming. Lightning flashed, washing the room in strobes of white. She scrambled backward, gasping. Air wouldn't fill her lungs no matter how hard she tried to breathe. Her shoulder blades connected with the wooden headboard, smacking it against the wall. Pain bloomed across her back. Another round of thunder fractured the air. Windows rattled, and the frames on the wall shook.

She curled into herself, wrapping her arms around her knees, rocking. "You aren't on that hill, you aren't," she whispered over and over again.

A sob tore free. Fat tears coursed down her cheeks. Rain lashed outside. She tried to focus on the sounds of the storm, to ground herself in the now and not the past threatening to pull her under. Fear settled like a heavy stone in her stomach. Her whole body trembled. Cold sweat dampened her clothes and made her hair stick to the back of her neck. Streaks of lightning barely warned of the following fierce boom, swallowing Cia's involuntary cry of terror.

Warm arms banded around her, pulling her against

a muscular chest. "Shh, *kovetka*, you're safe. Shh," Deklan whispered into her ear, stroking her hair and rocking her.

Cia wrapped her arms around his chest, her fingers digging into the supple muscles of his back. Deklan's juniper and sandalwood scent filled her nostrils. The heat of his skin helped further calm her. Safe. She was safe in his home. In his embrace. Another shudder wracked her body. A dry nose prodded her elbow, and Cia lifted her head enough to see Izia had crawled onto the bed with Deklan. She hadn't even noticed the mattress move. Some interceptor she was turning out to be. She lifted her arm for the wolf to snuggle into their hug. His large head squeezed between their bellies until he laid his muzzle on her thighs.

Deklan caressed her hair while the storm raged outside, squeezing her tight whenever a boom of thunder made her tense. Once the worst had passed, he relaxed against the headboard, putting enough space between them for her to see him in the low light of the dying fire heating her room.

"Thank you," she whispered.

He caressed her cheek to her jaw, fluttering his fingers over the pulse at her throat, tracing the path her tears had trailed. "Every storm?"

Vulnerability assailed her. She wanted to curl back into herself, but Deklan tightened her against his side, his hands overlapping on her hip. "Only the ones at night with thunder."

The storm continued to growl in the distance, no longer a threat to her sanity. The patter of rain joined the gentle crackle of the fire. Cia relaxed and folded her knees over his thigh, resting her cheek in the hallow of his shoulder. He traced a lazy trail up and down her left arm, his other hand cupped one of her knees. She could easily imagine them in this exact position after a night spent in a much more pleasant manner. Would he hold her the same after sating his passion? Cia squeezed her eyes closed. She wanted to find out with a desperation that hurt in her chest.

"Since the murders or your entire life?" he asked, resting his stubbled cheek on her head.

Fresh tears sprang into her eyes. "The murders," she managed to choke out.

Oh, how she hated even speaking about them. The pain never lessened. She swiped the hot, wet streaks from her face. "The first one I had to go through happened in those cells Uncle Vayden found me in. I thought I was going to have a heart attack. It was so dark and I was so scared."

All the screaming and crying children with her hadn't helped. Everyone was terrified, and as the oldest, she should have been able to calm them, but she'd been a useless wreck.

"You were locked away for how long?"

She sniffled. "Around three weeks from what they said when they rescued me. I spent most of it underground, waiting for someone to get me to start my supposed training."

"And you weren't scared there?"

"No." She shifted and let her head fall back against the headboard. Interesting shadows played on the ceiling from the flickering lightning outside and the weak fire within. "I know this is going to sound so selfish, but if I was there, in that underground cell, I didn't have to face what happened. They stole me away, screaming, covered in blood. I don't remember much else afterward but waking up clean and in one of the cells, where a man spoke to me from the shadows. I never saw his face, and he told me I was special and could get vengeance for what happened if I was patient. They gave me something else to focus on, and without my dad... I didn't have to think about Joshie and Mom... d-dying on that hill."

The moment her uncle delivered her into her father's arms, the grief she'd been denying herself had opened like a flood to drown her in sorrow. Two years later, she still fought the same tidal wave if she dwelled too long or too hard on the loss. Thoughts of her vengeance were the only thing capable of pulling her from the void.

"And every storm you've been alone," he murmured.

Deklan's fingers brushed her jaw, urging her to look at him. She rolled her head and met his darkened stare. The loneliness he spoke about threatened to consume. Nights of thunderous storms, in a house where no one could hear her tortured screams. Could offer any comfort unless she sought it out, which she would never do because of the pain she'd bring her father.

Tonight had been different. Because of him. "I'm not alone now."

His fingers grazed her jaw and trailed down her neck to her collarbone. Heat followed each curve he traced, awakening a curious pulse at her center. Her breath grew ragged. Never had she imagined such a simple touch could lead to sensual anticipation. He leaned closer, his mouth grazing the path he'd laid until he reached her neck, where he breathed deep.

A harsh exhale rasped across her throat. "Your scent drives me crazy."

Cia blinked, unsure how to respond. "My... scent?"

"Yes," he breathed against her skin, and she resisted

the urge to moan. "Like sweet jasmine floating on a midnight breeze."

The smooth texture of his tongue dragged along her pulse point, and Cia gasped. Sparks shot along her nerves, zinging straight to her core, where everything clenched with hot need. Nothing in her limited experience had prepared her for Deklan and the havoc he created among her senses without touching her in an intimate manner.

"Wh-what are you d-doing?" she managed to pant out, curling her fingers into Izia's fur to keep from grabbing his master.

"I don't know," he whispered, moving lower.

She couldn't stop the brazen response, lifting her breasts toward his questing mouth.

His tongue traced the faint swell above the neckline of her silk top. "I shouldn't have touched you."

Cia sighed, her head lolling back. The length of her unbound hair brushed the pillow lodged behind her. "I love it when you touch me," she murmured before she could stop the words.

Groaning, he pulled away, and she struggled not to grab hold of him and demand he stay close. The tantalizing glimpse he'd given of what she could expect at his hands wasn't near enough. He slid his arm free from around her waist and rose from the bed. Cold swept in where he'd been, and she shivered. The weak flicker of lightning added to the chill of his departure.

"Don't leave," she said in barely a whisper. The anxious knot in her chest intensified at the thought of him no longer being with her.

In the heavy shadows of the room, she couldn't make out his expression, only the stillness of his form as he stood beside her bed. "I can't stay."

Cia shifted on the mattress, sitting on her legs, her palms pressed to her thighs. "Why?"

He turned away, dragging his hand through his unbound hair. "I'm the arch guardian of Wolvenguard."

Cia scooted closer to the edge. Izia followed, belly crawling, his fur tickling the exposed skin on her legs. "I know who you are. What does that have to do with you staying with me?"

He spun around, hand still lodged in his hair. "If my staff sees me leave in the morning or catches me in here, there will be talk. Not the good kind. You're... no one, Lucianna. An unranked guardian and young." He sighed. "So young. What do you think they'd believe?"

Anger spiked through her. Stupidly, she'd believed they were past his hang-ups over her age. "I'm an adult, capable of making my own decisions."

"I know."

She sputtered and squared her shoulders. "You... do?"

Heaving a sigh, he dropped his arm. "Yes."

Shocked, she collapsed onto her butt, bouncing on the soft bed. "Oh. When did you, I mean, why did you change your mind?"

"My father came to see me and pointed out you were old enough to die for Sziveria, why did I not believe you were old enough to make any other decision concerning your future? He had a valid point."

Cia let his explanation sink in. "You spoke to your father about me?"

"He didn't give me much of a choice."

She laughed. "I'd apologize, but I'm not unhappy. I don't understand the problem then if I'm fine with you being seen with me."

"No one will believe *you* made the choice. I'm older

and in a position of high power, and you're in my home." He shook his head. "No, I can't stay."

"I don't want them to think that about you," she admitted. She wanted him to remain ached for him, but not at the cost of his reputation.

"And I don't want them to believe such about you, either."

That either of them would be willing to trade their body for influence, giving *or* taking. Only one way around such a ridiculous predicament. Cia slid from the bed and touched his arm. He turned enough for her to catch his gaze. Her heart pounded in her ears. Tingles danced along her skin. She swallowed away nerves.

"Contract with me. Promise to be my husband, and I promise to be your wife," she said.

Deklan swept a knuckle under her chin, his touch gentle, almost reverent. "Aren't I supposed to be asking?"

She grasped his wrist. "If we waited for you to ask, I'd have gray hair by then. Will you?"

His arm fell away, and the tendons along his jaw popped. "You don't know what you're asking."

"Sure, I do." Knowing she played a dangerous game, she stepped in closer, crowding his space, filling his senses with only her. "And I'll learn what I don't know or understand with time. With your help."

Faster than she could perceive, his hands dug into her hair, grasping her head and tilted her face toward his. "Forever Lucianna. With me. Could you handle that? Could you handle *me*? Because what you want, what will happen, won't be undone."

"Can you explain what won't be undone? My father," she licked her dry lips, "he wasn't comfortable

talking to me about the bond if that's what you're refer-
ring to?"

Deklan glanced around. "Now isn't the time."

"I am so tired of hearing that," she ground between
her teeth. "When will be the right time?"

He leaned close, his breath fluttering through the
hair near her ear. "When I won't throw you on the bed,
have my way with you and *show you* all about the bond
we will share."

Her eyes slid shut, and she moaned. "Oh please,
please, do that."

His hands fell away so fast she swayed from the loss
of his support. At the fireplace, he gripped the mantle,
his head hanging between his extended arms. The
incredible wolf tattoo on his back flexed and moved.
Cia wanted to retrace each detailed line with her fingers
and her tongue. She pressed her lips together. What an
odd urge. Yet, she couldn't deny the art called to her.
The wolf seemed to materialize from the fog-shrouded
forest just for her, stepping through the mist to reach
her. Beneath the mystical depiction, words in Ruthenian
were scrawled in neat lines.

"You are...." The words strangled in his throat and
forced her attention away from his back.

"Shameless? Mischievous? Too bold?" she offered.
She refused to say immature, though she figured she
was probably more than a little of that, too. They
seemed to have passed some great barrier concerning
her age, and she refused to bring it back to the forefront.

"All those things," he said, chuckling. "And
unaware of the future you're submitting yourself to."

Submitting. The choice of his word wasn't lost on
her. She dared to move closer to him. Near the fire, the
tortured expression on his handsome face became clear.

Cia wanted to ease his torment, to understand what he was having trouble revealing. "Am I really submitting when there's a promise of so much to be shared? When after you're done helping me learn about my Gen-Heir talent, you can also help me learn about our connection, and yours, with the wolves?"

"You'll have one, too," he said quietly.

"A connection?" She glanced at Izia, still draped over her bed, his front paws dangling over the edge. "To the wolves?"

"Just to one." He nodded at the bed. "That one."

Awe and excitement bubbled up within her. "Really? Like what you have?"

"You're full-blooded, Ruthenian. Izia may be able to connect with you as well if we bond fully."

Incredible! Had her father known? So many questions popped into her mind, and she struggled to filter out the most important. "How? How will this happen?"

His jaw flexed again while his fingers tightened on the mantle. "After we have sex, and I accept your bond."

Cia almost jumped into the air with a fist punch. Instead, she crossed her arms and figured the less enthusiasm she showed, the easier it would be for him to continue in the logical manner he seemed determined to take. "All right. Anything else?"

The tattoo shifted again under his flexing shoulders. "You'll carry my imprint. Proof for all other beast masters we're mated."

At that, her legs refused to support her, and she flopped onto the floor. "How is that possible?"

He shrugged. "How is any of it possible? We have no idea. It's a unique trait to beast masters and supposedly possible for anyone carrying even a hint of

Ruthenian genetics to accept. My mother carries my father's imprint."

The art spanning almost the entire expanse of his back took on a new meaning. It *was* Deklan to everyone from his father's nation. Unique to him. "What do the words mean?"

"The beast master's creed. All of us Ralston children with the beast master marker chose to show we took the responsibility seriously."

"Is that why you asked if I liked your tattoo?"

He nodded.

Slowly, she rose from the floor and went to him. Yielding to the impulse to touch the illustration, she trailed her index finger along the wolf's misty form. "You're more than a passing curiosity for me. I'm not like all the others. I'd be honored to wear this for my life, Deklan, if you'd wish. Will you accept me?"

18

Emotion clogged Deklan's throat. If he gripped the marble mantle any harder, the stone would shatter. Since his first attempt to find a mate at seventeen, no one had uttered the words every male beast master longed to hear. She'd said them, unaware of their significance. After years of failed attempts, he'd been forced to overlook the prejudice against his mixed heritage if a woman would accept his bond. By his twenty-fifth birthday, he'd given up hope. He'd been nothing more than a curiosity being appeased or perceived as weak and attempted domination. A mistake only one woman had made. All the others had used him for an experience.

Cia changed everything.

Deklan had to be the one brave enough to enter into something, not knowing how many years from now they'd be together. If they'd even like each other. Though, according to his father, their bond would make it impossible not to grow. Did he have the courage to risk the chance she'd come to hate what they shared? Or maybe she'd embrace the closeness. He'd never know if he didn't say yes.

Turning, he sat in front of the fire and braced his forearms on his bent knees. "You won't come to regret losing out on all the experiences you should be having at your age?"

She scoffed. "What experiences? Dances and the coy giggling games? Most girls *are* married by my age, you know."

"For one year, Lucianna. Rarely for life. And they go through two or three one-year contracts before deciding to do one longer or have children and commit to the eighteen years." He opened his hands. "You'll get no such option with me."

"Kevin and Raina married for life. They're happy."

"Raiventon's situation was unique. Most are like Kynhaven and your Uncle Vayden, who gave their wives one year to decide before they signed their second contract."

Cia laughed. "Uncle Vayden and Melody had a baby before their first year was up, and they're perfectly happy with the eighteen years. My uncle is already plotting for a way to make sure another eighteen years gets tacked on. They are not a good example."

"Yes, but they had the option at the start. The time to get used to being together for longer."

She let out a huff that conveyed her frustration and the patience she would likely lose. He swallowed away a grin. Life wouldn't be boring; he could at least count on that with her.

"Would you believe me if I told you I've tried to figure out a way to meet you for the past year?" she asked, tucking her chin, a sweet flush darkening her cheeks. "And then you show up in New Columbia, and you're… you."

He drew his brows together. "Me? What does that mean?"

She shrugged. "My team said one thing, everyone else said another. You were this mystery. Who to believe? I couldn't exactly walk up to you and ask who the *real* Wolvenguard was, no matter how much I wanted."

"And you think you know the real me now?"

"I'm learning. I'll learn more every day." A soft smile toyed at her lips. "You aren't what any of them thought."

"No?"

Her smile broadened, and she moved to him on her knees. The thin pink sleep set she wore did little to conceal her, no different than this morning when she'd been standing on her bed, a sexy, rumpled mess. Tear stains still streaked her cheeks, but the horror of the storm had long passed, allowing him to focus on the sensual female curves she had on display. Curves to be his for the taking if he acquiesced. Though the memory of her terror made him want to pull her back into his arms. Izia had been convinced someone had broken into her room under the cover of the chaotic weather. The enemy turning out to be her memories hadn't been any easier to handle than a live intruder.

He didn't stop her when she moved his hands to slide between his bent knees. Nor did he push her away as she ran her soft hands up his biceps to his shoulders, leaving a trail of sparks along his skin. Would her touch always feel electric to him, or would it calm after the bond was complete? His whole body tightened. Taking Cia, accepting her claim, while giving all of himself.

Everything. The thought left his heart drumming in his ears.

Her twilight gray eyes looked him over, exploring like a physical touch. "No one seems to realize how patient you are. Or kind. Or fiercely loyal. They only focus on your dedication to your position or how seeing you with three massive wolves makes them feel. They don't see *you*."

Gently, her fingers brushed his lips, over his eyebrows, and into his hair. She pressed a delicate kiss to his mouth and whispered, "I see you. Only you. And I want to know more about who I see. I want *you*."

Before he could respond, her mouth covered his. Distracted by the leisurely exploration of her lips on his, her tongue teasing for entry, he didn't notice her wrap around him until she rocked her pelvis. Pleasure condensed in his groin. Somehow, he kept silent. Forward women were nothing new to him. His first lovers had insisted on being the dominant partner, and being too young to know the game, he'd submitted. To a point. Cia was inexperienced and curious. For now, Deklan had no problem yielding control to her.

He slid his legs down, allowing her to straddle his hips easier. The firm tip of her tongue delved past his lips. He opened, and her confident exploration and teasing made him groan. She rose, her fingers tangled in his hair, her mouth slanting over his to take the kiss deeper. Deklan pushed his hands underneath the thin silk of her top to her bare skin. He cupped her shoulders, urging her back down, flexing his hips when she obeyed. She moaned into his mouth. Oh, how he wanted more. So much more.

Everything. All of her.

But not yet.

"Yes," he whispered into her mouth.

She sat back, brushing his hair from his temples, and searched his eyes. "Yes?"

Deklan took a moment to enjoy her passionate state. Glossy, swollen mouth. Flushed cheeks. Nipples straining for his mouth against silk. He didn't deny them, leaning forward and taking the sensitive nub through the fabric. She gasped, her hold tightening along his scalp. He traced all the delightful textures with the tip of his tongue while holding her breast in place with his teeth.

"Oh, summer sun," she rasped, arching her back.

"I should stop. I need to stop," he said, turning his attention to her other breast.

"You always stop. Don't. Not now." She grasped his face and lifted until his gaze met hers. "You said yes. That means you're mine."

Deklan closed his eyes as she caressed from his face to his neck and along his shoulders to clutch his back. Her fingers pressed into his muscles, and through the contact, the tingling of her bond called to him. Beckoned to be acknowledged and accepted. The beginning of the end. No going back.

He kissed her slowly, his tongue sliding along hers and exploring all the sweet secrets of her mouth. He savored each shallow intake of her breath. Her impatient squirming. And through it all, he allowed her to weave the first threads that would bind them for life. Delicate pearl flared through his veins, weak for now, an echo of what was to come. Her desire tugged at him, and from her sudden jolt, his beckoned to her as well.

She broke their kiss and leaned back, confusion widening her eyes. "What…?"

Deklan caressed down her back, dipping his hands

beneath her panties to cup her bare butt. Squeezing the firm globes, he guided her along his erection, straining the fabric of his sleep pants. "Our bond has started. You'll experience traces when I have extreme emotions. When I'm really angry, or happy, even scared."

"And lusty?"

"Especially that," he murmured, unable to stop kneading the handfuls of supple flesh.

She blinked. "Why?"

"There are many reasons, but the biggest one is to ensure we build a family. Theories abound that the first generation of Ruthenians built the empire all by themselves." When her brows furrowed and stiffened, he kissed her forehead. "You know how I feel about a family, but we won't start one until you're ready."

"What if I'm too scared to start one?" she whispered, tears shining.

Deklan wrapped her in a hug, all thoughts of sating desires forgotten. "You won't be, I promise. We'll work through your fears. That's what we're starting. What you asked for tonight. A partnership that will make both of us stronger."

She held his jaw between her hands, her gaze meeting his. "How could I ever make *you* stronger?"

Vulnerability shone in her eyes. Like an elusive mist, her apprehension floated through him, giving him a taste of what their bond was to hold. Deklan wasn't quite ready to expose any weakness. Too many years of rejection. Too much derision from women meant to see potential in him, only to sneer at the thought of sharing his future.

"Trust me?" he asked, pressing his forehead to hers.

She nodded.

He kissed her nose and then helped her from his lap.

A noise of protest escaped her at the exact moment her disappointment flitted through him. Deklan arched a brow. Her moods seemed to be as vocal as the rest of her.

"What—"

"I have to be gone before my staff arrives."

She moved on unsteady legs to the door, and Deklan suppressed a smug grin. "We can sign a contract. Right now."

"I don't have one." When she stared at him blankly, he stood and adjusted his pants. "Not all high-ranking guardians keep marriage contracts in our desk."

"Just Synintel?"

The arch guardian over intel teams was known for manipulating couples into marriage, including his daughter. That other couples working under him had ended up contracted only sparked further speculation about his meddling in the affairs of others. Many questioned if all the arch guardians controlled fate.

"I have no idea," Deklan answered. "Aside from the quarterly meeting with Queen Elect Arnica's advisors and the social functions I can't get out of attending, I don't know what the others on this street do or don't where the guardians who work under them are concerned."

"How many guardians are under you?"

Deklan pondered the questions. "Maybe twenty, including my team. The other beast masters may have teams, but they're responsible for them. I only step in if they get too arrogant to be tolerated."

She leaned back against the door. "Tomorrow, as soon as the records department opens, we go sign."

"No."

Her gaze narrowed, and she pointed at him. "You said yes, you can't take it back."

"I couldn't if I wanted to, but you will have a promising ceremony."

"We can still have one, after."

He shook his head. "Won't be the same."

She glared. "Why?"

"You've grown up, Sziverian. The promising ceremony always comes first with family. We can sign the contract immediately after instead of waiting like most couples do, but our families will be with us."

"I don't care about—"

"You will," he quickly cut in. "Trust me on this. You'll go to one for someone and wish we'd taken the time to have one."

When she glared at him, he sighed and raked his hand through his hair. "Look, I know you want…" He waved a hand at the bed, not trusting himself to speak what he wanted just as desperately. "And we will. Soon."

She crossed her arms over her chest. "How soon?"

"Meet my family this weekend. We can tell them and decide then."

Her shoulders straightened. "Your family?"

"Yes. All ten siblings and my grandmother."

THE RALSTON FAMILY. ALL OF THEM. WHEN CIA HAD blurted out her proposal, she hadn't been thinking beyond not being alone. Hadn't considered anything but finding a way to convince the very stubborn arch guardian not to leave her. Aside from a journalist and a matchmaker, every other Ralston served in a guardian role or one of critical support.

Not that Cia's family was anything to ridicule. She boasted an assassin father, her own intel guardian status, and a close relationship with the Shield Guardian Terravine. The Dossett's were family. Neither Cia nor Henry would have managed on their own after the murders without them.

But the Ralston's were a force unto their own. Respected, revered, and, in many cases, even feared. What would they think of her? Deklan had seen an immature teenager at first glance, would they as well? And what if the great Madeleine Fenwick, matchmaker extraordinaire, didn't approve of her? Cia pressed a hand to her aching chest. Not to mention beyond the numerous guardianships held by the family, she'd pretty much just committed to an arch guardianship of her own. Once she married Deklan, she'd share his title. Another round of panic threatened. What in the arctic had she been thinking?

"Hey, hey," Deklan whispered, his hands sliding up her bare arms. When had he crossed the room? "Calm down."

"Your grandmother…"

"Will love you."

"Your guardianship…"

"Isn't all you think it is." He squeezed her biceps. "Besides, it's too late to worry now."

"What do you mean?"

Cia couldn't make out his expression in the faint light, though she had the impression he was… bewildered. She pondered the curious insight.

"Until you," he said, "I didn't know a Ruthenian could repress their genetic inclinations or be so oblivious of them as not even to know they exist."

"What does that mean?" she asked, annoyed. "You're acting like I'm defective or something."

He barked out a laugh. Leaning in close, he kissed her. A swift brush of his lips left her following when he pulled away.

"No, I just wish I knew a quick way to help you learn your Ruthenian nature." He tucked a lock of hair behind her ear, caressing her jaw to her chin. "Or maybe you just need to know how to recognize that part of yourself, and the rest will happen."

"*Did* something happen?" she asked slowly, feeling as though she missed something vital.

"Remember when I said there was no going back?"

She nodded.

He laced his fingers through hers and held up their joined hands. Cia glanced from their hands to his shadowed face, trying not to get stuck on his chest and the sprinkling of hairs that covered his pecs and drew an enticing line to the waist of his pants. She'd been intrigued in the gym when he'd been damp with sweat. Now, she was close enough to touch and not distracted by his kiss. Then she realized she *touched* him. Had been touching him all night, and he'd allowed the contact. While little sparks still seemed to arc between their skin, they were muted.

A slow warmth spread through her. Comfort and contentment she couldn't claim as her own but was there all the same. Gasping, she pulled her hands free and looked at them. The sensation faded. She tried to recall their earlier passion in front of the fire. Had she felt something more then, too?

"Was that..." She licked her lips and touched his bare arm. The flicker of emotions returned, with amusement mixing among them. "Oh, it is! It's you."

Amazed, she grabbed both his arms and squeezed.

He loosened her grip, laughing. "You won't get more by puncturing my skin."

"So, I'm like a sympath with you now?"

"For now, yes. Once our bond is fully forged, you'll be able to sense my emotions the same way I can yours, without touch."

"All the time?" She blinked and pulled her hands free. "How will I know what's me and what's you?"

"You'll learn to isolate yourself from me like I can with the wolves. I'll teach you."

Cia tried not to be overwhelmed by the realization he hadn't been joking about their being tied together for life. While they may not be contracted, they might as well be. No going back, he'd said, and she was only getting a glimpse of what that meant.

"No second thoughts," he whispered, taking her face in his hands. "We're in this life together now."

No, she couldn't regret her impulsiveness, no matter what crazy changes were about to befall her. She would have arrived home bonded if she had her way back in New Columbia. At least she had a greater understanding of what their connection would entail. She had to hope, in time, the love her parents shared would form between them. Ruthenians sure had a backward way of forging relationships. First comes the bond, then comes the marriage…

Wrapping her arms around his neck, she pressed her body to his and rested her cheek on his chest. The faint dusting of hairs tickled her cheek. She closed her eyes and breathed his scent in deep. His heart beat a steady, strong rhythm into her ear.

"Please don't go. Stay with me tonight," she whispered against the warmth of his skin.

He hugged her. "Izia will remain."

She wanted the man and the wolf, but since she wasn't going to get her way, she nodded in acceptance. Glancing at the large canine lounging on her bed, she wondered if they could sneak into his bed. Would he kick her out if he woke to discover her curled around him? Or perhaps she could seduce him into staying. She worked her bottom lip. While no longer a hard mass jutting against her, there was no denying the thick, heavy length of his member resting between their bodies. If she…

"Whatever mischief is going on in that head of yours, stop," he said, exasperated.

Frowning, she leaned back. "Not fair. Am I an open book to you now?"

"You're very expressive."

"Great," she sighed. "The mystery is gone before we even started."

He curled a finger under her chin and tilted her head back. "Ah, Lucianna, I'm confident you will find numerous ways to continue to surprise me."

At her smile, alarm skittered across her fingertips.

"*Kovetka*," he said in warning, taking a step from her. "I will not have either of us dragged through the mud by gossipers. My staff isn't infallible, and *The Havener* pays good money for scoops from ranked guardian staff. We can't risk it."

Unlike *The Haven City Chronicle*, *The Havener* printed the latest and juiciest in scandals and rumors. They would indeed make the popular, unscrupulous publication. Sighing, she dropped her arms.

"Fine," she bit out.

"You can wait a week for our ceremony. Please."

She held up a finger. "One week. And we complete

the contract directly after. I'll wear the bracelet forever if you want, but our promise to be married will last only for how long it takes to sign the contract."

"Two-second engagement?" he asked, chuckling.

"Sure, I'll give you two seconds to relish the fact that you're getting married, then," she clapped her hands, "signy-sign."

He shook his head, grinning. "You're good for me." The smile slid from his face, and she felt more than saw his shift in intensity in the weak light. "Hopefully, I will be good for you, too."

19

THE MOMENT OF RECKONING HAD FINALLY ARRIVED. CIA drew a deep breath and clutched the bag with the books she'd managed to pilfer from Joel Blackbain and the few items she'd collected from the assassin attempting to kill him. At least she had an offering to appease the infuriated guardians about to confront her. A justified anger, which she wholly deserved. And they'd given her two days to wallow in her guilt.

"Well," she said to the wolf at her side, "I guess here I go."

He whined, his bushy tail flicking her thigh with each step.

She patted his back. "Yeah, I know. Me too. At least you get to play in the greenhouse. Lucky."

Deklan had knocked on her door a half hour ago to let her know everyone was waiting for her downstairs in the receiving room. The room joined an informal dining area, ensuring enough space for everyone to sit and eat while they waited on her. Though, if Deklan wanted, he could also have seated

259

them in the breakfast or formal dining room. She wondered if any of the previous Wolvenguards had used all three eating areas or if the spaces had been added to increase the square footage of the monstrous house.

At the top of the stairs, she slowed. Voices drifted from the open double doors at the front of the foyer. Calm, casual, and familiar to the team dynamics she'd become used to. For the moment, no one was frustrated or upset. Would that change when she walked in? Squaring her shoulders, she bounded down the steps, motioning for Izia to join the other wolves in the greenhouse. He knew the way and trotted in the opposite direction, his nails clicking on the marble.

Savory and sweet scents strengthened closer to the gathering. Cia licked her lips and hugged the bag to her rumbling stomach. She walked through the open double doors, and a hush fell over the room. Emotions flickered on everyone's faces. Katria smiled sympathy in her bright blue gaze. Beside her on the plush beige couch, comfortable enough for two, her husband Sean sat back and crossed his arms over his broad chest. Kevin shoved a fork full of something into his mouth and waved the utensil in her direction. The relief on Mason's face made tears sting her eyes. No one looked angry, only curious and… yes, disappointed.

"I'm sorry," she blurted, squeezing the bag tighter. "I should have said something. I should have trusted all of you."

Katria slowly set her plate on the coffee table. "Did you get the information you were hoping for?"

She shook her head.

Katria tsked. "How frustrating."

An understatement if one had ever been offered. Cia

sat cross-legged on the floor at the coffee table and dumped out the contents. "I did get this."

Mason joined her, giving her a one-armed hug into his side before picking up one of the books. He pressed a quick kiss to her head. "I'm glad you're safe, girly."

The gesture lifted a weight from her shoulders. She smiled at him. "Me too."

Cia met Sean's stare across the table. "Did you do okay seeing him?"

"I opted not to," Sean answered. "Nothing good would have come from our meeting. He was stable enough to be taken straight to Stonebreak, thanks to Wolvenguard's medical scientist. I was invited to be part of the guardian team returning him. I turned down the assignment."

"I wanted to go," Katria said, propping her chin on her hand. "Sean said no."

"Sean was ensuring his brother made it to the prison alive," Kevin said, dropping a chair at the end of the table and sitting.

"Shooting in close quarters is a notoriously bad idea. Bullets ricochet, you know that," Katria said and then smiled at Cia. "He would have made it to the prison."

"He would have made it two steps off the train," Kevin said, stabbing his fork into a ham cube.

Katria shrugged, reaching for one of the folded papers. Cia raised her hand and opened her mouth to warn her, but Kat had already opened the sheet. The assassin's cheeks blazed red, and she snapped the paper back together.

Sean plucked it from her fingers. "He must have been there awhile."

"Long enough to record the docks activities," Cia said, tapping the thinnest book.

Kevin set his plate down and leaned over to collect the journal. He thumbed through the pages. "I wonder if Raina can tell me anything about these."

"I bet they're researching other ports in the country since Port Tabria and Port Scarborough are being heavily watched," Mason said.

"I don't think they could use that port for their human victims," Cia said. "Too many stairs, they'd be noticed."

"Not if they load people into crates and lower them down the cliffside," Deklan said from the entry to the dining room.

Cia's heart leaped at the sight of him leaning casually against the doorframe, arms crossed over his broad chest, pulling the maroon sweater he wore tight. The sides of his hair were tied into a knot at the crown of his head, leaving the rest to brush his shoulders. She wanted to kiss him good morning and learn what he had eaten by his taste. His gaze shifted to her, full of heat and a warning. Too late, she remembered he could sense her emotions.

"That would be risky," Mason said, "if one of the crates fell."

"I'm not saying it'd be ideal, but it is plausible," Deklan replied. "If they're desperate enough, they may try anything."

"And we have to remember they aren't just dealing in the human variety of cargo," Kevin said, holding up the small vial of pink powder. "They're moving this crap, too."

"And bringing in stolen New Columbian timber as Thanzian cotton," Mason said.

"Among other things," Sean agreed. "However, they knew to watch that port for Joel's arrival."

"I can't keep my location secret," Deklan said. "Not with three Ruthenarc Wolves."

"Or your train," Cia said, smiling at him. She looked at her team. "Have you guys seen that thing?" She moved her hand in an arc. "Huge 'Wolvenguard is here' sign. Literally."

"So, the question is," Kevin began, moving the vial back and forth in the light of the window, "was the guy an assassin sent to spy or a spy given orders to attempt to kill Joel on arrival?"

Cia recalled the battle between her and the would-be killer and the sleeping area she'd investigated. "He could fight."

Kevin lifted a brow. "Better than you?"

"Everyone can fight better than her," Deklan said, throwing an arm out before she could answer.

Heat flushed across Cia's cheeks and through her body. She pushed papers around with her index finger.

"What?" Kevin asked in shock. "Did you forget all your training?"

"No, I remembered it all. I just had trouble staying calm." She shrugged and continued before he could reply. "His sleeping area was simple, so he could pack up in a hurry. He knew what he was doing."

Sean rubbed his forehead. "That could be a spy or assassin. Both can fight. Both know the long game."

"He was an embarrassing shot," Katria said, flicking at the dust on her black skirt. "I'm guessing a spy asked to fire a gun."

"The question everyone should be asking," Ryan said from behind Deklan, making Cia jump. Had he been there all along? "Is if this guy works under the FIO or the SNID."

Ryan brushed past Deklan and accepted the activity

log for the docks when Kevin held it up for him. Everyone waited in silence while Ryan inspected the journal.

"It's not formatted like our logs," Kevin said.

"No, ours are more organized. However," he said, turning a page, "this isn't random either. There's a level of training here." His attention shifted to Cia. "Did he speak to you at all? Have an accent?"

"No," she answered. "There wasn't anything specific to determine if he was, or wasn't, Sziverian."

Ryan leaned over and picked up one of the slips of erotic art. "Interesting fact about nudes. Cultures like different things."

"Do those contain a unique difference to our preferences?" Mason asked.

"Yes." Ryan held out the paper, pointing to splashes of color where the artist had shaded in sheer fabric draping around and across the woman's body from armbands on her biceps. "This is a Thanzian tradition. Married women wear the colors of their spouse's family."

Mason raised a brow. "And what family would allow their colors to be used for erotic representation?"

"Probably none. These may be his family colors."

"Personalized erotica?" Sean asked, brows raised.

Ryan shrugged. "Sure, why not? The eager partner, female or male, is one most people fantasize about. Imagining that said partner is yours alone is even better."

"If the images had been Sziverian in nature, what may they have been?" Cia asked, curious.

"Likely two people instead of one, with no indication of a commitment," Ryan said, refolding the paper and tossing it onto the small pile. "We may have come far in our acceptance and desire for fidelity since the human rabies epidemic, but we cling to the old ways of freer relationships, which is why curtain shows and the lusty book section at Mr. Harold's Book Emporium do so well. The fantasy of risky sex without any health dangers is a lucrative industry in this country."

"What about those parlors that cater to short-term affairs?" Cia asked, wrapping her arms around her knees.

"Those are very much underground and why we continue to have HRS outbreaks. That, and people visiting Old City Ruins for the same."

"Or The Rows," Deklan said. "Prostitution isn't exclusive to Old City Ruins."

"No, however, those residents are far more desperate than The Rows. An HRS containment unit isn't necessary for The Rows like it is for Old City Ruins."

Cia bounced her chin on her knees, something tugging at her mind. "This group, the V Alliance, deals in drugs, human and goods trafficking, and they all seem to crave a sort of sexual autonomy. All of them I have dealt with have had, or wanted, some form of erotica."

"Magic lily dust is said to help the user reach a more uninhibited state, to make it easier to shrug off societal constraints. It's popular among those your age," Ryan said.

"Not to mention they had no qualms freeing and working with a serial rapist," Sean ground out. "I agree there's a common thread among the group participants."

"Not all of them," Mason said. "There was no evidence Tamina Peyton took drugs or participated in anything sexual. Her involvement appeared to be a desire for power."

"Yes, she had access to you, a prestigious house in our country, and was likely offered something to bring you to their side. When she failed, she died for their cause in an attempt to eliminate you as well," Ryan said. "Which leaves me to believe someone has the authority to make these promises."

"You're no closer to discovering whom?" Kevin asked.

Ryan shook his head. "Anytime I think I have a clue, it disappears."

Like what had happened with the entire case surrounding Cia's kidnapping and the death of her mother and brother. If not for Vayden's close relationship with Henry and his remarkable investigative skills, Cia never would have been found. Vayden had given her what he and his wife Melody had been able to learn concerning the assassin, which wasn't much. The only link to the group was the ship she'd been bound for and a dried nasturtium flower that had been left at the scene of the murders. A calling card of sorts for the V Alliance.

While she knew finding the identity of the V Alliance's leader was important, Cia only needed the name of the killer responsible for taking away her family. Selfish as her goal may be, she couldn't bring herself to care about the rest. Not yet.

Cia gathered the two books she'd taken from Joel. "One of these has Sziverian radio numbers. The other, I'm not sure what to make of it."

Ryan grabbed the book. "Radio numbers?" He turned page after page. "I didn't think this many people owned radios in Sziveria."

"Maybe they give their people one for joining the cause," Mason said.

"It would make communicating any time of year much easier," Ryan said. "But the cost…"

"May be nothing with how much they're making with their deceptions," Sean said.

Ryan snapped the book closed, gripping it tightly enough to turn his knuckles white. "Radio numbers must be registered. But if I ask for a comprehensive list, someone will suspect I've learned something. Happens every single time."

Kevin smiled. "Tell me where they're located. I'll get you the list."

"What is the other book?" Katria asked.

Cia shrugged. "I have no idea. It's in some code, I think."

Ryan handed Kevin the radio code book and took the other from Cia. "Was this the only one?"

"No, but the others burned," Cia answered.

Ryan tilted his head in question.

Deklan moved to stand behind Ryan, looking over his shoulder at the open book. "New Columbia has these strange ash bombs. They destroy everything when they strike. Leveled the entire camp except for the cement cell they'd locked Cia in."

"Man made?" Ryan asked.

Deklan shook his head. "No. They seem to come from the UZs there. Most cities are well beyond the UZs. The camp was within the borders. I don't think the camp had experienced one before that night. If any former prisoners had known, they would have been fighting to get into the cell with us."

Katria touched her throat. "Everyone in the camp died?"

"Men were walking around when I entered the cell, and as far as I know, only Joel and his entourage left on his train. The next morning, there was nothing but ash," Cia said.

"That's terrifying."

Cia nodded. "But the next group won't know how dangerous it is to be there. Have to admit it's a great way to ensure all evidence is destroyed and no one is any wiser about the risk."

Ryan held the book out to Cia. "I'm going to ask you to take this to Ramsey Survaine. She and her husband, Caidon, are in the country for a few weeks. I'll get you their address."

"She knows what's written?" Cia asked.

"She's a cryptographer. If she doesn't recognize it at first sight, she will within a few days, or maybe even hours."

Thankful she wouldn't have to beg or demand to be part of solving the mystery, Cia took the journal from Ryan's hand. "I hope it contains something useful."

"Especially since you risked so much to get it," Katria said, leaning forward. "Did you think you weren't important enough to be missed?"

The lecture Cia expected when she stepped into the room had only been delayed. She set the book down, taking a deep breath. "At the time, it seemed the best option. I couldn't risk the information being sat on and debated over, therefore going to waste. I acted a bit impulsive, I know."

Mason swayed his large frame into her shoulder. "A little?"

Cia rolled her eyes. "All right, fine. I was very impulsive. Trust me, Deklan, never let me forget."

"None of us would have let you forget either if we'd

been the ones to catch you and bring you home," Kevin said. Leaning forward, he braced his hands on his knees and clasped his hands between them. "And had we been along, we may have been able to discover more. You're part of a team, which means we're at our best when *all* of us are working together."

"Neither Kevin nor I went it alone when our wives were kidnapped," Sean said. "Our strengths make us unstoppable, but only if we can count on each other."

And she'd let them down in more ways than one. "I understand. I'll be better in the future."

"There won't be a future if you do it again," Ryan said without a hint of emotion, just fact.

Cia's heart lurched. She had never considered they'd reverse her guardianship status, always figuring her talent permitted her to... what? Misbehave? Shame threatened to drown her, and she resisted the urge to drop her head in her hands.

Warm fingers kneaded her neck. A gentle calmness settled through her. Deklan's presence quieted her further, and she allowed him to shoulder some of her angst. Had he sensed her distress through their weak bond? She wanted to ask, but not around everyone. Talking about their newly forged connection seemed to do something primal to them both. Since Cia was all for taking advantage of any seductive moments she could, she wanted him very much alone when she brought it up again.

Sean, however, missed nothing. Not that Deklan could hide the fact he'd sat behind her and touched her in a very familiar way. Her team leader's amber gaze narrowed. "Get close to Cia while you hunted her, Wolvenguard?"

"I asked him to contract with me last night," Cia

answered before Deklan could. "He said yes. You may congratulate us."

Kevin's brows shot up. "*You* asked?"

"She's impetuous," Deklan said as if reminding everyone Cia had a marked lack of self-control.

"You didn't have to say yes," Sean said.

Oh no, Sean was *not* going to undo all her hard-earned progress. Cia glared. "Why not?"

Sean waved a hand. "Because you're...."

Cia hopped up and opened her arms. "I'm what? A woman? Women can't ask men to be part of their future?"

Sean pinched his forehead. "No, that's not what I was trying to say. You're young."

"I was eighteen when I contracted with you," Katria said.

"You didn't know," Sean said, looking annoyed at Ryan. "Neither of us knew."

Katria waved. "Semantics. I was still married at eighteen."

"This is your choice?" Kevin asked quietly.

Cia nodded, somehow avoiding reaching back in search of Deklan's hand.

"And yours?" Kevin asked, looking at Deklan.

Cia swallowed against the rise of nervous flutters in her stomach. What would he say?

"One of you thinks she's too young, a grievance of mine as well. The other believes she could somehow coerce me into a relationship." Deklan glanced at Mason. "What do you have to say?"

Mason carefully set the vial of pink powder aside. "I think Cia had to face the horrors of life too young. Younger even than Katria did. She's made many mature decisions since that fateful moment, some good, some bad. No one could accuse her of doing anything against her wishes, that's for sure. Every choice she makes is with an end goal in mind. Are you okay being part of that goal?"

Cia wanted to argue she hadn't asked Deklan to contract to help find the assassin. But could she deny his civil position wouldn't be a boon? She *would* have the power of an arch guardianship behind her. However, that wasn't why she'd asked or even why she still wanted a relationship. A very permanent one.

"I'm very aware of Lucianna's objective," Deklan stated. "She hasn't made her desire to find a killer a secret." His focus shifted to her, and Cia lifted her chin. "I'm hoping once she contracts with me, she'll see me as an equal partner and allow me to help."

"We all want to help," Katria said. "Me more than most."

Sean's hand slipped onto his wife's much smaller one. "This group has managed to be steps ahead, not just one or two, but sometimes it feels like every single step, for years. You were reckless, Cia, but your quick thinking to get to New Columbia ahead of any Sziverian official may have finally given us a chance. My brother fled at the arrival of Wolvenguard, which means he would have fled at our arrival as well. While you and Kevin could have snuck around the camp unnoticed, the rest of us don't have that skill. We would have waltzed in the front gate just like Wolvenguard, not knowing an element of surprise could have nabbed us an information prize."

"A mistake we won't make again if we find an encampment of theirs," Ryan said. "We'll do stealth recon first, then send in a team for high-priority capture."

"Blackbain wasn't the only significant escapee?" Deklan asked.

Ryan rubbed the back of his neck. "You know we don't only keep Sziverians in our maximum-security prisons."

"But once Sziveria accepts them into custody, they become our responsibility," Deklan said.

"Yes."

"And some of them are loose?" the Wolvenguard asked. "Which ones?"

As if debating whether to answer, Ryan worked his jaw for a moment. "Basil Vacek from Ravenna and Ethaniel Seeds from Latanus."

A tendon jumped in Deklan's jaw. A peculiar, muted burn flared through Cia. She raised a brow. His anger?

"The Feral Thief and The Chance Killer?" Deklan ground out. "You've lost a kleptomaniac murderer and a poison maker who likes to kill at random for fun?"

"We think they were released in hopes of looking for them over Joel," Ryan said.

"Except you took years to figure out the subterfuge, and priorities shifted," Deklan said.

"Something like that," Ryan grumbled.

"Any leads at all on their whereabouts?" Kevin asked.

Ryan shook his head. "No. We've only known about their possible escape for a few months. We're still hoping it's fake. Arch Guardian Praekasdian is doing a cell-by-cell search of each prison. A sort of prisoner inventory, if you will. He's discovered some on the transfer list weren't moved at all."

"Could the assassin be one of these released convicts?" Katria asked.

Ryan shook his head again. "I don't think so. Your

family's murders happened around the time Praekas-dian was initially asked to help the V Alliance. The murders were a message, and then when he still didn't comply...."

"Jessalyn was captured," Mason ground out, his hands fisting.

Thanks to the V Alliance and their wretched plans, Cia learned of each guardian's tragic history. Mason's wife Jessi had been captured by a contract killer who liked to play with his victims first. She'd managed to escape, deeply traumatized and forever scarred. Her abductor had also murdered Mason's twin sister. Mason had made quick work of the sadistic predator, who'd barely lived long enough to answer questions from Sean. A feat Cia envied.

"A message and an attempt to get a powerful Gen-Heir," Cia said. "Like with me."

"Yes. They do seem obsessed with procuring talent, which means they still don't have many powerful play-ers," Ryan said.

"Maybe if they quit using violence as a means of recruitment, they'd have better luck," Katria said.

Cia shared a sad smile with the sharpshooter.

"I agree," Ryan said. "Whoever runs things isn't a logistics talent, or they'd know better. I'm not sure what their talent is. Only they must have one to be in a posi-tion of high enough power to influence shield guardians and intimidate arch guardians. You don't get that level of arrogance by being weak."

"But looking at other arch guardians, or summer sun forbid, the monarchy and staff, would require a ridiculous amount of evidence," Sean said.

"Yes, it's a delicate rope to balance," Ryan said. "But I'll get across, one way or another."

Just as one way or another, Cia would find a cowardly assassin.

DEKLAN LEANED AGAINST THE WALL, ARMS CROSSED, observing inceptor training firsthand. Coated in a fine sheen of sweat, Cia screamed out her exhaustion, completing a flawless front kick followed immediately by a sweeping side kick. Kevin blocked them both, returning them with rapid punches, which he held. Had they been completed, Cia would be down. Until now, Kevin had mainly kept to kicks and defensive cardio. The sudden offensive move did what Deklan predicted Kevin wanted.

Cia froze.

Her breathing changed from rapid exertion to panicked gasps. Deklan straightened. Out in the greenhouse, Izia howled.

Cia is fine, Deklan said to Izia, hopefully preventing the wolf from barreling in to the rescue.

"And there it is," Kevin whispered, walking around Cia's debilitated form. "Now, how to get past it?"

Deklan joined him, touching the exposed skin of her lower back, slick with sweat. Tense muscles bunched beneath his fingers. "Come back, *kovetka,*" he murmured into her ear. "You're safe."

Inhaling, she blinked and shook her hands. "Sorry, I'm so sorry. I tried to stop it, but—"

"Better here than with an adversary again," Kevin said, giving her a light tap on the shoulder. "I meant for you to have an adrenaline spike. I've tried a few other things since we've started. Only a direct threat worked."

"But I panic instead of engaging," Cia said, spinning away from them in disgust.

Kevin sighed. "I'm not sure how to handle this. My talent happens immediately upon an adrenaline rush. I don't control it. I can ignore it, but I can't stop the transition. You don't do that. It's almost as if—"

"She has to make the choice," Deklan said. "Once she recognizes the sensation, it'll be as immediate as yours if she wishes. Or she can remain unaffected if, say, the adrenaline spike is caused by a heavily rocking train car or a close call with an idiot Ariot driver."

"It's different for her?" Kevin asked.

"She's full-blooded Ruthenian, like Katria. Access to our talents is voluntary. Weaker bloodlines, not weaker talents," he said at Kevin's glower, "have an uncontrolled response. A Ruthenian botanist can touch a plant just to feel leaf textures, whereas someone like Melody Dossett has no power to manage her reaction to touching the plant. She just," he clapped his hands, "experiences her ability."

"Interesting. I didn't know that."

"So." Deklan moved to stand before a still-brooding Cia. "You can look at your issue this way."

She met his stare, expectant. "Yes?"

Deklan held up both his hands. "When your adrenaline spikes, you have a choice. There's another sensation occurring that you're missing because your anxiety is ruling you. You can follow the panic or," he sent his hands in opposite directions on either side of her body, "you can follow your ability and see the world as you alone are meant to."

"How am I supposed to recognize my talent when I can't get past the panic?"

"As long as adrenaline flows, it's there, waiting."

Deklan glanced at the greenhouse. "Maybe we just need a natural adrenaline spike so you can feel it without the threat of danger."

"Doesn't fear produce a natural adrenaline spike?" Cia asked, accepting a hand towel from Kevin and wiping her face.

Deklan smiled. "There are other ways to bring on adrenaline."

Izia, Deklan commanded, *meet Cia at the greenhouse door. Neva and Nikita meet me there, too.*

Kevin draped a towel over his shoulders. "I'd love to watch and see how this works out, but if I'm no longer needed, I'll get back to my family. I missed Tanis walking for the first time. Raina is determined to keep Silas from taking his first steps until I can be there."

Warm memories of his younger siblings accomplishing the milestone made Deklan's smile grow. Someday, he'd experience the same with his children. He held a hand to the master guardian. "You're a lucky man, Raiventon."

Kevin grinned and gave Deklan a firm shake. "You'll hear no argument from me."

Dog noses pressed to the glass, catching everyone's attention. Bright eyes glittered with anticipation. Nikita dragged his snout, exposing his small front teeth and leaving a trail of clear snot. Cia laughed.

"That wolf is a mess," she said, still chuckling.

"They look ready to go," Kevin said. "Have fun, good luck, and I expect our next training session to be much different."

Deklan led the way to the greenhouse. Humid, earth-scented air rushed by as he opened the center door. Birds trilled, insects hummed, and small critters scuttled about in the undergrowth. Untamed green foliage filled the expansive glass house to the ceiling. Once a year, gardeners came in to ensure the wild growth didn't weaken the panels by attempting to expand beyond their habitat. The wolves had forged trails, which Deklan ran with them once a day.

A wide brick terrace offered the only semblance of order. Three outdoor couches framed a large table. His team and any guests he welcomed usually sat out in the greenhouse. Lanterns hung from hooks behind each couch, and a fire pit with a grate for grilling meat was on the far left of the gathering area. Walking into the natural space filled Deklan with comfort.

"We're going to play a game," Deklan said, playing with Neva's ears.

"A game?" Cia asked in disbelief.

Deklan smiled. "Trust me, this is unlike any game you've ever played. Take your leads from Izia. He knows the rules and will be trying to win."

"And how will this help me?"

He met her uncertain gaze and stifled a grin. "When your adrenaline surges, you'll be having fun. Pay attention. You'll feel *something*, I can't explain it to you, but it'll happen. Let it flow, sink into it, and pay attention to what happens next. You should win this game."

She shifted her attention to the dogs prancing around him in excitement. "Even against the wolves?"

"Yes, with Izia's help."

She worked her bottom lip, and he wanted to kiss her. Maybe he would. He cupped the back of her neck and dragged her close. She gasped, and he didn't waste a second sealing his lips to hers and delving deep. A sensual moan sounded from her, and he slanted his mouth over hers, his tongue battling for control. Her fingers dug into his hair at the base of his neck, her fingernails scratching his scalp. The little sting urged him on. She moaned again, longer, huskier, and pressed her chest to his, seeking to get closer.

If he didn't end the kiss, he would toss her on the nearest couch and see how far she'd let him go. Knowing her, she wouldn't care if his entire staff witnessed them, provided she had her way. The thrill of her passionate nature didn't help him draw his mouth from hers. She followed, pressing wet, teasing grazes across his lips until he couldn't stop from groaning in defeat and opening for her. Her nails dug harder into his scalp as she yanked him closer.

Desire flared through him, heady and tempting. Cia's uninhibited responses were everything he hoped for in a mate, and all she had managed to do was seduce him with her kisses. What would she do when he touched her for the first time? Really touched her, learning what brought her pleasure. The thought had his hands seeking out her firm butt and hauled her against his body. The rush of her gasp when she encountered his erection made him smile. Being the minx he'd taken to calling her in Ruthenian, she wiggled, exploring how they fit so close.

"No more," he grated at the cusp of his restraint.

A delicate shudder ran the length of her body, still pressed close enough for him to feel the hard buds of her nipples pressed to his chest. He took his hands off her body before he moved them to a new location. Oh, she was a sight. Hair mussed, lips swollen and glossy, chest, neck and cheeks flushed. He wanted to trace the bloom from her face to the swell of her breasts.

She took an uneven breath and stepped back. "I'll agree to shelve this for now, but next time—"

Deklan held up his hand. "I won't start something we can't continue."

The blush in her cheeks deepened, along with the hunger darkening her gaze. "Promise?"

He took another step away from her, needing more distance to keep from grabbing her again. "Yes."

She smoothed damp hair from her temples. "Very well. What game are we going to play?"

Deklan grinned. "Hide and hunt. Or as they call it in my father's native tongue, *srykat zre straes'ya.*"

Cia crouched high on the thick branch of a cork tree. The reddish bark reminded her of a sunset, and the sprawling branches made climbing much easier than the taller oaks and ash trees thriving in the massive conservatory. A sensual hum still vibrated through her body, making her squirm. For the second time, she'd missed her chance to feel the effect she had on him. Being pressed tight to his frame with his hard length trapped between them had excited her in ways she'd never imagined. The plan to sneak into his room before the week was out looked better and better with each passing minute. Or maybe she could convince him to sign the contract.

Tonight.

She should have bargained when he'd laid out the rules if she won his hide and hunt game; they contract tonight. Since snapping her fingers in frustration would give away her position, she suppressed the urge. The annoying pulse in parts of her body that had never suffered unsatisfied need before she met a certain arch guardian solidified her plan. Deklan didn't know it yet, but he *would* find himself with a wife and a mate before midnight.

In the bushes below, Izia hunkered down. Cia lowered onto her belly, hugging her knees and elbows to the limb, careful not to transfer any movement to the tree. The birds and insects quieted. Anticipation hummed through Cia, elevating her heart, and… then it happened. Fire zipped through her veins, and she let the foreign sensation flow. Her eyes closed as the tiny hairs on her arms lifted, and her scalp tingled.

A rustle of movement to her left snapped her into focus. Everything around her appeared brighter, more defined. Miniscule sounds made her head twitch in various directions as she tried to pinpoint where they came from and what made them. The area around her unraveled into a new experience, a dangerous distraction she would have fallen into if not for the even quicker onset of her reflexes. Leaves moving whispered feet from her, and she stilled. Through the dense brush, bright blue eyes stared intently.

Cia crept through the tree, carefully transferring her weight from one limb to another until she stood above Nikita. Weight braced on her hands, she lowered behind the still wolf inch by slow inch until her arms burned and her fingers cramped. She touched her bare toe between Nikita's shoulder blades.

"Gotcha," she whispered, then remembered the phrase she was supposed to say. Deklan had worked with her for several minutes until she could pronounce it properly. "*Chyvacen'ny.*"

Izia trotted out from underneath the brush, touching his nose to a whining Nikita. Cia dropped the rest of the way to the ground and faded into the curtain of a weeping elm. Using her hands, she caught Izia's attention and used sign language to bring Izia to her side. Nikita headed to the patio. Careful not to disturb any of the draping branches, she and the wolf crept along the cavernous interior of the tree. Listening closely, she crouched and inched aside the curtain of leaves.

A bird bounced from a low branch to the ground, twittering and fluttering its pale brown wings. Another bird flew in to investigate the linnet's findings. The vivid browns and creams of their plumage, paired with their quick movements, mesmerized Cia. Would she be fast enough to catch one? Izia lowered himself, his butt wiggling in excitement. Cia brushed her fingers along the back of his head. She wiggled her index finger back and forth when he looked at her. *No.* His nose trembled, and his ears twitched, but he remained otherwise immobile.

Cia did a quick visual sweep of the surrounding vegetation. Once she confirmed everything belonged, she eased from her shelter and took to another tree. She figured Deklan would do the same, so her hunt for the arch guardian would be tricky. Neva would be with her master like Izia stuck to her. A plan formulated in her mind, and she smiled. Glancing up, Cia plotted a treetop route.

Adrenaline raced through her veins, continuing to fuel her genetic ability. She sank into it like Deklan had instructed, using her new heightened senses to navigate the greenhouse. From her elevated position, she leaped, swung, and ran from tree to tree, ignoring the sting from unused muscles and unfamiliar actions. Below, Izia kept pace. She wished they were bonded enough to communicate. Soon.

A large branch quivered along the back edge of the greenhouse. Strong beams of light scattered through the plates of glass. The air was hotter where she ventured, beading sweat along her skin, dampening her bra and cotton pants. She ignored the perspiration sliding down her spine and gently stepped from one large branch to another. Reaching the suspicious tree, she lay on a stable limb and peered down.

Deklan crouched on a low, sturdy branch. His palm braced on the trunk while he studied the area around him. Neva sat below him. Excitement bubbled through Cia, and she grinned. Gripping the branch tight, she used her weight to swing wide. She released her hold and crashed into him, wrapping her thighs around his waist, she flipped as he let loose a bellow of surprise and pulled him down with her while she reached Neva.

"*Chyvacen'ny*," she said as they all crumpled to the ground. Rolling onto her back, she laid her hand across her belly and laughed.

Izia yipped their victory and danced around. Deklan pushed up onto his hands and knees, groaning. "I see you managed to acknowledge your talent."

She beamed up at him. "No anxiety."

He closed his eyes and dropped his head.

"What?" she asked, rising onto her elbows.

Sighing, he jumped to his feet. "Nothing."

She accepted his hand when he held it out for her. When she was up, he released her and motioned for the dogs to go ahead. Cia brushed away leaves and small branches. She trailed behind Deklan, not knowing her way back to the porch and enjoying the fluid way he moved through the manmade forest. He slowed until they walked together.

"What was it like?" he asked.

"My talent?"

"Yes."

Cia shrugged, pulling a leaf from her hair and flicking it away. "Intense. Like a fire inside me. And everything is *more*."

"We will continue to practice until the sensation is familiar enough to override your panic, and accepting it becomes second nature."

Cia rubbed her hands together, embracing the power. "No one will get the chance to hurt me again."

His large hand rubbed the back of her neck. "No one was going to get the chance anyway. Not unless you run off on your own again."

Cia puffed out a long breath. "Right. So, you'll go with me everywhere now? Like my own personal bodyguard?"

He cast her a sideways look. "You know I won't."

"Then your promise is a want, not reality. You *want* me to always be safe since I'll be in your care, but the reality is, we're individual people and won't always be together. I also want to make sure you're always safe." Oh, how she wanted that, with a fierceness that surprised her. Was that how he felt? Why he made such an irrational oath? "But we're on separate teams, achieving separate goals. It's an unrealistic desire for me as well."

He gave her another curious side glance.

"What?" she asked, defensive.

"Nothing."

Cia stopped and braced her hands on her hips. "You keep saying that, but clearly, there is something."

With his back to her, he stopped and tilted his head back, causing his hair to slide down his back. The slanting sun glinted off the deep red hue. Cia's hands twitched to slip through the silky length. The muscles in his back tensed beneath his damp cotton shirt. Cia took a small step closer, clasping her hands behind her to avoid reaching for him.

"Tell me," she implored.

Without turning to face her, he said, "I look at you, and you're so beautiful and...*young*."

Cia ground her teeth together. *Not this again.* "Deklan—"

"But then you say things that remind me you're not as young as I perceive. You can make adult choices and see the world from a mature perspective."

Cia flexed her jaw in annoyance. "Well, thanks, I guess."

He turned, his gaze dark and unfathomable. Gently, his fingers grazed her jaw to her throat. "And I'm allowed to feel very adult things for you."

She straightened. "Oh..."

"It's messing with my head. You're close in age to my youngest sibling, who I helped learn to walk and eat, and..." He pinched the bridge of his nose. "People are going to talk."

"People would say things regardless of who you contracted with. You're *the Wolvenguard.* I could be the princess of Ruthenia, and they'd still have something snide to remark about."

"Ruthenia doesn't have a princess."

Cia punched his arm. "You know what I mean."

Cracking a smile, he rubbed his left bicep where she'd landed a hit. "Yes, I know. And I'm trying."

"Try harder, arch guardian." She stalked past him and muttered under her breath. "Because your time is up."

20

"WHAT'S THIS?" CIA ASKED, ACCEPTING A FOLDED SHEET of paper from her father. He'd waved her down on her way to her room from a later-than-usual supper.

Henry stuck his hands into his pockets and rocked back on his heels. "A simplified contract."

Cia blinked. "A what?"

He pulled his hands free and signed. "A simple marriage contract. If either of you wish for anything more detailed, you'll have to file another. But this will make you legal for the interim."

Cia unfolded the paper and read over the basic provisions with blank lines for their names, years of agreed upon commitment, and a witness signature, which Henry already provided. Eyes wide, she stared at her father.

"Why?" she asked.

"Because he doesn't know you like I do. I know he wants a promise ceremony, but I also know you've already decided. He can have his ceremony still, and

285

you…" His hands fisted, and he glanced away. "Well, you know."

Cia flushed and refolded the contract. She waited until he had the nerve to meet her gaze again. "Can be my impetuous self?"

"Can be confident in your place in his life."

Cia reached for her father's hand and squeezed, ensuring he was looking at her. "I already am."

He leaned forward and pressed a gentle kiss to her forehead. "He will be a good mate."

A jolt of uneasiness rolled through her. "But will I be a good mate for him?"

"Why wouldn't you be? Yes, you're young, but you will grow together if you remember to be patient and compromise with each other."

She ran her fingers along the longest fold. "I'm not sure about… a family."

"Why not?" he asked, his motions quick.

She shrugged and sniffed away the burn of tears.

Henry sighed and drew her into a firm hug. "Lucianna, do not let one evil event rob you of the beauty of a family. Do not give them so much power over your future."

Cia clung to her father, the paper crumpling in her grip. She wanted to ask how she'd survive such a loss, how he'd managed to keep going, even for her. But he'd hear none of her questions, so she held tight until the worst of the fear subsided. Pulling away, she swiped at an errant tear. He squeezed her shoulders.

"When you're ready, you'll know. Don't put any pressure on yourself or your relationship. All will happen as it's meant to, in time," he encouraged.

Cia nodded. "Thank you."

"I'm going to stay at Terravine. You're safe here, and

I'm assuming you'll be a married woman in a few hours." He touched her chin, smiling, a sheen of tears brightening his eyes. "You don't need your father hanging around."

Cia regarded him, returning his watery smile. "I will always need my dad."

"Then you'll know where to find me."

After placing the contract in a safe place, Cia helped Henry pack what little he'd brought and load a waiting carriage to Grayson and Amari Dossett's manor house. The shield guardian's residence had become their second home, and Cia was thankful her father would be going somewhere secure and familiar. She waved as the carriage pulled from the curb and headed down the wide, vacant street. The only vehicles that ventured into the Arch District were those invited.

Returning to her room, she steeled her nerves for the night to come. She bathed, dressed in a robe with nothing underneath, found the contract, and then sat on her bed and waited. Hopefully, if her plan went accordingly, this would be the last night she called the room hers. Edginess made her leg bounce. Long shadows blanketed her room. Not much longer. Most of the staff left at sunset to beat home the cold of night, and Phin retreated to his rooms after checking in with Deklan. Cia needed only to wait until she heard Phin's retreating steps. The evening was between her and Deklan alone.

Finally, night descended in quiet darkness. Her room nothing more than shadows. Determined, Cia rose, tightened the sash of her robe, and headed down the hall, lit by two lone lamps. The dark stairs to Deklan's quarters loomed. At the bottom, she looked up. Faint golden light illuminated the wide opening and the landing. No sound filtered to her. She pressed her lips together, her fingers tightening on the contract until the paper crinkled. The thing wouldn't sign itself.

Cia bounded up the steps, clutching the length of her robe in her free hand to keep from tripping. At the top, she paused to get her bearings. She stood in an entrance of sorts. In front of her, double glass doors led to an open balcony overlooking the greenhouse. Glass panels were open above, letting in the cool night air. In warmer months, she imagined he left the doors open. The end of his spacious bed was visible to the left, along with three curious wolves staring at her from behind a wide gate.

To her right was a sitting area, and in the upper right corner, Deklan sat with his back to her, working at a desk. She entered the sitting room, her fingers brushing over the simple, practical leather chair. Two couches big enough for three were angled around a wide wooden table. Bookcases lined the wall, and a huge ornamental rug held warmth and added a touch of color to the otherwise masculine space. A beautiful slate hearth had a wood stove. The rich gray stone went to the ceiling and formed a raised base large enough to sit in front of if one wanted. No paintings or drawings hung from the sage green walls. The entire right half of the room was open to the house below. The area was essentially a giant loft. Cia wondered if Deklan saw the space as his or as all the other Wolvenguards before him: a temporary home.

A board creaked as she eased closer to him. His shoulders tensed, but he didn't look to stop his work. "What did you forget, Phin?"

"Hopefully nothing, that'd be awkward later," Cia said, smiling.

He spun around, gripping the back of the chair in a tight fist. "What in the arctic?"

Her smile held even as courage threatened to desert her. Raising the contract, she waved the paper back and forth. "You agreed to marry me."

"Now?" he asked in disbelief, his eyes wide.

"Yes."

"But we also agreed to wait a week for a promise ceremony."

She licked her lips, thrilled at how his attention strayed to her lips, and his grip tightened on the chair until the wood groaned. Emboldened by his reaction, she slowly crossed the space between them, sliding the folded slip of paper between her fingers. "See, here's the thing, I don't want to wait any longer to be your mate. I'm fine signing the contract the night we make our promises before our family, as agreed, but I'm not leaving your room tonight. So, it's up to you. Sign or wait? Either way, we'll be bound. One by Sziverian standards, one by Ruthenian. Do you want to be both, or is one enough?"

"Cia..."

Good thing she'd prepared for his reluctance. Cia might not be an experienced seductress, but collecting erotic content for her informants over the past few months had helped her learn a great deal about human longings. In every instance, they preferred the object of their desire to be naked. Aroused. Evocative. The most primal of needs on display for visual excitement. Which is where Cia wanted Deklan. Excited like her. Not uncertain. She *ached* for him. A persistent throb she knew intuitively only he could relieve for her.

She set the contract in front of him and untied her

robe. The edges fell open, and she raised a brow. "Well?"

DEKLAN'S TONGUE STUCK TO THE ROOF OF HIS MOUTH. The wall lamps above his desk glowed off Cia's exposed dusky peach skin. The robe gaped, and the edges caught on the gentle swell of her breasts. His fingers twitched to draw a line from the center of her chest down the flat plane of her stomach, over her little belly bottom to the exposed thatch of trimmed dark hair. Lust shot hard in his groin. A dark shadow drew a line between her thighs, pressed close in her obvious nervousness. Yet she stood daring before him, her hand trailing a shaky path along the lapel near her collarbone.

Pressing his index finger to the contract, he dragged it closer, never taking his eyes off her. "Will you always demand to get your way?" he asked softly.

Red blossomed across her already rosy cheeks. "Probably."

And he would *probably* give in whenever feasible. "You promise you won't regret not waiting?"

She licked those deliciously full lips of hers again, and the rest of his blood fled his brain. Then she blew his mind, perching on the edge of his desk, her legs falling open until the heart of her was exposed. "I might not know much about sex, but I've been this way since you kissed me in the greenhouse. You tell me, will I regret waiting?"

Deklan couldn't stop from touching her delicate, glistening flesh. She gasped, her legs opening further. He groaned. "You want me."

"Yes," she breathed. "Please don't make me wait any longer."

He somehow stopped touching her long enough to open the simple contract, already signed by her and Henry. He didn't contemplate the legality since no one would ever know it hadn't been done at the same time. He scrawled his name on the appropriate line. Then he dragged her onto his lap. She straddled him, her fingers tangling in his hair, her gaze searching his.

"No going back," he whispered against her mouth.

"Never."

The smooth skin of her rear filled his palms. He stood, and she locked her ankles around his waist. Deklan had never imagined he'd have a true marriage night. Ruthenians had different mating rituals, and taking a Sziverian had never been in his future. To have a Ruthenian mate partaking in Sziverian tradition was almost overwhelming. The first night of the rest of their life was about to happen. He paused before he crossed into his bedroom area.

She leaned back. "What is it?"

"The wolves."

"What about them?"

Deklan couldn't help laughing. "Do you want six eyes on us?"

She glanced over her shoulder and bit her lip. "Not really, but I want to be in your bed."

Reluctant to let her go, he eased her down his front. "I'll put them on the porch."

She stepped off to the side, keeping the path open to the balcony doors. "I guess I should be thankful this seems to be a new problem for you."

"I've never had a woman in my rooms."

She pulled the edges of her robe together and crossed her arms. "Never?"

Deklan went and released his wolves, calling over his shoulder. "You will be the only woman ever in here while this is my home."

A slow smile brightened her eyes. "The only woman ever. I like that."

Deklan did, too. Cool evening air swept inside as he opened the door to let out his small pack. Nikita whined and hesitated at the door. Deklan bumped his rump with his shin, urging the wolf outside with the others. Neva snapped at his jaw in reprisal. He growled in turn, and Deklan closed the door on their tussle. They rolled and bit, fur smooshing against the glass panels.

Cia stepped forward, perplexed. "Will they be okay?"

"Yes." He grasped her hips and pulled her into his body. Walking backward, he nipped at her lips and jaw. "You are sure? Last time I'm going to ask."

"I am so sure," she breathed, her hands sliding under his untucked shirt. She paused when they reached the edge of his bed, her fingers pressed into his flanks. Only the faint glow from a lamp in the wolves' den lit the open space of his room. Heavy shadows moved over her face, obscuring most of her expression from him. "What about you? I don't want you to second guess or regret, either."

Deklan smoothed his hands over both her cheeks into her silken hair, tilting her head back until he could meet her gaze. "I might worry for a time about all the experiences you'll miss."

Her fingers trailed a delicate path from his hips to his spine and back. "Like what?"

He lowered his head until his lips almost touched hers. "Stealing kisses at a party in the dark in a greenhouse."

"Then steal them from me the next party we attend. Drag me into the dark." A small smile curled her lips against his. "And we won't have to stop at just a kiss. What else?"

Coherent thought eluded him again, stuttering to a full stop with images of them tangled together in a clandestine tryst at some future party. Rushed and quiet, their passions unstoppable even with the threat of discovery. "You'd... do that?"

She pressed closer. "Have you ever?"

He shook his head.

"Then we'd have a new experience together. I want to have lots of them with you."

He closed his eyes and rested his forehead on hers. "I do, too."

"Good." She brushed her mouth to his in a slow, sweet kiss.

Deklan cupped her jaw, holding her for the kiss he really wanted. Devouring and claiming, taking them from gentle to outright surrender in long, deep pulls. Her body shivered against his, trying to move closer. Deklan spun them around and knocked her legs out from under her, sending her crashing to the bed. He followed, careful not to land on her, bracing his weight on his knees and forearms over her.

Delighted laughter escaped her into his mouth. Her knees parted to cradle his hips. He rocked against her, pleased when she mimicked the motion, her giggle becoming a gasp. Wrapping his arms underneath her shoulders, he held her to his chest, deepening their kiss once more. Her tongue slid along his as she writhed and wiggled beneath him until he worried they wouldn't even make it to the real thing.

The front of his thin cotton pants became damp with her desire, and he groaned, pulling his mouth free. No one had ever wanted him with such abandon, and the knowledge empowered him. He needed to touch her. Lifting his hips enough to slide his hand between them, he cupped her sex, his fingers caressing through her slick, swollen folds. Damn, she was so ready. Her hips lifted in a silent plea. Cold air brushed his butt. While he'd been distracted discovering how wet she was for him, she'd used her feet to push down his pants.

"Too fast," he whispered.

"Not fast enough," she argued, arching beneath him. "We have… forever. It's okay if we rush this time, right?"

Deklan gritted his teeth. His body screamed *yes* while his mind urged him to take things slow, to make sure her first time wasn't disappointing. He rose higher, looking down at her now mostly exposed body. The robe pooled on either side of her, framing her stunning curves. He wanted to touch and taste every inch of her. Find out what made her desperate for more. Discover with her what made her scream in pleasure. An unintelligible sound left him as her cool fingers wrapped around his hard length.

"Wow," she breathed, exploring his shape. She wiggled until her feet were braced on his hips. "I need to see."

Deklan stood, allowing his pants to fall the rest of the way off. He stepped free of them and shucked his shirt. Cia rose onto her knees and tossed the robe aside. Reaching for him, her hands trembled. He moved until his thighs touched the edge of the mattress but remained standing, allowing her to take in his much larger body. Her hands smoothed over his shoulders, biceps, and pecs to trace the line of hair to his groin. Instead of grasping him again, she kept going, touching his thighs and up to his hips. A trail of electricity followed her touch, like little arcs of lightning everywhere she explored. Deklan rolled his shoulders, taking her questing bond deep into himself.

"You are so beautiful," she said.

"Men aren't beautiful," he muttered, unable to stop from brushing his fingers across her pebbled nipples.

She inhaled and glanced down. "Do that again."

He complied, only went a step further, leaning over and taking her breast into his mouth. She shouted in surprise and would have fallen back if he hadn't wrapped his arms around her waist to support her. Needing to be closer to her again, he eased her back onto the mattress, continuing to lavish attention on her breasts with his tongue and teeth until she bucked in demand beneath him. Deklan slipped his hand between her legs again, not surprised when his fingers slid from her clit to her opening without any resistance. He stroked her, dipping the tips of his fingers into her just enough to make her pant for more. The more frenzied she became, the more her bond crackled along his nerves. Soon, his fingers became coated in her need, and he couldn't wait any longer.

Taking himself in hand, he eased into her tightness. Sweat beaded along his hairline and gathered between his tense shoulders. She grabbed his biceps, her nails biting into his muscles.

"Oh, oh," she gasped, her body tensing.

"Relax," he whispered into her ear and licked down her jaw to her neck.

She moved her head to give him better access. "How?"

Slowly, he rolled his hips, seating himself a little deeper in small increments. "Does it hurt?"

She pulled her knees up further and wiggled. "It's... not really pain, just weird."

Deklan paused and looked at her. "Weird?"

"Don't stop!"

He went a little deeper.

"Not bad weird, just new weird," she clarified, her words stuttered and breathless.

New and unfamiliar, he could handle. He knew a woman's first time wasn't always a great experience, no matter how good a lover a man could potentially be for her because of the pain. But he also knew every time after this would be different.

"I'll try to go slow," he gritted, moving until fully seated.

"I-I'm okay," she said, pressing her feet into the backs of his thighs. "I want to know you. It's okay."

He tested her words, easing back and thrusting forward. Her eyes widened, and her breath hitched. Not in pain. He did it again, aroused further by how slick she remained, how tight she fit around him until he wondered how long he could truly make this last for her. He pressed his hand under her hip and angled her to take more of him. She cried out, her nails digging into his arms. Her inner muscles clenched and worked him, taking him even deeper until his eyes almost rolled into the back of his head. Deklan increased his movements, paying close attention to her body language, to how she moved, seeking more and giving her all he could.

She exploded beneath him in a rush of wet heat, her

body tense, eyes squeezed shut, breath held. He moved faster, taking her higher until her breath left her on a ragged scream. Her hips bucked, her inner muscles spasmed, forcing his pleasure to mount, and he could no longer hold back. Hugging her to his chest, he let his release flow free. A sudden punch of energy took him by surprise.

Invisible threads wove between them. Heat built everywhere they touched. She trembled in his arms, her legs tightening around his waist. The echoes of her fading release whispered along his nerves, and he rose, staring at her in shock. The same disbelief widened her eyes.

"You feel that, too?" he asked.

She blinked and then shoved at his shoulders. "Let me up, let me up!"

Surprised by her sudden urge to leave his bed, he didn't move fast enough for her. She wiggled and pushed until he fell to the side, pulling free of the warm glove of her body. The loss made her grimace, and she glanced at his erection, dark and glistening in the low light. She reached for it, then shook her head and jumped to her feet on the mattress. She spun around.

"Is it there?" she asked, glancing over her shoulder at him.

Deklan forgot to breathe. His wolf tattoo covered her entire back, from the top of her shoulders to the sensual curve of her lower spine. *His mate.* "Yes."

She squealed and bounced off the bed, running to his bathroom. Deklan followed, lighting one of the wall lamps and then grabbing two hand towels. He dampened them while she twisted and turned in front of the mirror over the sink, scowling.

"I can't see all of it," she said, disappointed.

Deklan laid a towel on the tile counter and then hoisted her up. He gathered her hair over her shoulder and handed her his shaving mirror. Tears glistened as she took in the detailed work of art now gracing her body.

"Oh, Deklan, it's stunning."

"Yes," he agreed, his eyes never leaving her face.

While she stared into the mirror, he gently cleaned them both. He tossed the wet cloths into the tub. The cool washcloth had done nothing to ease his still rampant desire for her. Her back muscles made the tattoo reflection roll and dip as she moved to take in all the angles from her perch. The sensual motion fascinated him.

"Are you sore?" he breathed.

She wiggled. "Not too bad, why?"

He caressed her thighs to her hips and dragged her butt to the counter's edge. "I'm not done with you."

WARMTH CASCADED THROUGH CIA'S VEINS. HER ALREADY heightened nerves danced with new desire. Sex had been... *fantastic.* So much more than she could have ever imagined. That he wanted her again, now, when they'd barely caught their breath and sweat still clung to their skin, thrilled and excited her. Earlier, she'd been curious about what he felt when he touched her, and she'd wanted to learn how he'd feel once they'd finished. If she hadn't wanted to see her newly transferred tattoo, she would have stroked him. She wondered if these urges were normal or taboo.

She looked at her husband, her mate, bound to her. A new thrill raced through her body. He stared down, his hands kneading her thighs, his gaze transfixed. She followed his line of sight and flushed when she realized he stared at her sex. Damp curls glistened between her spread thighs. Transfixed, she watched as he slid his thumb along her clit. Pleasure burst from the contact, and she trembled, wanting more. He kept a slow pressure, working a finger within her.

"Does that hurt?" he asked, his words gruff.

Cia closed her eyes and took stock of how she felt. "I'm a little tender."

He pushed in a second finger, gliding them in and out while continuing the blissful motion on her sensitive nub. "Too much?"

"N-no," she moaned, parting her thighs further. "Feels... so... good."

His mouth captured hers for a long, wet kiss that only added to the mounting sensations at her center. The ecstasy she'd known earlier mounted again, a feverish, desperate pinnacle she needed to crest like she needed to take her next breath. She whimpered urgently, rocking her hips in sync with his skilled hand. In her mind, she screamed *oh yes, yes!* In reality, she could do little more than form incoherent guttural noises. Perhaps later, she'd be embarrassed. Or perhaps she'd give him one of those secret smiles she saw so often between the partners in her life. The ones she now understood meant *I know what you look like in the throes, and I can't wait to get you there again.* Oh yes... she'd do that.

She moaned his name. A plea for more or an end, she wasn't sure. When his hard length pressed into her, she almost melted into a puddle on the counter. Oh, summer sun, he felt amazing. He grasped the back of her neck and thigh, holding both so strongly she could do nothing more than take the carnal thrusts within her.

Panting, he breathed Ruthenian partnered with erotic words into her ear. Her body coiled and tightened. She would never have expected she'd enjoy hearing how she felt, how they looked while being pumped into, but from his mouth? An orgasm spiraled through her body. Evidently, they brought her to the tipping point and pushed her over.

Breathless and curious, she leaned back enough to look down. She watched as he disappeared inside her, only to slide back out, slick from her spent desire, thick from his own. Another burst of pleasure had her squeezing her eyes closed and throwing her head back. He growled and pumped harder, his damp chest pressing to hers. The soft hairs on his pecs teased her sensitive nipples, and she found herself grinding against him, trying to help him achieve what she'd already managed as yet another shattering orgasm claimed her. She screamed his name, a demand to join her.

Then it happened… he jerked and thrust hard, heat pouring into her while a flutter of satisfaction brushed her nerves. His release made real along their bond. She wrapped her arms around him and held tight, gasping for air. Her heart swelled as he returned her hug, squeezing like she was the same lifeline he was to her.

"I can't believe you were going to make me wait for that," she grumbled.

He laughed and leaned back enough to grasp her face. He swept damp hairs clinging to her temples back and kissed her. "Should I thank you?"

She swept her hands over his shoulders to his chest and patted his sweaty skin. "I think you've compensated enough. No thanks necessary."

He growled, pulled free of her, and tossed her over

his shoulder faster than she could react. She squealed and laughed as he swatted her butt and tossed her onto the bed. Legs and arms spread, she landed in the middle of the messy sheets. Another laughing shriek left her as he launched himself at her.

His large body covered hers. "Then allow me to continue to show my gratitude, wife."

21

CIA STARED AT THE DARK WOOD OF CAIDON AND RAMSEY Survaine's apartment door. The entrance was one of many in a wide, long corridor lined with beautiful paintings of Sziverian's natural wonders and padded blue carpet. The musky scent of age permeated the air. Nerves danced in her stomach. Answers might be found on the other side of this door, yet she couldn't bring herself to knock.

Part of her longed to still be in bed with Deklan, warm and treasured in his arms. While they hadn't made love again, something she didn't understand until she'd awoken this morning, hurting in places she didn't know could hurt, he'd still shown her a passion she hadn't known existed. When morning light had arrived, she'd been worried about being embarrassed by all they'd done. But awakening in his bed as his mate, with the wolves restless for their morning routine, had felt right.

"Go on," the man of her thoughts urged. Izia nudged the back of her knee.

The tomes she'd stolen from Joel Blackbain felt heavy in her grasp. "What if she can't read them?"

"She might not be able to right away, but given time, she will. That's how her talent works."

And then Ramsey might open the book and know immediately what every line contained. Answers could be Cia's the moment she dared to knock on a stranger's door. Deklan's arm snaked around and rapped a rapid staccato on the door.

"Hey!" she cried, pressing the journals to her chest.

His hand settled on her back. "Your impulsiveness rubbed off on me."

"Great timing," she mumbled.

He squeezed her hip. "Frustrating, isn't it?"

Cia resisted punching him in the stomach. The door swung open, revealing a man not much taller than her, with broad shoulders, damp black hair, arresting emerald green eyes, and built like her husband. A fact she couldn't help noticing since he wore no shirt and his pants weren't buttoned. She blinked.

"Yes?" Caidon asked, unabashed about his lack of clothing.

Deklan moved Cia to the side when she continued to stare at the assassin. "We're here to see your wife, Ramsey. Ryan Voklane sent us to ask for her assistance in deciphering some ledgers."

"Come in," he said, opening the door the rest of the way and heading down a long corridor.

Deklan followed first with Izia behind. Cia closed the door and took in the dim interior. The corridor forked to open into additional hallways to the left and right and straight into a spacious living area. Well-worn couches, chairs, rugs, and mismatched shelves of books filled the room. Sweet orange and spicy cinnamon scented the air. Floor-to-ceiling windows let in midmorning light and helped the plants hanging from the ceiling and potted on the floor thrive.

The apartment was massive and yet cozy. Lived in and reflecting the generations of families painted in an elaborate family tree on the wall leading to a large dining room. Cia was drawn to the detailed depiction of ancestors one family refused to be separated from. These people never wanted to forget where they came from. She noted Caidon's name, bound with Ramsey almost two years ago. Four other Survaines had yet to meet their mates, one close to her age, the other three too young for marriage. Though Cia was confident Henry had never met Christopher, she was aware of the other assassin. Just as she knew about Katria's father, Aleksandrov Nachemir.

"Isn't it wonderful?" a woman asked, coming to stand beside Cia. "I did the same thing the first time Caidon brought me here." She brushed her fingers over their names. "Someday, our children will branch from this tree, names never to be forgotten."

"It's amazing," Cia agreed.

She glanced at Ramsey. Coiled black curls were secured in a messy bun ponytail combination. A few escaped to frame a round, pretty face. A fluffy pale pink robe covered her from neck to toe, but there was no hiding the woman had generous hips.

Caidon stepped in behind his wife and wrapped his arms around her. "They need you to look at something. Ryan sent them."

Ramsey's brows rose. "Oh? How exciting." Her violet gaze met Cia's. "Do you think I have time to finish breakfast? My nephews stayed with us last night, and they'll be waking up hungry any minute now.

We're lucky the room they're sleeping in has no windows."

Cia looked at Deklan, who shrugged, hands in his pockets. "We're in no rush."

"Do you need any help?" Cia asked.

Ramsey smiled. "I won't say no."

In the kitchen, Ramsey set a bowl of shredded potatoes in front of Cia, along with the vegetables she wanted chopped to be added to a batter she'd mix the potatoes in and then fry. Onions, garlic, green peppers, and something leafy and green. While Cia chopped the vegetables, Ramsey coated the bread in butter and then pressed each side onto a plate with spiced sugar. The slices would be grilled in a pan, caramelizing the sugar, while the seasoned potato cakes were fried. All of it smelled heavenly already. A simple, comforting Sziverian breakfast.

Once Cia finished with the vegetables, Ramsey gave her peaches to cut into small portions. Caidon entered the kitchen, fully dressed, the cutest baby boy she'd ever seen perched on his hip. Blond hair curled around his ears, and dark blue eyes took in the kitchen with bright curiosity. He gnawed on his fist, drool coating a bib tied around his neck. Behind Caidon's legs, a young boy peeked around. Cia smiled at him, and he hid, clutching at Caidon's pants.

"Oh, there are my sweet boys! Good morning, Parker and Adrian!" Ramsey proclaimed, clapping her hands and reaching for the baby. The infant grinned and shrieked, waving his drool-soaked hands. Ramsey danced to the peaches Cia cut, picking up a small chunk. "Look what Auntie Ramsey made sure we had this morning. Mamma says they're your favorite."

The baby's eyes crossed as he tried to focus on the

sticky chunk of fruit held between Ramsey's fingers. Ramsey didn't give him any time to figure out if he was happy with her offering. She tucked it between his toothless gums and made happy eating sounds. His tiny arms flapped, and he squealed again, gumming at the soft fruit.

"See? Yum, yum!" She looked at the other boy. "Do you want some peaches, Parker?"

Parker peered out from behind Caidon's legs but didn't answer. Ramsey shrugged and went back to cooking. Before Adrian could tangle his hands in her hair, Caidon plucked him from her hip and tossed him in the air. The back and forth was so natural between them. A domestic dance they'd done before.

Cia glanced at the doorway and found Deklan watching the pair with a barely contained mask of longing. A pang tightened in her chest, from his expression or his bond, she wasn't sure. Either way, she realized his desire for a family was genuine. And from what she understood, he'd had no hope of ever finding the contentment of raising his own children. She, his mate, would gift their union with life if she could find the courage to bear a family in a world full of hurt and danger. Cia chewed on her bottom lip and returned to her peach slicing. Such deep thoughts were not welcome during breakfast prep.

Caidon ushered Parker into the dining room and set the baby into a high chair. She and Ramsey finished the cooking and plated everything to serve. Deklan stepped in sans a wolf, and Cia glanced around in alarm.

"Where's Izia?" she asked.

Deklan took two plates. "The boy panicked when he saw him. Caidon showed me to their small greenhouse. He's in there not freaking out children."

Cia frowned. "Poor Izia."

"He's fine. Lots of new scents and dark spaces for him to investigate." He leaned forward and whispered, "And mark."

Cia snorted, trying to contain a snicker. "Naughty."

His gaze heated. Lust seared across their bond. "I'm discovering I enjoy naughty."

Memories of their erotic moment on his bathroom counter flitted through her mind, making her want to squirm. Warmth suffused her cheeks, and she almost forgot they were standing in a stranger's kitchen. "This new you is going to take some getting used to."

"Not new," he whispered, pressing a chaste kiss to her lips. "Just exposed."

She grinned. "I like you exposed."

"If you are done with the newly married flirtations," Ramsey interrupted, good humor lightening her words, "our food is getting cold."

"Oh!" Cia started, equal parts embarrassment and mischief making her flushed cheeks burn. "Sorry."

"No worries." Ramsey laughed. "We aren't any better."

They ate, with both Ramsey and Caidon getting the kids to partake. A ritual Cia was familiar with thanks to Uncle Vayden, his young daughter, and three nieces. She waited until the kids were content to play or consume their food without adult assistance.

Pushing a peach slice with her fork, Cia asked, "How did you know we're married?"

"Aside from the wolf ears peeking out from the neckline on your back?" Ramsey asked, her violet eyes twinkling.

Cia gasped and touched the back of her neck. She'd had the oddest urge to wear a backless shirt, which she didn't own, to show off her new markings. Instead, she'd found a loose teal sweater that practically slid off her shoulders, playing peek-a-boo with the top edge of the tattoo.

Ramsey hitched her shoulder in Deklan's direction. "Pretty sure that's his. Plus, the little morning kitchen whispers gave you away. My brother and his wife were ridiculous after their marriage. I think it's a requirement."

Deklan laughed. Cia flushed, unsure how to feel about them being so... mushy. She didn't consider herself a romantic, but looking back on their recent behavior, she couldn't disagree they'd been the epitome of *sweet*. Since Deklan didn't seem bothered, Cia decided not to worry about their unprofessional conduct.

"Where's the rest of your family?" Deklan asked Caidon.

Caidon took a sip of tea before answering. "In Ruthenia. Until the..." He slid a glance at Cia, frowning. "Assassin threat is handled my sisters aren't allowed to return to Sziveria. He and my mother can only tolerate so many months apart."

Appetite gone, Cia picked up her plate and stood. "I can understand that. It's nice he has such an option."

"My paternal grandparents live there and accepted my mother. I am thankful they have a way to stay safe. My younger sisters are enjoying the cultural differences of Ruthenian society."

Ramsey gathered her and Caidon's empty dishes. "Let me take these to the kitchen, and I'll look at your books."

Caidon accepted a quick kiss from his wife and then turned his attention to convincing a now fussing Adrian to finish eating. Deklan helped before Cia could, clearing the rest of the table. Adrian shrieked and threw a peach chunk. The yellow fruit landed with a splat in front of Cia. She popped the fruit into her mouth and made happy noises. Adrian stilled, his dark blue eyes wide, his little hands fisted. He squealed again and picked up two handfuls of peach. Sticky juice oozed between his fingers. Caidon held one hand back while the little one shoveled fruit into his mouth. Apparently, he didn't like *his* food being consumed by someone else, even if he threw it away.

Parker slipped from the table and ran from the room. Caidon leaned back, watching, and shook his head. "Do you mind keeping an eye on little man here?"

"No, I don't mind."

Cia stood and moved to the seat next to Adrian. The baby went still again, his gaze turning owlish. She wondered how he did with strangers. If he'd be a screamer or an accepter of someone new. Fear of an unfamiliar person outweighed their innate curiosity, with most babies she had limited experience around. Adrian smacked his tiny lips and held his sticky fingers out to her, offering to share bits of peach. Laughing, Cia accepted the baby's offer, nibbling on his tiny hand and making snorting sounds, to his delight. He laughed, a squeal of joy, his chubby legs kicking underneath the tray.

A curious warmth spread through her. At first, she thought it was happiness to experience and participate in such innocence. To be reminded life didn't have to be horrific, but full of promise. Hope endured even the bleakest of heartaches. But the warmth grew, spreading through her entire body like honey. Viscous and sweet.

Gasping, Cia looked over her shoulder. Deklan watched her with unrestrained hunger.

You'd make a beautiful mother whispered through her as though on a balmy breeze.

The words were lovely, and she should have felt cherished, as he probably meant, but when she realized he'd just spoken to her without moving his mouth, in secret, all she could think was, *stars above, we're going to be unstoppable.*

"Okay," Ramsey said, her hands brushing the pages, "this one is a list of, well, I guess operatives would be the best word and their roles. Drivers, ship captains, bankers, record keepers, messengers, guards, drug brokers—"

"Assassins," Cia breathed, sliding to the edge of the couch cushion. "Are any listed?"

"Summer sun," Ramsey breathed, her horrified gaze locking on her husband, "this is a complete dossier of everyone involved in the V Alliance. Records keepers..."

"We knew they did," Caidon said. "There was no way for them to erase Parker's existence without help."

"Jonathon is going to be so upset," Ramsey whispered. "How many crimes has he tried to solve only for them to disappear? Now we have proof, complete proof, someone is behind it all."

Cia didn't know much about how the Records Department worked, only that different branches handled all the paperwork for the entire nation. From storing evidence logs to birth accounts and land titles to guardianship endowments. They not only had an incredible amount of responsibility but also of control.

One bad keeper... Cia's contract with Deklan could vanish forever. One bad keeper with a motive? A tremor of dread raced up her spine. They could do irreparable damage.

"Have they managed to falsify a ranked guardianship?" Cia asked, bracing her elbows on her knees.

Deklan shook his head. "Not that we're aware of. They've attempted to manipulate people into powerful rankings but haven't stolen one outright. Yet."

"I don't think they can. They'd also have to coordinate with the officials who release the annual Directory of Ranked Guardians. If they don't have their cooperation, the fraud would be immediately removed and detained," Caidon said.

"Still," Cia said, "it has to be a temptation they won't be able to hold out for much longer."

"We know they've managed to corrupt a few ranked guardians," Deklan said. "I don't think they're desperate enough to forge one, considering it'd have to be a low-ranking guardianship to go unnoticed for a year."

"I think stealing vital family histories is awful enough," Ramsey said, her gaze dark. "And who knows how many people they've done this to. How many families they've destroyed that no one will ever know any better because they're just... gone."

The vulnerability of that statement left them all quiet. No one was immune from such a devious scheme. Everyone sitting around the dossier had a record of birth on file. A marriage contract. If the V Alliance stole Cia away tomorrow, as they'd planned, they could erase her from Sziverian history. Everyone who knew her could be convinced they were crazy for saying she existed. Had that been the plan at the beginning? Had Uncle Vayden found her in time, rescuing her from more than being stolen from her father? The thought had panic burning in her gut.

A masculine hand engulfed hers. A tether pulling her from the mire of dark thoughts. Blinking, she looked at Deklan. He threaded his fingers through hers and squeezed. She took a calming breath and returned the gesture. She was safe. Had he experienced her anxiety through their bond? This new thing between them was wild. So many questions formed, and she couldn't wait until they were alone to ask.

"Can you write the translations in the book? Is there room?" Deklan asked Ramsey. His thumb stroked a soothing pattern on the back of Cia's hand.

"Not unless I write small. I'll transfer the information to a new journal."

"I can help," Cia offered.

"That'd be great," Caidon said before Ramsey could answer. "If someone is watching us or you, the less interaction we have between us, the better."

Ramsey hopped up to get a new notebook while Deklan checked on Izia. Caidon followed to make sure the boys were okay. The moment Ramsey returned, they set to work. Cia had to be careful not to pay too close attention to who Ramsey called out so she wouldn't lose focus. She knew, *knew*, the identity of her family's killer was within the book. At some point, Izia lay at her feet. The men were either with the kids or off talking somewhere else. Cia brushed her fingers along the wolf's soft fur.

"What's it like?" Ramsey asked while waiting for Cia to finish writing.

"What?"

"Having all the wolves around."

Cia glanced up. "I don't know yet. Deklan was separated from two of them when we met, and I've only lived in his house a few days."

Ramsey smiled. "Crazy how fast things can move, huh?"

Cia grinned. "Very. But so far, it's been fun."

They continued working. Lunch appeared on the table for them, but neither Caidon nor Deklan interrupted their flow. By the time they finished, the sun was low, casting rich golden rays into the apartment. The second book had turned out to be radio transmission numbers, as suspected, and Ramsey wrote the translated names into the margins, making the process faster.

When they finished, Cia flipped through the pages. "So many people."

Ramsey pointed to the right side of the page. "Yes, but look, not all of them are in Sziveria."

"And this was one of six books I grabbed."

"They were all the same?"

"Looked to be."

Ramsey shook her head. "We can only hope they were duplicates, maybe for other members."

"Is there any order? Like alphabetical, to know if we're missing more information?"

"Not that I can tell. And all the skills you'd need to run an evil empire are listed." Triumph brightened Ramsey's pretty face. "We're finally ahead. You have no idea what this means."

Cia knew precisely what it meant. She was one step closer to finally knowing the truth. To making her risks worth the chances taken. To justice, not only for herself but all the families ripped apart by someone else's agenda.

"Thank you," Cia said, putting all her emotions into the meager words.

Ramsey touched her hand and gave a weak, almost sad smile. "No need to thank me. I'm as eager for this information as you."

Deklan's scent reached her before he did. A thrill zipped through her. He moved behind her and rested his hands on her shoulders. "About finished?"

"Yes," Cia said. She held the completed book out to him.

He straightened and accepted the journal. "Did you find him?"

"I haven't looked," she whispered.

"Why?"

She shrugged. No answers came to her other than the moment she knew she'd feel obligated to act.

Deklan searched her gaze. "Worried you'll do something rash?"

"Maybe," she drew out, unsurprised he'd read her so well.

He brushed his fingers along her jaw before opening the book. "I'm proud of you."

"Even with a name, how will I find him? I know nothing about investigating."

"You did a decent job to get to New Columbia."

"I used information from others."

"That's all investigating is. Searching for information, usually provided by interviews." He returned his attention to the journal. "You didn't notice a name when you were helping?"

"I didn't concentrate on what she was saying specifically, so I didn't get distracted."

"Gotcha," he whispered, and Cia rose onto her knees to face him.

"He's there?"

Deklan flipped the book around and tapped his index finger over a name. "Berk Pherson."

Cia snatched the book and stared at the unassuming name. She'd expected a monstrous name to match a fiend. She waved a frantic hand behind herself. "Is he in the book? Ramsey, did you see a Berk Pherson in the radio book?"

"I don't… hold on…" Ramsey murmured.

Pages flipped. Izia whined a long, drawn-out string of sound. Sensing her excitement? Cia twisted on the couch and flopped to her butt. She wanted to grab the list and search for herself.

Ramsey blew out a long breath. She closed the book and handed it over. "No, I don't see his name in here. But you're welcome to look on your own."

Cia held all three of the journals to her chest. "I will. Thank you again so much."

Ramsey smiled. "No, thank you. Just be sure to somehow inform Ryan discretely. If you leave from here and go see him…"

"Someone will know we've discovered something important," Cia filled in.

"Yes." A sparkle lightened Ramsey's violet eyes. "They've had the advantage long enough. Let's finally take the lead, shall we?"

22

Delanee paced the marble floor of her brother's mammoth foyer, a rolled newspaper crinkling in her left hand. Wolvenguard had never been a big, scary place to her. All of the Ralston kids had grown up in the dark mansion, regular visitors to the residing arch guardian. Until Deklan, all the residents had been immigrants from Ruthenia, and her father, Markus, had maintained a friendship with each of them. Neva's claws clicked on the floor. The giant wolf matched Delanee's agitated strides.

When she'd arrived and searched for her treacherous brother, Neva had been staring into the training room from the greenhouse, her amber eyes bright and pleading to come inside. Never one to deny when she could spoil, Delanee had opened the door. Nikita had taken one look at her and bolted into the greenery. Ever playful, the silly dog would be disappointed to learn no one had chased after him. Oh well.

Voices echoed from the back of the house. Delanee stilled and put on her displeased sister face. Izia bounded out from Deklan's office, which meant they'd entered through the garage door. The two wolves did the obligatory greetings of sniffing before Izia moved on to investigate Delanee. He sat, ears twitching, tongue lolling, and waited to be loved.

A young woman walked backward into the foyer, her musical laughter teasing. Izia abandoned his pursuit of affection and bounded to the woman. He pranced around her, taken in by her excitement, adding his yips. The woman brushed her fingers along his fur anytime he glided within touching distance.

"If I win this time, I get to choose the reward," the woman said.

Her brother stalked after her in a predatory lope from his office, a stack of thin books clutched in one of his hands. "Why do I think this reward will benefit both of us?"

Delanee realized this must be the *wife*. Lucianna Castien, now Lucianna Ralston, Arch Guardianess of Wolvenguard. And as a sister, she needed to cut this little foreplay in the bud before it blossomed into something she didn't want to hear or see. Delanee cleared her throat.

Deklan's gaze snapped to her. He reached for his bride. A reaction he probably didn't even realize he'd done when the thunder in Delanee's expression darkened.

Delanee held up the twisted mass of paper clutched in her hand. "I read about your contract in the *Haven City Chronicle*, brother," Delanee gritted out, shaking the tabloid in his direction. "Why did I read about your marriage in another publication?"

"We only filed this morning," Deklan said.

"And you couldn't send me a message? Or drop by

after? Or..." She rolled her hand, leaving out all the other ways her very powerful brother could have notified his family.

His cheeks darkened. "We had somewhere important to be afterward. It didn't cross my mind."

Delanee dug deep for patience. "Do you know how this looks for me? *The Haven City Chronicle... The Chronicle*, Deklan! Beat me to a story about my brother! They are nothing more than a gossip and scandal spread, and I write exclusively for the society pages, which is nothing more than gossip and scandals, and they told Haven City about your marriage first!"

So much for patience. By the end, she seethed, her face hot, her blood boiling, surprised to find no broken glass after her screeching. For years, she'd attempted to prove she was worth more than writing titillating articles on the who's who of Haven City. Delanee wanted to write about things that mattered. She wanted to make a difference with her words. Tackle real problems and highlight actual social changes that need to happen. Like forgotten orphans and their unknown victimization to traffickers. Her big brother and his little bride may have cost her all the ground she'd managed since taking over the section after the death of the previous writer, Cora Dandridge. She hadn't been brave enough to go to the office to discover her editor's fury.

Gritting her teeth, she stomped to Deklan and whacked him on the shoulder with the paper. The action was cathartic enough that she did it until the pages frayed from the abuse. She punctuated each wallop with, "I. Can't. Believe. The. Chronicle. Wrote. About. My. Brother. First."

Exasperated, Deklan snatched the paper from her hand. "Enough!"

"What did they say?" his wife— wife! —asked, reaching around and taking the nearly destroyed tabloid from him. "My mother always enjoyed reading this over coffee. Said everyone's morning should start with a good laugh."

"That's because your mother knew all they wrote was worthless dribble meant to amuse rather than inform," Delanee snapped.

The woman's blue-tinted gray eyes widened. "Oh, how exciting." She smacked the rumpled paper against Deklan's arm. "We may have been tawdry gossip this morning, Deklan!"

"I didn't know there were spies for *Haven City Chronicle* at the records department."

"Informants," Delanee corrected. "Any journalist worth their pay keeps informants on hand for juicy tidbits and research. I will be finding myself a new one after this morning."

"Ohh." Lucianna's twitter morphed into a snicker. She waved her hand. "Listen to this— *We have it on good authority that the beastly master himself has taken a teenage bride.*" She laughed a full-bellied guffaw, slapping Deklan on the arm with the paper again. "They think I'm too young for you, too! Guess I'm the only one who never cared, huh?"

"I told you people would talk," he ground out.

Lucianna shrugged. "People would have talked no matter what. They don't know anything about us."

"They could have," Delanee said. "They could have known exactly what you wanted them to if you'd come to me. I didn't even know you were considering marriage, Deklan."

Lucianna blinked and looked between them. "Oh,

no, he wasn't. I sprang a contract on him last night and then jumped into his bed. End of story."

After landing that on Delanee, the little chit flounced away. "Wha—"

Deklan ran a hand down his face. "So. That was Cia, my wife."

Delanee opened her mouth, made an incoherent sound, tried again, and failed. She took a deep breath and forced focus. "She seduced you? You let a slip of a girl get the best of you? What is she after? Your ranking? Our connections?"

"Cia's an intel guardian under Ryan Voklane. She's not after anything. And *Ahty* convinced me not to let her get away."

"Our father?" Delanee asked in disbelief.

"Yes." Deklan blew out a long breath. "She's full-blooded Ruthenian but raised Sziverian."

"You can—"

Deklan nodded. "Fully bond with her."

And Cia would hold none of the prejudice all the other Ralstons had faced when searching for a mate with whom they could experience full matehood. Delanee hadn't even bothered due to the failures of her older brothers. She'd been too afraid. Sziveria had provided enough rejection and false promises to last a lifetime. She didn't need Ruthenia to do the same. She couldn't fault her brother for wanting what had been unobtainable before his wife.

"Congratulations, then." She chucked his bicep. "I hope you know I'll need a complete interview from you both before I leave. After the fiasco with The Chronicle, I need something to hand to my editor."

Sighing, Deklan ran a hand through his already disheveled hair. He glanced at the books he still held.

"Let me put these away, and I'll meet you in the greenhouse."

Delanee followed him instead of heading to the greenhouse. A cowardly course, perhaps, but she wasn't ready to spend time alone with his stranger of a wife. "What are those?"

"Something I need to try to figure out how to get to Voklane."

"I can do that," she said before she could stop herself. Somehow, she wiped the shocked expression from her face before Deklan turned around with one of his own. Had she really offered to meet with Voklane? Yes, she had.

"If you're seen leaving here and going to him, it will look just as obvious we've found something important."

Delanee kept her eagerness contained. The promise of helping in an important national capacity was the reason for her excitement, not getting to see the hand-some, tall guardian once again. "I won't. Give me some credit for knowing how to meet contacts. I *am* an investigative journalist."

Her brother smirked. "You're a gossip columnist."

She bristled under the term, accurate as it was. "Okay, so I'm trying to broaden my horizons. I helped Kynhaven a couple of years ago when I discovered magic lily dust was being peddled in his town. No one discovered my assistance. I can do this."

When he narrowed his gaze on her, Delanee tried again. "Look, I come and go from here all the time, and no one sees me as anything more than you do. Your sister and a gossipmonger. No one will suspect I have anything significant on me, let alone to share. I can meet with Voklane in a manner that seems random and get him what you need. Let me know what to tell him."

Deklan sighed, staring at her. Deciding. Delanee licked her lips and waited.

"Okay," he finally said, and she kept from pumping her fist in victory. He set down one and held out two of them to her. "These are the translations of the books Cia nabbed. I'm keeping one of them to ensure we don't have everything in the same place."

Before she could take hold of them, he yanked them back. His gaze turned intent. "Do not open either book, Delanee. I don't want you to be part of this."

Delanee hesitated before accepting the books when he held them out once more. "What are they? Diaries?"

"Doesn't matter. Voklane just needs to get them, all right?"

Delanee nodded. "All right. I'll make sure it happens. Do you want me to let you know after?"

"Voklane will, I'm sure." He wrapped her into a side hug and kissed her head. "Come on, I'll formally introduce you to my wife and get you that interview."

Delanee smiled though her mind was preoccupied. Deklan hadn't noticed her lack of promise not to look. At the first opportunity, she was definitely looking. Otherwise, she wouldn't be much of a journalist, would she?

SPINE STRAIGHT, FACE DEVOID OF EMOTION, CIA TRIED TO recall every ounce of training she'd received. Porcelain clinked. The delicate sound drew attention to the cup of sweet orange-scented tea Cia had yet to accept. She'd heard rumors from Melody about Madeleine Fenwick's infamous spiced tea, with *special* additions meant to help guests relax. Cia wondered if the location mattered or if the matchmaker laced her tea no matter where she offered a cup. The last thing Cia needed was the loss of mental faculties.

"Why so silent, child?" Madeleine asked, her voice strong despite her advanced years.

Nothing about the matchmaker said weak, old woman. She had to be pushing eighty, and yet her face was still beautiful. The deep lines of age only added to her regal demeanor. Her black hair was sprinkled with slate and silver and hung in a thick braid over her shoulder. Curiosity shone from her golden-green eyes over the rim of her cup as she took another slow sip of tea.

Madeleine wrapped both her hands around the rose and lilac adorned cup. "Are you worried I'll say you aren't compatible for my grandson?"

"No," Cia lied, the word coming out much too high.

Amusement sparkled in Madeleine's gaze. She motioned with her cup at Cia's tea. "Take a drink. Relax."

Knowing she couldn't continue being rude to her grandmother-in-law, Cia grasped the warm teacup and took a tentative sip. Warmed sweet spices exploded across her tongue. The tangy bite of orange almost concealed the bitterness of alcohol. Cia knew nothing about liquors, only knew she'd never had any, and the punch to her mouth made her grimace.

Madeleine laughed. "Well, at least I know you didn't get drunk and accidentally marry Deklan."

No, Cia had seduced him. And not accidentally. Clearing away the thoughts before she found her reckless tongue embarrassing her husband with yet another family member, Cia set the tea back on the table. "My contract with Deklan was intentional. I knew what I wanted. He took a little convincing."

"So his father told me." Madeleine placed her empty cup on the tray.

Cia couldn't handle the suspense any longer. "Why did you wish to speak with me, Mrs. Fenwick?"

"Would you believe Deklan pushed you in here without warning me?"

"What?" Cia asked, confused. "But he said—"

"I'm sure he said something very interesting, darling, but I had no idea we'd meet alone today. He knows I usually spend the night with Markus and Bella for our weekly family dinner, and he arrived early. Unusual for him." Sighing, the matchmaker refilled her tea cup. "My grandchildren are under the misconception that they require the same validation for their relationship that the rest of Haven City craves. I have myself to blame for that, of course. I've predicted too many successes and failures for them to think I don't have some mystical gift."

Cia blinked. "You... don't?"

"No," Madeleine stated, no hesitation. "What I have is a talent for reading people. Knowing when they're lying. When they're honest. When they're scared. When they're in a relationship for an ulterior motive." She sat forward, her eyes gleaming. "Power. Money. Social status. Even offspring all play a role in people trying to deceive others into marriage."

Cia chewed on her bottom lip. "Deklan would be impossible to deceive."

"Yes, as I said, my grandchildren don't need me. They'll know well before I do if their spouse is a fraud."

Well then... with judgment no longer on the table, perhaps Cia could relax a bit. Enjoy some relaxing tea before the main event. Dinner with the entire Ralston clan.

"Do you love Deklan?" Madeleine inquired, refilling Cia's tea.

Cia's hand froze on the way to her cup. "I... I'm..."

Madeleine smiled, returning the pot to the tray. "Love. Such a scary word, is it not?"

"No, it's just..." Cia struggled to center her thoughts. "I wasn't expecting anyone to ask me that."

"Why ever not? His parents are very much in love. They want nothing less for their children."

And Cia would never deny Deklan something so beautiful. Her love, a fledging seed with nothing more than a vulnerable quivering leaf in her heart, was too new to examine. Too precious to expose to anyone but him. The brilliance of their bond would feed her love until she knew Deklan would just become *aware* of how she felt one day. No words necessary. The thought made her smile.

"Ah," Madeleine sighed. "Very good. Until you're ready to tell him, and he will need to hear the words from you at some point, be gentle and patient with him. Many have disappointed him, and his heart is perhaps a bit more buried than yours."

Deklan's past relationships weren't something they'd discussed beyond the forced bonding. The hot stab of jealousy at the thought of him even kissing another woman, let alone experiencing what he'd given her last night, had her never wanting to broach the subject. But she knew he'd given up hope of ever finding a mate. Would he continue to cling to the fear of unacceptance? No, Cia discarded the thought immediately. She'd already accepted all of him. What she knew and what she still had to learn. Patience hadn't been part of their dynamic so far. Cia snickered. Why would she start now?

Cia took a sip of sweet, spiced tea. She relished the flavor before meeting Madeleine's curious gaze. "I think I'll continue to treat your grandson exactly as I have been. Like the man I want and the one I'm never going to be willing to give up."

"Wonderful," Madeleine whispered, a smile sparkling in her gaze.

Cia beamed. One down. Twelve to go. Not that she needed anyone's approval, but *not* being disliked by the in-laws was an admirable goal. No longer worrying about Madeleine Fenwick's opinion of her also helped. A burst of noise beyond the door made Cia flinch.

Madeleine's eyes widened, and she straightened. "Be a darling and help me set this tray up out of the way of little hands, would you?"

Faster than Cia would have thought an octogenarian capable of moving, Madeliene was out of her chair and to the door. "Gigi's here, my babies!"

Squeals and the pound of tiny feet echoed from the corridor. Smiling, Cia gathered everything onto the tray and looked for somewhere to place the set. Two children, a girl around five and a toddler barely walking, launched themselves at Madeleine. She drew them into a tight hug.

"Gigi missed you both so much."

The girl laughed. "You saw us last family meal."

Madeleine smacked a loud kiss on the top of her head. "Too long, much too long."

Porcelain clinked as Cia positioned the tray on a cabinet filled with unfamiliar objects. Leaning down, she peered through the glass.

"I'd like you to meet someone special," Madeleine

said, interrupting Cia's curiosity. A small face peered around her great-grandmother. Big blue eyes in a sweet face framed by pale blonde curls regarded her. "That is Lucianna. She's Uncle Deklan's wife."

The girl's blue eyes widened. "Uncle Dek got married? When?"

Madeleine brushed her fingers over the girl's head. "A few days ago."

Holding hands, the siblings inched closer to Cia. The girl pointed at herself and then her brother. Dark, wispy curls surrounded a sweet, innocent face. Dark brown eyes stared at her, uncertain. "I'm Rose, and this is my baby brother, Rowen. I'm helping him learn all his new things."

Cia crouched down, smiling. "That's amazing of you. I bet you're an excellent teacher."

"I am!" she proclaimed, grinning. Rowen let loose a loud, unintelligible noise that wasn't entirely happy. Rose frowned. "He wants our momma. Mooomm-mmmaaaa!"

"Rose, there is no need to shout," a woman called from somewhere in the house. "I can hear him just fine. I'll be there in a second."

"He wants you!" Rose yelled. Still staring at Cia, Rowen's bottom lip began to quiver.

Cia popped up and took a hasty step back. Was the baby crying because of Cia or another reason? Madeleine tut-tutted and reached for Rowen. A full-fledged wail erupted from the toddler. Cia grimaced. Rose slapped her hands over her ears and screamed for her mother again. Madeleine picked up the baby, who wiggled and squirmed to be put back down, his face turning an alarming shade of red.

"For the love of stars," Deklan said from the doorway, exasperated. "What is going on?"

He plucked the wailing child from Madeleine. "Rowen, little man, really?"

A frown too big for such a small face quivered the boy's lips. He pointed through the open doorway and made unhappy noises. Fat tears raced down his chubby cheeks.

In a move only someone familiar with holding a baby could pull off, Deklan had the toddler situated on his hip, a little butt supported by his forearm, little legs dangling. Deklan rubbed his nephew's back and leaned close. "What big guy?"

Rowen made the same urgent sounds, still pointing.

"Momma is busy with *Baki*. Do you want to go see them? Where's your dadda?"

"Dadda had to work," Rose said, holding her arms up.

Deklan leaned down and scooped her up. Rose grabbed handfuls of his shirt and held on. She wrapped her arms around his neck once he positioned her on his other hip. "Your wife is pretty."

Deklan glanced at Cia, and a tremor raced through her chest. "Yes, she is." Then he motioned with his head. "Come on, come meet my big sister."

"That's my momma!" Rose proclaimed. "Auntie Mira, Auntie Lanee, and Auntie Dyna are all your little sisters." She puffed out her chest and pointed at herself. "My momma is your only big sister."

"Yep, and she won't let me forget it, either," he grumbled.

Madeleine smacked between his shoulder blades. "Do you let the seven younger than you forget you're older than them?"

Cia observed the comfortable byplay between grandson and grandmother and smiled. She'd never known her grandparents, both having been Ruthenian. Often, she wondered if they'd ever known of her and Joshie. Her smile faltered. Now, just her. Perhaps it was for the best. She imagined her father or mother, whoever had chosen to leave, would have been blamed for the tragedy.

She followed them across the hall to a large study that doubled as a library. An archway opened into a spacious dining room that led into a kitchen, allowing all the family members to gather and still be able to speak regardless of whether they sat at the table or worked at a counter. Cia stumbled to a stop. So many happy, talking, and laughing voices filled the room. People sat at the table, on stools at an island, or worked on various dishes in the spacious kitchen.

Deklan made the kids in his arms bounce. "Dalila! I have your urchins!"

A woman Madeleine's height with short dark brown hair looked his way, wiping her hands on a towel in the kitchen. "You can keep them if you'd like."

Deklan set Rose down. She ran to another man, lifting her arms and jumping. Deklan held Rowen across the wide island in the center of the kitchen. "I think this one would object."

After throwing the towel across her shoulder, Dalila accepted the happily kicking toddler. "You little monster," she growled, then rained kisses on his cheeks.

"Where's your bride?" another woman asked, throwing chopped potatoes into a pot.

Deklan motioned to Cia, and she squeaked in alarm as everyone turned in her direction, silence descending. Madeleine gave her a side hug. All at once, the room erupted into shouts of excitement. As a collective, they descended on her, hands reaching, introductions she could never hope to follow being made.

"Quiet," Deklan said, then roared, "Come on, family, this is why no one ever brings anyone home until we're married!"

Everyone quieted again.

"*Baki's* already met her?" a woman asked, her arms crossed over her very pregnant stomach. "Why has *Baki* already met her, Deklan?" She gasped and dropped her arms to her side. "You didn't! You made her sit through the *Baki* test, didn't you?"

"And you didn't with Westen?" Deklan accused, holding up a finger. "Because I specifically remember you standing outside the closed door, chewing your nails until none were left on one hand, the day you brought him home."

Color rose on the woman's cheeks, and she glared. They broke out into heated Ruthenian, coming to stand nose-to-nose, Dalila and another man joining the argument. Cia's eyes widened.

An arm wrapped around her shoulders. Cia glanced to her right, her gaze meeting eyes the exact color of Deklan's. "Welcome to the family. I'm Bella, Deklan's mother, or *makyshka*, as they call me."

"Thanks," Cia whispered, still paralyzed by the noise and the attention.

"Let me introduce my crazy children to you." She angled Cia to the left and pointed. "Those two are my oldest, Darius and Dominik, twins. Then I had Dalila, followed by Deklan. My next set of twins are Deverick and Drayke. After them came Damira, Delanee, who I believe you've met, Donovan, Dustin, and my youngest, Dyna."

Cia blinked and tried to keep the names straight. She knew she'd fail. "All of the start with D?"

Bella laughed and released her hold. "Yes, it's... a long story."

"I hope I can hear it someday."

Bella touched Cia's arm, a smile on her face and brightening her eyes. "You aren't going anywhere. Another night, when it's not," she waved an arm around, "this."

Cia laughed. "All right. Anyone else?"

Bella took a deep breath. "Oh yes. Deklan's *ahtyshka* is outside with the wolves. His name is Markus. Dalila is married to Torian. You've met their children. Deverick is married to Sadie there. Their little girls Evaline and Jade are out with Markus. Damira is mated to Westen, and she's expecting their first."

Cia furrowed her brows. Mated, not married like the others. "Damira is a beast master talent?"

"Yes, equestrian. It's a little different than the predator talents like all my others, but she still bonds the same."

Cia looked at the beautiful woman caressing her round belly over a flower print dress, still yelling in her brother's face, and wondered what imprint she'd left on her husband and how the man had taken having to bear his woman's mark. If the way he leaned over and whispered something into her ear that made her snap her mouth shut and flush was any indication, well.

The siblings still quibbled. The others watched, throwing in the occasional jab or comment that Cia couldn't understand. One of the older twins Bella had pointed to, Darius, held Rose, who kept squishing the air out of his cheeks and laughing at the ridiculous sounds he made. They were all beautiful. Essential to each other and had gone on to act as if she already belonged. Not a stranger, but someone able to handle their crazy. Maybe even someday add her own to the mix.

"Thank you," she whispered to Bella. "Thank you for such a wonderful family."

Bella hugged her again. "Thank you for making us even stronger."

23

"You're getting better," Deklan said, flopping onto the oversized couch on his balcony. They'd spent the weekend home, with her practicing and decompressing after meeting his family. They'd accepted her into the fold, something he hadn't doubted. He'd been teased about the age gap and the quick, zero promise time between them. But since he wasn't the only one to have jumped into a relationship in the family, they weren't upset by the lack of formality.

Cia took up half the space, her head on a pillow and her legs kicked over the arm. Loose yellow silk flared on the couch around her, barely covering her hips, teasing the fact she lounged in nothing more than an oversized shirt. She turned a page in the book she read. "Is that what your wolves said?"

"Yes."

She tilted her head back and looked at him. "Would have been better if you'd trained with us."

Deklan grabbed the end of her braid and tugged the band free. He undid the plaits and ran his fingers through the silken length of her hair. "I had a lot of work to catch up on. I've been gone for weeks."

She laid the open book down on her stomach. "I've been thinking."

Deklan raised a brow but kept the *uh-oh* to himself.

"If our bond grows and we can communicate like you can with your wolves, wouldn't I be better suited on your team?"

Deklan stilled. "You've caught some of my thoughts?"

She swiveled on the couch to sit. Her hair slipped from his hand. "You mean you didn't speak to me that way on purpose? The words were just like conversation."

Deklan tried to recall when he would have projected thoughts to her and came up empty. "How many times?"

"Once," she said, setting the book on the smoked glass coffee table.

"Where?"

"At the Survaine's." She chewed on her bottom lip. "So, it was an accident?"

"I don't know." Deklan ran his hand over his face. "Technically, our bond will be stronger than what I have with my wolves, but I don't know much of how it works since every bond is as unique as the relationship."

Determination slid across her face. Her shoulders wiggled as she straightened her back. "Let's see if we can. What do I do?"

How did he explain how something he'd instinctively accomplished worked? He'd been able to help her discover her genetic talent, and this wasn't much different. Deklan closed his eyes and instructed her to do the same. "Our bond will be like a glowing thread in your conscious. My wolves are their eye color, while you are…"

He hadn't sought her thread because he hadn't known she'd have one. Embarrassment filled him because he should have. She was more important to him now than his wolves. He sorted through the connections and realized with a start Cia wasn't a thread but a path all her own. She became a presence in his mind at the mere thought of forging a link.

"What am I?" she whispered.

"You," he breathed.

A frustrated growl left her. "I can't see, find, sense, or whatever, anything."

Maybe the bond was one-sided. But he didn't think so, not knowing she'd be able to establish one with Izia. If she could accomplish that, she could share the same with him. Maybe they needed to start with the wolf so she could experience an extrasensory pairing. Traditionally, the bond was done with family present, celebrating the accomplishment. Deklan would be the first to bring a spouse into the bonded Ralston beast master fold. He wasn't sure how his family would feel if he took the tradition from them. He'd already compromised on their promise ceremony. However, his mother's bond with Lunah had been unconventional, and they might understand.

Deklan opened his eyes. "How important is this to you?"

Cia slumped forward, elbows on her knees. "I don't know. I was excited about us being an unstoppable team. It's silly."

Warmth spread through him, bringing a small smile to his lips. He brushed his fingers from her shoulder to her hand and pulled her close. "Not silly. But you have no idea what I do or the dangers of my job."

She threaded her fingers through his, her gaze on their joined hands. "Can't be much worse than what I'm training to be for an intel team."

The softness of her skin distracted him. Made him want to play and tease. He couldn't help but draw his hand back enough to trace the lines on her palm. Her gaze remained riveted as she visibly swallowed.

"I imagine there won't be much of a difference," he agreed, caressing the line from her thumb to her wrist. "Would you mind running with my wolves? Would you want to chase down criminals and dangerous suspects?"

"Am I not doing that now? Hunting down serious threats to Sziveria?" she asked, her words hitching as he lengthened his touch to the sensitive skin of her forearm.

Gently, he dragged his short nails along her inner wrist. An alluring flush blossomed across her cheeks. Her breathing turned ragged, parting her tempting lips. He leaned close and kissed a trail from her jaw to her ear. The sweetness of her arousal sizzled along his nerves from their bond.

"And I suppose," he whispered, tracing the shell of her ear with the tip of his tongue, "you envision us doing our hunting wordlessly."

She shivered. "We'd be..." She swallowed and took a deep, uneven breath. "A very powerful couple."

Deklan shifted until his face was level with hers. He grasped her chin and met her unfocused gaze. "And you want to be powerful."

Vulnerability replaced the haze of lust he'd woven

in her eyes. "I don't ever want to be weak again," she whispered.

"Lucianna," he breathed, an ache splintering through his chest. He spread his hand across her neck, his thumb rubbing along the underside of her jaw. "*Kovetka*, weakness is perceived, and you need never feel that way again. We will work through this fear."

Her mouth captured his in an aggressive kiss. The tip of her tongue speared between his lips, licking the inside of his mouth, demanding more. A seal of his vow to her. Deklan devoured her, sinking his hands into her hair and angling his mouth over hers until she moaned for more. She climbed onto his lap, wasting no time working her hips to ensure he lost his mind.

Deklan leaned back, breaking their kiss long enough to look at her. A sensual flush bloomed across her cheeks and chest. The fullness of her lips glistened from their embrace. She smiled, cupping his jaw in both her hands.

"I can't believe you're mine," she whispered.

He slid his hands to her hips and squeezed. "We are each other's."

A tightness pinched her face. She pressed a fist between her breasts. "I have this... discomfort at the idea of being away from you. Is that normal?"

Deklan eased a hand beneath hers, pressing his palm flat on her sternum. His other continued to cradle her jaw. The silk of her shirt warmed between their skin. The gentle swells of her small breasts tempted his splayed fingers to move in either direction. She wrapped her hands around his forearm and wrist as he rested his forehead on hers. Their breaths mingled, a little erratic, a lot restrained.

"Another reason to want to work together?" he asked.

"Yes," she admitted, her grip tightening on his arm. "Is that normal?"

He pressed his hand firmer to her chest and searched her anxious gaze. "There is no normal, not for mates. Our bond is as unique as our relationship will become. Ours alone. If your half of our connection is loath to separate, then we will remain a pair. It'll become a condition of my assistance. *Our* assistance."

"You don't… feel the same?"

"I haven't contemplated being away from you," he said honestly.

Her lips flattened into a line. "Contemplate it now."

Deklan caressed his thumb along her jaw and kissed her. Closing his eyes, he reflected on time away from his wife. Of separation. From her. A punch to his chest almost sent him careening off the couch. Cia's hold on his arm kept him from falling. She gasped and clutched at his shoulders.

"Deklan? What happened?"

Gulping air, Deklan rubbed away the sharp ache. "I thought about being away from you."

A smile quirked her lips. "I guess you liked that about as much as I did."

"You can be confident I feel the same," he said, frowning at the lingering discomfort.

She climbed onto his lap. Straddling his hips, she wound her arms around his shoulders. "If we can't be apart, and we can figure out how to communicate through our bond, we'll be the ultimate Wolvenguard."

Deklan gripped her hips and yanked her against him. Growling, he caught her bottom lip between his teeth. "You sound power-hungry again, *kovetka*."

A shudder raced along her spine. Her hands framed his face. "We'll be unstoppable…"

Unease made him shift on the couch. She settled further onto his lap, her knees bracketing his hips. The position put her exactly where he wanted her. Craved her. He had to stay focused and put a halt to her fixation. Settling back, he took a deep breath and waited until she met his gaze. "Do you know why this arch guardianship has succeeded?"

She shook her head. Her fingers found the unbound hair at his nape and fiddled with the strands.

"We aren't usually in the position long enough to be compromised. Either through death or burnout, most Wolvenguards don't last longer than a decade. I'm the first to make it to the fifteen-year mark. I don't know how much longer I'll remain in this position. Though I'll always serve in some guardian role, I won't always be the Wolvenguard."

"They'll never be able to replace you," she said, her touch sliding along his neck through his hair.

Deklan forced concentration on their conversation and not her innocently seductive caresses or the disappointment attempting to creep into his consciousness. "While that may be true, a bond to a wolf is the only requirement to hold this position, and the willingness to lead a team who is prepared to lay down their life to keep Sziveria safe from the criminal element. That's it. My younger brother Donovan will fit this role better than I ever could. Once he's fully trained, I plan on making the recommendation." He tried to keep his expression and voice devoid of emotion. "If you contracted and mated with me in the hopes of being one of the most powerful people in the nation, you'll be dissatisfied in a few years."

Damn it, Deklan had *needed* her to be different. He'd figured—hoped—she would be. But there was no denying a relationship with him *would* catapult her to the echelons of authority after mere introductions. Like him, she could walk into any government building and demand an audience with anyone she chose, and they could hold little back from her. Knowledge, influence, whatever she wanted, she'd be given. Arch guardians were selected very carefully, and it was trusted they'd be just as wise when choosing a spouse.

How could he have been so wrong? The sudden need to put space between them, to consider the implications of why she'd been so obsessed with a relationship, had him trying to move out from under her. Her hands gripped his shoulders, and she clamped her knees to his sides.

"Deklan."

He had no hope of undoing what had been done. No hope—

"Deklan!"

The warmth of her hands pressed to his cheeks, and she snatched his face close to hers until their noses touched. "Look at me," she demanded.

He did, and her focused dawn gray eyes held him captive. A sense of calm flowed through his system.

"I am not those other women. *I'm not.* Do you understand? Nod if you do."

He nodded.

"Good. I might be young and inexperienced, and yes, I might be a little too excited about this sudden influx of resources at my disposal. I am hunting a murderer, you know, but I didn't marry you for those reasons."

His heart slammed against his ribs, a reminder of

the narrow miss with a panic attack, but the anxiety faded into an echo of discord. Her grip softened until she brushed her fingertips across his cheeks and jaw.

"Good," she whispered, fluttering delicate kisses across his nose, mouth, and chin. "That's good, baby. Now, I want you to listen to me because this is important."

Deklan returned his hands to her hips, caressing her thighs to her waist, allowing her to continue to ground him.

"During training with the wolves this morning, I thought about why I constantly tried to bond with you before I knew what was happening. I mean, that requires some serious emotional commitment, right?"

"Yes," he croaked out.

She gently brushed her fingers along his jaw and feathered kisses across his face. The unceasing connection gave him something to focus on, along with her words.

"That's what I figured."

An expectation settled between them. Something important lingered in her explanation. Something she wanted him to realize. Her first attempt to bond with him had been on the train when he'd given in to temptation and kissed her and anytime thereafter when she'd been in his arms. So, she… cared about him even then?

"You didn't know me well enough to know if I'd be a good mate," he said.

"That's true," she conceded, pressing closer to him. "However, since I knew nothing about this mate business, I was following my heart. Which you have owned since the moment you walked into the Terravine ballroom last Wintervail. I saw you had no idea who you were, but I knew I wanted you. Melody, Vayden's wife, informed me I might as well hope for a star to turn into a diamond in my hand. And that you were too old for me."

Deklan glared.

Laughter bubbled from her. "Yeah, I had that response, too! See, I'd already decided I was going to have you. When you rescued me, you sealed your fate. You're mine, Deklan Ralston. Because you're *you*, and I love you. All this other stuff, it's a bonus for what we already have."

The truth of her words flowed along their bond, sincere and comforting, like warm honey in his veins. And he realized that wasn't the first time he'd had the sensation since they'd forged their connection. He responded in kind, unable to stop the surge of emotion from welling up within him. She was everything to him. His heart. His life. And had she turned out to be a power-hungry imitation of the woman he'd thought her to be, his heart would have continued to break until... He took a breath and allowed the toxic thoughts to exit. He no longer needed to allow such poison into his mind or his relationship.

"I love you," he whispered.

She beamed at him. "I won't forget if you don't."

"Forget I love you?"

"Yes." Her arms wrapped around his shoulders, pulling their chests together tight. "I've heard it's a risk of a long-term relationship."

"Life will be different for us." He slid his hands up the back of her loose shirt, reveling in all the softness beneath his palms. "If I get out of line, you won't need words to remind me. Same if you ever want anything from me."

Her back arched, and her hips rolled in a provocative move, instinctively feminine, that made everything instinctively male in him take notice. Her tongue licked a path to his ear, where she whispered, "Show me."

CIA HAD EXPECTED HER HUSBAND TO ROLL THEM OVER AND take her with the same intense passion he'd shown her the first night they'd been together. He'd been cautious since, wanting her fully healed before they engaged again. Though they'd done other, deliciously wicked things, she was ready. So ready. But he didn't. His fingers traced each shallow dip and rise along her back and low front as if memorizing her form until she squirmed. The hard length of his arousal hit her in the perfect spot, and she moaned. Fine, if he wouldn't move them along, she'd take things into her own hands. Literally.

Reaching between their bodies, Cia grasped him through his pants. His fingers tightened on her hips as his own bucked against her questing touch. Desperate to feel him, she fumbled with the buttons pulled tight from the strain of his erection. In moments, he sprang free into her waiting hand. Soft silk over hard steel. She shuddered in pleasure. Taking him would be a matter of quick moves. All she wore was a shirt and panties, which wouldn't even need to come off to make the rest of her day awesome.

However, Cia had discovered a few things about herself during their short marriage. She enjoyed the lead-up to sex as much as the act. The teasing and tempting. The desperation built by fingers and tongues. Which was all she'd had access to for several nights. Deklan was a generous lover, and she knew he'd continue to help her navigate all the pleasures of their relationship.

"Oh, I want you," she confessed, gasping as her fingers encountered his slick tip.

Naughty impulses made her hips rock. She wondered as she took his mouth in a heated kiss if he'd let her explore her urges. Her cheeks flamed at the thought of asking. If she didn't inquire, then how would she know? He certainly hadn't been shy when he'd used his mouth on her last night, asking over and over again how much she liked his tongue. He hadn't allowed her to be embarrassed, and then she'd been too wrapped up in pleasure to care about his questions or where he'd buried his face. The warmth in her cheeks increased at the memory.

Then she realized this was the perfect opportunity to try the talking-without-words method she desperately wanted between them. Maybe if she could *think* the words to him, she'd be less anxious about his reaction to her desires. As her tongue tangled with his and his taste caused her body to throb even more, she searched for the illusive bond. He'd said she felt like herself to him, so Cia needed to search for Deklan within her. She delved into her consciousness, searching for...

Deklan.

She sighed into his mouth. And there he was, a comforting presence hovering in her mind's heart. Pulling free of their kiss, she rested her forehead on his while her hand continued a lazy up and down journey along his shaft. A heady pulse ached at her center, made worse as she imagined what she would attempt to tell him she wanted through their connection. Nerves tangled with arousal, causing her heart to pound. She could do this. She could be bold in her sexuality, safe in their space, and knowing they belonged to each other.

Taking a deep breath, she formed words along their bond. A graphic description of exactly what she wanted. He froze beneath her, and she did the same, not even breathing. Oh no. Maybe she wanted too much. Maybe her desires were too—

"What are you waiting for?" he rasped.

She blinked, blush flooding over her entire body. "Y-you heard me?"

"Loud and clear, *kovetka*," he growled. "Now, do it."

Emboldened by his clear anticipation, Cia wiggled out of her panties, dropping them on the ground beside her book. He worked on the row of buttons down the front of her shirt, peeling it open. His mouth went to work on her breasts, sending delicious arcs of pleasure down her belly. Cia almost lost focus, her fingers tangling in his hair, dislodging the small knot at the top of his head to free the silken strands. The strands brushed the heated skin of her chest, and she arched into his kisses.

His fingers found her, sliding along her slickened skin, and she cried out. He pushed one, then two, fingers inside her, stretching, testing. Inhibitions long since gone, Cia rode his hand while he lavished attention on her breasts. The sharp sensation of his teeth biting and sucking joined the fevered motions of his fingers working her. Despite the ministrations being one-sided, they both seemed to need her to finish.

And finish she did, coming in a rush all over his hand, her body trying to curl into itself as wave after wave of ecstasy flowed within her. Before she could float down from her release, Deklan flipped her onto her back, pulled her knees up, and surged into her.

Another orgasm ripped through her, and she gritted her teeth against the onslaught, only to fail at containing herself, screaming as the pleasure reached critical heights.

Deklan showed no mercy, pounding into her until sweat dripped from his face onto her chest. One of his hands gripped the armrest above her head while the other held her thigh so tight she knew she'd be marked when they finished. Which was fine by her. She planned to do a little marking of her own. Sliding her fingers underneath his shirt, she caressed the shifting muscles of his back. Little arcs of lightning met her fingertips, and she swore the leaping under her touch was the wolf rising from its skinbound prison to meet her roving hands. The visual made her arch beneath him, seeking to get closer.

Sudden emptiness made her gasp, but Deklan flipped her onto her stomach and yanked her hips up and back before she could comprehend what'd happened. The shirt she'd been wearing was shoved around her neck and shoulders, and his lips trailed delicate, reverent kisses down her spine to the small of her back. His large palm kneaded her butt before gripping her hip.

"I had to see it again… had to…." He slowly sank back into her from behind, and they both groaned. "Touch you."

Cia wrapped a hand around the edge of a cushion and the armrest, gripping both until her knuckles hurt. His hips moved in short, quick rolls, and the intensity of his thrusts left her panting. Banding his arms around her ribs, he pressed close to her, the soft tickle of his chest hair telling her he'd ditched his shirt at some point. He kissed her shoulder before gently biting, and she trembled as a ribbon of pleasure unraveled through her. His heavy breaths brushed her ear and neck. Each powerful thrust of his hips sent her rocking forward. All his muscles tightened around her, his arms squeezing, his abs contracting against her low back, and with one final, hard thrust that forced a keening cry from her, he trembled and groaned.

Long after the hot rush of his release left him, he continued to hold her, his big body wrapped around hers, supporting them both. Kissing her shoulders, he eased away from her, and Cia collapsed onto her stomach, her arm draping over the side of the couch. Deklan slipped under her legs, arranging her thighs across his. The soft trail of his fingertips traced the outline of the wolf on her back. Cia moved enough to be able to see his face. He was boneless like her, splayed upright, his chest heaving, sweat glistening along every inch of his exposed skin. He still wore the shirt but had unbuttoned it. His pants were open and rumpled around his hips.

Another shiver of awareness heated her blood. How? She was depleted, exhausted, and yet... yeah... she wanted him again. Unconcerned with her nudity, she rolled onto her back and threaded her fingers through his. "I think it's only fair we get a mirror above the bed," she said, somehow without cracking a smile.

He rolled his head to meet her stare, his brows drawn tight. "Why?"

"I want to see your tattoo. Seems to be important to you, I want to know what that's like."

Surprise and desire flared in his eyes. "That's...." His voice failed, and he cleared his throat. "I'm not sure what to say."

Cia grinned, feeling bold and a little naughty, a state

she was learning he brought out in her in the best way. She climbed onto his lap and wrapped her arms around his shoulders. "Say yes, wife, I shall love to provide your every wish in our bedroom."

He gripped her hips and laughed. The sound warmed her insides. Caressing from her hip to her upper thighs, he shook his head.

"What?" she asked, winding hair at the base of his neck through her fingers.

"I just, I never expected this," he whispered, his eyes serious yet sparkling with happiness.

"Expected what?"

He squeezed her thighs and then motioned around the open space of the balcony. "Passion, fun, spontaneous sex."

Cia frowned. "Why not?"

"I don't know. I mean, my parents have a healthy relationship, and the few siblings in my family seem happy enough. I just never expected that for myself. I'm…" He cleared his throat and looked past her to the greenhouse. She didn't rush him, content to look over his handsome face and play with his hair. When his gaze returned to her, a fierceness glowed in his ocean eyes. "I love you."

Happiness sprouted wings in her chest. She hugged him tight. "I—"

"Hey," a male voice called from below. "If you two are done, don't get started again."

Deklan cursed and closed the edges of her shirt while dislodging her from his lap. Cia laughed.

"He can't see anything," she said, rebuttoning the shirt. However, she wasn't sure how she felt about the man having heard them.

Deklan tucked himself into his pants on his way to the railing. "What in the arctic are you doing here?"

"I need to check Izia's stitches," Tate said.

Cia joined Deklan at the rail. She waved at the medical scientist. He returned the gesture, grinning.

"Hey, arch guardianess, congratulations!" he called up. A medical bag was clutched in his hand.

Cia beamed. "Thank you!"

"Izia's on his way," Deklan said.

Foliage rustled deep in the greenhouse, and within moments, not one but three wolves came to greet the team member. Barks and excited whines echoed in the open space. Deklan turned from the railing.

"To be continued?" he asked.

Cia drew him away from their guest's line of sight and kissed him long and deep. "Definitely. And you're going to agree to that mirror."

24

Delanee tried to get comfortable on the hard chair
with no padding. The delicate spindle legs creaked
from her efforts, and she stilled. Breaking furniture that
didn't belong to her during an interview wouldn't go
over well. She flipped the page in her notebook and
focused on her subject. Fione Faneline, a true orphan.
The young woman tucked a long strand of red hair
behind her ear for what Delanee figured was the
hundredth time. A nervous habit and Fione's hair was
cut too short at the sides for the strand to stay in place.

The girl would never escape her orphan status, her
last name telling all of Sziveria she was born without
being claimed by a family. Abandoned on the doorstep
of the orphanage that would raise her. The name Faneline could not be passed on. If two Fanelines ever
contracted, they instead took the first name of their
spouse as their last name, forming a new family
together. If they had children, they'd decide whose
name would carry on to the next generation. Fione had
not married, and as Delanee looked around the

350

elegantly feminine parlor decorated in pinks and creams, she wondered if the girl ever would.

"What else did you wish to know?" Fione asked, pressing a handkerchief under her nose. She had assured Delanee she hadn't been with her patron in almost a month, and the sniffles were allergies, not because she'd potentially been exposed to human rabies syndrome. A real risk given her means of employment.

Delanee hated that the girl had to clarify a runny nose. Had to live with the fear of what that might have meant if she'd slept with her benefactor within the last two weeks. Pulling her thoughts together, Delanee glanced back over the notes she'd taken so far. "How often do you recall other orphans disappearing from the home?"

Fione sniffled and dabbed again. "As I said, we weren't well watched. If we kept to ourselves, they didn't much bother us. If someone went missing, we figured they left on their own."

"So the other kids didn't look out for each other?" Delanee asked, curious about the dynamics between the other orphans.

Already, she'd learned education was sporadic. If a child was driven to learn, they could when a teacher volunteered. But volunteers were sparse, maybe two or three weeks a year, leaving most children illiterate. The kids relied on an older orphan to arrive and become the teacher if they wanted to learn to read or do simple math. Fione had never seen the point, and it was too late when her time at the orphanage ended. She'd squandered any chance and was left with limited employment choices.

Fione shrugged. A sage green knit shawl slipped off her shoulder, and she tugged it back into place. "If we bonded to a kid, we watched out for them. But otherwise, no. We were discouraged from getting attached. No money to help with sickness, and it's not like we could go with each other if someone found a new home."

In other words, the threat of loss wasn't worth the effort of forming friendships. Delanee scribbled in her notebook. "When someone showed up to take a child to a new home, how were they vetted?"

Fione blinked in confusion.

Delanee searched her mind for an easy way to explain. "How did the head of the orphanage know the child would be safe?"

"Oh, um, I don't think they cared. One less mouth to feed, you know?"

Delanee's heart cracked. The reply was what she'd feared. "Did you ever worry about someone coming to take you?"

Fione shrugged and picked at the edges of the hankey. "Sometimes. I figured if someone came to get me, maybe I might be fed better, you know? Maybe I might get medicine when I got sick. But no one ever did."

"Who seemed to disappear or leave the most?" Delanee asked gently.

"The boys. When they reached their teens, they'd just walk out the front door, and no one would stop them. The younger boys disappeared a lot, too."

Delanee's journalistic side sat up and took notice. "How young?"

"Less than ten, but not babies," Fione answered.

"Are babies adopted a lot?"

"Yeah, especially the last few years. The nursery never had many. But we could see people leave with them during the day from our windows." Fione pulled the wrap tighter across her chest. "I think most of them were families waiting for records to confirm relations."

And no one ever came for Fione. Delanee swallowed and decided it was time to move on. "The boys that went missing, can you tell me anything special?"

Simple sleuthing had brought Delanee to the door of Ms. Kimber Odekirk, the owner of one of the most established pseudo-brothels in Haven City, in search of Fione, who'd grown up in an orphanage on the outskirts of town. Brothels were illegal due to the health risks, though many still existed deep underground, and prostitution was a foundation stone in The Rows and Old City Ruins. People like Ms. Odekirk managed to get around the prohibited aspect by having her patrons enter into a shadow contract for a duration of their choosing with an individual on the property.

The patron paid a large sum to keep the woman, or man, to themselves. Should they wish someone new, a new contract was drawn. The arrangement only worked if both parties were honest in the terms. The owner would not allow anyone else to see the contracts chosen, and the contract would not engage in relations for at least two weeks before crossing the threshold. Odekirk had a reputation for human rabies syndrome, never affecting her workers. She had a thorough method of ensuring honesty, and as a result, one had to be referred for employment or consideration for a shadow contract. Fione considered herself fortunate, and the money she made would ensure her choice to do what she wanted in a decade. A fair trade for a financial freedom she never dreamed she'd have.

Fione had to be a whore to afford to choose her destiny. Delanee hated the disparity between them and wanted a change. She only hoped the nation would wake up and care when her article was finished. Between the lack of opportunities for orphans due to the neglect of a country and the obvious trafficking of their most vulnerable, Delanee hoped with everything what she wrote would matter.

The subtle chime of a bell brought their attention to the entry. Ms. Odekirk's skirts rustled as she sped down the hall to greet her newest guest. Four men and one woman had arrived to visit their courtesans since Delanee had begun her interview.

"Mr. Pherson, how lovely of you to visit with us this evening. Please, if I may see you for a moment in my office?" the owner asked, her voice pleasant yet firm to ensure no argument.

On the way past, Mr. Pherson ducked into the parlor, smiling the second he saw Fione. He pressed a quick kiss to her lips. Dressed in brown slacks, a matching brown open vest, and a white shirt, he looked completely ordinary and not of the same wealth class as the others who'd sauntered through the door. His medium brown hair was parted at the side and neatly combed. He was perfectly average in every way.

"I will be but a moment, my darling." An unfamiliar accent stilted his words.

Fione's demeanor changed from tired and sickly to excited and attentive. She smoothed her hands down the buttons of his shirt and accepted the tweed hat he handed her. "I've been waiting for ages, Berk."

"I know, things have been…" He noticed Delanee and cleared his throat. Something about him tugged at her mind. "Anyway, I will return. I think I know what Ms. Odekirk wants. It is time for my renewal."

"With me?" Fione asked, brushing her fingers across

her chest, which she'd revealed in the short window of Berk's arrival, allowing her shawl to fall to the seat and unbuttoning the first few buttons of her top.

Berk took hold of her hand and pressed a kiss to her fingers. "Only with you, my darling, only ever."

A delicate blush bloomed across Fione's cheeks. "Do you still have my drawings?"

He cleared his throat. "I should like new ones. With my um, colors, if you remember."

She swatted at his bicep. "I knew you'd ruin another set." A deeper flush brightened her cheeks. "And, of course, I remember your colors."

Clearing his throat again, he straightened. "Right, well, meet you in your room?"

"Yes," she purred. "I'll be waiting for you."

Fione rose, and Delanee followed. "One more quick question, if I may?"

Fione sighed and reached for her discarded shawl. "Yes, quick, I know Ms. Odekirk won't dally on the contract. Berk has been my patron for two years. He will expect me to be waiting for him as I said I would."

"Of course," Delanee said and poised her pencil to write. "Do all the patrons pay the same fee?"

"Yes, though if a woman arrives a virgin, she gets more for her first patron for the duration of the contract." Fione smiled, folding the shawl into the bowl of Berk's hat. "Berk has been my only lover. I know it's silly of me, but I keep hoping maybe..." She shook her head. "I've been very lucky."

Fione grasped Delanee's hand to stop the writing. "You can't publish his name," she whispered. She glanced at the opening into the foyer and leaned forward, her tone still quiet, "He's a secret guardian, doing very important work for the government."

Dread swamped Delanee. She didn't know how to tell the young woman there was no such thing as a secret guardian. Even Survaine, who held a seat for his role alone with First Intelligence, wasn't a secret. He had a page in the Directory of Guardians. Something continued to niggle at the back of her mind.

Fione's hand tightened around Delanee's. "Promise me you won't reveal his name."

"I-I won't," Delanee said.

On her way out, Fione pulled the pins from her flaming red tresses and disappeared up the stairs, a bounce in her step. Delanee carefully closed her notebook, suddenly wanting to be inconspicuous. Danger rang across her nerves, and she didn't know why.

The patron appeared in the hall, pausing at the foot of the stairs. His unremarkable brown gaze locked on her, and Delanee found herself pinned. The stare was cold. Calculating. Not at all the man who'd been present minutes before with his young lover. He looked her over at how she clutched her notebook, her hand frozen halfway to her bag. Recognition hit her, and it took everything in her not to tremble, anxiety slicing an icy path in her stomach. Just as swiftly, he dismissed her, taking the stairs two at a time until he was out of sight. Delanee had no doubt he'd be asking Fione who she was, and Delanee needed to be good and gone by the time an answer left the courtesan's lips.

Shoving her belongings into her well-loved messenger bag, the same bag her mother had once carted all over the inhabited world, solving the unsolvable with her beast master husband, Delanee tried to keep her hands from shaking. Breath sawed from her lungs as she swallowed against the fear drying her throat. Oh, summer sun, she had to leave *now*. Grasping the bag to her chest, she all but flew out the front door, hailing the first cabby she saw on the street.

"Arch District," she instructed.

"I can only drop off at the—"

"I'm aware of the rules," she said, "just go, now, please."

He tipped his black hat, and she finished climbing into the worn-out interior. Rough, scarred benches took up most of the small space. She kept her bag hugged to her chest, her knees pressed together. The gross scent of unwashed bodies, old urine, and cheap tobacco barely registered. The trip was short, the carriage rocking to a stop less than fifteen minutes later. The cabby knocked on the side, and Delanee exited, his fair already in hand. She paid him and walked the street to her brother's house. Deklan would be angry with her, but he'd get over it.

Phin had the door open before she reached the top step of the walkway. He bowed low to her and stayed bowed until she passed him into the foyer. "They're in the arch guardian's office, Miss."

"Thank you, Phin."

"Always my pleasure," he murmured.

Delanee rushed through the foyer, past the stairs, and back to her brother's office. The door was closed, and she hesitated at the handle. The last thing she needed was to walk in on her brother enjoying his new marriage. Leaning forward, she pressed her ear to the door. Voices rumbled on the side, masculine, and she recognized both. Blinking, she straightened, her heart pounding for a new reason. She took a second to compose herself, not wanting to appear frazzled.

Not bothering to knock, she swung open the door and stepped inside. Conversation halted, and the room occupants stared at her. Cia sat sprawled across a chair in front of a low burning fire, Izia's head on her stomach. The gray wolf didn't even lift his head in greeting, the traitor. The other two wolves curled up in front of the fire at least acknowledged her with tentative tail wags, hopeful for a word or motion from her to let them know they had permission to rise. Deklan leaned against the front of his desk, legs in black slacks crossed at the ankles, arms crossed over his chest, pulling the tan fabric of his knit sweater tight across his biceps. Cia must love the view. Sitting casually in a chair before the desk, Ryan Voklane had twisted around to see who'd interrupted. His pale brows shot up, but that was the only indication her appearance had surprised him.

"I'm in a meeting." Her brother motioned at Ryan. "I'll be out in a few. We're almost finished."

"Actually," Delanee said, taking another bracing breath, "I'm glad he's here since he'll want to hear what I've come to say."

Cia swung her legs around to sit upright and grabbed the back of her chair. Izia grumbled and sank to the floor, his muzzle on his front paws. Delanee patted the bag, still clutched to her chest, and wondered where to start.

"I interviewed a young woman raised in an orphanage. She works at a shadow contract house, the one owned by Ms. Kimber Odekirk?" When the men both nodded, Delanee returned the gesture and continued. "Right, well, a man arrived toward the end of our conversation. Turned out he was Fione's, that's the orphan's name, patron. His name was Berk Pherson."

Cia sprang from the chair. "The name from the book?"

Delanee nodded. "Yes, the same."

"I told you not to look in that book," Deklan growled.

"Actually," Ryan began, "if she hadn't looked at the book, she wouldn't have known to come here, and we'd never know she was in danger from hearing his name spoken. He'll learn she's a journalist, and he can't afford for her to know his name, even if he thinks she won't know what to do with the information."

"Danger?" Delanee squeaked. She'd known she needed to get out of the building. She never considered that wouldn't be the end. "What… who is he?"

"An evil man," Cia whispered. Her stark gaze shifted to her husband. "She's not safe."

"No, she's not," Ryan agreed.

Delanee's heart jumped into her throat. She touched her clavicle and tried to even her breathing to keep the fear away. All the color drained from Deklan's face. Faster than she could realize his intent, he crossed the space and snatched her into his chest. His arms banded around her, crushing her into the hard planes of his body. He buried his face into her hair, his large body trembling. His palpable anxiety magnified her distress.

"She's okay," Cia said, her voice soothing and gentle. "Deklan, do you hear me? She's okay. Everything is all right."

What must his mate be feeling along their bond? Not something good, Delanee figured, with the way her brother continued to cling despite Cia's attempts to calm him.

"And she's going to stay safe," Ryan said. "She'll leave with me. We'll take the back route to Synintel's and leave in one of his carriages, and I'll play a shell game from there. My Ariot is parked at the FIO. No one will know where to find her."

Delanee pushed against her brother's solid chest. "Wait a minute, don't I get any say in this? What about my work?"

"How will you work on anything if you're dead?" Deklan all but roared into her face.

"Baby, you must calm down," Cia said, her fingers curling around his upper arm.

"What can you remember about the man?" Ryan asked, stepping into her limited line of sight, squashed as she still was against her brother.

Under her cheek, his heart pounded a thunderous beat. She finagled her bag free and handed it to her sister-in-law. Deklan didn't seem capable of releasing her yet, and the buckles had been pinching her chest. Arms free, she returned her brother's hug. His hold tightened, and she rubbed soothing circles along his back.

"Everything about him was average," Delanee said. "Brown hair, brown eyes, brown clothes."

Ryan's silvery eyes flared. "What shade of brown? Light or dark?"

Delanee lifted her hands from Deklan's back in thought. While unremarkable in color, Berk's eyes had been shiver-inducing. She'd never forget them. "Um, neither. A very mundane brown, like mud. Why?"

"No variation in colors? No grays or greens or blues?"

"I didn't get close enough to stare at them, so I can't honestly say, but no, they looked uniform."

"Touch talents have lighter eye shades. In the brown family, they tend to be shades of amber, honey, or golden." He looked at her as he said the last color, and she resisted the urge to look away.

"Raina has light brown eyes," Cia said, her hand still gently smoothing Deklan's bicep.

"Her eyes are more the color of wet sand, and she's a logic talent," Ryan said.

"You think he's a logic talent, this Berk man," Delanee surmised.

"Now, yes. Something that he can utilize behind a gun to give him some accuracy. A mathematical talent, perhaps." Ryan turned slightly, his attention shifting. "Can I speak with your sister alone for a moment, please?"

Cia unpeeled Deklan from around Delanee and tugged him from the room. "The wolves stay," her brother snapped, and Cia sighed.

"Yes, beast master, your sister will have guards. Now come on."

Deklan pointed at Ryan, who threw his hands up. "What am I going to do to her, Wolvenguard?"

"Deklan," Delanee said, meeting her brother's wild stare. "I'll be fine. Ryan won't hurt me. Ever."

The door closed quietly behind the couple, and Delanee took a deep breath. She turned to face Ryan, who had an odd look on his face. "What?" she asked.

He shook his head. "Nothing."

Closed in the room with him, the space suddenly seemed smaller. Intimate. She rubbed her arms and drifted closer to the fire. "What did you need to talk to me about?"

He mirrored her motions, closing the short distance between them. "I was just wondering…"

His fingers brushed along the top of her hand to her inner wrist, leaving a trail of electric awareness. Delanee's lips parted, and she glanced up at him. Why did every nerve within her leap to life whenever they touched? She met his stare and swore currents of white bled into his already pale irises. But then she blinked, and his gaze was normal, if a little heated, and she blushed, pulling her arm away from his questing hand.

"What were you wondering?" she asked, massaging the point on her wrist where the tingling remnants of his contact remained.

"If you'd agree to stay with me until the assassin situation is handled," he said without hesitation.

She blinked. Many times. Her eyelashes flap-flap-flapping like all the silly girls she detested at societal functions. Perhaps she should give them some slack, now understanding how a vacant brain felt. "I'm sorry?"

He braced himself on the arm of the chair opposite her, crossing his arms and his ankles. The chair was solid mahogany and barely creaked under the uneven weight. "Here's the thing. You're a public figure. Anyone who reads *The Haven City Chronicle* with any regularity knows your name. You provide gossip to the entire population, a much-needed distraction from the daily grind of life. Where you live, and who you live with, is no secret either—"

"My *baki*," Delanee gasped, covering her throat.

"Don't worry, Deklan and I will make sure she's safe, too. But you can't stay there, even sequestered. This guy is an assassin. He'd target you through one of the many windows in that apartment. And you can't stay with your parents, your siblings and parents would become targets then, too."

"They won't if I'm not there?"

"I don't think they will, no."

"Why? Why would my being there change anything?"

"Because targeting them outside of you would be foolish. Chances are this guy isn't going to tell anyone he's been compromised, and assassinating the Wolvenguards family won't go over well with anyone. But he has to do something about *you*. He'll likely plan it carefully, make it look like a robbery gone wrong like they did for Wystone many years ago. And, like Wystone's case and Lucianna's family, all the records pertaining to it will simply disappear after you're dead."

"My brothers would never stand for that," Delanee said, anger surging through her.

"No, but that won't stop it from happening if you don't take measures to protect yourself and, therefore, your family. Don't make them go to war against the Ralston's. It'll be a bloody battle with losses on both sides."

The seriousness in his gaze and the softness of his voice made her take a step back and evaluate her options realistically. Whoever was creating turmoil, kidnapping for profit, and distributing drugs for the same wouldn't hesitate to decimate her family to maintain their power. And while yes, as a collective, the Ralston's would be an admiral opponent, they would suffer losses. Even one was too many. Ryan was giving her a means of protecting herself and all her blood. "It wouldn't be... proper... for me to live at your house, no matter how short term."

"No one has to know. Only Synintel knows where I live, and the two old biddy's who live next door to me won't say anything to anyone. You won't leave the house from the front door for anyone else to know you're around. And why would you be with me anyway? No one knows we have any sort of relationship."

"I left a party with you," she reminded him.

He smiled, a shallow upturn of his lips, and Delanee suddenly wanted to make him really smile. She bet he'd be beautiful. "No one knows who I am. If I am noticed, I'm Synintel's assistant, nothing more. I'm not important enough. I doubt that idiot chasing you the other night even bothered to look at my face, he was so focused on you."

Delanee recoiled. "That's ridiculous."

"Not really."

"I meant about you not being important."

"I know."

Delanee opened her mouth, but nothing came out. She snapped it closed and growled. She wanted to demand an explanation for why he felt he wasn't important. Without him, Synintel would have no personal connection to all the teams who worked under him globally. She knew enough FIO guardians to be aware of his vital function. Then she realized perhaps his significance was purposefully skewed. He couldn't become a target if he had no value outside of an assistance role. Even his office was among all the other support staff for the FIO. Delanee forced herself to calm down. Her anger had no justification anyway. Ryan wasn't hers to defend.

"Why would you let me stay with you? You don't know me or owe my family anything."

For several silent moments, he looked at her, his gaze seeming to take in every subtle curve of her face until her cheeks warmed, and she had to shift her focus to the crackling fire. The wolves lay in a content pile of fur and tangled paws.

"They don't get to take another life from a family. They don't get to take *you*, Delanee."

The *I won't allow it*, went unsaid, hanging in the air between them. And somehow, she knew he not only meant the declarations but was more than capable of ensuring her safety. She clutched the back of the chair.

"All right, I'll agree, providing I'm allowed to continue working on my article. I'll need all my research. And you'll have to deal with my brother," she said.

Ryan's ghost of a smile returned. "Consider him handled."

25

Soft light danced along Cia's naked torso, cast from the woodstove and the single candle burning on the nightstand. Deklan sprawled across her lower body, his damp cheek resting on her slick stomach. They were sweaty, winded, caught in the aftermath of his need for distraction.

"How…" Deklan managed to croak free, though he couldn't bring himself to form the rest of the heart-breaking question.

Cia knew, however. Either through their bond, their recent activity, or the weakness in his voice, she didn't need him to clarify. Her fingers brushed through the damp strands of hair near his temple, easing the length behind his ear and across his shoulders. "I'm still not over their deaths. Not completely. I may never be. But every morning, I wake up. I breathe. I eat. I live. Now more than I ever did before."

That made two of them, and he didn't have the excuse of a tragedy to explain why he'd allowed himself to become a shell before her. Hugging her hips, he pressed a kiss below her belly button. He sighed and laid his head back down on the pillow of her stomach. "She will be safe with him."

Again, he didn't need to specify. "Of course, she will. Now, whether he'll be safe with her..."

Deklan lifted his head again. "What do you mean?"

A wicked light danced in her gaze. Her legs parted further, her knees bracketing his shoulders. Both her hands sank into his hair. "Do you think Ryan's concerns are valid?"

Deklan licked the salty skin beneath her navel. "Answer mine first."

She arched, arousal sizzling along their bond. He lifted his hips to adjust the sudden hard length caught between his hips and the mattress. Would they always affect each other like this, or would the newness wear off once they discovered all the tantalizing ways to pleasure each other? If he had his way, he'd put to good use everything he'd learned about her every chance he had.

Then she reminded him he wasn't the only one discovering secret places and subtle ways to seduce. Her toes caressed his flanks while her hips rolled beneath him. Deklan shifted enough to bring his hand underneath her roving thigh, knowing what he'd find but still groaning with satisfaction at finding her core swollen and wet to his touch. Her legs spread wider, her feet moving to settle on his shoulders, and Deklan wasted no time.

First, he used his fingers. Then he couldn't resist using his mouth. Only when she begged, demanded, and finally threatened did he slide into her, savoring how she moved, the sounds she made, and the way they fit so perfectly together. He kept them on the edge of beautiful release. Passion flared between their bond, amplifying every sensation, from the way his skin slid along hers to the way she tremored deep inside. When he could no longer hold back, he took her with him, intense ecstasy seizing his muscles, his bellow joining her scream.

Panting in his ear, she hugged him. "I think your sister likes Voklane."

Deklan laughed and dropped his forehead to the bed, his chin resting on her shoulder. "Now, you answer my question?"

Her shrug bumped his jaw. "I wanted you again."

Groaning, he pulled free of her and rolled onto his back. Staring up at the ceiling, he tried to catch his breath. "We need showers."

Cia grunted as she sat up and looked around them. "And new sheets."

Deklan laughed again and scrubbed his hands down his face. "Right. Come on. We'll continue this discussion after we're clean."

They showered, limiting their touches to teasing and quick kisses between rinsing. Afterward, Deklan changed the sheets while Cia let the wolves back in and settled them in their gated space. The domestic simplicity had him stopping mid-snap of the top sheet. They hadn't even discussed the routine after they'd dried off. Neither had bothered to put clothes on. He'd grabbed clean linens from his closet while she'd gone to care for the wolves. She gave each wolf individual loving, scratching under chins, between ears, and using her toes on bellies until they all settled on something fluffy in the open space. The gate closed with a delicate *snick*.

"You know," she said, hands on her hips, her lean

body all kinds of visual distraction while he tried to finish making the bed, "if we built a half wall here instead of this fence thingy, they wouldn't have to go out."

"They'd add to the acoustics," he said, smoothing the blanket into place.

"Eventually, they'd stop, though, don't you think?"

He tossed the pillows against the headboard and shrugged. "I don't know, maybe. They're okay going outside."

"Except…"

"Except what?" he asked when she didn't continue. Tossing the blankets back, he sat on the clean sheets, facing her. She sauntered toward him, a slow roll of her hips, her fingers dancing over her flat belly. Eagerness flooded along their bond. More than Deklan's spine straightened. "What are you doing?"

She climbed onto his lap and locked her arms behind his neck. "What happens when I want you again, and they're back inside?" she whispered into his ear before taking the lobe between her teeth and biting.

Groaning, Deklan fell back, his legs dangling over the edge of the mattress. He gripped her hips, holding her in place against his abdomen. "Half wall, huh?"

She glanced over her shoulder. "I think a thick curtain would work too, don't you?"

Deklan couldn't think of much as she took him in hand and reduced him to base noises. By the time she finished with him, he was thankful Phin lived far below so the racket that exploded from his room wouldn't be heard.

"For the love of stars, *sesay tikhil'ste!*" he roared when the wolves continued to howl and bark like a squirrel ran across the ceiling.

Silence descended, and Deklan let out a breath of relief. Cia lay sprawled across his chest, panting, her arms loose at his sides, falling to the mattress. Then she chuckled, rolling off him and flopping over until only her legs remained draped along his.

"Well, that was interesting."

Deklan dropped his arm over his eyes. "Never again. I *told* you what would happen, and I wasn't wrong."

She laughed, punching him in the arm. "No adventure in you."

"That wasn't adventure, that was insanity." He turned his head and glared at the wolves resettling in their space. "They know better."

"Maybe a whole wall... turn that into an actual room. What was it before?" she asked, propping her chin on his bicep.

"It was always the space for the guardian's wolf. The only difference is that I added all the cushions along the room's edges." He took in the open space, a room with only three walls and the half-fenced wall so he could see them and vice-versa. "No, no full wall. The curtain may work, though."

She lifted herself and patted his chest. "I know! Accordion doors. We can close them when we want privacy and open them when we don't need any."

"I don't know if that will muffle enough sound."

"They'll adjust," she said, then dropped her chin into the hollow of his shoulder. Her fingers brushed through the fine hairs across his pecks. "Do you think Ryan's concerns are valid about us working together?"

Ah yes, the conversation they didn't have much, much earlier. He laced his fingers through hers and kissed her hand. "Anytime one of us is in danger, it will affect the other, no doubt. However, my parents successfully worked together for decades, so I know it's possible to overcome. At least enough to continue to function on the job."

Her fingers caressed between his, and she shifted until she half laid across his left side. "I'm willing to try, are you?"

"You're not going to miss your team?"

She tucked their joined hands underneath her chest, close to her heart. "I'd miss you more."

Deklan laughed at the sugary statement and hugged her tight, squeezing until she yelped in protest. "What am I supposed to do with that?"

"Be happy you're stuck with me?" she asked, wiggling until he loosened his hold.

"I'm very, very happy to be stuck with you," he admitted, all traces of humor leaving him.

"And I adore my team, I do. They gave me purpose when I was at my most selfish, but they didn't know what to do with me. No one did." She rose and brushed her fingers across his bottom lip. "Not until you." Tears shimmered in her eyes. Regret and a hint of shame floated along their bond. "I know if I don't have you to help ground me, I'll return to being that woman."

Deklan shifted until the headboard supported his shoulders and pulled her onto his lap. He took her face between his palms and kissed her gently. "You won't ever be that woman again if you don't want to, Lucianna. You're in control of the decisions you make. All I did was help you see what you couldn't, or wouldn't, see in yourself."

She shook her head and swiped away a fallen tear. "No, I know I have trouble seeing my impulsive nature. I probably always will. Just like you'll always be more cautious than is necessary." She snorted and rolled her eyes. "Between us, we'd make a normal person."

"No such thing as normal, you know," he said, brushing away another stray tear. "But okay, we'll find a way to work together. We'll have to utilize another team to help train away our aversion to the other being in danger so we don't cause further issues in the field."

"I agree."

"And you'll need to be bonded to Izia."

She looked over at the resting wolves. "What will that be like? Does it hurt?"

"No, not for you, it shouldn't." He rubbed her goose-bump-covered arms. "He's almost completely bonded to you already. Just have to do the final step."

"What if Ryan finds out about the assassin before we can?"

"Izia will still go anywhere you do," he said without hesitating. "He's…" Deklan glanced at the beautiful gray wolf, who'd raised his head, his silver eyes intent on Cia. "Yours anyway."

She recoiled. "Mine, as in only? No, that can't—"

"No, no, that's not how it works," he assured her. "He's still under my bond, always will be, but he'll defer to you first unless I command him otherwise, individually or with the group. The connection between the two of you can't exist without me."

"I am so fascinated by this," she murmured, easing down until she lay on him like a human blanket. "I can't wait."

While he knew she spoke of the bonding with Izia, he couldn't help but feel the words also pertained to finally discovering the assassin's location. Nerves bunched in his stomach. Hunting Berk Pherson was likely the first test of how they'd fair as a bonded couple working together. He hugged her to his body as if he could always pull her into his very frame and keep her safe. But he couldn't, and she wouldn't want to be placed in a bubble any more than he would. How had his father managed all those years working with his mother and managed to stay sane?

26

Sean bolted awake when his hand encountered cold sheets instead of his wife. He almost fell out of the bed in his haste to get free from the tangle of blankets. Nude, he rushed across the short distance to the adjoining door. The room that had belonged to his wife for a very short time had been turned into a nursery for their daughter while they'd been stuck in Italyssa during the pregnancy. They'd returned a complete family to the improvements, and Sean's home, once full of nightmares, had become a haven filled with new memories.

Sean eased into the room, knowing better than to rush inside with an assassin. That particular lesson had been learned. His gaze went first to the crib. The rose curtains draping from the corona affixed to the wall had been pushed back, revealing stuffed animals in an otherwise empty baby bed. In the dying firelight, the stitched golden letters of *Anyka Margaret Blackbain* on the front of the canopy shimmered softly. Sean let his fingers trail on the door, pushing it open. The hinges were silent, like his steps.

No other light sources illuminated the spacious bedroom. Listening to the quiet *pop* of the logs in the fire and the creak of the house settling, Sean tried to discern any other sounds. A delicate snuffle and murmur had him moving across the thick carpet to the left side of the room. Barely concealed by a black silk robe, his wife had crammed her and their toddler in the small space between the changing table and chest dresser. Her left hand rested on the fully assembled rifle lying on the floor. Nyka slept, draped across his wife's torso, her little hands opening and closing.

Oh, Katria.

Sean returned to their room to slip on cotton pajama pants. Back in Nyka's room, he crouched before his reason for life, brushing his hand along Katria's bare calf. Tears streaked her cheeks, spilling over to race to her jaw. Fear, grief, and a sense of helplessness filtered to him from his touch. He sat, moved the gun out of reach, and scooted forward until he could gather his wife and baby girl into his arms. Katria didn't resist or reach for her weapon, which Sean counted as a win. Nyka's short crown of black curls tickled Sean's bare chest, and he swept the mass from her small face.

"Why are you doing this to yourself?" he whispered, looking up from his daughter.

"I can't... lose her," Katria managed between choked breaths. More tears spilled, and she squeezed her eyes shut. Her cool hand slipped around to clutch his back.

"Kat, love," Sean breathed into her hair, his hand cupping the back of her head. "Sweetheart, you aren't going to lose her. She is safe. *You* are safe."

She pressed her face into his chest. The heat of her tears dampened his skin and broke his heart. Hard tremors wracked her shoulders, but her sobs were silent. Nyka squirmed and whimpered in discontent, and not for the first time, Sean wondered if his daughter had inherited his ability instead of her mother's. He slowed his respiration and closed his eyes, willing them to calm.

As Katria relived the darkest days of her life and their precious child rested between them, Sean held them both and rocked gently. His wife had to get through the panic on her own, and when she did, they'd both be here. A visual reminder all was well, his promise of safety a truth she could believe in because she knew he never lied. Not to her.

Eventually, the shuddering ceased, and the hot splashes on his chest dissipated. Sniffling, she lifted her head. Her vivid blue eyes always had the power to steal his breath. Tonight was no different, despite the swelling from crying. She ensured Nyka was in his arms before leaning back, her weight supported by his bent leg.

She scrubbed her face and kept her head in her hands, still sniffling. "I swear, I see things in every shadow, knowing the scab is so close. In this city, right now."

"Voklane is going to find him," Sean said quietly, rubbing Nyka's back.

Katria shifted until she rested against the wall, head tilted back. The weak light glistened off her damp cheeks. Only the belt of her robe kept enough of the silk in place to cover her breasts, the thin cover split to her navel and parted at her side, displaying the entire length of her leg from hip to toe. Sean glanced away, knowing if he looked much longer, he'd use his toes to unravel the wrap completely.

"I know he will. I do. And I know we'll be there when the hunt finally begins. But in the meantime..." She covered her face again, her chest expanding on a deep breath.

"You need to realize this guy, Berk Pherson, has no idea who we are. At no point have we been hunted by an assassin in that capacity. You've been targeted, yes, but not by him. Whatever they use him for, it's not for people like us."

"That could change."

Sean shook his head and stood. Nyka's legs dangled against his hip, and her little arms flopped at her sides. He swayed gently when Nyka rubbed her face against his chest and fussed. He brushed her soft curls and rubbed her back, marveling not for the first time how big his hand was compared to her tiny frame. Even though she was no longer a fragile infant, she was still so small to him. He figured she'd always be his little girl, his daughter in need of protection. "They don't even know he's been compromised. Stop making trouble where none exists, Kat. Stop doing this to yourself."

Her hands dropped to her thighs, and she stared at him. Silence stretched between them, and her words were a mere whisper when she spoke. "I love seeing you with her. I love you. My whole world in one space."

A faint smile curled his lips. "I was thinking that same thing when I found you."

"Really?"

The smile faded as he kept her gaze. "You know what you mean to me."

She rose onto her knees, retrieved her rifle, kept the barrel pointed down, and stood. Not bothering to fix her now gaping robe, she stood before him, her focus intent. "Everything."

No ego in the statement, only truth. Sean's heart nearly burst in his chest. He closed the short space between them and kissed her, his tongue sliding along hers, seeking, claiming, until they both panted for air. Her fingers dug into the bicep holding Nyka, and his hand had somehow undone the robe completely, wrapping around her bare hip and pulling her against his thigh. The rifle bumped his leg, and Nyka muttered syllables known only to her in her sleep. They remained close, lips touching, sharing the very breath between them.

"I love you," Sean whispered. "Nothing is going to happen to our daughter."

Her hand found his hair curling into the length behind his ear. "I know because I'm going to make sure he dies."

OLD CITY RUINS
   Three days later

SWEET TOBACCO SMOKE CURLED IN THE FRIGID NIGHT AIR. Ice sparkled on the decaying bricks in the narrow alley. Leaning against the wall, a booted foot braced on the crumbling façade, the silhouette of their guide barely separated from the rest of the darkness.

"Thaine?" Deklan whispered, holding his hand out to keep the rest of the members of the combined intel and Wolvenguard team from closing in and spooking the man.

The orange tip of a cigarette glowed in the hazy air. The silhouette moved into a shallow pool of light cast by the moon. Not much changed, except Deklan now perceived a height near his own and a form that meant youth or undernourished. Perhaps both. Voklane had given Deklan a single name for the man who'd lead them safely through Old City Ruins without specifying if it was a first or last name.

"I'm going to tell you the same thing I told the other." The silvery light gleamed off Thaine's dark hair, which looked cut by hand with the blade of a dull knife. Uneven hanks framed his face and curled faintly near his shoulders. A loose wool jacket fell to his knees, buttoned up over dark pants. "The only reason you're being allowed here is because we were told the guy you seek killed two kids. We don't protect those who take our futures from us."

"Understood," Deklan said, having been told as much by Voklane.

"You don't stop at any other locations. You don't talk to any other residents," Thaine instructed. "We go straight to the building I've scouted, and I'll remain with you until your business is completed."

"What are you, the king of the ruins?" Cia asked from behind Deklan.

A burst of orange glowed, illuminating a young man's face. While his jaw had yet to fill out completely, and his cheeks still possessed a hint of adolescence, his pale eyes were older than Deklan's. He blew out smoke on a long exhale, the earthy sweetness floating around them. Using the brick beside him, he ground the burning nub before dropping the unused portion into his jacket pocket.

"I'm whatever they need me to be," Thaine stated. "This way."

The group followed behind their guide, sticking to the shadows when he did, crossing roads and slipping between gaps in walls older than anything else in Sziveria except for pre-cataclysmic remnants. Why the oldest section of Haven City had become abandoned to the lost and forgotten was a mystery. Deep into the guarded community, Thaine ducked into an uneven doorframe, the wooden support along the top skewed to the point that it appeared any bump would send the stone it supported tumbling down. Everyone bent lower than necessary to follow. He stepped on a jutting concrete slab and jumped, grabbing the lip of a hole in the second floor.

Deklan glanced around at the stone building, from the stairs to the floors above, the structure had mostly stood the test of time. The same could not be said for the newer buildings in Haven City, generally constructed of wood and brick. No wonder the outcasts of society had taken residence in the crumbling ruins. The buildings may be decrepit, but they still managed to function and provide a means of shelter if one could handle the lack of modernity. He followed Thaine onto the second floor and then laid belly down to hoist up Neva and Nikita with the assistance of Tate and Galvin below and Thaine beside him. Izia remained home on Tate's orders, not wanting the wolf to tear his stitches or compromise the job due to the healing injury. After the wolves were up, he helped Katria and Sean. Tate handled himself, the only member of Deklan's team, a second medical scientist never hurt. Mason, Kevin, and Cia remained downstairs.

Thaine motioned for them to continue following, and they went up an additional story, this time on narrow stairs. He took them through a roofless area, the walls jagged along the top and missing all together in sections. The moon's pale light glittered off frosted surfaces and patches of ice along the floor. Fragments of walls spoke of smaller rooms, and they stepped over or through them to the end of the floor, where Thaine motioned for everyone to crouch. He pointed through a fissure. Deklan shifted on his heels and peered through the gap. A two-story house with boarded openings and smoke curling from a hole in the roofline came into view.

"This is where the guy spends his time here," Thaine said, shifting until he was in the cover of the wall and took out his cigarette. He used the stone surface to strike a match, shielding it with his hand to light the tobacco. A long drag and equally long exhale sent a puff of fragrant smoke into the air around them. Neva sneezed. Thaine smiled and scooted further away.

"Is he alone?" Deklan asked, checking the bulky com-unit affixed to his belt.

Thaine answered after another drag, the orange glow of his pull illuminating the space for a second. "I've spent the last three days watching him to make sure I could give you accurate information. I noticed no one even visited. He left once, for a few hours."

Deklan shifted from his position and motioned for Katria to take his place. She did without hesitation, laying out her rifle case and assembling the impressive BACR-18, known simply as a *baser* to anyone in the field. The black weapon absorbed the silvery light. Only the glass of her scope caught a reflection. Her involvement was a quick resolution if the assassin happened to escape not one but two interceptors, which would be a feat. The dogs were there if the scab managed to evade the interceptors *and* Katria's bullet. He would not outrun the wolves. They were taking no chances. One way or another, Berk Pherson's connection with the V Alliance ended tonight.

Deklan pressed the transmit button on his com-unit. "Guide has confirmed target location. Building is behind this one, north side."

A round of *affirmative* crackled into his ear. Wanting to pace but not knowing the safe areas to step, Deklan settled for finding another gap in the third-level wall and looked out over the expanse of Old City Ruins. He braced his hands on his upper thighs and took in the view. Weak golden glows broke up the darkness. No streetlamps. Only glittering stars and the moon provided the inhabitants with any sense of light. Deklan's breath released in a steamy puff. Hard to comprehend he was within the same civilization, separated only by a river.

"Door is barred from the inside," Mason's voice said inside the earpiece.

Deklan found himself wandering closer to the wall Katria lay behind. Neva brushed his thigh, her nose bumping into his hip. He curled his fingers into the thick hair between her shoulders.

She will be fine, she will, Neva said along their bond. *Strong, she is strong.*

"No movement on the bottom floor. Subject appears to be upstairs. Advise our interceptors go in through the back window," Mason said. *"Busted covering shows the room is used for storage."*

"Do it," Sean replied, his words echoed through the radio.

Go time. Deklan's muscles bunched with unfamiliar anxiety. He paid close attention to Cia's emotional state along their bond. They'd opted to keep their communication limited to emotions only so she wouldn't be sidetracked. There hadn't been time for them to learn the ability between them, and it still took a lot of concentration to forge the link. If, at any point, she changed from a combination of nerves and anticipation to fear, his wolves would be unleashed.

Stepping onto Kevin's braided hands, Cia allowed herself to be hoisted to the window located too far above to reach on her own. Her fingers grabbed at the narrow opening, the cold brick stinging her skin. Parts of a board used to keep out the elements had rotted, and pushing the remaining fragments away proved simple. Kevin kept her stable as she yanked pieces of wood free and dropped them to the ground, ensuring the interior room wasn't compromised by sound. Mason conveyed the process in hushed tones across the radio. Their small group was outside of the visual field of the rest of the team.

While Cia wouldn't communicate with her husband, his bond was strong. Nervousness. Impatience. Love. They buffered along her peripheral, a sense of comfort that even when she went into the dwelling, she would not be alone. The intensity of his feelings when she'd separated from him had taken her by surprise. Any powerful emotions from him since their bonding had been in his presence, and she'd been feeling mostly the same, so they hadn't registered as foreign. The sensations he broadcasted now could overshadow her concentration if allowed. She couldn't afford any distractions. She monitored his reaction, pleased when nothing changed as she shimmied into the small room. Deklan trusted her to care for herself. She wouldn't let him down.

The closet-like space contained essentials. Cia used the shelving as a ladder, slowly climbing down to avoid disturbing the food and household objects. Kevin would not be following. All intel indicated the assassin lived alone, a reclusive existence in the most hostile environment Sziveria had to offer, second only to the Northern Boundary. A chance to prove herself was being offered to Cia, and she hoped to make everyone, including herself, proud.

On silent feet, she dropped to the stone floor, waiting to ensure the sounds she *had* made went unnoticed. She eased from the storage room, opening the door enough to squeeze free into a kitchen area. No candles, lamps, or fires burned to illuminate the darkness. She pulled a glow tube from her pocket, quickly combined the components, and then shook the glass to mix the ingredients. A green glow revealed a sparsely furnished space. No rugs covered the floor. No curtains hung from the shuttered windows. Cia glided across the living room, searching for a way to the second floor. The narrow stairs were against the left wall.

Leaving the glowlight on the floor at the base of the stairs, she crept up, keeping her body angled so her back stayed against the wall. The upstairs offered the same sense of desolation. A thin mattress with a rumpled blanket lay behind a red velvet chair positioned so close to the fire it posed a hazard. Even from the back of the room, gnaw marks were visible on the stained and worn seat. A man half laid in the wing-backed lounger, one leg tossed over an arm. Golden light danced around the room from the fire. Berk Pherson must loathe the cold.

The whisper of a page turning joined the faint crack and pop of burning wood. Cia pressed her back to the stone wall at the top of the stairs and waited. Berk's foot bounced. Another page turned. Soon, his foot would no longer bop around. The book he read would fall to the floor, never to be picked up again. An absurd vision of her mother's book lying spine up on the arm of their couch popped into Cia's mind. She swallowed, realizing with a punch of clarity *she* didn't want to be responsible for a lost life, no matter how deserving.

But the beauty was, she didn't have to be the one to tender justice. Someone else was capable. Willing. Cia just had to give her the opportunity. New plan in place, Cia straightened from the wall and closed the distance to the man who'd stolen so much from so many.

"Must be nice to think you're safe," Cia said, her words pitched low.

Berk vaulted from the chair, his eyes wide. The book went flying. Loose pages scattered and fluttered to the floor. The man she'd fought and almost lost against in Port Ice Hollows stood silhouetted by the fire.

"Surprise," Cia whispered, smiling.

He sneered. "Back for seconds, little one?"

Cia didn't dignify his question with a response. She leaped for him, sending a solid kick to his chest. Adrenaline flooded her system. She embraced the flare, letting the fire burn along her nerves, pushing out the unwanted spike of panic that threatened to undo all her hard training. Berk spun but recovered swiftly. Not quick enough for Cia's now enhanced reaction time, however. She delivered punishing blow after punishing blow.

Each kick and punch steered him in the direction she needed him to move. He attempted to fight back, shielding the vital parts of his body with his forearms and risen knees, executing sloppy kicks that Cia was embarrassed had once defeated her. She easily evaded his defensive moves, made aware by subtle cues of what he would attempt to try next. And when he aligned with the window, she spun, gathering momentum, and sent a strong kick into his chest. He flew back, the weight of his body shattering the wooden shutters. Teetering in the opening, Berk grabbed at the stone frame.

All the anger, the grief, the pain of what this man had taken from her left Cia's mouth on a scream as she launched herself at him. Forgetting his precarious situation, he lifted his hands to ward her off and lost his balance. Cia grabbed the frame to stop her forward momentum. Her upper body swung forward, out the window into the cold night. Berk's yell echoed in the narrow space between the buildings. He landed and struggled to rise. A useless endeavor.

The harsh crack of a rifle shot blasted through the icy air. Cia flinched from the noise and the hard jerk Berk gave in death. Without warning, tears spilled from her eyes. She lifted her gaze to the shadow that rose across the distance, blocking a gap in a cracked third-story wall. While Cia couldn't see the assassin, she figured the same wet tracks threatened to freeze on Katria's cheeks.

An enemy had been eliminated.

Vengeance had been delivered.

Swiping the tears from her face, Cia turned and

searched the barren room. She found the rifle on the fireplace mantle, wrapped in burlap. The second she touched the cool metal frame, nausea rolled through her stomach. Snatching her hand away, she took a moment to compose herself. Her father deserved to know the threat was gone, his family avenged. The killer's weapon would deliver the message in a way nothing else could but the body. Cia forced herself to pick up the gun, securing it under her arm. She left the house through the front door, tossing the bar aside. The narrow wood beam clattered on the floor, loud in the empty room. She didn't bother to close the door. No one lived there anymore.

Before even his wolves could reach her, Deklan was in front of her. He touched her shoulders, upper arms, her face, and hair. Despite the moment's seriousness, she laughed and grabbed his right wrist in her free hand.

"I'm fine," she said. He didn't stop. His panic and relief fought for domination along their bond. Cia squeezed and moved in close to his body. "Baby, look at me. I'm fine."

Finally, he paused long enough to meet her stare. She raised her brows and opened their bond further like she remembered doing on the balcony days ago. *See, I'm okay. I'm fine.*

He kissed her. Hard. "Not knowing what you were doing drove me crazy, but I didn't want to distract you."

"I know. We'll practice."

He sighed heavily and nodded. The rest of the team arrived. The wolves waited behind Deklan, ignoring the dead body only a few feet away.

Katria stopped in front of Cia. "Thank you."

"I couldn't do it," Cia admitted, and Deklan pulled her to his side and hugged her.

"That's not a bad thing," Katria said softly. She motioned to the burlap-covered rifle. "May I?"

Without a word, Cia handed the weapon over.

Katria unwrapped it. Disgust and contempt twisted her pretty face. "A Siber rifle. What a piece of crap." She flipped the rifle to hold like she would to use it. "It's rusted in the barrel, and this pathetic little scope isn't even calibrated."

"Would explain a lot," Sean said, wrapping an arm around his wife's waist.

"This is an embarrassment," Katria said, returning the rifle and fabric to Cia. "No self-respecting sharp-shooter would be using a Siber anything. They are the worst weaponsmiths in the inhabited world. Everyone knows that."

"They're cheap," Kevin said. "Siber's number one export is arms. They supply the Vativarsan's and the Imperial Qu'in's with guns."

"And that makes both those neighbors equally matched. If either Sziveria or Ruthenia decided they wanted those lands, there'd be no battle," Katria said.

"Shows the V Alliance doesn't know much about strategy when it comes to weapons, at least," Mason said. "We can use this information."

The sweet fragrance of Thaine's tobacco drifted over Cia, and she glanced in the guide's direction. He leaned against the wall, a foot braced on the stone behind him. The orange glow of his cigarette drew her gaze to his face. He was young, Cia's age, and years from now, his looks promised to rival all the men standing around her. His stare met hers, and she wished for more light, the color of his irises a mystery.

"Does anyone claim anything of his?" Thaine asked.

Cia held up the rifle. "Only this. For my father."

Katria produced a shell casing, held upright between her thumb and index finger. "I have all I need." Her attention shifted to Cia. "For my father."

They shared a somber look between them. Sisters in tragedy.

Tate clapped the guy on the shoulder. "Whatever you want is yours."

Thaine tilted his head back and blew out a long exhale of smoke. "I think I'll take the building. There was a completed second story?"

Cia nodded. "Yes, the floor is made of wood. Not much furniture, though. Lots of food."

Thaine nodded. "Thanks. Do you need help finding your way back?"

Deklan moved to stand near Berk's booted feet. "My wolves can lead the way if you prefer."

"I need to stake my ownership on this property before sunrise, or I'll lose it," Thaine said.

Deklan held his hand out, and Thaine accepted. "Thanks for everything."

Thaine maintained the grip for a long moment. "If you need help again, just ask to find me."

"Appreciate that," Deklan said and released his grip.

Her husband regarded the body again, sighing, hands on his hips. "Damn, I really don't want to carry a dead guy." He lifted his head and glanced at their small team. "Any volunteers?"

Sean laughed. "You outrank all of us, Arch Guardian Wolvenguard. All you have to do is assign one of us to manual labor."

Shock slapped Deklan's face as though he'd forgotten his position.

Thaine chuckled and motioned to the house behind him. "I'll find a way to make a sled, and then two people can drag him. I don't think anyone wants to carry him. You'll be covered in blood by the end. Not something I recommend."

Kevin and Tate went to help Thaine. The small group returned with a door and a sheet. Thaine used a large knife to make notches in the wood while Kevin and Tate twisted the sheet to resemble rope. They handed the length to Thaine, who threaded the roped sheet into the notches, holding it in place while Kevin and Tate handled the body. Kevin lifted Berk's head by his hair and promptly dropped it back down.

"We'll want to leave him this way," Kevin said, grappling with the dead man's arms.

"I can imagine," Tate said.

"You don't want to," Kevin muttered.

Together the men heaved Berk's weight onto the makeshift gurney. Thaine secured the body and then held out the two sheet ends. Deklan took one, and Mason accepted the other. Neva and Nikita moved to flank Cia.

"We ready?" Deklan asked.

The wolves led the way, never more than a step ahead of Cia. They followed the same path Thaine had guided until they reached the alley they'd found on their own. Deklan took over leading, exchanging his place, and hauling the body with Kevin. Neva shifted to the beast master's side while Nikita remained with Cia.

A familiar figure waited for them across the river. Ryan peeled away from a stone retaining wall, meeting them before they reached civilization.

"You were successful," he said, stopping next to the body.

"Your contact came through. I hope he was rewarded well," Deklan said.

"Very well. An insider for Old City Ruins may prove invaluable in the future, now that we know the V Alliance may favor hiding within its anonymous streets."

Deklan took Cia's hand and waved Tate to join them. "Our part is finished here." He squeezed Cia's fingers and looked at her. "We have somewhere else we need to be."

In the blistering cold, Cia had stood in front of Terravine Manor, staring at the frost coated door until the pink glow of dawn sparkled on the dark wood. The rifle had become heavy in her arms. Ever supportive, Deklan stood behind her, silent. Waiting for her to find the courage to knock. The wolves had been cloistered into the hired carriage with the driver bundled under his layers of clothing.

She'd done things she shouldn't have for this moment. And now that she stood here, the proof of her success in her arms, she couldn't seem to bring herself to rip open the wound for her father. Did he even want the closure? Would it matter to him? Deklan rested his hand on her hip and pulled her back into his solid chest. He propped his chin on her head and then knocked hard twice. Apparently, their bond had conveyed her cowardice.

"You have nothing to be ashamed of," he whispered, kissing her cheek, his lips cold and dry.

"What if he..." A hundred bad reactions swam in her mind.

"Shh." He hugged her close. "No what-ifs. You need to do this, so we're doing it."

The door swung open to the Terravine's bright housekeeper. She beamed a smile, her fluffy orange robe sweeping the floor. She took a step to the side to allow them to enter. "Morning, Miss Cia. Are you here to see your father?"

"I am," Cia said and motioned to Deklan. "This is my husband, Deklan."

"Ah." The housekeeper's smile grew, deepening the wrinkles at the corners of her blue eyes. She closed out the cold. "It's Mrs. Cia now, how wonderful. Congratulations. I'll go get Mr. Henry."

"Thank you," Cia said, leading Deklan from the entry room to the grand foyer.

Stairs curved up to the second story on their left, and pillars divided the entry from the grand hall, which led to all the social rooms on the first floor. The living quarters were upstairs. The spacious manor had been Cia and Henry's home for the entire winter after she'd been rescued. The first time she had seen Deklan was in this house, in the massive ballroom. Her feet carried her closer to the memory.

Through the pillars and down a short stretch of hallway, she found herself standing outside the cavernous space. Chandeliers dripping with crystal twinkled in the blooming morning light. An empty platform took up the far-left wall. Shield Guardianess Terravine loved live performances and often hired singers for all her hosted events.

Deklan's presence shifted the air behind her, a comforting warmth. Cia leaned against the entry, watching the glow of sunrise slowly brighten the space. "I fell in love in this room."

Deklan braced his forearm on the wall above her, the heat of his body washing over her back. "You fell in curiosity. You didn't know I was worth loving. Not yet."

She tilted her head back against his chest and met his stare. "Sure, I did. *The* Arch Guardian of Wolvenguard, powerful, honorable, and a leader worth following. There were plenty of things I didn't know yet, but how you made me feel wasn't one of them."

Bare feet slapping on marble interrupted the moment. Henry skidded around the corner of the hall, his gray robe fluttering out behind him. Striped pajama pants and a plain blue t-shirt covered him. His hair stood at odd angles, and his face held the harsh lines of being yanked from sleep. Concern shone in his eyes, and his fingers moved in rapid motions.

"Are you all right? What's wrong? What's going on?" Henry asked.

Words died in Cia's throat, and she could only hold out the burlap-wrapped rifle like the offering it was. Her father stared at the fabric covering for a long moment. Slowly, he undid the folds, revealing the gun. His eyes lifted to her in question, and she nodded. Silent tears raced down her cheeks, her heart fracturing all over again.

Henry took the weapon from her. The burlap slid to the floor. Cia waited until her father lifted his gaze. She signed, "He will never take from another family again."

Henry handed the gun to Deklan, freeing his hands. "He can get another rifle. Perhaps a better one."

Cia squared her shoulders. "He can't get another face."

Henry's brows popped up, concern returning to his eyes. "You?"

"No, not me. Katria Blackbain."

Henry took a deep breath and swiped a hand down his face before answering. "Nachemir's daughter. Good." Henry's gaze shifted to Deklan, and he spoke, "I didn't want that for my daughter."

Deklan nodded. "I know, but the choice was hers either way. She opted to give Katria the shot."

Henry grabbed Cia and pulled her into a tight hug. Cia wrapped her arms around her father's broad back and squeezed. She had no way to communicate with him, so she held on, offering and accepting the comfort they both needed. Deklan's hand brushed the hair from her neck and gently kneaded the tense muscles. His touch grounded her further, something she suspected would always be the case. Her family may be broken, but they were on the mend, growing and forging new paths.

EPILOGUE

RALSTON FAMILY HOME
  One week later

"WILL IT HURT?" CIA ASKED. AGAIN.

Deklan massaged her shoulders, his thumbs squeezing into the bare skin of her back. "No, though you may feel odd for a moment while the bond is completely forged. Don't worry, beast masters surround you. We won't let anything go wrong. And Izia is more than ready."

An understatement. The wolf lay on his back, paws curled into his chest, his back end shimming back and forth in his excitement. A happy, upside-down smile made him appear more vicious than joyful. Cia sat cross-legged at his head, Deklan behind her, his thighs bracketing her hips. The loose amber folds of the traditional Ruthenian dress she wore puddled on the floor around her. A sheer silk layer over a thicker under gown of the softest wool she'd ever touched. The back was open to showcase her bonded status. However, her anxiety had caused Deklan to relocate, and now the dress design mattered little since no one could see her imprint.

Nerves danced under her skin and fluttered in her belly. Cia pressed a hand to her stomach and took a calming breath. She glanced around, meeting her father's gaze. He gave her an enthusiastic thumbs up. Beside him, her Uncle Vayden did the same, and soon everyone who'd arrived to support her was holding up their thumbs and making goofy *you can do it* faces. Cia laughed, and across from her, Markus smiled. Next to him, his wolf Lunah lay with her head on his thigh.

"Are you ready, my daughter?" Markus asked. Like all the Ralston men, he was shirtless, the strong lines of his body unhindered by age.

Cia took another bracing breath and lowered her hands to her knees. "Yes."

Deklan dropped his hands to her sides and squeezed. "All right," Deklan said slowly. "Then let us begin."

They almost did the bond at home. They couldn't start working together until Cia was connected with Izia, and Cia was ready to begin that part of their lives. Deklan had gone to the Northern Boundary to handle an escapee without her, and the separation had been difficult for them both. But Cia had taken the promise ceremony from Deklan. She wouldn't take this away, too. The symbolism was beautiful, with the Ralston family forming a circle around her and Izia. Her father and Uncle Vayden's family formed another ring.

"Izia, *k'te* Lucianna," Deklan commanded.

Izia flipped onto his stomach and wiggled to Cia until his muzzle brushed her outstretched fingertips. A new wave of stress rolled through her. She hadn't figured out why she was so nervous about bonding with the animal when she couldn't wait for one with Deklan. Perhaps the unknown or the finality. Neva and Nikita stretched out on either side of them, their nostrils flaring.

Deklan's arms wrapped around her waist. He hugged her to his chest and kissed the side of her neck. "Sink your hands into the fur at the side of his face deep enough to touch his skin. He'll hold still."

Cia obeyed, her eyes meeting Izia's beautiful golden stare. His tail thumped like a drum beat on the wooden floor.

"Ready?" Deklan whispered for her alone.

Cia nodded, her heart pounding in her ears.

"Izia, *sza'vnica*."

The last thing she noticed before her eyes closed and her body seemed not to be her own for a moment was every beast master straining under an unseen weight. A force punched through Cia's mind. A new pathway, a thread of silver connecting her to another life force. The delicate thread shivered, strengthening in brightness, until a voice called her name over and over again.

Cia, my Cia, my Cia, Cia!

She groaned and slowly came to, opening her eyes to find herself staring at the ceiling. A tissue was pressed under her nose. The shouting continued in her head, and she patted Izia's head.

"You don't have to yell, baby," she croaked.

Markus laughed. "Why do they always shout first thing?"

"Excitement," Deklan said.

Izia whined and pressed into her side, laying his muzzle on her stomach. *Sorry, I sorry.*

"Oh wow," Cia whispered, tears burning her eyes as she met Deklan's proud stare. "This is amazing. I really can hear him."

"Yes. And he'll be able to hear you once you learn."

He dabbed at her nose some more, and Cia blinked. "Am I bleeding?"

"A little, it's normal. If he hadn't been so excited, you might not have. Any pain?"

She touched her forehead and analyzed how she felt. "No, none." She shifted her gaze to meet his stare. "You're really okay sharing him?"

Deklan leaned close and pressed a gentle kiss to her lips. "I'm more than okay. I can't believe I have you, have what we're sharing. I love you. So much."

Tears spilled from her eyes, sliding past her temples into her hair. She laughed and cried at the same time, not something she would have thought possible before this moment. She wrapped her hands around his neck and kissed him again. "You're stuck with me forever now."

He smiled against her mouth. "Forever sounds good to me."

www.ingramcontent.com/pod-product-compliance
Lightning Source LLC
Chambersburg PA
CBHW010546170726
48285CB00011B/2781

* 9 7 8 1 9 5 5 2 9 3 1 9 8 *